Curse of the Mardale Skull

George Luckman

Pen Press

First published in Great Britain by Pen Press

All paper used in the printing of this book has been made from wood grown in managed, sustainable forests.

ISBN13: 978-1-78003-340-2

Printed and bound in the UK
Pen Press is an imprint of
Indepenpress Publishing Limited
25 Eastern Place
Brighton
BN2 1GJ

A catalogue record of this book is available from the British Library

Cover design by Jacqueline Abromeit

Dedicated in loving memory to my son,
Dr Steven Paul Luckman 1973–2010
and to my wife
Maureen Rose Luckman 1940–2011
Forever in my thoughts

Acknowledgements

W R Mitchell – *The Lost Village of Mardale*
J A Brooks – *Ghosts and Legends of the Lake District*
Geoffrey Berry – *Mardale Revisited*
Godfrey Watson – *The Border Reivers*
Keith Durham, Angus McBride – *Men-at-Arms Series – The Border Reivers*
Archivist, Carlisle Castle

About the Author

George Luckman was born on 24th May 1934 in Birmingham. After completing National Service in the R.A.F he married a schoolteacher, Maureen, and several years later their son Steven was born.

After starting up a small Garden Centre in the Midlands the family eventually moved to Keswick in Cumbria, where they again went into business producing needlework kits. It was during this time that George was inspired to write by the reappearance of the lost village of Mardale, which emerged from the Haweswater reservoir during a prolonged period of drought.

Now retired, he lives in Torquay, Devon.

CHAPTER ONE

13th July 1994

"Bloody hell!"

Joy Elliot sprang up anxiously from the spot where she had been crouching, consternation etched on her pretty face. In her haste to retreat from the scene, her feet almost abandoned the wellington boots that seriously impeded her progress in the ankle-deep sediment surrounding her. Not normally prone to such utterings, her words took on an added emphasis. Turning ashen faced to Professor Merlin Reid, the man who accompanied her, she pointed to the area of mud she had so speedily vacated. "Look!"

The man stepped forward to do so, almost recoiling in a similar manner when observing the object that had caused her so much distress. Under a thin film of water, barely covering the rock-strewn, silted base of the reservoir where they stood, the vacant eye sockets of a human skull appeared to be staring back at him. Being by profession a medical man, he was not unaccustomed to looking death in the face, though under normal circumstances he would have expected that face to retain its human form – not to be devoid of an outer covering of flesh and skin. Quickly recovering his composure, he returned to the still shaking young woman. This was hardly what they had expected when journeying to this place.

Haweswater – the man-made reservoir they were visiting – was sorely depleted. Severe drought conditions had caused the water level to drop so significantly that Mardale – the isolated, once beautiful village which had nestled at the base of this valley – now lay almost totally exposed once more. Formerly secure in the embrace of the surrounding mountain ranges, the tiny hamlet had eventually been swamped by the rising tide of water that engulfed the area on the dam's eventual completion some sixty years previous. The homesteads, so long ago forsaken, now lay in ruins, strewn like broken toys in the cloying silt.

The professor took hold of the young woman's arm. "Nothing to get alarmed about. I think we may have just stumbled across part of a body disturbed at the time of the flooding."

She was still trembling, her face white as the crisp blouse tucked into her faded jeans. For a moment he hesitated, loath to desert her, but the authorities clearly had to be notified. He gently led her a short distance away, hoping that he might calm her.

"I realise that came as a bit of a shock, Joy, but I do need to phone and report this. Would you mind hanging on here while I return to the car park and use the car phone?"

"Sure. I'm fine now." She made a great effort to sound confident, though she was still struggling to pull herself together. Something about the find had disturbed her beyond reason. What that something was she found difficult to put into words: "It was just so awful suddenly seeing that horrid thing right before my eyes," she explained. "It seemed evil somehow; almost as though it were grinning up at me."

The professor nodded understandingly. "Sure you don't mind remaining here then?"

"No, it's okay – you carry on."

He hesitated. "There is just one thing. It would help if you could discourage anyone from tampering with the skull before it's been examined by the police."

She gave him a nervous smile. "I'll do my best." Thoughtfully making his way back along the firmer, mud-baked track which wound off in the direction of the car park, Professor Reid paid scant attention to the other groups of people viewing the scattered ruins. His mind was concentrated on one salient fact. Not wishing to disturb the young woman more than was necessary, he had chosen to conceal the reality that the skull she had found was almost certainly not some remnant washed out of the Mardale cemetery. To his knowledge, all of the bodies originally buried at Mardale had been exhumed and reinterred at Shap – a larger village some eight miles away. It would appear that the skull in question – and possibly the body which may also lie concealed beneath the sediment – could only have found its way to the bottom of Haweswater as the result of an accident, or some form of villainy. No doubt an acquaintance of his in the Penrith police force would be as intrigued by the mystery as he was himself.

As predicted, once apprised of all the relevant facts, Inspector Grey quickly reacted to the story of the grim discovery.

"You say you're certain all of the bodies were moved out at the time of the exodus?"

"Read your history books, Inspector. Apart from the fact that the residents of Mardale would no doubt have wished to see the bodies of their relatives reburied elsewhere, you can hardly imagine the authorities allowing corpses to remain in place at the base of a reservoir."

"Point taken. Bit of a health hazard to be sure."

"As you say. And the skull really is much too far away from the old graveyard to really be a likely contender as an item accidentally mislaid during the original exhumations."

The professor had good reason for arriving at his conclusions. The layout of the village had been quite obvious from the coverage given to Mardale's reappearance by the local television broadcasts. The tell-tale stumps of the ancient yew trees adjacent to the ruins of the old church had been quite easily identified.

Grey accepted the professor's judgement without question. He had long since come to respect the reliability and resourcefulness of the man during the course of several investigations. "Right, Prof. I'm on my way. I'll get the pathologist to accompany me. You say you're close to some ruins at the water's edge?"

"That's correct. Just follow the main track. Bear off to the left once you hit the softer ground. You'd be well advised to wear wellingtons."

A smile crossed Grey's face as he replaced the phone. Was there anything here that 'The Magician' could lend a hand with? Grey had conferred the singularly appropriate title on the professor after the last of their encounters. The man had an almost uncanny ability to produce something out of the hat whenever he was allowed anywhere near a case such as this. Still smiling, the inspector set about making the arrangements.

"Sergeant, get hold of the pathologist. And contact Missing Persons. I want anything they have on any disappearances in or around Haweswater and the surrounding area over the course of the last twenty years or so. The Magician's come up with another one."

The sergeant chuckled. The professor was well known at the station. "What's the old boy hit on this time?"

"Skull at Mardale. No traces of flesh present, so it's been there a while. Grab some digging equipment and shove it in the boot of the car. I expect we'll find the rest of the body buried under the sediment. Give me a shout once the pathologist arrives."

Professor Reid slowly retraced his steps. In his late fifties, suffering from the onset of rheumatoid arthritis, he no longer moved with the effortless ease that youth once endowed. Pausing to rest for a moment on the seventeenth-century packhorse bridge, restored to use once more by the water's dramatic decline, he marvelled that the ancient structure still remained intact, carrying the old road to the ruined hamlet. The stream – also now fully restored – flowed below the rough stone parapets, winding its leisurely way to join what remained of Haweswater reservoir. Shimmering like a jewel in the bright sunlight, it had reverted to more or less its original size prior to the damming of the valley.

There was no denying that this spot was the ideal site for a reservoir. Surrounded on all sides by a stunning array of crags and mountains, a natural basin had been carved out during the ice age as glaciers gradually lost their frozen grip, dragging rocks and rubble in their wake as they slowly receded. Just a narrow opening at the far end of the valley had allowed the escape of all but the beautiful stretch of water which finally became trapped at the lower level. Only with the eventual addition of the huge dam – which had plugged the outlet from Mardale so effectively – did the original body of water vastly increase in size.

"Amazing sight, eh?" Another elderly visitor had stopped to marvel. "Makes you wonder what this place was like in the past."

"It does indeed." The professor had himself been reflecting on the character of the vale. "Small wonder that an isolated spot like this originally attracted hardy settlers."

"I'll say! Plenty of land to cultivate by the look of it. Fish in the lake too, no doubt."

The professor nodded in agreement. "Clear mountain springs, pastures for the cattle, deer running wild in the forests."

The old chap alongside chuckled. "Sounds idyllic when you consider the state of the world today. And just think of all that rock lying around just begging to be used for building their cottages and barns."

Plenty for dry stone walls too, the professor thought, looking at the scene spread before them. Though it was remote from civilisation, this place must surely have been a wonderful haven for the small community who once lived out their lives here. Sad then that it finally came to this: obliterated in order to supply its precious liquid resources to the inhabitants of distant conurbations.

Bidding the man goodbye, Reid now returned to the scene of the discovery, relieved to find his young associate had managed to keep order. She had been joined by a small group of curious onlookers, whose numbers were increasing steadily as a stream of sightseers arrived to view the remains of the lost village. It was proving quite an attraction to locals and tourists alike. No doubt there would be a handful of past residents among them, drawn back by evocative memories of the place.

A very pleasant girl, Joy Elliot was normally quite self-assured, though it was nevertheless apparent that she was still somewhat unsettled by the discovery of the skull. Her clear blue eyes lacked their usual sparkling enthusiasm, the smile that was normally never far away having deserted her. The tiny snub nose was now flecked with perspiration, the brow furrowed. Blonde hair – drifting in the breeze – framed her taut face as she engaged in animated conversation with the group of people gathered around her.

Suddenly becoming aware of the professor's presence, she was clearly relieved to relinquish her position of responsibility. Still strangely disturbed by the discovery of the gruesome remains, she had not dared to return to the location of the find for a second look. The feeling that some malevolent force was emanating from the object would not leave her. She tried to think logically. Professor Reid might well regard her as a fool if she let on how much it had affected her. Silly thing! She was eighteen years old now – not a silly schoolgirl! It was time she acted her age. Moving out of the knot of people surrounding her, she crossed to where he stood.

"Am I glad to see you back," she whispered. "It wasn't easy persuading that lot to keep their distance. I had to mention you had connections with the police, otherwise I think someone may have dug the thing out." The thought obviously distressed her.

"Sorry I had to leave you like that, Joy," he apologised. "I'll take over now until Inspector Grey arrives."

Joining the inquisitive gathering, he was intent on ensuring that nothing was disturbed. It was no problem living up to the image Joy had created. An imposing figure, tall, slim, greying, craggy of face and with an air of authority, he gave the impression that he was not a man to be trifled with. Though clad casually in tweed jacket and twill trousers, he nevertheless appeared totally in command.

"Keep back please. A police inspector is on his way. Nothing much to get excited about. Just an old skull."

The group accepted his instructions without question.

"Funny place for it to turn up!" A man in hiking gear seemed to be taking a keen interest. "That's the remains of the old church over there isn't it?" He indicated the rubble strewn area a good distance away. "Can't see him legging it all the way from there."

Reid smiled. "Well certainly not in his condition."

The people close by chuckled good humouredly.

"Think some poor sod saw himself off?" The question came from somewhere in the crowd.

"It's possible." Reid was not prepared to conjecture.

"Maybe someone saw him off!" The heavily laden hiker eased the pack from his shoulders. "Good place to dump a body."

The man was almost voicing the professor's own thoughts. Reid considered the possibilities. Conceivably the rest of the body still lay beneath the sediment. If that proved to be the case, the pathologist would want to remove the muddy residue layer by layer, ensuring no disturbance was caused to the angle and placement of the remains. The posture of a corpse – or even a skeleton – could often give some clue as to the possible cause of death. If it were a case of murder, someone, somewhere, could be in for an unpleasant surprise.

Having established his authority, he returned to Joy Elliot. She was still looking pensive. "Pop back to the car while we're waiting for the police to arrive," he suggested. "Get yourself something to eat. There's a flask and sandwiches on the back seat."

She nodded. “Thanks, I think I will.” Taking the car keys, she plodded off through the mud to the firmer track, pleased to distance herself from the scene of the discovery.

It was only as she made her way back that Joy suddenly realised she and her tutor had failed to complete the task that they had set out to perform. The uncovering of Mardale – though fascinating enough in itself – was not the only reason for their visit to the lonely backwater. Joy was a student at Brandley Hall and was attending a course there run by the professor, who had forsaken his medical career to teach. Together with a further group of students, they were attempting to uncover a few of the mysteries associated with hayfever and its related allergies. A technique had been developed at a nearby research institution, which made it possible to identify pollens laid down over thousands of years. The almost indestructible material could be recovered from the base of a lake by taking out a core of the sediment existing there. Each type of pollen could then be categorised and dated as to its approximate age. The drying up of the lake at this time was a heaven-sent opportunity to conduct an experiment within a definite time span. Since the village of Mardale was known to have disappeared under the waters some sixty years previously, there could be no doubt about the authenticity of the resulting data.

Arriving back at the car, she unlocked the door, gratefully sinking down on to the seat. Removing her wellingtons, she deposited them outside. She would go back and join her tutor later – preferably when Inspector Grey had taken charge of the situation. She would have a bite to eat and a cup of tea first. That might help settle her nerves.

In spite of her determination not to dwell on the subject, her mind kept returning to the shock of seeing the skull. As the professor’s ailment restricted his movements, she had volunteered to undertake the task of crouching down to extract the core of sediment. What she had not envisaged was to find that hideous object apparently staring directly up at her – only inches away from her face. The Prof. would have to finish the job himself or get someone else to collect the steel tube and mallet she had been equipped with. She shuddered yet again. She wanted nothing more to do with the gruesome relic. Let the police clear it out of the way – then perhaps she would feel a little happier. Why did she have this overpowering conviction that something dreadful had occurred in this seemingly peaceful valley? And that something equally as dreadful may be about to happen once more?

The professor had also finally come to realise that he and the student in his charge had failed to complete their task. The tools still lay where Joy had dropped them when effecting her sudden withdrawal. A thought occurred as he awaited the inspector's arrival. The sample he and Joy had been attempting to collect could well prove to be of interest to Grey. As it was possible to determine the ages of the different layers of pollen present in the sediment, so should it prove equally feasible to estimate how long the skull – and possibly the remains of a body – had been lying in that position. Anything that assisted in pin-pointing the time of its arrival there could be of tremendous benefit to the investigating team. Grey was not the type of man to resent his suggestion that this was likely to be of value. He suddenly became aware of the hiker tugging at his sleeve once more, apparently keen to attract his attention.

"If the police are turning out, surely they must think there's a possibility that a murder's been committed."

Reid shrugged his shoulders. "They have to investigate any incident such as this. Could just be an accident. Some poor devil may have drowned a few years back."

"Wouldn't they have checked on that before now?"

"Plenty of people go missing in this area. Climbers and the like. There are occasions when their bodies turn up years later, frequently in a secluded gully on the mountains or some other out of the way spot."

"Doesn't rule out murder though."

The man clearly hoped for some extra excitement to enhance his visit.

In spite of the professor's interpretation of the events, he too had considered the possibility of the skull being part of the remains of someone killed unlawfully. If that proved to be the case, the perpetrator of the crime must surely by now have come to the conclusion that his wrongdoing would never come to light. This skull was surely no recent arrival here and only the extreme drought conditions leading to the depletion of the huge reserves of water could ever have made the discovery possible.

His musings were brought to a halt by the sight of the unmistakable stocky figure of Inspector Grey, determinedly making his way through the clinging, glutinous mud. As was his usual custom when involved on official police business, an ancient briar pipe was clamped firmly between his teeth, the bowl – polished by constant use – gleaming bronze-like in the bright sunlight.

Reid smiled to himself. Grey always puffed away furiously whenever angry or excited. He was puffing well at the moment – though that might be mainly as a result of the exertion.

"Over here, Inspector." Spotting his quarry, Grey surged forward. Alongside him the pathologist and a police sergeant were valiantly struggling to keep up. The sergeant was equipped with spade and trowel, the pathologist with his usual bag of tricks.

A large, formidable looking character, Inspector Grey appeared every inch a policeman. Dark piercing eyes stared out severely beneath heavy, bush-like brows, drawn together below the creased forehead. Those eyes had seen more than their fair share of the suffering that all too often accompanied the crimes he was constantly combating. One of the old school of policemen, he was a dedicated copper who'd pounded the beat many years before securing his present position. Reid had a great deal of admiration for the man.

"What's all this then, Prof?" Grey's greeting, though business like, lacked none of its usual cordiality.

Leading them to where the discovery had been made, the professor pointed out the skull. "See for yourself. As I indicated on the phone, there's little left to identify the person involved."

The pathologist – having had more dealings with items of this nature – crouched down above the barely submerged skull for a closer inspection, eventually making his thoughts known.

"We've certainly got something pretty ancient here, Grey. I'd have banked on finding at least a trace of hair alongside in this sediment if this character had arrived here in the past few decades."

Grey started to chuckle. "Poor sod could have been bald, Bob."

The pathologist laughed out loud. "Bloody sceptic! I might have expected that from you."

Grey was known for his sense of humour. No doubt he needed it to relieve the pressures of the often harrowing tasks that had to be undertaken. Bob Hargreaves concentrated once more on the skull.

"Looks as though our friend here had a good set of teeth – even if he were bald. Could be useful for identification."

Grey nodded. "From what I can see, there's no sign of damage to the front of the skull. Could we allow the sergeant to gently scrape away some of this silt?"

"Sure." The pathologist moved aside. "Let's see if we can unearth anything more under there."

Reid quickly stepped in before too much disturbance took place.

"Could we get the sergeant to take out a core of sediment first? As you can see, we were about to do that when Joy came across the skull."

"No problem." The inspector indicated that it should be done.

Reid explained about the possibility of dating the sample.

"Sounds fine to me." Grey handed over the tube and mallet once the task was completed. He was quite satisfied that it was in safe hands. He would be able to call upon any evidence that came to light.

The sergeant now switched his attention to the unpleasant task of searching for the rest of the remains. With great care he began to remove the softer top layers of mud. Nothing solid impeded his work, though it was difficult to make out any real details – the thin film of water that covered the area filling in each trowel full that was displaced. Painstakingly, he continued the task. Still nothing. It began to look as though the rest of the body was not present. The pathologist called a temporary halt to the search for the trunk and limbs.

"Can you concentrate on the skull, Sergeant?"

More of the softer layers were removed from around the object. Soon it was free.

"OK. Just leave it there." The pathologist took over. Donning gloves, he gently eased the skull from its resting place, placing it in a polythene bag.

The professor suddenly became aware that the once small crowd of onlookers had grown rapidly in size. He recognised the photographer from the local newspaper snapping away. No doubt he was there to record the uncovering of Mardale. His editor would be in for a pleasant surprise. An on-the-spot report of the events now taking place would be even more newsworthy. There would undoubtedly be plenty of speculation as to how the human remains came to be there. And no one would be keener to learn the answer to that mystery than Merlin Reid himself.

"Right. Would you like to use the spade now?" The pathologist had carefully laid the skull aside.

Cautiously the sergeant continued. It was a slow and difficult task, the mud giving up no further clues. Eventually the pathologist was satisfied.

"OK. Nothing else here. We'd have turned it up by now if there had been."

Grey nodded. “Strange. You’d assume a body sinking to the bottom of a lake would remain more or less intact. There wouldn’t be much to disturb it at such a depth.”

“Could have been a dissection job.” It would not have been the first that the pathologist had dealt with. Shading his eyes against the bright sunlight he scanned the surrounding area. “No sign of anything else. Case of wait and see if something turns up I imagine. Though judging by the appearance of the skull, I’d say it’s a bloody long time since this item found its way here.”

“We’ll concentrate on that before we waste time searching for any other remains then.” Grey responded. “Get me a report in as soon as possible and we’ll take it from there.” He turned his attention to the professor. “We’ll take a sample of the sediment from inside the skull and compare it with the one you have there. As you suggest, it may help to establish how long it’s been lying here. Looks like we’ll have to probe a fair way back to trace this blighter though.”

Joy Elliot had been observing the action from a distance. Once the inspector and his entourage had vacated the area, she waved to her tutor, who had also been about to leave until the reporter stepped forward.

“Is it right, sir, that you discovered the skull?”

“Not exactly.” Reid beckoned Joy to join him. “This young lady was the one who actually spotted it. It gave her quite a shock… Are you feeling well enough to speak to this reporter?” he inquired as she arrived.

“Yes, I’m fine now.” She was still not intending to let on that she felt shaken by the experience. “What exactly would you like to know?”

“Well, Miss. I think our readers would be interested in hearing your account of the discovery.”

She hesitated a little, still uneasy about relating her actual feelings at the time of the event.

The reporter smiled encouragingly. “Just give me your name and address first, then we can carry on from there.”

She forced herself to relax, explaining why she and her tutor came to be there, and then recounted the discovery of the skull.

It quickly became apparent that the journalist placed a great deal of importance on the find. Almost to the extent that it appeared he already suspected the identity of the person involved. Yet how could that be?

"Are there no other students with you?" He was at last coming to the end of his questioning, clearly seeking the final crumbs that might draw his report to a conclusion.

"No. I'm only here because my parents are out of the country at the moment. I stayed on in the hope that I could be of some help to the professor."

"I imagine your friends are going to be a bit miffed at missing all this excitement then?"

She nodded. Her friends would no doubt have loved to be involved.

"May I take a photograph for publication?"

"Sure, why not?"

The reporter strategically placed her with the excavation in the background. Wouldn't the others get a surprise. And maybe she was over-reacting to some extent to the event that had taken place. To be honest, it was quite exciting being the central character in such an intriguing case – in spite of the trepidation she felt.

The professor tactfully avoided making any mention of the discovery of the skull on their journey back to the Hall. It was clear that the young student had not yet recovered her composure. Strange that she should be so affected.

Joy was also unable to comprehend the emotions that now filled her mind with fear and apprehension. Later, on retiring to bed, all manner of images disturbed her dreams. Had she been fully aware of the macabre history of the skull, her dreams may well have turned to nightmares.

CHAPTER TWO

29th October 1589

The reivers (Scottish Border Raiders) had spent the day sleeping rough. Secure in a wooded hollow, high in the mountainous region of Westmorland, they had little fear of the March Wardens, nor of any troopers who might accompany them. Their confidence was born of regular incursions over the border into England, for this was a way of life to these men. Breaking cover from their chosen place of exile: the Debatable Lands – an area adjacent to the borders of both Scotland and England – they had ridden throughout the hours of darkness, silently and swiftly, to reach this place. Through the salt marshes of Solway Moss their trusty, sure-footed 'Galloways' had carried them, the sturdy, shaggy little ponies, unshod and unkempt, keeping a good pace by the fragmented light of the moon. Across the border, negotiating burns, stony outcrops, bleak fellsides, bogs flecked white with cotton grass – by unfrequented byways and passes they had travelled. Arriving before dawn broke, they had taken a meal of oats and dried venison, encamping during the hours of daylight till dusk began throwing its blanket of shrouding mists and lengthening shadows over the mountainous terrain once more; the drab mantle of nightfall being their only ally in this alien territory. On this occasion, they had penetrated deep into English territory, encountering scant sign of sheep or cattle on the way. Rich pickings were becoming as rare as pigs taking wing!

"Time we were awa'." Robbie Armstrong was keen to press on further into the wilds of Westmorland. His kinsmen, along with Duncan of Crieff – a rogue who had earned his place among them by running his sword through a Moss Trooper about to spike an Armstrong – needed no urging. Unless they rapidly availed themselves of some form of booty, their raid may have to be aborted. A quick strike and a speedy retreat were required, ere the night lost its grip and daylight exposed their nefarious activities.

The thick blanket each man carried was speedily rolled and affixed to the rear of his saddle. 'Jacks' – loose-fitting tunics, quilted and covered with hide above an inner canvas stitched with metal plates – were donned. Weapons: short Scottish sword, lance and long-handled axe, were strapped in place or carried. A 'Steill Bonnet' or helmet, plus riding boots, completed the outfit. No man went reiving these days unless he was prepared to fight for his life. And though life was cheap on the border, no man laid his down without a mighty battle.

"Aw ready?"

"Aye!"

These were men of few words. Each was acutely aware of the risk they took. An encounter with a warden could mean a dance at the end of a rope – or a bloody fight to the death. Reiving days were almost done now, the authorities slowly but surely stamping out a practice which had endured throughout the course of the Border Wars – a long drawn out confrontation which seemed finally to be coming to an end; leaving the erstwhile combatants to fight to scratch a living from the land. With little else but battle experience, small wonder that men on both sides of the border had turned to thieving and cattle rustling to exist. It was a way of life that had made many small farming communities so vulnerable that they had either joined forces with the reivers or banded together in some place that afforded a modicum of safety. Only some distance from the frontier did the brave or the foolish now consider it a risk worth taking to leave their animals unattended.

For some miles the reivers travelled the hills in silence. As on previous occasions, that silence proved to be their saviour. Hearts beating like drums within their chests, they caught the murmur of distant voices carried on the wind. The troopers could well be on the prowl. A hand on the muzzle of each nag was sufficient to quieten the beasts as they were drawn to a halt. The voices grew louder. Thank the Almighty that he had seen fit to almost totally blot out the night sky with copious clouds. But for that mercy, the game would already be up. Still the sounds drew nearer. Swords were slid gently from scabbards. There was no time to cut and run.

The warden and his men were taken completely by surprise. Only four troopers accompanied the official as this outing was purely a gesture of authority. So far from the border, they were not expecting trouble. They could not have been more mistaken.

Set upon from all sides in the gathering gloom by the eleven desperate raiders they stood little chance, though they fought like tigers. Swords flashed as a fleeting beam of moonlight illuminated the gory scene of carnage. Swords that ran red with blood! Faces and limbs split open by the savage welter of blows, one by one the troopers crumbled, inflicting little more than minor cuts and bruises on their attackers. Finally each man was cut down without mercy and put to the sword.

"Guid work, me laddies!" The evil Robbie chuckled with delight. A few dead troopers would cause him no loss of sleep. "Tether their nags. They'll drive hame wi' the cattle on oor return."

The ponies were led to a small thicket and secured; bark being hacked from the tree nearest the track, ensuring its recognition in passing. Stripped of all weapons and valuables, the bodies of the troopers were unceremoniously tossed down the fellside to lie part hidden amid the massed sweep of purple heather and sun-bronzed bracken.

"Let's ride, Robbie." Duncan of Crieff was impatient to be off. They had even more reason now to conclude their business with all speed.

"Aye, man, haste ye on."

They were dropping down towards more fertile land now. Shap and its abbey lay some distance ahead, around its perimeter a scattering of farmsteads. Deep into Westmorland, some unsuspecting folk may have failed to take adequate precautions.

And so it proved.

Sheep were still on the higher ground, cattle below in the walled enclosure alongside a small farmstead. Well-fattened animals that had partaken of the summer bounty of sweet grasses. Fit animals that would drive at good speed over the mountains and through bog and mire to their new quarters.

No time was spent in discussion. Each man knew his appointed task. The cattle were the first priority. Quietly and stealthily, desperate not to give warning by disturbing either sleeping men or dogs, the riders made their way down. Two horseman stood by on either side of the gate as it was swung wide. The remainder eased their way inside the enclosure, slowly coaxing the cattle to their feet. No sudden manoeuvres took place. A gentle nudge from a ponies muzzle was sufficient to stir the animals into action. A delicate touch with a lance was all that was required to move any laggards forward. With little more than a snort, twenty or more animals were lifted from under their owner's nose as if by magic.

Up the hillside they were driven, like some broad shadow cast by the clouds in the dispersed light from above. Faster now, as the reivers hastened them on. Too fast maybe, as the silence was suddenly shattered by barking echoing from below. The hooves of the cattle had struck rocky ground, disturbing an alert sheepdog.

The light of a lantern soon appeared, followed by the roar of an obscenity. At the rear of the group, Duncan of Crieff turned his mount, preparing to do battle. His duty was to hold off any retaliatory action which might be forthcoming while his comrades made good their escape – in the process, adding to the plunder by rounding up as many of the plump Swaledale sheep as could be managed.

The sheepdog, followed by a giant of a man, came rushing forth from the farmhouse. Like a shot from a gun, the dog came bounding towards the intruders, attacking Duncan's pony from the rear once it came within distance. One lash from a massive flailing hoof sent the unfortunate animal, broken and yelping, across the side of the fell. The dog's master was now charging up the incline as though intent on tackling the raiders weaponless and single-handed. The reiver sat astride his mount observing the heroics with growing amazement. The man made no attempt to slow as Duncan raised his border lance. Straight on he came, cursing and screaming at the top of his voice. Only at the last moment did he attempt to dodge the thrust of the weapon. It was to no avail. Deep into the muscular upper part of his torso the lance struck, seemingly only prevented from piercing directly through his body by the massive shoulder-blades. Just the merest grunt escaped the huge man's lips, though he was clearly badly wounded. Grasping the lance, he tore it free from his shoulder. Then with an almighty tug, he almost unseated Duncan, who was forced to relinquish his hold on the weapon. In a flash, the lance was turned on its owner, thrust with such force that it penetrated both padded jacket and armoured lining. Deep into Duncan's side it sank, tearing through flesh and bone. Almost involuntarily, knees goaded the sturdy pony into flight. Neither reiver nor smallholder were in a fit state to continue the fray. No further challenge came from the silent farmstead as the giant staggered and fell.

In spite of his injuries, Duncan refrained from calling out to his fellow raiders. A man accepted his fate as he accepted that others might suffer in the same manner. Left arm now crushed hard into the savage wound that shot searing pain with every jolt of the pony's hooves, he resumed his position at the rear of the troop. The tide of animals, swelled now with the addition of the sheep, were driven forward at a pace that was fast though not furious. Could he keep up?

Keep up he did, till they hit the High Street range of mountains once more. Gradually now, he began dropping back, loss of blood weakening his pain-racked body. Still he endeavoured to drive the small group of cattle and sheep that had fallen back with him. In the gloom that came with a night sky barely illuminated by the fickle, shrouded moon, his companions were unaware that he was adrift. Espying a remote valley, lit by the grace of a momentary gap in the clouds, Duncan gathered all of his strength, heading the animals in that direction. He desperately needed some place to hole up. Strength, unfortunately, now failed him, though he had succeeded in his effort to force the beasts part way down the narrow, stony track. Pitching from his pony, he was unconscious before he hit the rocky ground.

30th October 1589

Molly Grieves was up with the lark. Herbs and wild flowers were sweetest when picked fresh with the morning dew and herbs and potions were her livelihood. Venturing forth from the cave where she occasionally sheltered overnight when some distance from her mother's home, she was startled to discover sheep and cattle grazing what tufts of grass struggled to survive on the rock and boulder strewn mountainside. Neither shepherd nor herdsman appeared to be accompanying them, though that too would have been surprising, since no one had lived in the hamlet of Mardale for several years. The settlers who had once inhabited the fertile area of land at the base of the secluded vale had long since fled their farms and fields when reivers first began their plundering. Too few in number to put up anything more than a token resistance, they had been stripped of all but their most meagre possessions. Sheep, cattle, even household goods had been taken. Faced with starvation, those who had survived the attacks had been forced to throw themselves on the mercy of friends or relatives who lived in the comparative safety of larger communities.

So what was now afoot? With some trepidation, Molly ventured a little further from the cave. No sign of life in the valley. With the exception of the animals, no sign of life anywhere. Emboldened by the absence of any other human presence, she took up her basket, heading towards the higher ground where she knew she would find the ingredients necessary to ply her trade. Molly was the local 'healer' – a vocation passed down through her family for as long as she could remember. Looked upon with some awe by the uneducated farming folk, the family had gained a reputation for being in league with unnatural forces – for how else had they gained their powers? Molly was content to foster that belief, now prescribing to both humans and animals alike; a rare gift that ensured she and her mother would never starve. Plucking the odd leaf and herb along the way, she kept a wary eye open.

Almost attaining the more level area of ground that topped Kidsty Pike, Molly stopped in her tracks. Ahead, a lone pony gave her but a cursory glance as it cropped the grass. Saddled and bridled, it had clearly not been put out to pasture. As the pony moved off a little way, the prone figure of a man became apparent on the rocky track. Even from a distance, Molly could see that all was not well. Still dressed for combat, the man lay crumpled on the ground. Gingerly easing her way forward, she could hardly fail to notice the blood-stained protective jacket.

Like others of her calling, Molly normally considered not the reason nor the rhyme of how a man had acquired his injuries. That this man would die if not attended to appeared inevitable. But this man was clearly a Scot – and the penalty for aiding a reiver was the gallows. She hesitated. Though she had cared for many others in the past who had suffered injuries such as this, they had always been her own kinsmen. Border folk knew little else but war and feuding, death and destruction being accepted as part of their lot.

Kneeling at the fallen reiver's side, she assessed his condition. Unconscious or not, she would never manage to raise him to his nag. Nor was he likely to survive a journey atop of a pony with the ugly blood-caked gash in his side. To be sure, it was most unlikely that he would survive whatever action she took. Quickly reaching a decision, she drew his sword from its scabbard. Rising to her feet, she realised his eyes were now open. Seeing her armed, he was sure that he had breathed his last. Not a finger could he lift.

She smiled down at him. "Now, me bold buckaroo, rest ye there while I see to your carriage."

Duncan breathed easily once more – or as easily as his pain-racked body would allow. Mercifully, unconsciousness overcame him once again.

Molly wasted no time. Sword in hand, she strode to the nearest birch tree. Slashing at a long, slender branch, she finally brought it down. Now she attacked another, felling that in the same manner. The obedient pony put up no resistance as she took up its reins, leading it over to the fallen timbers. Unfastening the blanket from its moorings, she now used the belts to good effect. A branch was securely attached to either side of the saddle, the less bulky, twiggy material, trailing out on the ground to the rear. Taking a corner of the blanket, she knotted that to the top of one branch, stretching it then to repeat the process on the opposite side. Affixing the lower corners in the same manner, she managed to bind twigs and branches together, forming a hammock-like structure. A makeshift contraption to be sure, though a wounded reiver was not likely to complain.

Heaving the unconscious man on to the rough carriage was no easy task, though it was eventually accomplished. Molly was a strong lass. Reins in hand, she now led the pony back down the track, drawing up close to the cave entrance. Untying the blanket, she used it to drag the man over the uneven ground. Just as well he was not conscious of the fact. Exhausted now, Molly collapsed on her bed of bracken and hay.

Recovering shortly, she hauled the man on to the soft bedding, laying him on his uninjured side. The first priority was warmth if he were to survive after a night out on the open fellside. Cautiously opening his blood-soaked jacket, she managed to avoid disturbing his wound. Now shedding her own loose-woven garments, she pressed her naked body to his, covering them both as best she could with her discarded clothing and the portion of blanket that he was not laid on.

It was many hours later before a groan announced the man's return to consciousness. Molly smiled at the startled look that crossed his rugged face as he realised his situation.

"Lie still now, ye be safe here."

"Water." The appeal came out in a hoarse whisper.

She drew away from him, wrapping him quickly to conserve his body heat. Taking her clothes and dressing hurriedly, she was aware that his eyes followed her every move. She took up a mug from among the few belongings she stored at the cave.

"Bide ye there." The instruction was hardly necessary.

Leaving the cave with caution, in fear that someone might observe her, she sought out the nearest cow. It was ripe for milking. Molly was used to turning her hand to almost any task. The mug was soon full to the brim with the warm liquid. It would benefit the man more than the ice-cold water from the nearby gill.

She eased up his head on her return, pressing the mug to his parched lips. "Sip it gently now."

That was clearly all he was capable of, the pain in his side causing him to gasp even with that small effort. Gratefully, he drank till every drop was gone.

"Rest yersel'." She made him as comfortable as possible. "Ye'll be needin' tae pass water by now?"

He nodded, humiliated by his situation, yet aware that he was totally incapable of movement.

She had noticed a pack on his saddle as she led the pony down. A bowl of some description was apparent among the contents. Quickly she collected the baggage, seeking out the vessel. Meant to contain the meal of oats the man also carried, this would have to serve a new purpose. Loosening the belt around his waist, she eased down his breeches at the front. "Nae blushes now, I've done this afore."

She assisted him as best she could, replacing his clothing with the same care. "Tell me when ye next need help. Ye'll nae move till I say. I have nae dragged ye here tae lose ye now."

He forced a weak smile. Never would he have imagined he would come to this.

She took up the bowl and mug, heading out to the sparkling gill which cascaded down through rocky outcrops on its way to join the stretch of water in the valley below. No one need want for anything in this place. Returning the cleaned vessels to the cave, she removed the saddle from the pony, stashing both saddle and axe inside. The man was barely awake, though she could see the relief in his eyes. Any sign of his presence would almost certainly mean death – probably for the two of them!

She read his mind. "The animals need drivin' down tae the valley bottom afore they start to wander. If they're sighted, we're done for, like as not."

Taking the mug once more, she topped it again from a cow only too happy to lighten its load. The wounded man would need a regular supply of nourishment if he were to thrive. She must collect a pail when next making her way home.

Having ridden bare-back since childhood, Molly mounted the pony, heading the cattle and sheep down towards the valley below. The track was narrow for most of the way, ensuring an easy progression. Studying the lie of the land as she rode, her eyes lit on one of the fields that was least likely to be spotted from above. Still outlined by the almost indestructible dry stone walls built by the original settlers, it was lush with the uncut hay that had remained ungrazed all season. With Mardale Beck running alongside, the animals would find both fodder and water there.

Persuading the animals to enter the enclosure proved no easy task, though once one was enticed it became a procession. From force of habit, both cattle and sheep played follow my leader. Molly heaved a sigh of relief as she propped the rickety gate in position, quickly attending to any cow which had not had its milk released. As she did so, her mind strayed to the owner of the animals. Should he now be in pursuit, he was unlikely to suspect that they would be secreted here. But for the injury the reiver had sustained, the booty would now be en route to Scotland; indeed, perhaps most of it had already arrived there.

Tethering the pony near the water's edge, she tackled the climb back with consummate ease. Long, muscular legs, used to such terrain, carried her swiftly to the cave, safely set well back into the mountain where few ever strayed. Duncan still lay in excruciating pain, any movement threatening to set the blood coursing from his wound once more. Congealed by the close contact with shirt and jacket, only those materials had stemmed the flow sufficiently to keep him alive. He gingerly raised his head as she entered.

Taking up the mug, she once more pressed it to his lips. He would require a steady supply to restore his strength. Fortunate for him that he had held on to the cattle, the milk being an ideal source of nutrition. Once more he drained every drop, shivering with cold as she eased his head down. Once more she stripped naked before uncovering his upper body and easing herself against him, covering them both as she did so. A grateful smile crossed his lips momentarily before he slipped, exhausted, into a deep sleep.

31st October 1589

Both Molly and Duncan had slept until dawn. Worn out by her efforts of the previous day, Molly had still managed to maintain close contact throughout the night. Her reward was the warmth that now emanated back from the man lying alongside her. It was a warmth she welcomed for its own sake. A warmth she had never experienced before in this way. Gently drawing away, she saw his eyes open as she did so. Eyes that spoke volumes. Eyes that expressed his thanks without need for words, though words finally came.

"Yer an angel, lassie. What name are ye known by?"

She gave him a wry smile as she took up her clothes, sensing her breasts tingling under his unblinking gaze as she dressed.

"D'ye always sleep wi' your lassies afore ye inquire their names?"

He would have laughed at her jesting had his injuries not prevented him doing so. "Nay, lassie; ye be the first."

She chuckled. "Just as well! I'm Molly Greaves – if it please ye. And what might your name be?"

"Duncan McKade – Chief o' the McKade clan – what few there be left o' us after the wars. Called Duncan o' Crieff by most o' my ain folk."

"Right, Duncan. Bide ye there whilst I fetch more milk. I'll attend tae your other needs once you're fed."

Though it was a fair trek, she was not long away, tarrying only for the time it took to milk the cows for their comfort and for her requirements. Mixing Duncan's stash of oats with the tepid liquid, a palatable meal soon appeared. Having helped him raise himself once more, she now spoon-fed him like a baby. He would need all of his strength a little later when she came to clean his wound. Shirt and jacket may have conserved his lifeblood, but infection could soon set in. Not daring to risk any disturbance of the wound prematurely, by now it was rapidly becoming a necessity.

Having fed him, she proceeded to carry out the more intimate tasks. Sick he may be, she quickly realised that there were now signs of some recovery. Strength was beginning to return in at least one region! She smiled as she readjusted his breeches. Clearly she was not the only one to find the situation a little unsettling. Maybe if he were not such a fine specimen of a man she might control her own emotions more easily. Auburn hair and beard framing his bronzed and weather beaten face, that face was hardly drained of its colour in spite of his loss of blood. A powerful man, broad as he was brawny, it saddened her to see him laid low. He was clearly greatly embarrassed to be tended by a young woman; yet she felt no discomfort in his company, only a growing attachment to this stranger. In the process of providing him with the warmth of her naked body, it was the first time she had actually lain in that way with a man. The sensation still lingered, both in her mind and body.

"Rest agin while I'm awa' tae my mother's cottage. I've potions and ointments there that'll heal your wounds."

With his improving health came bemusement. "Ye'll nae dee yersel' any favours, lassie. Ye ken the risk ye'll be taking?"

She shrugged her shoulders. "Should I let ye die, Duncan? I'd nae more desert ye than turn my back on any suffering creature."

He was hardly used to such treatment. Brutalised by the Border Wars, he expected no quarter. "I'm a reiver, Molly. I either kill, or get killed. Ye'd be best leaving me here tae seek my ain way oot o' this."

"And die out on the fells? Or be cut down by the troopers? Ye'd bleed tae death hardly afore ye set foot outside this valley. Bide ye here till I heal your body. What ye do then is your ain concern."

He gave her a weak smile. "Off wi' ye then, lassie. Hasten ye back."

She returned his smile, her own lighting up a face that was both bonny and suddenly flushed beneath its healthy tan. She had waited many moons for a man to be concerned that she should hurry back to his side.

Setting off homeward, she contemplated Duncan's words of warning. Only now did the full force of the commitment she had undertaken cause her concern. To risk her own life may be foolhardy, but she also had a mother to support. Like herself, her mother had been a healer before her, though even she had been unable to totally fight off the effects of a stroke which had left her partially crippled, and dependent on Molly in so many ways. Twenty-three years of age, Molly had never wed, though her looks and figure had turned many a head. Flaxen haired, tanned by sun and wind, a body toned by constant exercise, she would have made any man a worthy wife – though who would take on a wife when he would need to support her ailing mother too? Not many in this impoverished area. Predominantly farming folk, a man valued a woman mainly for the labour she could provide. Another mouth to feed was sufficient to deter all but the most dedicated suitor.

"What kept ye, lass?" Molly's mother was accustomed to her daughter's absence when seeking out her herbs and berries, though this time she had tarried longer than normal.

"Sorry, Ma, but I've a tale tae tell that ye'll nae wish tae hear."

"Are ye unwell, lass?"

"Not I, Ma."

"Then who? I've had Abraham Jowett's kin here seeking potions. They've not long gone. Is it he ye've been treating?"

Molly knew Abraham Jowett only too well. A bad-tempered oaf, he had recently struck his wife so severely as to break her arm, though the poor woman was five months pregnant. Molly had tended her, with little thanks and no payment from him. Alice Jowett was now with her ageing parents while she recovered.

"Not he, Ma. Tis another who's sorely wounded."

"Wounded ye say? So too is Abraham. He were found not long since out on the fells wi' a rent in him that would hae killed a normal man. He could barely speak, though he reckoned it were a reiver who'd pricked him. They robbers took off wi' his cattle an' sheep too."

Molly could hardly sympathise with the man. Built like an ox, he refused to join his neighbours in herding his animals with theirs in a place of safety. They say no man is an island, yet he came as close as dammit!

"That could mean trouble, Ma."

Her mother raised her head questioningly. "It's not a reiver ye've been aiding?"

Molly nodded. "I could nae leave him to die. Ye'd have done the same."

"Heaven help us! There's a warden and four troopers found dead upon the fells! Are ye mad, lass?"

Molly threw her arms around her mother. "They'll nae find him. I've hid him safe in the cave under Kidsty Pike. He's some o' the sheep and cattle wi' him, but I drove 'em down into Mardale. Who's tae see 'em? The vale's sae isolated hardly none but me ventures there."

Her words of reassurance fell on deaf ears.

"Someone's bound tae see 'em sometime. Ye'll no evade the troopers!"

"He'll be long gone afore they catch on, Ma. Once he's fettled, he'll be off like a hare."

"He'll be the death o' us, Molly. If they take ye, I'll nae survive for long."

That was Molly's main fear. "Nae use worryin', tis done and that's that! I'll just make ye comfortable, Ma, then I'll be awa'. I'll keep poppin' back tae see you're OK. Jest tell anyone as asks fer me that I'm lookin' after aunt Bessie."

Molly's mother knew better than to argue. Molly had gone her own way for too many years to challenge her decisions.

Finally satisfied that her mother's needs were provided for, Molly was on her way. Laden with blankets, provisions, pots and potions, she kept well away from the few farms on her return journey. Best if she went unseen.

No sign of any intrusion as she approached the cave. Pushing her heavy bundle out of sight before going forward, she broke into song. Should Duncan have been discovered, she was ready with her excuse. Her herbs hung drying in the cave – and who would suspect a young woman happily singing along with the birds of the air?

Her subterfuge proved unnecessary. Duncan lay where she had left him, a faint smile playing around his lips.

"Ye sing like a dove, Molly."

She doubted that, though it pleased her he should think so.

"Shush yer mockin' while I bring in my wares. Ye'll be the one singin' once I set tae work on that wound."

She fed him once all was unpacked. A bottle of her mother's Elderberry wine relaxed him, subduing the ache in his side a little. It was as well. The time had come to attend to his injury.

"Ye'll nae enjoy this, Duncan, so grit yer teeth!"

She had filled a pail from the stream while he drank; her ointments were readily to hand. Leaves of comfrey lay waiting to cover the wound once treated. The ice-cold water she applied to loosen the blood-caked clothing caused him to gasp with its freezing intensity. Cruel it may seem, though it should cause his blood to flow less freely, the flesh contracting to counter the influence of the icy drenching. As soon as it appeared feasible, the clothing was peeled back as it softened around the wound, revealing a truly ugly gash. Gently she bathed the area, aware of Duncan's extreme discomfort – though he fought hard to disguise it. Spreading the ointment thickly, she carefully pressed the comfrey leaves to hold it fast, securing all with strips of fabric wrapped around his body. Drying him well, she stripped once more, happy to provide him with her body heat in order to restore his own, sapped by the treatment he had received. There was no way she dare risk lighting a fire.

Crushed between her breasts, the sachet of lavender she had prepared before leaving home – and which now hung from a thong around her neck – mingled its fresh fragrance with that of the hay and bracken as they lay together. His body odour aroused a great yearning in her. How she desired to become more than a mere comfort to this man!

CHAPTER THREE

November 3rd 1589

Days had passed without sight or sound of troopers, nor, for that matter, any other intruder in the secluded valley. That the reivers would have been pursued after their murderous attack on the warden and his men was in no doubt, though with their head start and the knowledge of every twist and turn that might throw off their stalkers, it was unlikely the perpetrators of the crime would be taken. Presumably no thought had crossed the mind of the troopers that one of the reivers' band may have fallen by the wayside. If such a thought had occurred, any search had evidently been conducted elsewhere.

Duncan was healing well. Very well. As Molly awoke after yet another night cradled in his arms, breasts pressed firmly to his receptive body, she felt a stirring between her thighs. The clothing he still wore around his lower limbs failed to restrict the movement. Duncan was clearly becoming aroused. Fully awake and gazing deeply into her eyes, his own eyes were aflame with passion. One hand encircled the nape of her neck, gently drawing her to his lips. She made no attempt to resist, crushing her mouth to his. Having risked death for this man, she would not deny him the pleasure of her body. Nor would she deny herself the pleasure of his!

Eventually his mouth broke contact with her own, only to seek out the firm contours of her breasts. The low moan that broke the stillness was not the sound born of pain that had echoed around the cave in recent days, rather the expression of a woman desperate for fulfilment. Just as well no intruders were within hearing distance, as Molly's cries gradually intensified with each stroke of his tongue, each contact made by his hungry lips. Struggling now to help strip off the breeches that restrained him, she pressed herself to his body once more – this time a body as naked as her own.

He did not rush her, caressing, kissing, stroking, as he whispered words of endearment in her ear. His every action appeared motivated by a desire to cater to her needs as much as to his own, though clearly his injury restricted too vigorous an approach. She instigated his entry when she could control her desire no longer. Fully aware that he might well undo all the healing that had taken place, she took matters into her own hands, forestalling him from exerting his body by her own undulating movements. Gratefully, he allowed her to continue until both of them, lips and bodies crushed together in a passionate embrace, came to their climax. Locked in each other's arms, no thought was given to what the future might hold in store as they lay exhausted by their efforts.

Molly was the first to show signs of recovery. Kissing his eyes, his cheeks, the tip of his nose, his lips, she chuckled out loud. "Well, well! Ye seem tae be comin' on, laddie! 'Tis clearly time we got ye on your feet. If that wound o' yours can take such punishment, it's fit tae be tested wi' a little more exercise."

He still held her tightly, forcibly returning her kisses, chuckling too as he came up for air. "Ye be a hard lass, Molly! Would ye turn a man oot o' his bed afore he's had time tae catch his breath?"

She silenced his complaint by pressing her lips once more to his.

"Get ye up then when ye be ready, Duncan. Ye'll hae my body agin' once I'm sure ye can manage it."

He actually contrived to laugh. "Awa' wi' ye, lassie! Ye drive a terrible hard bargain!"

She grabbed up her clothes and towel, casting a cheeky grin in his direction as she did so. "Awa' I be then. Stay abed till I get back fra the gill, then I'll cut ye a crutch."

He followed her naked form with joyous eyes until she was out of sight. Joyous, smouldering eyes that endeavoured to miss not one iota of sinuous, sensual flesh.

Plunging under a rocky prominence, Molly braved the icy waters that cascaded down the mountainside towering above, gasping as her body was engulfed. Invigorated and refreshed, she towelled herself briskly after her dip, the chill soon abating – though she hardly noticed its presence. She felt naught but delight. Delight that Duncan had wanted her. Delight at finally becoming a whole woman at last.

Gazing down at her breasts – firmed even more by the effect of the icy drenching – she was happy with the sight. Duncan had rejoiced in her breasts. She had rejoiced in his pleasure, for the nightly contact with his body had been inordinately tantalising. So tantalising indeed that it had proved almost impossible to endure. And though it may be but a short while before common sense decreed that he should move on, she was now certain that she would give herself to him whenever he desired her. Whatever time was left to them, she would grasp each single moment of happiness while she may.

Dressing now, she made her way back. Duncan still lay abed, a smile of contentment playing around his lips. Unfortunately, he could not be allowed to remain inactive. Molly was only too aware that such inertia could lead to congestion of his lungs – especially with winter's chill increasingly extending its icy fingers to probe every inch of the cave's interior.

"Don't get tae comfy now. I'll fetch ye a stick tae lean on, then we'll see about gettin ye on your feet."

She took up the axe, ignoring his playful plea that she leave him in peace. A branch that forked into two was soon lopped off the nearest tree and cut to size. Duncan would not realise it until he came to stand, but his confinement and loss of blood would render him weak in the legs. A strong lass Molly may be, though she realised she would struggle to take his weight for long.

As she had foreseen, it was a difficult task raising him. Helping him to his knees first, she gave him the crutch for support as he gingerly forced his body to respond.

"Easy now! Let me help ye. I want nae heroics."

He made no answer, gritting his teeth with the effort as he rose. "Lean on me."

He was forced to do so. "Can ye bear my burden, Molly?"

"Aye. Wedge that crutch under your shoulder and let me gie ye an arm tae hang on tae."

He didn't argue. "God, but I've nae much strength left, lassie. Ye'll hae tae tack it easy wi' me – I'm nae used tae being molested afore breakfast."

She could hardly bear his weight as she shook with laughter. "Gie ower, Duncan! Ye'll hae the pair o' us down if ye aren't careful."

His laughter was cut short as he attempted to move. She held on tight. "Easy now! One step at a time."

One step at a time it was. Shuffling steps maybe, but progress was made. With much grunting and a little cursing, Duncan finally made it outside.

"Well now, de ye think ye can see tae your ain personal needs this morning?"

He smiled down at her. "I may need a wee hond."

She could hardly refuse.

4th November 1589

Molly was delighted. The previous day had gone well. Duncan had fought to regain the strength in his legs, eventually managing to walk a short distance aided only by the crutch. On inspection, the gash in his side appeared to be healing rapidly. Molly had strapped him tightly around, ensuring the wound should come to no further harm. He had demanded payment when night came for achieving the task she had set him. She had been only too pleased to acquiesce. Now that morning was once more here, it was time for further progress.

"We need tae move fra here soon, Duncan. Wi' winter on its way, I think we should seek shelter down in the valley. There's monie a farmhouse as needs nowt more than a bit o' thatching."

He nodded, "Aye, we could risk a fire tae warm us there. A wee bit o' smoke might gae unnoticed at that distance."

"Ye'll need tae look the part o' a local man. If we're sighted, we'll hae nae chance wi' ye dressed like that. I'll awa' tae my mothers and fetch some o' father's clothing. Ma's kept 'em in spite o' his being dead these seven summers."

"Will they fit me?"

She looked him up and down. "They will wi' a few tucks an' tackings. Da was a big man tae. I'll bring needle and thread along wi' me. Soon hae ye lookin' like a real farmer."

He grimaced. "What next, Molly? Have ye nae pity?"

She grinned at his teasing. "Ye be thankful I can stitch. Ye might hae ended up in one o' Ma's dresses!"

He broke into hearty laughter, this time hardly needing to clutch his injured side as he did so. As she left she was not sure if she were happy or sad. The signs were that he would soon be well enough to travel on.

"What news, lass?"

Molly's mother was clearly concerned.

"Nowt tae bother ye, Ma. Naebody's been near us and Duncan' s fettlin' grand. Another week an' he'll doubtless be awa'."

"Another weck and ye could be caught!"

Molly shrugged her shoulders. "I'll nae let that happen if there's any way tae prevent it. If I can tek some o' father's old things, I'll dress him so he might pass as one o' us."

Her mother didn't hesitate. "If it'll git him awa' fra here wi'out the pair o' ye bein' caught, ye can tek the lot!"

Molly kissed her cheek. "I knew ye'd not deny me, Ma. Now, tell me how ye be faring."

"Nae bad. Ye could fetch some logs in fra the pile afore ye leave though. I'm nae much use when it comes tae carryin'."

Molly was well aware that her mother would never complain. "I'll cook us a stew up too while I'm here and bide awhile. I can pot some o' it up in the hay box tae keep warm fer Duncan. He's nae had a hot meal since I found him."

That appeared to pluck at her mother's heart strings. "Poor man! Take owt ye need, lass. I reckon as how he's nae worse that many o' our ain kinsfolk."

* * *

That was hardly the sentiment which burnt in the heart of Abraham Jowett! He too was growing stronger each day – and vowing to avenge himself in some way once his wound was healed. The troopers may have failed in their attempt to apprehend the reivers, but he was determined someone should pay for his losses. A man was nothing if he had neither cattle nor sheep to sustain him. Better death while seeking his revenge than penury. He would risk all to retrieve his animals.

Molly had inquired of Abraham Jowett's progress as she and her mother ate.

"He's on the mend. That wife o' his has gone back tae him – more fool her! She were here askin' fer ye. I told her Bessie were ill an' ye could nae attend tae Abraham. I think she thowt ye would nae treat him on account o' his mean temper."

Molly chuckled. "She's not far wrong! I got not one penny out o' that mean sod fer treatin' her."

It was Molly's mother's turn to chuckle now. "Don't ye worry, lass. I made 'em pay afore they ever got a mite o' medication out o' me. An' I charged 'em double fer it!"

"Great, ma!" Molly had never expected to collect her debt. "That auld bugger would gie ye nowt but a scowl if he could get awa' wi' it."

Collecting up the dishes now, Molly washed them before saying goodbye. Loaded with as many useful household items as she could manage, she slipped away along the more remote tracks, intent on getting back before Duncan's meal cooled in its nest of hay. The welcome she received on her return was well worth the effort.

"What would I de wi'out ye, Molly?" Duncan hugged her as best he could, a look of grim determination on his weather-beaten face. "I'd be laid in my grave were it not fer ye. I'll nae walk awa' fra ye once I'm healed. Tis more than I could stand."

She was still uncertain whether that commitment was precisely what she desired. To stay meant he would never be out of danger. "We'll see, Duncan. Come eat up this stew while we talk."

He took the hot food from her hungrily. "There's nae need tae talk, lassie. I'd rather be caught an' hanged here than gae back tae my auld ways. I'll nae tek ye back to my land either. It's nae life fer a woman amongst a gang o' cut-throats."

She clung to him, tears filling her eyes. "I surely love ye, Duncan, but it'll never be safe here. I doubt we can hide forever."

He grinned as he ate appreciatively. "We'll manage, Molly. Ye'll nae get rid o' me now. I've never tasted stew like this afore in my life!"

She punched him playfully. "So it's just my cookin' as has stolen yer heart?"

He looked unblinkingly into her eyes. "Nae, lassie. Tis ye an' aw ye bring abed wi' ye!"

5th November 1589

Molly had spent much of the previous day sorting and stitching her father's clothing to fit Duncan. Dressed now in his new attire, he was ready to move out.

"Reet, lassie, lead on."

She had brought up the pony from below, loading it with all it could reasonably carry. Duncan was best on his feet, not subjected to the jolts and jars that might come had he ridden the nag.

"Call out if ye be in pain. We can stop whenever it suits ye."

He had no intention of dallying unless the pain became unbearable. Away from the protection of the cave they might easily be spotted on the less shielded track leading down the mountainside. Though hardly fearful for his own safety, he was, nevertheless, fearful that Molly might be taken. She was risking her all for him. And this woman had shown him the only real affection he had ever encountered since taking up his life as a reiver.

They travelled with no further word passing between them, each aware of the need to be alert for any sight or sound of other human presence. They need not have concerned themselves. Only the cattle and sheep below occasionally disturbed the tranquillity of the vale with the odd baa or bellow.

On reaching the base of the valley it soon became apparent that the farmhouse alongside the penned animals was eminently suitable for their needs. Sheltered from view by the tree covered slopes, neither they nor the cattle and sheep would be easily observed from the heights of the surrounding peaks. Molly took charge.

"Sit ye down on yon rock, Duncan. I'll see tae unpacking the nag."

It was abundantly clear that the effort of moving had drained him. He made no attempt to argue.

Molly went forward to examine the solidly built structure. The oak lintel above the door bore the legend 'Oxtors Farm'. She forced her way in, a mighty shove causing the creaking hinges to relax their longstanding grip. As she had surmised, damp and musty though the place proved to be, only the roof needed urgent treatment. It must wait awhile, for a fire was still the immediate priority. Quickly unburdening the pony, she collected hay and kindling nearby, soon producing a welcoming blaze in the hearth. Collecting up more of the dry fallen timber from the wooded slopes, she took the axe to the larger branches before stacking the logs inside. Any green material which might cause their discovery with its tell-tale pungent smoke was quickly discarded. Now she busied herself gathering hay and bracken for their bedding while the house became aired. Duncan may be recovering well, but his day's efforts would have weakened him. She wanted no chill to undo all the good work of the last few days.

"Come inside, Duncan." She called to him once all was prepared. November's crisp commencement was a harbinger of winter's bleak hold on all of nature's creatures. Unless she and Duncan quickly established themselves in this place they would not survive for long. And once the house was renovated, the byre for the cattle would also require attention. The animals needed nourishment and protection too if they were to provide supplies through the coming months.

The journey down to the valley bottom had clearly taken its toll on Duncan. Shivering now, he was pleased to feel the welcoming warmth emanating from the crackling fire, the scent of the pine logs quickly driving the musty odour of dampness and decay from the confines of the room.

"Sit ye down on the bedding, Duncan."

She helped him prop himself against the wall, a thick blanket protecting his back from the rough stone surface.

"I'll get ye some food now. Ma let me raid her larder afore I left. It's hot victuals ye'll be havin' tae build up your strength."

He smiled up at her. “Lassie, ye hae the makings o’ a grand wife. I’ll treat ye well once I’m up an’ aboot. If it’s a farmer ye be set on I’ll nae let ye doon.”

She ran her fingers affectionately through his ruffled mop of hair. “We’ll see. Best ye get fit first.”

It was a simple meal she produced, though well accepted. Once equipped with more adequate cooking facilities Duncan would come to realise her true worth.

“Stay there in the warmth. I’ll attend tae the shutters afore night falls. There may be naught but a few folk as might see the light fra the fire, but we’ll take nae chances.”

He nodded. “If ye need help call me; I’m recovered enough tae gie ye a hond.”

She managed the task without his assistance. In spite of the deterioration that had taken place over the years, the structure of the building was still sound. A branch here to support the weight of a sagging frame; a packing of bracken there to eliminate any sign of the glowing fire within. Before dusk cast its mist-embroidered mantle, all was secure.

Morning, 14th November 1589

Hot food and warm surroundings had worked wonders. Duncan was up and about and working hand in hand with Molly as though nothing had ailed him. Tempered by the rigorous lifestyle he normally pursued, he had fought off the effects of his dreadful injury with growing confidence, revelling in his renewed energy. During the nine days they had spent in the vale, he and Molly had restored the farmhouse almost to its former glory, adjacent outhouses having provided a wealth of rusty tools, either left there by the former tenants in their haste to depart, or perhaps as a result of those tenants being murdered during the course of the raids. Whatever the reason, hammers, pickaxes, spades, forks – even an ancient plough – all had been abandoned. Once cleaned and restored they would be put to good use.

As he made his way now towards the byre to begin work there, Duncan waved goodbye as Molly headed once more in the direction of her mother's home. Not yet quite self-sufficient, they were in need of more provisions, though Molly carried a leg of lamb from one of the beasts they had slaughtered, intending to exchange that with her mother for whatever she might have to spare.

Pausing momentarily on her way in order to collect the herbs that would by now have dried in the airy confines of the cave, Molly noted she would need to replenish them. Her mother would still require a regular supply of ingredients to make up her potions if she were to keep body and soul together. Life would become impossible without some form of income.

"What news, lass? Has he moved on?"

Molly had guessed correctly that the only thing on her mother's mind would be Duncan's departure. Her question had come even before she responded to Molly's cheerful greeting.

"Nae, Ma."

The answer was received with stony silence.

"He reckons he's staying."

"More fool he! And more fool ye! Are ye both out o' your senses?"

Molly shook her head. "He's mine now, Ma. We're as one together."

The message was understood. "Then that's an end tae it! Ye'll nae doubt rue it, but 'tis time ye had a man. Come hither an' gie me a kiss." Her wrinkled face broke into a warm smile.

Molly threw herself into her mother's arms. "He's a grand man, Ma, ye could nae help but like him. Reiver or no', he's a fine brawny lad wi' a grin as would melt butter. I could nae sooner gie him up than I could gie up breathing!"

"Then ye hae my blessing, lass. All I ask is that ye both tek care."

Molly's mother's blessing came none too soon! Abraham Jowett was healed and obsessed with seeking revenge. Word had reached him of the tell-tale cry of a bleating sheep emanating from some point below the crags of Riggindale. And as Molly had left the valley that morning, Jowett was close by, observing her every move. He had allowed her to pass without disclosing his presence, uncertain whether the bundle she carried was merely her usual collection of herbs and berries. Once she had moved out of sight he quickly made his way to the valley below, the lance he had ripped from the hands of Duncan McKade now held firmly in his own grasp.

There was no longer any doubt in his mind once the cattle and sheep came into sight. These were his animals! And not far from them stood a man engrossed in the business of repairing a byre. A man who, in spite of his coarse garments, was no more a farmer than he was a prince. This man Abraham had last seen astride a nag. This man had thrust his lance deep into Abraham's flesh, tearing open the massive wound that was, even now, barely healed. The vow that escaped the huge man's lips proclaimed that this man was about to die and was to meet his death by the very weapon that had felled Abraham himself. Only one of them would live to see the light of another day.

The roar of anger that burst forth from the lungs of Abraham Jowett shattered the peace of the vale, compelling Duncan McKade to spin on his heels. The giant charging towards him with the pace of a raging bull, face twisted by rage and fury, was a sight to put the fear of God into any man. With speed born of desperation, Duncan raced to avail himself of the sword he always kept nearby. He barely made it.

Immediately, Abraham Jowett was upon him, the lance ripping though the outer flesh of the arm that Duncan was forced to throw up in defence. Adrenaline coursing through his entire body swamped Duncan's awareness of the pain. He retaliated with a slash of his sword as the giant's impetus brought him within range. There was satisfaction as blood gushed forth from his opponents shoulder. Another roar of rage and frustration from the huge aggressor almost deafened Duncan. With a blow from a flailing arm, he was swept aside like a child, hardly managing to maintain his footing. Amazingly agile for a man of his size, Abraham now spun around, the lance once more driven forward with devastating effect. Only a desperate glancing blow from the hilt of Duncan's sword forced the lance below its intended target, though that was but a momentary consolation. Like a searing hot skewer, Duncan was aware of the sharp steel shearing through his thigh. Even as the lance was ripped out to continue the attack, he desperately threw himself forward into close contact with his massive assailant, plunging his sword into the man's side. It appeared to have no more effect than a blow from a fist.

Duncan was stumbling now, conscious only that his strength was fading fast. His legs finally refused to respond to his insistent demand that they move. A swift glance indicated why. The last lunge of the lance had clearly severed an artery, blood pumping from the gaping wound in an unstoppable torrent. There was to be no deliverance! Only the thought of Molly left to fend for herself kept him standing. He raised the sword in a last desperate attempt to rid himself of his attacker.

Sensing victory, Abraham stepped back, a triumphal gleam in his eyes. Out of range of Duncan's sword, there was no need to rush in for the kill. Steadying himself, he drew back his arm, driving the lance forward with all the power he commanded. Through Duncan's chest it plunged, flinging him back like a rag doll. Though the man was undeniably dead from the moment the lance struck home, Abraham was not finished with him yet. Taking up the fallen sword, he dealt a massive blow to the neck of the spread-eagled figure, decapitating him with one stroke. Still Abraham was not satisfied. Tearing the lance from Duncan's body, he bent to take hold of his gory trophy by the hair, staggering to the farmhouse with both lance and head in his grasp. Weakened by the battle's injuries, he nevertheless managed to drive the blunt shaft of the lance into the yielding ground. Duncan's head was then forcibly rammed aloft on the point of the weapon. If any reiver or other usurper came to this valley, he would surely realise a new ruler reigned here. For, like many before him in the wilder, lawless parts of this border region, Abraham Jowett had formally claimed this vale as his kingdom. Even the authorities would not deny him that claim in the face of his dispatching one of the reivers who took part in the murder of a March Warden and his troopers.

He savoured the moment. The reiver lay slaughtered and the fate of Molly Grieves – the treasonable slut who had given succour to this fugitive from the law – now lay entirely within his hands. He would consider precisely what that fate should be as he awaited her return.

CHAPTER FOUR

Late afternoon: 14th November 1589

Molly Grieves sang quietly to herself as she made her way down into the valley; her mother was coping admirably and Duncan appeared well on the way to full health. The tiny hamlet of Mardale, barely visible as the last of the daylight hurried from the sky, was no longer to be a place abandoned by all but the wild creatures. Duncan awaited her return there. Duncan – the man she was desperate to hold within her arms once more. Her step quickened as she drew ever closer to the farmhouse. He would be worried that she should be returning with the light fading so fast. A fresh wind driving dark clouds over the rim of the surrounding mountains now stole the last remnants of that light. Only the fire's diffused glow emanating from the cracks around the farmhouse door gave her her bearings. She should not have allowed her mother to keep her chatting for so long.

"I'm back, Dun—" Her words were cut short as the door she had rushed to open was torn from her grasp and slammed shut behind her. A huge hand struck her back, impelling her forward, causing her to sprawl in a heap on the floor. Before she could even gather herself, she felt the steely tip of a sword pinning her down. Abraham Jowett had heard the sound of her approaching footsteps and had dragged his protesting body up to spring his unpleasant surprise.

"Welcome home!"

With heart-stopping terror, she recognised the voice. The cynical, sneering tones sent a shiver down her spine. This brutal man had come for his revenge. But where was

Duncan? She hardly dare consider that unspoken query. Surely if he were alive he would never have allowed this monster to enter their home. Anticipating the thrust of cold steel that was almost certainly about to end her life, she sent up one last prayer that her lover had died swiftly and awaited her on the other side.

The tip of the sword lifted, seemingly indicating that her attacker was about to strike. Molly braced herself.

"Get up!"

The curt command came as a total surprise. Frozen into immobility by her fear, Molly could not respond. A jab from the sword made sure that she did. What had he in mind for her? She regained her feet before he had chance to draw blood once more. Turning slowly, she faced him.

Now she was amazed by the fact that he was even able to stand. Blood seeping from a wound in his left shoulder soaked the whole sleeve of his jacket, dripping steadily from the cuff. His right side was so inadequately bound that the rough bandaging hardly stemmed the flow from an even more horrendous injury. Duncan had clearly made his huge adversary pay a high price for his incursion.

"Treat my wounds, wench, or I'll cut ye tae ribbons!"

For a moment she almost chose death. But was there just the merest chance that Duncan might still be alive? If so, he must be so dreadfully wounded that he would need her help even more than the brute standing before her. The hope that her lover may have survived held her in check. Prepared as she would have been to join Duncan in the afterlife had she been certain of his fate, that fate had still to be confirmed. And what use was it to throwaway her own life? She could not bear the thought of her mother being left to be hanged or jailed for her part in the crime of assisting a reiver.

"If I tend ye, will I hae your word my ma won't be named?"

Abraham had had adequate time to consider his course of action. He now held the power of life or death over this woman and her mother. If he chose to spare them, their knowledge of the healing arts could prove invaluable. Having already decided he would claim this fertile valley in place of his own insignificant smallholding, the women would be a powerful asset. Forcing them to take up residence in the vale would mean others who relied on their services would be driven to seek them out.

"Aye. Ye'll both hae my protection – but ye and yer mother shall dwell in this vale. Ye'll hae food and drink, but ye'll dae my bidding. I'm King o' Mardale now!"

"Then sit ye down." Molly was aware that she had little choice. If she failed to attend to this man he would surely kill her and hound her mother to her grave. Built like an ox, she judged he would survive whether she treated him or not – though he appeared uncertain of that fact. She would play on his fears.

Leaning on the sword for support, he struggled to lower himself on to the bedding. She made no offer to assist.

"I'll make nae promise I can save ye wi' the amount o' blood ye've shed."

He glared up at her. "Ye saved the reiver."

"He were nae sae badly cut."

She had made her point. Blood still oozing from between the bandaging he had struggled to apply, she saw for the first time the doubt in his eyes. He had clearly come close to death as a result of the wound he had incurred on the first occasion he had clashed with Duncan McKade. He would not wish to risk his life again.

"Fer pity's sake, get started!"

She responded quickly, seeking out the ointments that had healed Duncan. First she attended to the huge man's shoulder, bandaging him firmly. The wound to his body was too severe to unwrap at this stage. She made up a pad of material, securing that with more bandaging. That should prevent any further serious loss of blood. She rose from her knees, sickened that she should be caring for this ogre.

"Is Duncan dead?" Though she was fairly certain that he was, she had to have confirmation.

"Duncan is it?" Abraham Jowett spoke the name with loathing. "Aye, he's dead right enough. Ye can bury his body when ye hae a mind tae it." A grim smile played around his lips as he wallowed in her despair. "Ye'll leave his head on the lance that slew him though. Nae man shall pass this spot wi'out knowin' the same shall happen tae him if he trifles wi' me!"

The cry that escaped Molly's lips was born of anger, revulsion and contempt. She leapt forward to strike the grinning face that confronted her, but the sword that flashed to fill the space between them stopped her just in time.

"If ye wish tae join the reiver, I'll nae stop ye. Though it be best ye get used tae the sight o' his head where it be. I'll hae yer hide if ye disobey me!"

For the first time since her father had passed away, Molly was moved to tears.

"Stop the snivelling, wench, and put more logs on the fire!" He showed neither remorse nor sympathy. "Ye'll stay here this night an' see tae my needs. Tomorrow ye shall saddle that nag an' bring my wife here."

She was too distraught to answer. Building up the fire, she moved as far from her tormentor as she could possibly manage, squatting down on the floor. The very thought of Duncan and his awful fate filled her with total despair. Though she had prepared herself for the possibility that she and Duncan might be discovered, never had she envisaged that the end would come in so brutal a fashion.

15th November 1589

Molly had hardly slept. Even before dawn had etched its silver traces across the morning sky, she had stretched her chilled body and risen from her cramped position. Abraham Jowett still lay in a deep sleep, the injuries he had received clearly having drained most of his strength. Moving to the fire, she heaped logs on the smouldering embers, warming her aching limbs as the flames licked through the dry timbers. She had spent the sleepless hours considering her position. Duncan was gone – and nothing she could do would bring her lover back. Like so many other women before her, she had lost her man in yet another of the constant border conflicts. And, as had those other women, she too must adjust to her new situation. To thwart Abraham Jowett's wishes would merely place her mother at his mercy.

Screwing up her courage, Molly ventured outdoors. It was as well she had been warned. Not ten feet away, Duncan's lance stood upright in the ground. In the gloom of a morning scarcely illuminated by the cold light of day, she could not bear to allow her eyes to rest on the gory sight that topped the weapon. Clutching the saddle and material that had wrapped the bundle she carried last evening, she sought out the body of her lover.

Duncan's mutilated form was not far from the byre. The sight that met her eyes made her physically sick. He had clearly suffered terribly before the end had come. She turned away, unable to approach him until she had gathered her shattered wits. She would saddle up the nag and construct a bier to carry his desecrated body. As on the last occasion, branches from a birch tree made a suitable form of transport. For the second time in what appeared just a few short days, she struggled to lift Duncan onto a makeshift carriage. Were it not that it was a labour of love, she could never have born the pain of moving him. But move him she must. She had already planned his final resting place. He should lie close by the cave where they had first made love. And should she eventually be allowed to retrieve his poor head that too would rest there. Equipped with spade and pickaxe, she led the pony up the steep incline to seek out a suitable spot.

After much toil she concluded her task. It had been with great difficulty that she had found soil of sufficient depth to bury his body on this fairly barren mountainside. It now lay in a shallow grave in a sheltered grassy spot between two boulders – a large one near his headless shoulders, a small one at his feet. She would never again lose him. Covering the disturbed soil with bracken and fallen branches, she headed to the gill to clean up. She would carry on out of the valley once she was tidy, bringing back the wife of Abraham Jowett. That unfortunate woman could tend to him henceforth. Medication Molly would supply, though nought else, to the appalling monster who had slain the only man she could ever love.

Alice Jowett was concerned to discover Molly Grieves on her doorstep in such a state. Blood-stained, white and shaking, Molly's gruesome morning's work had left her devastated.

"Whatever is it?"

The woman's quavering voice indicated that she had correctly associated Molly's appearance with the fate of her own husband. Molly could feel no enmity towards her. She was merely another victim of the border conflicts.

"Abraham has sent me tae collect ye. He's injured, but he's safe at Mardale."

"Thank God!"

Molly would have thanked God had it not been so.

"What happened?"

"There's been a battle. He slew a man."

Alice Jowett was too shocked to speak. Molly put an arm around her.

"Abraham says ye are tae move tae Mardale. There's a farmhouse an' land there along wi' some o' his animals."

Alice shot an enquiring glance at Molly, still unable to comprehend. Molly could not bring herself to explain the precise circumstances.

"We're tae load up the nag wi' as many o' the things ye'll be needin' there tae get settled. The rest's tae follow later."

Alice could hardly take it in.

"But we're settled here! I'll be havin' a bairn soon!"

Molly pitied her. "Ye should nae worry. I'll be on hand when ye need me. I'm tae settle at Mardale too – along wi' my mother."

Confusion brought forth the tears. “I don’t understand. What’s tae become o’ us?”

Molly took her arm. “Dinnae fret yoursel’. I’ll help ye collect up your belongings an then we’ll be off. Abraham will explain.”

What goods and chattels could be accommodated without causing the pony too much discomfort were soon loaded. The two women walked, leading the laden animal. It was a fair trek, until finally they were about to make their way down into the valley. Molly had avoided speaking of all that had occurred, though she could no longer hide the truth.

“Prepare yoursel’ afore we get tae the farmhouse, for a lance stands there wi’ a human head speared upon it.”

Alice gasped at the words, shaking from head to toe as she stumbled to a halt.

“Nae point in dawdlin’. Jest steel yersel’ not tae look upon it.” Molly saw no point in mentioning that she herself had not done so and could hardly bear to speak of it.

Alice seemed rooted to the spot. “Was it Abraham’s doing?”

Molly nodded. “Aye. An’ he’s set on it stayin’ there. He reckons by killing a reiver an’ layin’ claim tae his possessions, he’s earned the title King o’ Mardale. He’ll nae let me bury the head wi’ the body though. He wants everyone tae see what he’s capable of.”

Alice appeared finally to comprehend. Clearly Molly had not been away from home tending her aunt. And Abraham had butchered the man she had been shielding. It was Alice’s turn to feel pity now. No wonder Molly had been so quiet and withdrawn. She must have formed a true attachment to this man. Alice reached out a hand. “I’m truly sorry! Will these men never cease tae battle wi’ each other?”

Molly hugged the woman, who was clearly as distressed as herself. “Tis time they did. How many more wives and sweethearts must cry for their departed?”

15th December 1589

A month had quickly passed since Duncan's death. With news of Abraham Jowett's victory over the reiver who had raided his land and taken part in the massacre of the troopers, folk were now treating him as a hero. There was already talk of settlers coming back to the valley under his protection – though there would be a price to pay. Jowett had laid claim to the land and all buildings that stood upon it. Self-declared 'King of Mardale', no one dared dispute that right.

Molly had forced herself to accept her new situation. Throwing all her energies into renovating a tiny cottage that had been allocated to her and her mother, she had worked all the hours God sent to make it habitable. Under the threat of revelation of her part in assisting Duncan, there was little else she could do but comply with Abraham Jowett's demands. In truth, she had never wished to leave the valley anyway, since it now held Duncan remains – and the constant workload had helped obscure the pain of losing her lover. Pleading for the head of Duncan whenever she encountered the man who still displayed his nauseating trophy, all her entreaties fell on deaf ears.

"I must try again, Ma."

Her mother shook her head. "He'll never part wi' it, lass. Can't ye see he wants tae gloat ower it?"

Molly wept, determined never to give up. "I'll nae rest till it's laid wi' the rest o' Duncan's body."

"Then ye'll never rest, lass. Just try an' take it wi'out his permission an' the pair o' us will pay dearly!"

Molly grudgingly accepted the wisdom of her mother's words. Even Alice Jowett could not persuade her husband to give up his gory souvenir, although she had made the attempt. Molly would have to bide her time a little longer. Surely Jowett would tire of his sport eventually? Besides, Molly now had something of much more import to occupy her mind. With growing delight, she was aware that her monthly cycle had been interrupted. The passing weeks soon brought joyous confirmation of her state. Without doubt, Duncan's seed was now growing inside her. Her lover would live on in the body of his child. One day it may even claim back the rights to rule this valley, for had not its parents been the first to resettle the deserted vale?

* * *

When Molly's time came she was delivered of a son. Nothing could have pleased her more – but for the fact that Duncan was not there to see his child. Nevertheless, from this day forth she would take the name McKade as her own, for in all but the eyes of the clergy, she had been a wife to that man. And the baby should also proudly bear the name Duncan. No one would ever be allowed to forget that her former lover had been chief of the McKade clan.

* * *

Twenty years later, Abraham Jowett lay upon his deathbed. Molly McKade had tended him to no avail. For the last time, she made the plea that had passed her lips so many times before.

"Will ye reconsider? Please let me take awa' Duncan's skull for burial."

The skull, picked clean by scavengers so many years ago, had finally been placed in a niche in the wall of the farmhouse.

Jowett glared up at her, defiant to the end. "That skull remains here in this house. My son shall nae part wi' it either. So long as a Jowett lives, I swear ye'll ne'er unite it wi' the reiver's body!"

Molly had come to the end of her tether. "Then I curse ye an' aw your descendants. If I'm nae tae have it, then whosoever of ye shall move it fra this place shall suffer death and ruination. Till it lies wi' Duncan's body, nae one o' your family shall disturb it wi'out suffering the consequences. By nature's wrath shall they perish!" With that she turned on her heels and departed. Jowett's wife and son would never forget the look in her eyes nor the words she had spoken. It would be many years later that other members of the Jowett dynasty would also have cause to remember those words.

* * *

Summer, 1768

Though almost two centuries had passed, Duncan McKade's skull still occupied its niche in the farmhouse wall, casting its eyeless, malevolent grin over every move that was made. Though the McKades never stopped pestering for its return, Sarah Jowett – wife of the latest 'King of Mardale' – was strictly forbidden by her husband to ever hand it back. The feud between the families had never ceased: the head of each new Jowett household swearing to retain the skull as a token of their power; the male line of the McKades equally dedicated to reunite it with the rest of Duncan McKade's remains in the secret grave known only to themselves.

But eventually Sarah could stand it not one moment longer! Taking up the skull, and prepared even to ignore the curse that accompanied it, she paused only momentarily to ensure that she was not observed. Silently, she slipped from the house, making her way to the large expanse of water that covered the lower levels of the valley. Sparkling in the light of the morning's sun, the lake looked a place of total tranquillity. It would be a fitting spot to finally dispose of the disgusting relic, inherited from an age when open warfare ruled the Borders. With all her might, she hurled the skull far into the lake.

Trembling after her defiant act, Sarah returned to the farmhouse, plucking a bunch of wild flowers from the meadow on her way. Placed in her best vase, they would grace the recess which formerly held the abhorrent object.

Surely her husband would agree that the time had come to end this foolish dispute.

Sarah was to be desperately disappointed. On seeing the vase of flowers after returning from the fields, Nathan Jowett howled in rage, sweeping it to the floor.

"Have ye given that skull tae the McKades, woman?" he roared.

Sarah recoiled in terror before his stinging onslaught. "I would nae disobey ye in that way, Nathan!"

"Then where is it?"

She wept in the face of his fury. "I cast it into the lake."

For one moment she thought he was about to strike her. Luckily, he withheld the blow, for like every Jowett before him, he was a huge man with a matching temper.

"Then back ye go! Ye'll nae enter this house agin' wi'out it! Ye know full well the curse it carries!"

She could see he would never relent. His word was law. Without even contemplating a plea that he reconsider, she hurried away back to the water's edge, desperately attempting to seek out the very spot where she had stood previously. In her haste to rid herself of the skull, she had given scant thought to her surroundings, merely acting on impulse and despatching it as soon as she had reached the lake. Now plunging in with little regard to her safety, she soon regretted hurling the object with such force. The water was up to her waist before she drew anywhere near the area she judged it to have landed. Before long the water was up to her neck. Despairingly, she ducked beneath the surface, holding her breath as she frantically struggled to search the floor of the lake. Each time she came up, gasping for air, she was empty handed. Still she continued, the weight of her sodden clothing dragging her down. Disorientated, she realised she had strayed out of her depth. Never a capable swimmer, she struggled to fight her way back to the surface, managing it but briefly. Lungs bursting for air, only the waters of the lake entered her body as she failed to take the vital breath in the fraction of a second before she became engulfed.

Help arrived too late. Though her struggles were spotted by one of the farm labourers, his valiant attempt to reach her failed. Able only to judge approximately where she had disappeared below the waves, it was some time before he made contact with her lifeless body. Dragging her to the shore, he made a futile attempt to revive her before heading off to break the tragic news.

"Good God!" The blood drained from Nathan Jowett's face. "Show me!"

The pair ran back to the spot, Nathan then making his own desperate attempt to breathe life back into his wife. It was a pointless exercise. Despair and fear clouded his face.

"Get the nets an' boats here!"

The labourer hesitated. Had he heard correctly?

"Get them, man! The bloody skull's out there! There's nowt I can dae fer my wife, but I'm nae risking the curse on me an' the bairns too."

Everyone in the vale was aware of the existence of Duncan McKade's skull and of Molly McKade's curse. Those who had doubts about the effectiveness of that curse would now be forced to reconsider. The labourer sped off to do Nathan's bidding. He had seen proof enough to convince him.

Two boats and the nets were quickly brought to the spot. Attached to the rear of each boat the larger of the nets was spread to drag the base of the lake – a procedure normally reserved for the taking of fish. Nathan hurried the men to begin. He was not prepared to take the risk that the death of his wife had not been brought about as a direct result of the curse. And there was no telling if this was precisely where the skull had entered the water. There would be no let up until it was recovered.

Only after several hours was the operation successful. Nathan Jowett had refused to leave the scene until the skull was safely in his hands. Others had had to remove his wife's body. Now he hurried home, intent on replacing the object before further damage could be caused. Sceptical up to this point, he would take no further risks. The skull would be walled up in the farmhouse, lest someone else should seize it and it should be lost forever. The almost instantaneous demise of his wife after her foolhardy action had shaken him to the core. Would her death alone be an end to the matter?

CHAPTER FIVE

Mardale: 24th May 1934

"Good God!" The Rev. Bramwell Thursby almost collapsed. "Surely not!"

Mary Jowett steadied him, a hand stretched out to his shoulder. "I'm afraid 'tis true, vicar. Margaret's body were found at the base o' Harter Fell within the last hour."

The vicar slumped down in despair on the nearby pew, tears welling in his eyes. "How can that be? Surely she should have been busy with her chores?"

Mary Jowett appeared as mystified as he. "So she should have. When she failed tae appear this morning, the other maid went seeking her. Her bed had nae been slept in an' the maid said she'd heard her walking the floor till well after midnight."

The vicar shook his head, sobbing in his anguish. Margaret Thursby was his eldest daughter and worked full time for the Jowetts, living in with the family at the extended farmhouse. He was aware she had not been entirely happy there, but positions were hard to come by in the valley and a vicar's stipend hardly covered his own living expenses. He looked questioningly at the woman alongside him. "How did she die?"

Mary Jowett had been dreading the question. "It appears she slipped fra one o' the crags on Harter Fell."

"Slipped?" The vicar looked up in disbelief. "She knew the fells around here like the back of her hand! And why would she be up there at such a time?"

The woman appeared almost evasive. "She's nae looked well fer some time, vicar. I've caught her weeping a couple o' times, but she'd nae say why. She never did complain, but she were hardly cut out fer hard graft. 'Tis a pity she were never found more suitable employment."

The vicar's sobbing now racked his whole body, for he alone was responsible for directing Margaret to work for the family. "Oh, God above, how could you allow this to happen?"

Mary took hold of the man's shoulders once more. "'Tis little consolation, but I'm told her death would hae been instantaneous."

News spread quickly throughout the small community. Isobel Thursby raced home to the vicarage to seek out her father. He had lost his wife – and the girls their mother – some years before. Now tragedy had struck their family again, though Isobel could simply not accept the suggestion that her sister may have committed suicide. Bursting through the door, she hardly dare ask for confirmation. "Tell me it's not true, Pa!"

The vicar shook his head. "God has taken her, Isobel."

She rushed into his arms, weeping copiously. Not Margaret. Not her sweet sister. Not the beautiful girl who had charmed everyone she had ever encountered.

Her father hugged her close. A fairly distant man, hollow-cheeked and sallow of face, he was not normally prone to show affection. It saddened her that it had taken Margaret's death to finally bring his paternal feelings to the surface for the first time in many years.

"Where is she?" Isobel finally drew away to ask the question.

He almost choked on the words, hardly able to look her in the eyes. "The Jowetts have taken her back to Oxtors Farm. Mary Jowett said it would be best if we remembered her as she was. The fall damaged her terribly."

Isobel was distraught. "I must go to her! I can't stand the thought of her lying there without ever saying goodbye."

Her father hesitated, then broke down. "Go then, Isobel, for I can't bear the thought of seeing her disfigured."

Margaret's body lay in a tiny attic room upon a spartan, roughly constructed bunk. Just a portion of her face was exposed, the rest of her discreetly covered with a clean white sheet. It was clear that the other maidservant in the Jowett household had lovingly tended to her before Isobel arrived. It was also apparent that Margaret's injuries had not been exaggerated.

Isobel shook with pent-up emotion as she bent to kiss the ivory cheek. What possible reason could there be for her sister to be lying here, cold and immobile? How could someone so full of life have that spark snuffed out for no apparent reason? Though toiling as a maid in the Jowett household was nothing short of drudgery, Margaret had struggled to maintain a positive outlook, sharing her secret with Isobel that Jack Tweedie had promised they should marry as soon as he was in a position to support her. Though they both realised that would take time, he could hardly wait to take her away from her unrewarding toil. Jack was a grand lad, a hard-working young man who could have taken his pick of all the girls for miles around. How would he survive this awful tragedy? Shocked as Isobel was by the death of her beloved sister, her thoughts now centred on him. Had he been informed? His dreams of a lifetime spent with Margaret would be shattered.

Isobel glanced at the few pathetic belongings that Margaret had left behind. Not much to show for her brief span on this earth. Not even a message saying goodbye. Had there been such a note, someone must surely have seen fit to dispose of it. That this family were in some way to blame for Margaret's death, Isobel could not drive from her mind.

Ellen Jowett was awaiting her as she left Margaret's tiny room, the tear-stained face of the young woman a picture of misery.

"I'm so sorry, Isobel!" The words were uttered almost as though she felt personally responsible. "There's none of us can believe how it came about."

Ellen was the Jowetts' daughter and much younger than Margaret, who just turned sixteen, though the two of them had become close friends from the moment Margaret entered service there. Isobel was aware that Ellen and her mother had done all in their power to make life at the farm as acceptable as possible for her sister, though the father, Adam, and son, Herbert, were hard taskmasters. Still claiming the title 'Kings of Mardale', they ran the valley and its residents with scant regard to aught but their needs and ambitions. No one dared to cross them.

Isobel struggled to keep control. "What about Jack Tweedie? Has he been told?"

Ellen nodded. "I ran and told him mysel'. I knew he and Margaret were walking out together."

"How did he take it?"

Ellen shook her head. "He could nae speak at first. I thought he'd been struck dumb. Then he started cursing my father and Herbert. He said it were aw their fault. He told me Margaret had been so unhappy here, but she could nae tell your father. He was the one who'd sent her tae work here and she had tae stick it out."

That sounded like Margaret. A sensitive girl, she would not complain to her father no matter what.

"Did you not realise how unhappy she was?" Isobel could scarcely bring herself to believe her sister would take her own life, however depressed she may have become.

"She had been very subdued over the past few months. Ye'll be aware spring is always a busy time on the farm. I think father's had her caring fer the new lambs as well as doing aw the housework and helping cook fer the extra farmhands. She's had little or no time tae hersel' as far as I can tell."

That meant she would have had little time to see Jack. And Jack was the one person who could have kept her sane. Isobel could barely contain her grief. Margaret was never cut out to be a skivvy. She had been determined to become a teacher eventually, though her father had never encouraged her. Like so many of his generation, his concern was merely that she sought out a husband and made him a good wife. That was career enough for any woman.

Ellen Jowett burst into tears. "I'm awful grieved if it were anything my father did as could have caused Margaret tae take her own life. Neither I, nor my ma, could ever utter a word o' protest about how he treated the servants."

Isobel could only feel bitterness in her heart that they had not at least made more of an attempt. Poor Margaret must have been driven to despair by these people before she could ever have considered suicide. And how tragic that she could not have held on until the day everyone was moved from this valley. Soon now the dam that was under construction would be completed and the Jowett's tyrannical reign would finally come to an end. The village of Mardale, which had grown over the centuries into a thriving little community, would be no more. At least Margaret would now be spared the pain of seeing their beautiful vale drowned beneath the waters of the reservoir.

27th May 1934

The service was conducted by Margaret's own father. He would not have had it otherwise. The tiny church, dedicated to the Holy Trinity, was overflowing. Margaret had been loved by almost everyone in the small community. Isobel was aware that most of the congregation were in tears. She had persuaded Jack Tweedie to stand alongside her for support. In truth, she realised he may be more in need of her support. Devastated by Margaret's untimely death, the young man had spent every spare moment carving a memorial to her on a boulder close by the spot where her body had been discovered. Inconsolable, he had barely been able to keep his hands off Herbert Jowett, the swaggering son of the domineering family he despised, for Jack believed him to be the most likely candidate to have contributed to Margaret's death. Herbert had a reputation for treating the servants as his personal property, and though Margaret had never actually accused him, Jack believed she may have hidden the fact that he was constantly attempting to force himself on her. Afraid to voice her complaints, she may finally have decided to end the misery of her drudgery and his attentions. But for the fact that he had no proof to back his suspicions, Jack would have tangled with the man – though he would probably have had cause to regret it. Set in the mould of his forebears, Herbert was a powerful youth and dwarfed all in the village but his father.

20th June 1934

Isobel could not believe the words spoken by her father. "You can't mean that!"

The vicar stood his ground. "You're almost fifteen now. Your schooling's coming to an end and you are much stronger and sturdier than your sister ever was. You would be much more suited to the work than Margaret."

Isobel could hardly deny it. Regular exercise competing in fell races and helping out on local farms, had ensured that she was in excellent health.

Despite that, she still protested. "But Margaret chose to die rather than continue working at that place."

"We can't be sure what was in her mind, child. God moves in mysterious ways. Who knows what possessed her? Margaret always had a delicate nature. Anyway, how else am I to put food on the table now that she's gone?"

"But surely there must be someone else who could take me?"

Her plea fell on deaf ears.

"Who else is there but the Jowetts? No other family in the valley can afford to set on a maid."

"You said one day I'd be allowed to do missionary work." Though that had always been Isobel's desire, still she couched her words with care, appealing to her father's faith.

"Time enough for that later. You're much too young to send out into the wicked world."

She made one last attempt to sway him. "I really need to answer God's call."

There was only a moment's hesitation. "You shall answer His call when we leave this valley. Till then, you will best serve God by obeying my wishes."

Isobel resigned herself to the fact that nothing would alter his decision. By now she was totally convinced that one day her father would have as much cause to regret this harsh decision as he must surely have had about despatching Margaret to her fate.

CHAPTER SIX

14th July 1994

Joy Elliot awoke perspiring heavily. It was a great relief to see the morning sunlight streaming through her bedroom window and to erase the memory of the nightmares that had plagued her. She shuddered as she recalled those tortured dreams: disembodied heads floating on dark waters, seeking sanctuary at a church that was no more. Her discovery of the skull at the depleted reservoir the previous day still turned her stomach. Quickly rising from her bed, she took a refreshing shower. That felt much better. She could face the day with renewed confidence now. Dressing and making her way downstairs, she sought out the morning's papers.

"MYSTERY AT MARDALE" The headlines blazoned across the front of the local newspaper caught her eye even before she became fully aware of her own presence on the page. Yes, there she was, along with images of the skull's removal from its muddy resting place and its subsequent unimpressive departure in a polythene bag. Her depiction was not particularly flattering – due primarily to the fact that she was attired in wellingtons and jeans – but at least they had spelt her name correctly. She smiled at her own vanity. Just like a woman; but then, she quickly assured herself, she was not exactly meant to be modelling the latest fashion. Now – what had they got to say?

The interview with her was only slightly embellished, though the rest of the article looked to be a complete flight of fancy.

'IS THIS THE MARDALE SKULL?' The reporter had certainly gone to town on the story. 'The ancient skull discovered at the lost village of Mardale yesterday, could finally confirm the truth of a legend handed down over the course of several centuries. Buried in the sediment surrounding the scattered remains of the village – and directly adjacent to the crumbling walls of Oxtors Farm – the skull, apparently confirmed as being of great age, may well be that of 'Duncan of Crieff'.

'Slain by Abraham Jowett in the battle to be acclaimed 'King of Mardale', the victor of that encounter was said to have struck off the head of his foe, impaling it on a lance as a grisly warning to any other would-be aggressor. Left to be picked clean by a variety of scavengers, the gory trophy was finally retrieved, later to be placed in a niche in the walls of Oxtors Farm – the building commandeered by Jowett at the time of the conflict – and there it remained!

'Cursed many years later on his deathbed by the woman who had nurtured Duncan prior to the battle, Jowett was issued with the dire warning that, since he refused to give up the skull, any member of his family who thereafter allowed its removal from its resting place would suffer dire consequences; 'By nature's wrath shall they perish!' had been the malediction.

'While it would be pure speculation to deliberate on the effect the curse had on the family involved, and indeed on whether it was actually taken seriously at that time, an incident occurring many years later apparently reinforced belief in the latent power of the imprecation. The wife of one of Jowett's descendants, unnerved by the constant presence of the skull, chose to ignore the threat of retribution and attempted to dispose of it. Her death was attributed to that attempt. Quickly retrieved, the skull was then reported to have been walled in to prevent any further disturbance. Since that time no other tragedy that could be attributable to the ancient invocation was ever recorded, though the Jowett family appear to have long had cause to remember the incident. Could it conceivably be that the crumbling remains of Oxtors Farm has finally spilled out the skull of Duncan of Crieff? And that it has lain undisturbed on the bed of Haweswater for much of the last sixty years? The pathologist taking part in the investigation was heard to remark; 'We appear to have something pretty ancient here.' Would it be too outrageous to suggest that the legend of the Mardale Skull may now be proven to be fact? We await confirmation from the powers that be.'

"Wow!" Joy shook her head in disbelief. Could this man be serious? Surely not. Yet she could hardly deny the horror she had felt at the moment of discovery, nor the lasting effects that the incident had induced. Was it any wonder she had been unable to erase the fears from her mind? She recalled the reporter's excitement the previous day. He must have been aware of the legend at that time. No wonder he had questioned her so searchingly. A shiver ran down her spine. What if it were true? But had the Prof. not said that the skull must simply have been washed out from the cemetery? That still sounded a much more likely explanation. She would pop up to her tutor's room and find out what his reactions were.

Merlin Reid had also been amazed by the article. It came as no surprise to find Joy at his door.

"Come on in." He indicated a comfortable chair. "Sit yourself down. I imagine you've been reading the sensational account of your discovery. It's a fascinating interpretation of the events that may have brought the skull there and no mistake."

The cosy oak-panelled study had always had a reassuring effect upon Joy. Here was a pleasant aroma of ancient books, polished leather furniture, and just a trace of Old Spice. The professor's personality was thoroughly imprinted on the place. Bookcases were crammed predominantly with medical tomes, though historical and geological textbooks concerning the Lake District also abounded. A various assortment of works of fact and fiction regarding crime and criminal behaviour denoted his interest in that subject also.

She took a seat, smiling nervously up at him. "You don't imagine there could be any truth in the story?"

"It would come as some surprise if there were." He attempted to sound positive, though he could hardly bring himself to completely rule out the possibility. He was well aware that there were a great number of myths and legends associated with various out of the way corners of the Lake District. There seemed little point in trying to fudge the issue. "I have to admit that there are elements of truth in the tale. The mere fact that some of these vales were so remote, did lend itself to the leaders of such communities taking on the title of 'King'. Up to the time of Mardale being dammed and flooded, I believe there was a family still in existence who continued to retain the title. I suppose we'd have regarded them as the old 'Lords of the Manor'. No doubt they would have laid claim to all of the land at some point in the past and the tenants of the farms thereabouts would have to pay their dues – and their respects."

"But what about the skull, Prof.? I thought you said it had most probably come from the graveyard."

He had been expecting the question. "Well, actually that was just my way of making light of the discovery. I sensed you were shaken by the incident and thought you might be even more distressed if you realised the skull could have belonged to an accident or murder victim. If you had reached that conclusion, you would probably have assumed that the rest of the body possibly lay there too."

Joy nodded. "To be honest, that thought had originally crossed my mind. I had visions of kneeling above the remains of that person as I gazed down at the skull."

He realised just how much that must have affected her at the time. "I must admit my own first reaction was a similar one, especially as I was aware that all of the bodies originally buried at Mardale had been exhumed and reinterred at Shap."

"So that was why you were so keen to inform the police?"

"That and a few other factors. Unless the people who were concerned with removing the bodies from the cemetery could have mislaid a skull, there certainly appeared to be a mystery as to how it came to be there. Inspector Grey felt the same way when I pointed out the facts. At least there will be a proper investigation now, and he did promise to keep me up to date with events."

"So we should eventually learn the truth?"

"I imagine so. We'll just have to bide our time and see what he turns up. Meanwhile, I think we should get our core of sediment over to the boffins at Windermere. We may be able to kill two birds with one stone. We should get our pollen results and Grey should get an approximate idea of the length of time the skull has lain at the bottom of the lake."

Joy was looking flushed and excited by the news. "You mean to say the story in the paper could actually be true? That skull could conceivably have been part of the remains of this Duncan of Crieff?"

"There's no doubt that it did look pretty ancient."

"Good grief!" She could still hardly believe her ears. "And I was the one to find it. If the legend is true, then no one would have set eyes on that thing since it was walled up. No wonder I felt there was something evil about it." Her pensive face suddenly broke into a large grin. "Inspector Grey's not going to have much of a job trying to solve this case if they are right, is he?"

"I shouldn't think so." Reid chuckled too at the thought of Grey tracking down the ancient killer. "Somehow I doubt this is going to turn into a murder hunt."

Subsequent events were to prove just how wrong this prediction would be.

* * *

The pathologist had also come to the conclusion that there was no crime to solve. Having carefully removed the sediment from inside the skull, he had then turned his attention to the skull itself. In spite of its prolonged immersion, it was entirely intact. The teeth were certainly in excellent condition. No sign of extractions or fillings. That ruled out the checking of any dental records. Closer inspection confirmed the pathologist's original conclusion that the skull was indeed of ancient origin. The molars gave every indication of grinding on much coarser materials than would be found in a modern diet. The remaining teeth showed almost no sign of attack from the softer, more sugary meals consumed during the present century.

Directing his attention to the base of the skull, the pathologist had quickly become aware that some damage had occurred in that area. A crushing of the bone structure indicated that a blow had been delivered with some force. It was not inconceivable that an axe or sword could have been the implement in question. The legend associated with the tiny hamlet of Mardale could not be ruled out.

Missing Persons had failed to unearth anyone who could remotely be connected with the case. This was hardly a surprise. Their records were unlikely to stretch back far enough to encompass the person involved. A search for the rest of the remains now appeared inappropriate. Any foul play that might have occurred had clearly taken place in the very distant past.

* * *

Inspector Grey was as good as his word. He had promised the findings would be conveyed to Merlin Reid.

"That you, Prof?" A quick phone call had caught the professor at home. "No chance for you to do any sleuthing this time. Not unless you're keen on archaeology. Our man's been deceased for a few hundred years by the sound of it. We're not seeking out a murderer this time. Still, I don't expect that'll stop you nosing around."

Reid chuckled. Grey knew him only too well. And the result of the pathologist's enquiry had only served to confirm that there might be some basis in the report of the legend. "So you're off the case for good now?"

"Sure enough. It's all yours. But try not to get me involved again. I might end up having to charge you with wasting police time!"

"Bloody cheek!" The professor roared with laughter. Grey would no doubt bait him over the subject for some time to come.

Replacing the phone, he considered the implications to be drawn from the conversation. He would go and impart the news to Joy.

* * *

Joy Elliot was reading the newspaper account of her gory find yet again when she heard the knock on her door. Springing up from her seat, she invited her tutor in. Quickly clearing books and files from the chair opposite her own, she made room for him to sit. The study was by no means small, yet she did manage to spread herself and her belongings over a wide area.

"Sorry for the mess." She had not been expecting a visit or she would have tidied up a little.

"No problem." He smiled at her discomfort. "I was a student too in the dim and distant past you know."

Having put her at her ease, he broached the reason for his call.

"I just thought I'd pop in and let you know what the police have turned up."

She looked at him expectantly.

"The story in the newspaper may not be as incredible as we first thought."

Her eyes lit up with excitement. "You're not saying that reporter might actually have got it right?"

"Well, Inspector Grey has confirmed that the skull doesn't appear to have belonged to anyone born in this century. The pathologist seems to be of the opinion that it could even be two or three hundred years old. That does imply that unless some joker got hold of an ancient skull and buried it at Mardale, or tossed it into the reservoir a good few years ago, there doesn't seem to be any other logical explanation for its appearance there."

“Good grief!” She was clearly becoming more thrilled by the minute.

He had to admit to a tingle of excitement himself. “Even if we could bring ourselves to believe that someone might have thrown the thing in there, it would have to be a remarkable coincidence for the skull to come to rest alongside the remains of the farmhouse. You can bet your boots that reporter did his homework before writing the article.”

“I guess so.” She was slowly accepting the fact that the story could not be totally discounted.

Reid had already come to that conclusion. “From the manner of his interview with you yesterday, it was obvious that that man knew he was on to something significant. I’m sure he’s got most of his facts right. It wouldn’t have been difficult for him to search back through the papers archives to establish exactly where the building was located. There was bound to have been a great deal of media interest at the time of the valley’s flooding.”

“You are serious then, that this report has some credibility?”

He could see she could hardly contain herself.

“Let’s just say I’m prepared to keep an open mind. It would be easy to dismiss the whole story as just a silly myth, but it does have a certain ring of truth to it.”

“So how do we go about finding out if it is true?”

He smiled at her growing excitement. “Well, what I’d really like to do would be to speak to some of the people who actually lived at Mardale. Admittedly, any of them alive today would have been little more than children or teenagers at the time of the flooding, but childhood memories are the ones that last. The tales handed down to them would certainly be more instructive than any interpretation by an outsider.”

She was nodding thoughtfully. “Yes, I see what you mean. And if there are any surviving residents, they must be even more intrigued by this than we are. I imagine some of them are going to be drawn back to the area by this story, even if they could have overcome their natural curiosity to revisit Mardale and rekindle their memories of the place."

"That's what I was banking on." He could see that the young student's fascination with the legend far outweighed any uneasiness about delving into the facts of the case. "You can lay odds that they'll almost certainly never get another chance in their lifetime to return to the spot again. I just wonder if we couldn't make use of the occasion to try to seek out one or two of them. They may have a fascinating tale to tell."

"Sounds great to me." Her eyes were sparkling at the thought of the adventure. For the moment her fears appeared to have been pushed to one side. "You did say 'We'? I assume that means I am invited to join in?"

"It certainly does. You're the one who set the ball rolling – and it could prove to be a riveting diversion."

Their conversation was cut short by the ringing of the telephone.

"Hang on, I'll just answer that, then we can decide how we're going to proceed."

He headed for his office. It was not long before he returned.

"It's for you. One of the national papers has got hold of the story. They'd like to hear your comments on the matter."

"You're kidding?" She was stunned by the news. It took a moment or two before she could pull herself together. "I can hardly believe this. They must think there's something in the story then, or I don't see why they'd want to contact me."

"Oh, I reckon it's quite newsworthy." He beamed across at the surprised young woman. "If you're prepared to talk to them you can use the phone in the office."

"Well, why not?" She was clearly adapting to the idea of becoming a celebrity. "If they're that keen, I'll just go and see what they have to say."

Whatever they had to say took a little while. Eventually she arrived back, looking even more flushed and excited.

"They want to come and interview me," she said breathlessly. "They're sending someone over to cover the story and to take some pictures."

"A star is born!" he chuckled, unable to resist ribbing her a little.

She smiled at his comment. "Don't speak too soon. The reporter may decide he wants to interview you too."

"I doubt it. There's not much I could add to your version of the events. In any case, if you don't mind, I would like to get our sample of the lake sediment over to Windermere. I know it's not going to help with the police investigation now, but we are going to need the results for when the course starts up again."

She had all but forgotten about their original reason for visiting Mardale. "Of course. You carry on. I don't mind at all. I'm almost beginning to enjoy this."

Reid took her at her word. She was a level-headed girl who should handle the press without any problems. "Fine. You have your moment of glory and we'll talk about our plans once I get back."

He left her to prepare for her interview, never suspecting how fateful the final outcome of that meeting might be.

CHAPTER SEVEN

Ellen Braithwaite was horrified to read of the reported discovery of the Mardale Skull. For the past sixty years she had hardly given a moment's thought to the sinister object which, to her belief, lay entombed in the walls of her former childhood home. The home which had been totally submerged deep at the bottom of Haweswater for what seemed an eternity.

Formerly Ellen Jowett, she had been one of two children born to Mary and Adam Jowett. Her parents had long since passed away, as had the man she wed some forty years ago. But finally the past was coming back to haunt her. Though now in her seventies, she was far from a frail woman, yet she shuddered at the thought of a predicted death in the family should the skull ever be moved from its resting place. Possibly the fact that an act of nature had spilled the object from its concealed crevice had prevented any repercussions at the time of that occurrence, but what of this new situation?

It had now apparently been physically removed from alongside the farmhouse. What catastrophe might now befall her loved ones? Though it seemed absurd, in her own mind she could not rule out the possibility of some terrible retribution. The fact that the threat of such retribution could now become a reality caused her to break into a cold sweat, her normally ruddy cheeks paling to the colour of marble. She had a son and daughter to consider. And what of her brother? She tried to remember how the curse had been phrased. As a child she had been informed by her grandmother that any member of the family who allowed the skull to be moved from the precincts of the farm – and thereafter failed to reinstate it – was liable to be struck down.

Perhaps it was not too late to make amends. She must contact her brother. Being slightly older than her, he may well have a better recollection of the legend. He had certainly always had an almost unhinged dread as a child that someone might one day steal away with the skull and that he would be the one to suffer as a consequence of that act. Only once the valley had been flooded did that fear gradually subside.

Picking up the phone, she dialled the code that would swiftly wing its way on the long journey to South Africa.

After a surprisingly short length of time, his gruff voice came on the line.

"Herbert Jowett."

"Hello, Herbert." The tone of her voice carried no sign of affection. "It's Ellen. How're you keepin'?"

"Not bad." He was clearly surprised to receive her call. "It's a gay lang time. How's yersel' an' the bairns?"

She smiled wryly at his reference to 'the bairns'. Her children were both now in their thirties – in spite of which her brother had never set eyes on either of them, nor they on him. She noted that though he had long since left England's shores, he had still not lost his old Westmorland accent – though by now there was a slight element of the clipped tones that came from his association with the Afrikaaners.

"We're getting by." She answered him in the same stilted manner, imagined him sighing with relief, though it would not be out of consideration for their well-being. His only concern would be that she might be about to press him for money. Quickly getting down to business, she outlined the events that had occurred at Mardale and her fears for the immediate future.

"Good God!"

That had shaken him.

"Are ye tellin' me, lass, that this is really the skull fra the auld farm?"

"There's laal doubt in my mind." She had no sympathy for his feelings on the matter. "What are we gaan to do?"

The silence that followed had nothing to do with his failure to comprehend her now somewhat unfamiliar accent. Finally he spoke, his voice carrying every indication that the fears of the past were coming home to roost.

"We're gaan to get the damn thing back fra the police, then bury it deep in the ruins of the auld house. Get on to 'em reet away, an' demand they return it. I'm comin' ower on the next flight. If we don't get the job done afore the valley fills wi' watter agin, it'll be too bloody late. I allus knew this was gaan to happen one day."

She heard the phone replaced with a crash. He had not even had the decency to say goodbye.

A smile replaced the somewhat sombre expression on her face. She had to admit that the chance to ruffle her brother's feathers had given her immense satisfaction. She had gleefully sensed the consternation that had seized him on hearing the news. His decision to return only emphasised the nature of his concern. Pity the curse wasn't directed specifically at the old bugger himself she thought. If anyone deserved to suffer, he did.

Dragging her thoughts back to the present, she attempted to think logically. She didn't much fear for her own safety, though the dread of something happening to her children still rankled. It might be an illogical fear, but there was no doubting her brother's belief in the prophecy.

She took up the phone once more, putting through a call to the Penrith police station. The sergeant who answered passed her on to Inspector Grey.

"Grey here. Can I help?" He had been informed about the nature of the enquiry.

"I hope so." She felt slightly embarrassed when dealing with people in authority, always feeling at a disadvantage. "I realise this may sound foolish to you, Inspector, but I'm ringing about the skull that was discovered at Mardale. I was formerly Ellen Jowett and my parents were the owners of Oxtors Farm."

"Ah yes, the 'Mardale Skull.'" It had passed through Grey's mind that any living descendant of the Jowetts might take an interest in the find.

"As you say, the Mardale Skull." She was relieved to hear him describe it in that way. "I've just spoken with my brother and we both feel that we're entitled to retrieve the skull and rebury it on the original site."

Grey considered her plea. He could well understand that anyone of a nervous disposition might be experiencing some concern. "Would you mind putting your request in writing, please?" He was attempting to be diplomatic. "I assure you that we will treat it seriously, but there are one or two investigations still in progress."

She sensed she was being tactfully obstructed. "I'll do that, Inspector, but you must realise that we want this matter resolved quickly. You may think we're paranoid, but if the rains come soon we'll never be able to lay this ghost to rest."

"Just so." Grey was aware that the woman was in some distress. "Leave the matter with me. I'll get back to you as soon as I'm in a position to do so."

It appeared she had to settle for that. If her brother wasn't satisfied he would have to take up the matter himself. After all, he had taken control of the family's affairs ever since the death of their father. That was a long time ago, yet Ellen had cause to remember it well. Their mother had also become quite ill herself following the bereavement and too weak to resist the demands of her son. The considerable sum of money that had come to the family as compensation for leaving their home – not to mention all the land that they had held title to – he had taken and invested in various schemes designed to make easy money. Little, or none, was used to benefit anyone other than Herbert himself.

Following the rapid demise of their mother, Herbert had taken off to South Africa, 'To make them all a fortune.' And make a fortune he certainly did – mainly at the expense of the poor blacks he exploited – yet Ellen had seen precious little of that money. Any request from her for financial assistance had been met with a deaf ear. The money was always 'tied up in the business.' Just a small pittance came her way, despite the fact that she had lost her husband early on in the marriage and was left to bring up two small children.

Finally she had grown tired of asking for assistance, realising that only on her brother's death was she ever likely to be able to claim any money due to her. At least he had never married, which meant there was no one to dispute her claim should she outlive him. The miserable sod had always managed to get what he wanted from women without ever giving anything in return.

It all came back to her now. The cavalier way he'd treated the girls in the valley. All he'd ever considered was his craving to satisfy his own needs. Thankfully, most of the young women realised it, steering well clear of him. No wonder he'd remained single. Any woman with an ounce of sense would have left him well alone.

She drew her thoughts back to the present. Maybe she should have a word with her son. If he had seen the revealing report in the newspaper, he may well be wondering what all the fuss was about. Since the legend of the skull had been long forgotten, with the farm apparently safe at the bottom of the reservoir, Ellen had never considered it necessary to worry her children by passing on the morbid details of the ancient curse. Now that the facts had been brought out into the open, the time for its disclosure seemed to have arrived. Once more, she reached for the phone.

"You must be joking, Ma!" Ralph Braithwaite had listened in amazement to his mother's outpourings. She had caught him just as he was about to set off to complete work on clearing a dyke. His fist clenched tight around the handset, dirt grimed fingers whitening as his anger grew. "You mean tae say that bloody auld skinflint's comin' over here?" Ellen was relieved to hear that her son appeared more angry at the thought of his uncle's arrival than concerned by the legend's prediction. "He is, son. Just shows how scared the auld sod is. He's never gotten over the fear that he was gaan tae be the one tae suffer if the skull ever got moved."

"Serve him reet!" Ralph laughed out loud at the thought of his miserable uncle's terror. "Well, he's the last one tae carry the actual Jowett name. And if anyone deserves tae get his comeuppance, that bastard certainly does. We all have tae die sometime, an' he's been a terrible long time gitten round tae it."

"You don't really believe in this prophecy then, Ralph?"

His mother sounded badly in need of reassurance.

"Course not, Ma! Load of old twaddle! I don't think we should say owt tae Jean though." Jean was his sister and the type to worry over almost anything. "We'll try tae keep it tae ourselves. If she asks ye anything about the curse, tell her it's all rubbish made up by the Press. You can say her uncle's just coming over tae have a last look at Mardale now that it's reappeared if she does gets suspicious."

"What about the skull though, Ralph? I still think it should be returned tae the farmhouse."

"Let him deal wi' it." He was angry that his mother should still be concerned to do her brother's bidding. "He's done bugger all for us in the past. Let the bastard sweat a bit. Maybe it'll teach him a lesson."

Replacing the phone, he felt his anger mounting once more. Hadn't his mother suffered enough trying to scrape by all these years? She could well do without this latest upset. Only her determination to outlive her skinflint brother, and perhaps one day receive 'her just dues, had kept her going through the bad times.

He recalled the promises she had made to him and his sister. They were never to have to scrimp and save once they grew up, as she had been forced to do. It had hurt her more than them that she had never managed to fulfil those promises. What should have been their inheritance was still in the hands of their scheming uncle. With no funds to pursue her case – not to mention the fact that her brother was out of the country – it was not surprising she had failed in all her attempts to gain redress. How dare the old bastard show his face after all this time! Ralph determined to have a showdown if the opportunity presented itself. There was no way his uncle was going to walk away unscathed. He was certainly not going to evade his responsibilities this time. Somehow, he had to be taught a lesson. Maybe the curse could be turned to the good of the rest of the family – with a little cautious assistance.

* * *

Angus McKade and his son Rory had also been getting their heads together. Angus was an old man now and becoming rather frail. In spite of that fact, there was a fire in his eyes as he spoke to the younger man.

"I never thowt we'd ever see this day, lad. That's Duncan McKade's skull right enough."

Rory McKade nodded. "You're reet, Da'. It's taken a long while commin', but we've the chance tae sort things out now."

"You'll not have forgotten where the rest o' the body's lain, son?"

Rory gave a grim smile. "Dunnae fret yoursel' about that. Just alongside the cave at Kidsty Pike, a big boulder at his heed an' a laal one at his feet. I can see the spot still, just like the day you first showed me."

The old man's eyes shone brightly in the lined, time-worn, crumpled face. "Good lad, Rory. We McKades have allus sworn tae put the skull back wi' the rest o' the remains – an' by God we're gaan tae do it now. I'll go tae my grave happy if we can redeem our pledge at last."

"We'll have tae deal with the Jowetts first." Rory guessed there would be opposition to their plan.

"Sod the Jowetts!" The old man's face contorted in outraged resentment. "If one o' them dies, like the legend foretells, I'll certainly shed nae tears. We should have been Kings o' Mardale, not they bastards; we should have walked off wi' all the money when the vale were sold." He shook with pent-up emotion.

Rory took hold of his father's thin shoulders. "It's the end o' it now, Da'. We may have lost out tae they thieving bastards in the past, but at least we should be entitled tae claim the heed back now. I don't see how they can stop us. It'll surely be o' nae use tae the police once they realise it's nowt tae do wi' a recent murder. We've carried this burden long enough. I'm not layin' it on my lad and I'm buggered if I'm lettin' this chance slip by now!"

CHAPTER EIGHT

Right! If a national newspaper were intending to carry her picture, Joy was not prepared to be portrayed in wellingtons and jeans. Though she struggled like the rest of the students to live on her grant, she had managed to acquire at least one presentable outfit. It was reserved for any interviews she had to attend and for occasions such as this.

Sheer, near-black tights; high heeled shoes to counteract her lack of height; a straight, pencil-slim skirt of Black Watch tartan; a smart, black, tailor-made jacket, worn over a white silk shirt. Not bad if she said so herself. If her friends were going to see her in the newspaper she was not going to appear looking like a bag lady.

Her outfit reminded her of the interview she had attended after applying to take part in the course at Brandley Hall. Professor Reid had been suitably pleased with her qualifications to offer her a place there and then. She had been overjoyed. Apart from the fact that this was a prestigious seat of learning, the establishment's location could hardly have been bettered. Set in an elevated position, about one mile from Keswick itself, the Hall overlooked the pretty little market town and the two lakes which took up most of the remaining area at the base of the valley. Impressive mountains, their lower slopes softened by a proliferation of conifers, deciduous trees, bracken and shrubs, formed a dramatic boundary on all sides, with Derwentwater – the most attractive of the two stretches of water – nestling almost directly below.

She could still scarcely believe her luck at being accepted to spend a whole year studying in such splendid surroundings. She recalled the professor's explanation of how the Hall came to be used for the studies carried out there. The former owner, Cynthia Moresby, had been a celebrated plant physiologist. Her death had prompted her son to set up a trust in her name to enable young people such as Joy to make use of the facilities there. Laboratories, together with a huge supply of plant materials, were available on site and the professor had been persuaded to take over the running of the establishment. He now lived there on a permanent basis and was, so he informed the students, equally delighted to have acquired the post. The work fitted in perfectly with his own research into the side effects of prescribed drugs.

Having ceased both reminiscing and admiring her reflection in the mirror, Joy now decided she should perhaps concentrate on her notes. There was always plenty of revising to do. She would carry on with that until the Press boys showed up.

* * *

It was a while later before the doorbell finally rang to announce the arrival of the reporter and cameraman. She swiftly made her way down to greet them.

"Miss Elliot?" A young man stood on the doorstep accompanied by an older companion weighed down with photographic equipment.

"That's me!" She held out her hand to take the one he proffered. "Won't you come in?"

"Thanks. I'm Tony Hoskis and this is Ray Jacobs. We're from Today's News – as I told you on the phone."

"Fine." She shook the somewhat gnarled hand of the photographer as it was thrust into her own. "Nice to meet you, Mister Jacobs."

"Same here. I must say you're situated in a beautiful spot." He stood for a moment admiring the view. "By the way, just Ray and Tony please. Let's not be too formal."

"Right, Ray; in that case please call me Joy,"

She led them into the students' communal lounge and library, where the older man divested himself of the heavy equipment before flopping down into an armchair.

"Can I get you a coffee or anything?" She glanced from one to the other.

"No thanks." The young man smiled across at her. "We popped into a pub on the way here and had a snack. We'll get straight down to business if you don't mind."

She didn't mind at all. She smiled back, rather bashfully, at the dishy-looking, dark-haired Adonis. He appeared to be just a few years older than her. Indicating that he take a seat, she carefully arranged herself opposite.

"OK, Tony, fire away. What would you like to know?"

"First of all, I'd like you to give us your own version of how you came to find the skull." He brushed back the lock of hair that had fallen across his handsome, virile-looking, tanned face, impeding his view of the notepad balanced on his knee. "Then if you could provide a little bit of background information about yourself, plus, of course, anything you know about this legend."

She attempted to disengage her mind from its preoccupation with the young reporter's appearance. He certainly was an attractive man, the sensual mouth parted in a smile that displayed pure white teeth to die for. Glancing across at her now with his sparkling, clear blue eyes, he waited patiently for her to begin. She found herself struggling to find the words – he almost took her breath away. Smiling back at him now a little hesitantly, she began to explain how the discovery came about, but had to admit that the first she had heard of the legend was on reading the report in the local newspaper. "I can tell you one thing though. The police have confirmed to the professor that it is a very ancient skull and that they're not considering taking any further action."

Both men took a keen interest in that news though the older of the two appeared slightly sceptical.

"It's not just going to be a skull left over from the old graveyard at Mardale, I hope."

Joy shook her head. “Not according to my tutor. Professor Reid has a pretty good knowledge of Mardale, and he’s convinced that all the bodies buried there were exhumed and reinterred at Shap cemetery.”

“That’s great!” The dishy reporter had pricked up his ears and was now scribbling away furiously. “If your man is correct, we could be on to a hell of a good story here.” He fell silent for a few moments as he finished writing up his account.

“Now, can you explain briefly how you came to be at Mardale in the first place.”

She detailed the events that had led to her tutor and herself visiting the depleted reservoir, going on to explain about the course she was attending at the Hall and the significance of the sample they had finally collected with regard to the studies being carried out there.

The young reporter was clearly delighted with all the information. No doubt with a little more research he could expand on the story the local paper had run. Eyes bright with excitement, he smiled dazzlingly at the young woman. “Just what we need, Joy. You’ve certainly came up with the goods. You haven’t been in touch with any other reporters have you?” The final query appeared to come as an afterthought.

“No. Only the local man I first spoke to at the time of the discovery.”

“Great!” He was giving her that flashing smile once more. “Would you mind letting us have it as an exclusive from now on then?”

“Why not?” She was in no mood to refuse him anything.

“You’re a treasure!” He reached across, squeezing her knee warmly. “Can I hand you over to Ray now? He’s the best in the business. Not that he’ll have much of a challenge making you look photogenic!”

She shyly accepted the compliment without comment. The touch of his hand had not been unwelcome.

The photographer had been busily setting up his equipment in readiness for the shots.

"I wonder if we could have you seated by the window with a book?" He settled her in position, ensuring that the shaft of sunlight entering the room channelled directly onto her golden hair. "We might as well run the student angle and the view behind you is pretty spectacular."

He rattled off several shots from different angles.

"Can we have you standing now? That's right. Just glancing out of the window as though you're deep in thought."

This was more like it. She hadn't got all dressed up to hide behind a table.

The camera whirred into action once more.

"What about your own study? A few shots there might be useful."

They trooped up the stairs with the equipment.

Joy quickly pushed any unsightly items out of the range of the camera's prying lens.

A few more shots seated at her desk, with books and files, and then the proceedings were over.

"That should be fine." Ray Jacobs thanked her for her patience, adding, "We should get a couple of good pictures out of that lot. We'd best be away now though. The editor will want this lot for tomorrow's edition."

She showed them out, sorry that the good-looking guy wasn't staying around a while longer. She had to admit that she had been exceedingly attracted to him. Was she wrong in assuming that he might have been similarly attracted? Possibly, but unfortunately that was something she would probably never come to know. Never mind. At least she had a great tale to relate to her friends when they arrived back – and weren't they in for a hell of a shock if they happened to pick up the relevant newspaper tomorrow?

"Nice bit of crumpet that." Ray Jacobs was busy loading his equipment into the back of the van. "I reckon you've pulled there – yet again!"

Tony Hoskis grinned at the comment. "She seems a smart girl. Not bad looking either. I wouldn't have minded getting to know her a little better."

"Play your cards right and you may get the chance." Jacobs was a wily old bird. "We might get an extension if we can persuade the editor this is worth following up on. With a bit of luck he may decide to allow us to stay over. I wouldn't mind exploring around here – it's a great part of the country." He grinned at the youngster. "Mind you, I reckon you'd be more interested in exploring that young woman, eh?"

"You've no soul," Tony Hoskis answered with a chuckle, jumping into the driving seat. "My intentions would be strictly honourable."

"Yeah, and I'm the Queen of the May!" Ray Jacobs scoffed. "Anyway, let's get over to Mardale and suss out the lie of the land. Sounds like a fascinating spot, even without the intriguing facts that are now coming to light." He took out the map as the young man engaged gear and moved off.

* * *

Merlin Reid's visit to the research institution's laboratories had been greeted with a great deal of interest. Everyone, it appeared, had read the report regarding the skull. It had not gone unnoticed that Joy was a student at Brandley Hall. The professor was forced to recount the entire details of the discovery before being allowed to get down to any form of business.

"And what about this, Prof.?" The white-coated boffin in charge of the department, who knew Reid well, had waved the article under his nose. "We thought we were helping out with a murder investigation here – or at least a missing person. Inspector Grey sent over the contents of the skull to see if we could determine the age of the sediment. We were getting quite excited by it all. He said you'd be along later with the sample you'd taken nearby as a further guide."

"It's here." Reid handed over the specimen. "You will remember though that the primary reason for collecting it was to establish the pollen content over the past sixty years or so?"

"Of course. Anyway the inspector rang in to say he has no further use for the information. It seems they're satisfied the skull's so ancient that it's gone past its 'investigate by date', as he put it. He did indicate though that you might be keen to hear the results. Said you enjoyed poking around with the odd mystery. Reckoned it might keep you out of his hair for a few weeks!"

Reid chuckled at Grey's interpretation of his interest. "The impudent old reprobate! Still, I have to admit I'm somewhat intrigued by this case. If you could establish whether the sediment from the skull corresponds with the sample I've bought along, it should at least rule out any possibility of it being planted there by some practical joker. There's surely no way anyone could fill up a skull with matching layers of sediment – even if they could be bothered to try."

"That's true. Anyway I'm sure it's no hoax." The still smiling boffin led the way over to the bench where Grey's sample had already been undergoing tests. "The pathologist had performed a pretty meticulous removal of the contents of the skull. The consistency of the sediment would have been entirely different had it been tampered with. You can take my word for it that the skull's lain where you discovered it for a considerable length of time. Once we compare your sample with this one, we should be able to establish fairly accurately just how long."

"Exactly what I was hoping for!" Reid was delighted by the pronouncement. "You know, the more I become involved in this case, the more I'm convinced that there is some substance in this legend. There surely has to be a good reason why such a tale came to be handed down over the centuries."

He could see that even the pragmatic technician was considering the possibility. Promising to keep them all up to date with his findings, he left them to their work. He would return to the Hall and inform Joy of the new developments.

On his arrival back, he was just in time to see the two pressmen departing. He was not exactly sorry to have missed them. His interest lay in discovering the true facts behind the bizarre mystery, not in providing the media with speculative gossip.

His journey back to the Hall had been spent contemplating how best to uncover those facts. He had come to the conclusion that a visit to Shap cemetery would prove to be the ideal starting point. Any headstones of the reinterred bodies from Mardale could provide evidence of the names of the past occupants of the village. The church register might also confirm any such findings, if it were still available. An event such as the one that had taken place would surely not go unrecorded.

From what little he could recall, the bodies occupied what had become known as the 'Mardale Corner' at the Shap graveyard. The sectioned off area had been designated solely for the purpose of accommodating all of the remains in one parcel of land, presumably in the hope that the relatives of the deceased might find some consolation in retaining a semblance of their former burial ground. It was a fitting location. Until the eighteenth century – when Mardale's churchyard was consecrated for burials to take place there – all deaths occurring in the vale had entailed a journey to Shap for burial. With the coffin strapped to the back of a hardy Lakeland pony, the cortege had to ascend a laborious zigzag track which wound over mountain and fell for eight miles to its destination. To this day, the track was still known as the 'Corpse Road.' A journey such as that in the winter months must have been hard to endure. It had to have come as some relief to the villagers when they finally acquired permission to begin burials at Mardale.

Reid drew his mind back to the present. What was needed now was a little luck in tracing one or two of the remaining descendants of the original villagers. It was possible someone might be prepared to recount any recollections they had of life spent in the vale. He doubted that many of the past residents would have moved far afield. A close-knit farming community, who had lived in virtual isolation, were hardly likely to have suddenly spread their wings and gone their separate ways. It was probable that the water company who had appropriated the land would have made provision close by for most of them. Shap and Swindale would appear to be the most likely parishes to have catered for the relocation of the villagers.

* * *

"Hi, Prof." Joy was pleased to see her tutor back. She had not exactly been over keen to return to her revision. "The journalists have already been. It seems they were working on a story close by when they picked up on this one."

"Yes, I saw them leaving. Did you give them all the gory details?"

"Oh yes. I told them all about you!" She chuckled at getting her own back for his earlier teasing.

"You cheeky young minx!" He joined in with her laughter. "I suppose I deserved that. Still, you might at least have changed into something smart to have your photograph taken."

She took a feigned swipe at him for his impertinent retaliation. "You beast! I thought I rather impressed the young reporter." She almost blushed at her lack of modesty.

He was still chuckling. "I'm sure you did. Sorry about that, Joy. I must say you do look very elegant."

"That's better!" She knew him well enough to engage in an exchange of good-humoured banter. "Anyway, now that we've done with the insults, what have you been finding out?"

He related all that had occurred at the Windermere laboratories. "So you see we do have a genuine mystery on our hands," he concluded.

"I'll say!" Joy was still in two minds whether she was pleased or disturbed by the news. This latest indication of the skull's antiquity only confirmed her worst fears. Keen though she was to get to the bottom of the affair, she intuitively came to the conclusion that the episode could well have some unwelcome effects on her hitherto uneventful life. It was fortunate that she was totally unaware of the devastation that it would wreak on the lives of others.

CHAPTER NINE

Once lunch was over, Joy and the professor quickly agreed that a visit to shap cemetery should be the immediate priority. Reid decided a little preliminary detective work might be called for, while the young woman took the opportunity to change into more appropriate clothing.

A call to the Allerdale Borough Council immediately gained Reid the information that he had the wrong authority. Shap came under the jurisdiction of the Eden District Council. Fair enough; he tried again. This time he met with a little more success, being directed through to the department that dealt with all enquiries relating to burials. His explanation that he was seeking evidence of any record of the exhumation and subsequent reinterment of the Mardale corpses met with a moment's hesitation.

"Can you hang on a minute? I think you may need the records office at Carlisle Castle if you're digging back that far." There was the sound of the phone being placed on the desk, followed by the rustle of papers. A buzz of conversation continued in the background. After a few minutes the lady returned. "Right. You could try Carlisle Castle, or perhaps one of the local funeral directors who deal with the Shap area. Their records go back a good way."

"Sounds fine to me." He was pleased to be getting somewhere.

"I can give you the name and number of the undertakers. We have a list." The young lady appeared very efficient.

"Yes, please." He made a note, thanking her for her assistance.

"You're welcome." She rang off after insisting he call again if he were unsuccessful.

A call to Carlisle Castle saw him passed on to the archivist. She too was extremely helpful, though unable to discover any record of Shap's parish register covering the 1930s. "It might be possible that they're stored at the Kendal Records Office," he was informed.

Expressing his thanks once more, he opted to contact the undertakers first. Previous dealings with council departments had convinced him that such a process might well be time consuming. Yet again his queries were answered with good grace, and in this instance with the very information that he sought. "The vicar of Saint Michael's in Shap," he was advised, "will be a fount of knowledge on the subject."

It soon emerged why he would have reason to be, since he was the son of the last schoolmaster to teach at Mardale. Though only a babe in arms at the time of the evacuation of the valley, it was revealed that he had never lost his interest in the dale. "Probably got a good few records you could sort through," Reid was told. "Nice chap; he'll soon put you right."

The professor was furnished with the vicar's name and telephone number. This was more like it. He seemed to be getting ever closer to his goal.

Fortunately, the Reverend Anthony Studley was at home to take the call. He listened with growing interest as the professor explained the nature of his enquiries and his desire to visit the final resting place of the bodies removed from Mardale.

"Do call in and see me," the vicar invited. "If I'm not in the church, you'll find me in the vicarage close by. Are you familiar with Shap? Do you know where the church is situated?"

"I'm afraid not. I'll be travelling through from Keswick."

"Right. You'll find that once you're on the A6, the road goes directly through the village. You'll see a turning on your left almost as soon as you enter Shap. It's sign-posted to Screedale. St Michael's is about 200 yards along, and if you're wanting to see the plot where the Mardale remains were interred, carry on about another 200 yards up the hill. You'll find a raised, walled enclosure immediately on your left as you enter the graveyard. All one hundred and four bodies were laid to rest there. It was necessary to consecrate a new parcel of land to accommodate the sudden influx of so many bodies at one time."

That was not hard to understand. A village the size of Shap at that time could hardly be expected to have provision for mass burial. "That's very good of you, Vicar. I look forward to meeting you."

The vicar expressed the same sentiments.

Though it had been necessary to keep Joy waiting, at least Reid now knew precisely where he was headed. The young woman had been fairly patient, though she was clearly relieved to see him finally put in an appearance.

"Oh good, you're here. I can hardly wait to get going."

There was no mistaking her desire to uncover the secrets that lay behind the legend. He explained the delay as they headed for the car.

"Well that's great!" She was bouncing with excitement. "Sounds as though the vicar could be a real help."

Opening the doors to allow some of the heat to escape before they entered, he glanced up at the cloudless sky. "Well, we've another nice day for it, Joy. There seems no end to the drought for the moment, though they are forecasting a change. I reckon Mardale should be on view for a little while longer. I think we might manage a return visit if we decide on it. Even when the rains come, it'll take a while for the ruins to disappear again. That is," he added, "unless we get a hell of a good downpour."

Joy nodded. "I hope you're right. Wouldn't it be terrific if we could get to speak to some of the people who'd lived there and were old enough to remember it? They must have some fascinating tales to tell."

"That's true." He settled himself behind the wheel as she joined him. "It's unfortunate the vicar was too young to have any recollections himself, though there is a possibility that a few of the others are still around. Problem is, anyone with memories of life there would have to be in their late sixties or older by now. In a small community such as that, there may only have been a handful of young people who'd have survived this length of time."

They moved off, with Joy still considering his words.

Quickly emerging on to the busy motorway that bypassed Keswick's narrow streets, Reid pointed the car in the direction of Shap. There was no travelling as the crow flies in this terrain.

On the left, Latrigg – one of the smaller prominences in the region – rose to a height of twelve hundred feet, its low levels clothed in dense forestation. The steeply sloping flank that faced the road plunged deep into the rocky ravine below, carved out over aeons by the rushing, tumbling waters of the river Greta as it careered down into the valley.

Beyond Latrigg, Lonscale towered majestically on the skyline, the gentler slope of its southern flank stretching out ahead towards the massive bulk of Blencathra – a sombre spreading giant of a mountain, known locally as 'Saddleback' for its unusual topographical features. As a motorway, this one would take some beating, surrounded as it was by so many imposing scenic features.

It spite of the glorious passing panorama of mountains and fells, Joy had been sitting quietly, oblivious to the view. It was clear that she had something on her mind. "I was just wondering, Prof. What do you think will become of the skull? Are the police likely to keep it as a curio? Or will they give it a decent burial?"

Reid had never given it a moment's thought. "I imagine they may carry out a few more tests first, just to make sure it is as old as they think. It might then end up in one of their 'Black Museums', along with some of the other macabre bits and pieces they gather along the way."

"I hope not." She sounded genuinely concerned. "I think it ought to be properly laid to rest. In a way, I feel sorry for ever having disturbed it."

The professor made good time along the motorways, arriving at Shap in about forty minutes. Spotting the signpost the vicar had mentioned, he turned into the narrow lane. St Michael's Church stood out on the right, with the additional cemetery mentioned by the vicar a short way ahead on the more open, higher ground. A parking area was conveniently provided opposite the wrought-iron gates which gave access to the graveyard.

It was with some relief that Reid now stepped from the car. Arthritic joints still bothered him, seizing up to some extent after any term of confinement. He stretched himself, happy to stand for a moment enjoying the fresh breeze that blew across the meadows.

"Carry on, Joy." He could see that she was impatient to seek out the burial site.

Not rushing to follow, he took in the scene. It was a very open spot here, with the land to the east rising gradually towards rocky limestone outcrops some distance away. A profusion of dry stone walls – clearly constructed from the same material – separated patches of rough pasture land containing small groups of lethargic Swaledale sheep. Their bleating, along with the strident croak of the rooks that seemed to abound in the area, were the only sounds that disturbed the silence.

Crossing to enter the graveyard now, he caught up with his companion, once more hesitating for a moment to glance across to the west and the distant mountain ranges which encircled Haweswater, Caldbeck and Ullswater. Shimmering in the heat of the afternoon sun, they made a fitting backdrop to the small village of Shap, spread sparingly across the sweeping canvas of fields and fells some distance below – the church dominating the scene. It seemed a far cry from the beautiful vale of Mardale to this exposed hillside, though the people lying here were hardly likely to be aware of their changed surroundings.

"Take a look at this." Joy was contemplating a memorial tablet that stood on the outskirts of the elevated, walled enclosure where Mardale's dead had been reinterred. It emerged that the grassed over patch of land was now in use for scattering the ashes of some of those members of the local community who chose cremation as their method of disposal. Presumably, relatives of the people buried in this spot would be the most likely to opt for this site as their destination.

A few stone steps led up to the higher level, where the small number of gravestones removed from the Mardale cemetery were lined up around the walls of the plot. Just fifteen headstones commemorated the departed, though 104 bodies had been laid in their final resting place here. Though it seemed rather tasteless to walk the ground above the remains, a bench had been provided in the far corner, seemingly encouraging entry.

"Is it okay for us to walk around on there do you think?" Joy appeared apprehensive.

"I'm sure it is." He made his way up the steps. "We'll just make a note of the names on the headstones in case it proves to be of interest."

That certainly turned out to be the case. The name 'Jowett' appeared several times, along with those of the more notable residents. Past schoolmasters and vicars were commemorated, as was to be expected, since they represented the hierarchy of such a small community. The poorer families had clearly been in no position to erect tombstones to the memory of their departed.

Joy was busy with pen and notebook. "This Jowett was a real person then," she said excitedly. "His descendants warranted headstones, so he must have been quite important. If he did, in fact, claim the title of King of Mardale, it appears that his line was carried on for several centuries – certainly judging by the dates here."

"I was just thinking the same thing." Reid had been studying the ages that most of the members of the family had attained before finally expiring. "They seem to have been a long-lived breed. Into their seventies and eighties, at a time when most people would hardly expect to survive beyond their sixties. They must have led a healthy life in spite of the hardships they probably endured as a result of their isolation."

Joy had completed the task of jotting down the details. She now stood quietly, clearly thinking back to the date of the exhumations.

"It must have been an awful time for the people of Mardale. Imagine having to watch all the bodies of your loved ones being disturbed, and knowing that you had to leave that beautiful valley forever. I suppose it was all in the name of progress, but I wonder if the people of Manchester ever realised the sacrifice these people made."

"Probably not." Somehow the professor could hardly bring himself to believe that the recipients of the clear mountain water ever gave it any thought. "As you point out though, it must have been a fairly traumatic time for the villagers. It does make you wonder if they ever adjusted again to their new surroundings." He made his way back down the steps, still musing on the subject. "Anyway, we may be able to discover a little more about that. We'll pop down to the church and have a word with the vicar. It sounds as though he could be the man to enlighten us."

Joy tagged on behind. "Are we going to look around the graveyard there first?"

"Most definitely!" He set off on the short walk with Joy now at his side. "It should prove enlightening if there are any tombstones of an earlier period relating to the Jowetts down there. We know for certain that Mardale's dead were interred here before the land at Mardale was consecrated for burials, so it could give us a better idea of how far back the dynasty stretched."

Making their way out of the cemetery and heading down the hill, ancient sycamores – from whence the boisterous chattering of the noisy rooks mainly emanated – almost hid St Michael's from view. It was a pretty little church, its architecture giving the impression that it may have seen some changes down the centuries. No doubt it had expanded in size as the population gradually increased. Reid recalled that at one time a monastery had also been situated in the parish of Shap, until it had been desecrated at the time of the Reformation.

The graveyard surrounding the church was not very spacious. This certainly explained why the additional burial ground had become a necessity. A walk around the plot quickly established that no recent burials had taken place there. The headstones all bore testimony to the age of the site. And here was what Reid had been seeking. In the shade of an ancient, gnarled yew tree, a group of headstones disclosed more of the history of the Jowett family. The first recorded burial had taken place early in the fourteenth century.

"Look at this, Joy!" He was rapidly becoming convinced of the truth behind the saga of the Jowetts. "All of these bodies were brought here from Mardale for burial. Proof indeed that the family were around at that time. It does seem to indicate that the legend of the original Jowett hacking off the head of the unfortunate Duncan of Crieff could have some basis in fact."

She shuddered at the thought. "I suppose it does tie in. It's no wonder. It still turns my stomach to think of those people living in the same house with it."

"Yes, it's hardly the kind of thing you'd want to see every day, is it? You can imagine how that woman who finally cracked and attempted to get rid of it must have felt. I suppose once it was walled up after her death it may have become a little more acceptable, though even then none of the Jowetts were likely to want to tempt fate by removing it from its hiding place again. Folk in those far off times weren't as worldly wise as we like to think ourselves today."

"Well, I'm not sure about that, Prof. but I don't think you could blame them." Joy was still not completely convinced that the curse could be discounted so easily. "If they had moved it, and one of the family suddenly died, the people responsible would never have forgiven themselves, would they? They'd naturally assume it was to do with the prophecy. You can see why the story was handed down. After the woman who originally disturbed it died, there must always have been some fear of the same thing happening again."

"Have you found what you were looking for?" The vicar had suddenly appeared from around the side of the yew tree, interrupting their conversation. "I spotted you from the vicarage. You must be Professor Reid." He shook hands enthusiastically. "And this must be the young lady you spoke of." Again a hand was genially extended. "We don't get many visitors to this churchyard now. It's quite a while since any interments took place here. I imagine you've already been up to our current burial ground?"

"Yes, Vicar." Joy pushed the notebook away into her handbag. "There surely can't be many graveyards with a history like that one." She smiled awkwardly at the tall, dignified-looking, grey-haired man.

"Indeed not." He smiled back at her, eyes twinkling in the depths of his rather gaunt face. "Nor many that can be so bleak in the winter. I've hurried through many a burial ceremony at the graveside when the weather's been foul, I must admit."

Reid rather liked the man's down-to-earth honesty. "No doubt to the relief of the grieving relatives, if truth be told."

"One hopes so." The vicar's face broke into a grin once more. "I almost envy the ones in the wooden overcoats at such times." For a moment he looked rather embarrassed by the words that had slipped so casually from his lips. "That's not too disrespectful, is it?"

The professor chuckled. "I don't think so. I imagine you need a sense of humour in your profession."

"It helps." He seemed relieved by Reid's reaction. "Some people frown on any attempt by a vicar to show his human side. I guess they think we're a different breed of men." He shook his head. "But, to quickly change the subject, I wondered if you'd finished your viewing here. If so, I'd be interested in listening to your story of the discovery of the skull. I originally learned about the legend from my father's own lips, though I'm not sure he ever took it seriously. The skull had been walled up for such a length of time when he came to hear of it that no one knew for certain whether there was any truth behind the tale or not."

"What about the other villagers?" Reid inquired. "Were they as convinced by the story?"

"Well, the only people who never doubted it were the Jowetts and the McKades. The McKades were the direct descendants of 'Duncan of Crieff' – or Duncan McKade, to give him his proper title. The story goes that they were always determined to retrieve the skull and to reunite it with the rest of the remains. It was believed that the headless corpse had been buried somewhere on the fells and that only McKade's descendants knew of the secret place. They continued over the years to make every effort in their power to persuade the Jowetts to give up the skull, but the Jowetts never got over their fear of moving it. Only when the valley was finally flooded did it put an end to the arguments. Everyone then had to accept that the feuding was over."

Merlin Reid was intrigued. This was the first he had heard of the McKades. It was remarkable to reflect on the family's persistence in handing down through the centuries, presumably from father to son, the knowledge of the hidden burial site of their notable ancestor. Was it possible that one of the descendants still lived – and retained that information? It was certainly another interesting avenue to explore.

Accepting an invitation to take tea with the vicar, he and Joy made their way inside.

Their account of the happenings at Mardale were related to their attentive host as they enjoyed his hospitality.

"Quite extraordinary!" He downed the remains of the contents of his teacup as he considered the story. "There's no doubt in my mind now that this is the skull of Duncan of Crieff. While I've no recollection of Mardale myself, I have done quite a bit of research on the village. Your description of where you made the discovery of the skull makes it clear that you were alongside Oxtors Farm. I'm convinced that all of the doubters who've poured scorn on the legend in the past are going to have to eat their words now."

Reid exchanged jubilant glances with Joy. This was just the confirmation they were seeking. He turned back to the vicar. "You mentioned the McKade family. Have you any record of them after they moved out of Mardale?"

"Oh yes." The vicar smiled at the professor's mounting excitement. "They came to live here at Shap – and they're here still; or at least the son of the original villagers is. He has a grownup son of his own now and a grandson. The old man's wife died a few years back, but the son and his wife and child still live on the smallholding with the old chap. There's little employment in this area to draw them away. Only farming, and catering for the tourist trade."

"Do you think they'd mind if I had a word with them?" Reid was hesitant about pressing the vicar for information. "Would it be an impertinence to ask you to reveal where they live? I wouldn't, of course, go bothering them without first checking if they'd be willing to talk."

The vicar appeared slightly hesitant. "I don't mind passing on the address, but I doubt you'll have much success there. They're a strange family – very introverted." He rose from his chair to collect a pen and paper. "They never seemed to integrate into the community here, unlike most of the others. The best person you could talk to about anything to do with Mardale would be old Joss Pattinson. You can find him any day at the Kings Arms around lunch time. He always sits in the corner alongside the bar." The vicar looked thoughtful for a moment, but then continued, "He must have been just into his twenties when he was uprooted and brought here by his parents. He still retains a marvellous store of memories of old Mardale though, in spite of the fact that he's not much grasp of what goes on around him now. Buy him a pint and he'll regale you with tales of the valley till the cows come home."

Just the job! Reid was delighted by the news. This was certainly preferable to sorting through piles of old parish registers. "So you think he would be prepared to help us?"

"Just mention my name. We've become great friends over the years, though he hardly ever attends my sermons." The vicar chuckled heartily. "He always complains that the pews are too hard, but I reckon the real reason is that he feels if he's reached his age without resorting to prayer, God must be taking good care of him anyway."

Joy giggled at the vicar's words. He did appear to be a slightly unorthodox member of the clergy. Not the stuffy type of person she would normally associate with that office. "Joss sounds quite a character," she remarked.

"Indeed he is. You'll find him a very engaging old chap. He can come up with a few incredible tales, but on the whole you can trust him to stick to the facts. I owe him a great deal myself for filling me in with details of my own family's life in the valley. My father was headmaster at the old school, and taught Joss and the other children there. It was a time of paraffin lamps, slates and chalks, and corporal punishment. Far removed from today's comprehensives I'm sure, though it seemed to turn out good honest citizens on the whole." He smiled apologetically. "Sorry if I'm getting on my favourite hobby horse. I'm sure you've listened to enough of my ramblings. I really shouldn't delay you any longer."

They thanked him for the tea and advice, then were shown out through the hall, where the professor's eyes were drawn to a picture of St Michael's Church dated 1898. It purported to be the last likeness before restoration and enlargement took place. It was interesting to note that the sycamores, which still graced the churchyard, were in place at that time and contained a rookery then as they did today. It was gratifying to realise there was such continuity. Maybe if he and Joy returned to Shap tomorrow, old Joss might be able to enlighten them as to whether the same kind of continuity existed in Mardale up to the time of the flooding.

CHAPTER TEN

The day was not going well for Inspector Grey. First Ellen Braithwaite had taken up his valuable time; then the *Today's News* reporters had pestered him for a statement as to whether a murder inquiry was to take place. He had assured them that no such inquiry was necessary. Pressed to verify the antiquity of the skull, he had let it be known that its age was the reason for the case to be terminated. He refused to be drawn on the subject of exactly how old the skull might be, or to make comment on the legend associated with it. He was far too wily an old bird to lay himself open to ridicule in the national press.

Having eventually satisfied the reporters' queries – without giving way to the overwhelming desire to reveal that he regarded them as blithering idiots – he now had Rory McKade on the line. Listening patiently to the man's tale, he finally sat shaking his head.

"You do realise that at this moment in time we are not totally convinced that this is the so-called 'Mardale Skull' – or that this legend has any basis in fact? Our enquiries are still at a very early stage."

"You'll not deny though that it could be the skull of our ancestor?"

Grey felt there was little point in doing so. "We have more or less established that it is quite an ancient relic. However, there is one point I have to make…" He guessed that the man was not going to be pleased. "I've already had a member of the Jowett family laying claim to the skull. Their justification is that since it originally came from the farm, they should be entitled to replace it there."

“I thought they buggers would be after it!” Rory McKade was in no mood to yield to the Jowetts. “That skull belongs back wi’ the rest o’ the remains. Oor family’s been pledged tae liberate it fer centuries. We’ll not rest till we’ve honoured the undertaking that were made by our forebears. The bloody Jowetts can’t get away wi’ it this time. It’s ours by rights!”

Grey forcibly stabbed the pen he was grasping on to the papers before him. This was all he needed. Two nutters arguing about the skull of some long dead combatant.

“Look, Mr McKade. I can only advise you to do as I suggested to the other family. Send in a request in writing and I’ll consider it along with theirs as soon as our investigation comes to an end. If the pair of you can’t then come to some form of agreement, you’ll just have to fight it out in the courts.”

“Oh, bloody great!” Rory McKade could see where that would lead. “Wi’ the money that family have, they’ll walk all ower us. We can’t take the buggers tae court. We’ve not the cash tae go tae law.”

Grey was rapidly losing patience. “Send in your request, Mr McKade. There’s nothing more I can do at this stage. You’ll have to excuse me now, I’m a very busy man.” He replaced the phone without awaiting a reply.

“Bastard!” Rory McKade sent his parting shot down the dead line. “We’ll see about that!”

Grey had hardly replaced the receiver before the pathologist was ringing in with his final report.

“I was correct in my assumptions, Inspector. That skull has to be at least a couple of hundred years old. Nothing there for you to trouble yourself about.”

“Not bloody much!” Grey’s ironic reply adequately conveyed his feelings. “I’d rather have got my teeth into some gory murder that have to admit that that skull really did belong to this Duncan of Crieff. I’ve got a member of each of the feuding families attempting to claim ownership.”

“Good grief!” The pathologist found it difficult to comprehend that such a feud could be sustained over so long a period of time. "They must be crazy. I don't envy you the task of deciding who gets the trophy."

"I've no intention of getting involved!" Grey was in no mood to appease either of the parties. "Now you've completed your examination, let me have the skull back. The silly buggers can get their solicitors on the case if they're so minded. By the time they've haggled over the issue the ruins have every chance of being under water once more. That should settle the bloody argument once and for all!"

Grey was reckoning without the steely determination of the people involved…

"They'll not hand ower the bloody thing, Da!" Rory McKade's face twisted with anger as he reported to his father. "Jowett and the Braithwaites have already tried claiming it. We're gaan tae have a reet fight on our hands."

The old man crushed the newspaper he had been reading in frustration. "I bloody knew it! I reckoned Jowett would come scurryin' back here as soon as he heard o' it. He won't let it rest, Rory. The bugger'll have it afore we know what's what!"

"Not if I have owt tae do wi' it." Rory was fighting mad. "How're we gaan tae stop him?"

"Well, not through the bloody courts, that's fer sure. If the bastard gets his hands on it an' I hear tell o' it, I'll have it off him somehow – even if it means beatin' it out o' him. If I'd had any sense I'd have done that afore he buggered off abroad!"

The old man knew there had been no chance of that. His son would have been no match at the time Jowett left. Jowett was in his prime then and Rory just a youth. "You be careful, lad. Jowett may be an old man, but by Christ, he's a big 'un."

Rory ignored the warning. "He's still got all the money that should rightly have come tae our family, Da. I know it's too soddin' late tae ever change that now, but neither him nor the Braithwaites are havin' the bloody skull too. I swear it's gaan tae join the rest o' the remains. I'll rot in hell afore I'll let that lot get the better o' us agin!"

* * *

Ellen Braithwaite's daughter, Jean, was endeavouring to convey to her husband the fears that now clouded her mind. "I'm scared, Cedric. Ma reckons there's nowt tae these tales o' a curse on our family, but I can tell she's worried. She can't hide it from me. This story o' hers that my uncle's comin' ower just tae visit Mardale agin is just a load o' rubbish."

Cedric Bull pricked up his ears. So Herbert Jowett was coming back. The bastard who had skipped off with all the money was finally coming back. And there was a curse on the grasping old swine. Cedric had cursed him enough times himself in the past to have put the man in his grave if there were any justice. Jean could have been a rich woman if her mother hadn't let that brother of hers get away with it.

"It's true what the papers say," Jean added, clearly troubled. "Ma's never let on anything about this curse afore, but Da let something slip just afore he died. I thought he were ramblin' at the time but it's comin' back tae me now. He said we were still tainted by what happened in the past."

Cedric allowed himself a wry smile. Jean was still the weak-minded woman he had married in the hope that one day she would come by her inheritance. He made no attempt to reassure her. "I guess you're right. Your uncle wouldn't be on his way here if he didn't believe in this curse, would he? Do you think he'd risk your brother gettin' hold o' him? You know Ralph's always said he'd swing fer the bastard if he ever set eyes on him."

"That's another thing that bothers me." Jean nervously twisted her handkerchief. "You know what a temper Ralph's got. I'd hate him tae get into trouble."

"Well, he's big enough tae look after himsel'." Cedric gave a grim smile. "I hope he does have a go at the thieving bastard. It's about time somebody in your family stood up tae the old sod. How the hell your mother's let him get away wi' it up tae now amazes me! If it were my cash, I'd have dragged him through every court in the land."

"Ma's never had the cash tae do it." Jean was aware that her mother had tried everything in her power to get justice. Unfortunately, Cedric had never accepted that fact. It was pointless attempting to make him understand. Cedric was a bitter man; Ralph was not the only one with a fiery temper.

CHAPTER ELEVEN

Joy Eliott had been waiting impatiently to get her hands on the morning papers. How had her previous day's interview gone?

There it was. Tony Hoskis had made an excellent job of padding out the story that had appeared in the local press. She glowed with delight as she read:

> This attractive young student, under the watchful eye of her tutor, Professor Merlin Reid, was stunned by an incident that occurred as she made ready to carry out an important experiment at the site of the crumbling, long-lost village of Mardale. Finally restored to the light of day by the exceptional drought conditions prevailing in the area, this tiny outpost, which had disappeared below the waves some 60 years previously, was host to a grim reminder of a brutal past. The sediment-covered base of the reservoir held in its clinging, muddy depths the skull of 'Duncan of Crieff'. About to take a sample of the sediment, Joy crouched, tools in hand, to come face to face with the gruesome relic which stared sightlessly up at her from below a thin film of water.

There followed a full account of the legend, which was accompanied by a report of an interview that had apparently taken place at Mardale. An elderly past resident had been located who verified that the ancient folk tale was no flight of fancy. As if to confirm the account that Joy and her tutor had heard from the Reverend Studley, the old man concerned had stated that everyone who had lived at Mardale prior to its destruction had been well aware of the feud between the Jowetts and the McKades. Speculation was now rife over the likely outcome. Old hatreds were expected to flare once more.

Photographs of Mardale and the area where the skull had been unearthed were prominently displayed, along with one of Joy seated at her desk. She was quite pleased with the result, although a little disappointed that she had hardly been shown off to her best advantage. She smiled, realising that she was, perhaps, being overly fussy. At least she did look tolerably chic and Tony had described her as 'This attractive young student.' She almost blushed at the thought of what her friends might have to say.

She was soon to find out. The morning was taken up by a succession of incoming calls from friends and relatives alike. All were keen to hear her account of the events that had taken place.

Her fellow students, needless to say, had pulled her leg mercilessly over the 'attractive' label, but nevertheless were devastated to have missed all the fun. Most of them had gone away on their breaks feeling a mite sorry to leave her behind on her own. Now envy had replaced that sentiment.

Having said goodbye to the latest caller, she went in search of her tutor. He had looked in a short while before to remind her that it was time they were making tracks. He was obviously extremely keen to have a few words with 'Old Joss', and she was just as determined to be part of the action. The newspaper report had only served to heighten her curiosity. It still seemed almost like a dream. It was difficult to accept that all of this was happening simply as a consequence of her chance discovery.

The professor had been waiting for her in his study. They quickly decided it would be best to get a meal at the Kings Arms once they arrived at Shap. It should give them the opportunity to seek out Joss and ascertain whether the old chap could shed any more light on the past history of Mardale. Joy was fascinated by the prospect of meeting someone who had actually spent his youth in the valley. What else might they learn? Each new fact that emerged seemed to confirm that Mardale still held dark secrets that remained to be unearthed.

Reid timed the journey well. They arrived at their destination shortly after noon.

The Kings Arms turned out to be a charming old coaching inn which appeared to have survived the passage of time with little or no change in its appearance. The roughcast, whitewashed exterior, laced together with massive, blackened, twisted oak beams, still retained images of its past. A small flight of three worn stone steps that jutted out from the front wall of the building bore testimony to decades of use. One might assume that, in the dim and distant past, they had been installed there to enable inebriated patrons of the inn to mount their horses after a night of drunken excess.

On entering the bar it was abundantly clear that the assumption of the inn clinging to its old traditional image was not misplaced. Smoke-stained ceilings were supported by more of the sturdy oak beams, their rough-hewn sides copiously festooned with genuine horse brasses dulled by the patina of age. Rough plastered walls were hung with cartoons of local huntsmen and hounds. A huge fireplace – thankfully not in use – took up a large expanse of one wall, copper pots and artefacts gleaming alongside in the shaft of sunlight which penetrated through the bullseye window panes, illuminating at the same time the somewhat gloomy interior of the building. Benches, stools and tables, all looked to be from a bygone age, showing signs of continuous wear.

At one of the tables beside the timeworn, elbow-polished bar, an elderly gentleman – looking almost as ancient as his surroundings – sat nursing a near empty pint glass. He matched exactly the description that the vicar had provided of the man they had come to see.

So this was Joss. Luckily he was alone, as Reid had hoped he might be if they arrived early enough in the day. Ordering two ploughman's lunches, he nodded across at the old man. "Afternoon. Could I get you a drink – and perhaps my companion and I might join you at your table?"

The old chaps eyes sparkled. “That’s gay kind o’ ye. I’m allus glad of a bit o’ company.”

The vicar was obviously correct in his assumption that a visit would not go unrewarded.

“What’ll it be?” Reid was delighted to have crossed the first hurdle.

“Bitter, please.” Joss emptied the remaining contents of his glass in one gulp, passing it over for the refill. “Are ye just passin’ through?”

The professor decided to come clean. “Well, to be honest, we really came here to see you. You are Joss Pattinson, aren’t you?”

“That’s reet.” The old man looked a mite confused. “I don’t know ye, do I?”

“No.” Reid smiled across reassuringly. “We got your name from the vicar at St Michaels. He assured us that you were the man to talk to if we wanted to find out anything about Mardale.” He set the pint of foaming bitter down in front of the man.

The eyes lit up once more in the weather-worn face. “Ah, Mardale. The auld vicar would tell ye tae come an’ see me. We have many a good crack about Mardale.”

Reid handed over the food to Joy, joining her and Joss at the table. There seemed little to be gained by not coming straight to the point.

“I don’t know whether you’ve seen the papers, but this is the young woman who found the skull – Joy Elliot. I’m Merlin Reid by the way.”

Joss studied Joy carefully for a moment or two. “I thowt I’d seen ye somewhere afore, lass. You’ve stirred up a reet hornets’ nest. Them Jowetts an’ McKades are gaan tae be back at each other’s throats as sure as eggs is eggs.”

Joy was a little taken aback. “I hope not. Surely they can’t still be feuding, can they?”

“Dunna fret yersel, lass.” Joss patted her arm. “I thowt there’d be trouble as soon as I heard tell the lake were dryin’ up. If you’d not found the skull, I reckon the McKades would like as not have gone lookin' fer it. If they'd known there were any likelihood it had broken loose fra the house when the waters arrived they'd have bin there afore anyone else."

Joy was finding it a little difficult following the conversation. Coming from the south, she found the old chaps strong Westmorland dialect not the easiest to understand. Winking at her from behind his pint glass, the professor took up the conversation.

"The vicar mentioned the McKades to us. He said they were still living locally, but that they probably wouldn't welcome anyone attempting to question them about the past."

"They'll not hardly speak tae anybody." Joss took a long swig from his glass, settling back into the creaking confines of his favourite bar-side nook. "The young un's almost as bad as his da'. They allus thowt they were better than most folk, but they'm all descended fra cattle thieves. Duncan o' Crieff were nobbut a bloody rogue. Tis said he were one o' they border reivers. Ye might have heard of 'em."

Reid nodded. He was well aware of the bloody history of the border counties and of the violent part the reivers had played for much of the sixteenth and seventeenth centuries.

Joss was well into his stride now. "They buggers used tae hole up in what were known as the Debatable Lands. It were a territory where law and order had almost broken down entirely. So close were it tae the English border that they could sweep down fra Scotland an' attack wi' out much fear o' reprisals. They'd seize any booty they could lay hands on an' be off afore anyone knew. It were a desperate time fer the farmers an' homesteaders who struggled tae survive hereabouts."

"So they probably raided Mardale too?" Joy was fascinated by the tale.

"Aye, lass, naebody were safe." Joss smiled, clearly enjoying his role as storyteller. "The place were raided so monie times in them days as everyone cleared out. That were why in were empty when Molly found this Duncan o' Crieff. Twere said he were chief o' the McKade clan. He an' his band o' robbers had been pillagin' all round the spot here when he were wounded. Happen he were badly smitten, 'cause he never made it back over the border. Word was, he fell behind the other raiders an' lost his bearings altogether. He were driftin' in an out o' consciousness, due tae losin' so much blood fra the gash in his side. Finally, he fell fra his pony wi' the life ebbin' out o' him. Just by chance, this lass who were out early in the morning collecting herbs, stumbled across him. He'd have died if she hadn't known what tae do. She were the local healer an' well respected by all the folk around there. She took pity on him, knowing he'd be butchered if he survived an' were caught. Somehow she managed tae get him into the cave close by, under Kidsty Pike, then went an' drove the cattle he'd stolen and managed to hold on tae down into the vale. She told no one but her mother an' they nursed him fit agin. By the time he were well, he an' the lass were bonded."

Joss stopped to draw breath, reaching automatically for his pint. After consuming a considerable quantity, he returned his gaze to the rapt faces of his attentive audience. It was quite a while since he'd had the chance to reminisce with anyone who showed quite such an interest in his tales.

His listeners sat back, expectantly awaiting his resumption of the fascinating account of the ancient happenings.

Wiping a skinny hand across his thin lips, Joss gave them a somewhat toothless grin before recommencing.

"The cattle had stayed safely in the vale – where there were plenty o' grass an' watter – so the lass an' Duncan McKade (or Duncan o' Crieff as he were then called) decided tae settle there. They reckoned it were fer enough away fra civilisation fer 'em tae make a new start. The vale were empty o' folk, so they had it all tae themsel's. Farms an' buildings that stood there had been abandoned fer years on account o' the reivers constant attacks. Ironical that, but as it turned out, it were just about the time the raids were finally comin' tae an end. Most o' the reivers had been forced tae gi' up their lootin' an' pillagin' by the middle o' the seventeenth century when all this were takin' place."

Joss directed his attention to Joy. "It were a bloody time on the border hereabouts then, lassie. Them as put up any resistance tae the reivers would like as not have bin butchered where they stood."

For a moment the old man faltered, his mind clearly wandering back to those days of savagery. "Did you know how the word 'bereaved' came about?" He didn't wait for a reply. "Twas on account o' they villains. So many folk lost their loved ones in skirmishes wi' that gang o' cut-throats that the word became part of the language."

The old man could see that he had impressed the youngster with his account. "Anyway, tae get back tae the story, it seems as though Duncan o' Crieff an' the lass laid claim tae Oxtors Farm. They got on well fer a while till Abraham Jowett heard about 'em. He reckoned some o' they cattle were his'n, so he set out tae confront McKade. Jowett were a giant o' a man, 'a yard across the shodders' it were said, an' McKade stood nae chance. They fought a bloody battle, wi' Jowett finally slaughterin' McKade an' declarin' himsel' King o' Mardale. He struck off McKade's head an' kept it as a trophy. McKade's lass were forced tae tend tae Jowett's wounds, or he'd never o' let her live either. He must hae feared the lassie's powers though and tis said she finally cursed him an' all his descendants as he lay on his deathbed. They surely thowt she'd some mystical way wi' her."

"So that's where this legend came from?" Reid was riveted by the tale.

"Aye." Joss plunged back into his account of the events. "The lass took off wi' the headless body after the battle an' buried it somewhere on the fells. She were wi' child when McKade were slain, an' bore him a son about eight months later. Jowett allowed her an' the bairn tae stay in the vale, on account o' her being useful as a healer, but he'd taken possession o' the farmhouse an' all the rest o' the land there. She had tae earn her keep tendin' cattle an' treatin' folk an' animals fer sickness. Jowett were a bully o' a man. Once he'd taken control o' the valley, he persuaded some o' the folk who'd left tae come back an' rebuild their lives agin, but they had tae pay him fer the use o' the land. No one ever got the better o' him, though as the McKade lad grew up he never gave up tryin'. There were allus bad blood atween the families that lasted right down the ages."

Joss leaned back, taking up his glass and draining it completely. He made no protest as Reid removed it, heading for the bar to replenish the supply.

Turning his attention back to Joy, the old gentleman pointed a bony finger in her direction. "Think thyself lucky, lass. In the auld days at Mardale, lasses all worked as hard as the menfolk. Most o' 'em were up at five in the mornin', gettin' the men off tae work an' seein' tae all the chores. I mind lasses as used tae serve the Jowetts. They were allus washin' an' scrubbin', wi' the clothes out on the line by seven o'clock. Parson Thursby's daughters were among 'em too, but that made no difference. The Jowett's worked them as hard as all the others."

Again Joss paused, clearly probing the confines of his memory bank.

"Good clean lasses the Thursby girls were, even though they'd nae mother tae look after 'em. She were taken when they were just bairns. The auld parson never gave 'em much thought though. He reckoned it were the will o' God for all folk tae work hard." He paused again, a sad expression contorting his face. "The oldest lass met her death not long afore the vale were flooded. 'Tis said she jumped off Harter Fell on account o' how young Herbert Jowett an' his father treated her. They were just as mean as all the Jowetts afore 'em."

The old man's story was interrupted by Reid's return. An overflowing glass was once more set before the aged raconteur. "Thank 'e."

Joss raised the glass to his lips, sampling the brew before resuming his discourse. "I was just tellin' the lass here about the Jowetts. None o' 'em were ever any bloody good." The professor nodded. "Yes, I heard. From what you were saying, it sounds as though that Thursby girl must have been in some state for her to resort to such a drastic course of action. Was there never any inquiry?" Joss shook his head. "Not as such. Mardale were so cut off nobody ever paid much mind tae us. Anyway, there were no one who'd dare blame the Jowetts fer causin' her death. It were taken as an accident, but Jack Tweedie never believed it. He were taken wi' Margaret – that were the lassie's name – an' he allus swore the Jowetts drove her tae her death. He toiled many an hour carvin' out a memorial tae her on a boulder close by where she fell. He were broken-hearted about it an' never did forgive the Jowetts."

"Did the parson not make any attempt to follow it up?" Reid asked, amazed that anyone could let such an event pass without question.

Joss shrugged his shoulders. "The auld parson did nowt. All he said at her funeral service was that God had taken her into his loving arms. He were as affeared of offendin' the Jowetts as everyone else in the valley. He never spoke a word agin 'em. He even sent his younger daughter, Isobel, tae skivvy fer 'em in Margaret's place, though she pleaded agin it."

"Sounds like Mardale was a harsh place, as well a beautiful one," Joy remarked.

"Ay, it were that." Joss resumed his story without much prompting. "We all had plenty o' work tae keep us busy an' not much money tae spend, but they were good times in spite o' that. Young folk these days get their money fer doing nowt, an' they're still not happy. We made our ain pleasures an' got on wi' it. Shepherds Meet were the best time o' the year. Shepherds would gather from all around, comin' ower the tops tae get there. It nearly allus took place on the High Street range o' mountains an' once sheep had been sorted as tae who owned which 'uns, there'd be hoss racin' along the auld Roman Road, hound trailin' an' wrestlin'. When all the events were over, there'd be a Merry Neet at the auld Dun Bull pub that could last a week or more. There'd be huntin' songs, an' drinkin' till nobody had a penny left. There'd be that many there, that they'd sleep in barns, or anywhere they could lay their heads. Nobody ever caused much trouble though an' they usually all parted in the best o' spirits."

"So there'd be plenty of regrets when you were all required to leave the valley at the time of the flooding?"

Joss nodded solemnly at Joy, "Aye. Most folk wanted tae stay put, but the Jowetts would have none of it. The villagers had no choice. They all worked fer the Jowetts, or rented out land fra 'em. They were all pushed out, one by one, till only the McKades an' the Jowetts were left. The Jowetts had been promised an awful lot o' money from the Manchester Watter Board fer the land and had no intention o' being dissuaded. Even the McKades were finally driven out. They'd put up a gay struggle, but it did 'em no good. They went wi' their tails atween their legs eventually – just like all the rest. No one had a good word tae say about the Jowetts, but it were like watter off a ducks back." Joss grinned at the unintended pun. "It were watter everywhere by the time the Jowetts had finished."

Reid smiled at the old man's words. "So you and your parents moved here?"

"Aye, us an' some o' the others. We'd no choice. The watter board rented some land tae us where we could run our sheep an' a few cows an' chickens, but it were never like auld Mardale. The Jowetts were the on'y ones who ever benefited from the move. They were set up fer life."

Joss fell silent for a moment as he lit up his pipe.

"I used tae go tae school wi' Herbert Jowett," he mused, sucking away, then emitting a large cloud of grey, pungent smoke. "He were nearly twice the size o' anyone else there. Schoolmaister used tae say he were nobbut too big fer his boots, but that he'd never have enough sense tae fill his head. There were none o' us very good scholars, 'cept the parson's daughters, an' they never had any chance tae put it tae use.

Margaret were allus wantin' tae be a teacher, an' Isobel said she were gaan tae be a missionary. The auld parson soon put a stop tae all that though. He reckoned as how education were wasted on lassies an' they were destined tae serve God by servin' man. Isobel had tae wait till we all left Mardale afore she got her chance. She took off tae join a nunnery, an were just about tae start on some missionary work when her father took ill wi' a stroke. She came back here an' nursed him, but it were a long time afore he died. She seemed tae lose heart after that. Never married, though she'd have made someone a good wife. Kept her father's house as clean as a new pin – an' hersel'."

Reid took advantage of the lull in the conversation to steer the old man back to the tale of Duncan of Crieff. "Did everyone in the valley believe the story of the skull?"

Joss appeared surprised by the question. "There were never any doubt about it, lad!"

Joy had to hide the smile that sprang to her lips. The thought of her tutor being addressed as 'lad' was almost too much to bear.

"We all knew it were true!" Joss bristled at the suggestion that there could be any doubt. "It were the on'y thing Herbert Jowett were ever really afeared of. His sister used tae taunt him about it whenever he played her up. She reckoned he'd be the one tae suffer if it ever got stolen. He believed it in the end. His parents had a hell of a job convincing him no one would ever find it. I remember as how they'd never let on exactly where the skull were walled up in the auld farmhouse in case someone did break in an tek it. That's why they stayed there right up tae the last minute afore the valley were flooded. They kept an eye on the house even then till it were under watter. Nobody would have done that unless they were certin' sure about it."

Well that appeared pretty conclusive. Reid could see that Joy was equally convinced. There was now little doubt about the skull being the authentic article.

Joy was clearly intrigued by the past lifestyles of the Mardale residents. "Were there many families in the valley?" she asked.

"On'y nine when I were a lad there." Joss replied. "Quite a few had left over the years. There were the Jowetts, McKades and Thursbys. Us Pattinsons of course – an' Mr Studley, the schoolmaister an' his wife an' baby son, Anthony. You've met him. He's the vicar here now."

Joy and her tutor nodded.

"Then there were the Tweedies, Ma Dixon an' her lass, Rollinsons, an' Atkins who kept the Dun Bull pub. About fifty souls in all. It were a gay quiet spot, wi' on'y farmin' tae mek a livin' fra. Everyone mucked in wi' each other though, laal ones helpin' out wi' haymeckin' an' milkin' cows an' such. They were long, hard days, but we all enjoyed it. There were no 'lectric or television, so we sat around the fireplace at neet, wi' women spinnin' an' knittin', an' menfolk tellin' tales o' days past. Many's the neet I've fell asleep by the hearth an' woken up in bed the next morning."

The old man sighed as he recalled the happy memories. "All these newfangled devices might suit some folk, but we never had any desire fer 'em. A good day's work were better than all o' these sleepin' pills. Folk have forgotten these days how tae enjoy themsel's. They race round like mad things, an' never take time tae lay down in a meadow an' listen tae the birds an' insects, or look close at a buttercup or a wild violet. They reckon as how we were simple folk, but we never needed psychiatrists. Them as needs 'em are the ones that have gone wrong."

Joy realised the old man was a bit of a philosopher. "It can't have been easy for you to leave Mardale, Mr Pattinson. That must have been an awful time for everyone."

"Aye, it were that, lass." Joss rubbed his gnarled old hand over the grizzled stubble sprouting from his lean chin like tiny shreads of silver. "It took us all a gay long time tae get over it. I reckon that were the on'y time any of us ever needed a head doctor." He gave her a wan smile. "Maybe the

Jowetts might have needed a doctor if some of us had had our way. Feelin's were runnin' high agin' 'em. There were a lot o' bitterness."

Joy was hardly surprised. "Are there many of the old residents still alive?" she asked.

"Nobbut a few." Joss screwed up his face in concentration. "Ellen Jowett married a Braithwaite, an' she's still alive, but her husband died a good while back. She's got two children, a lad an' a lass. Her brother Herbert were supposed tae have gone off tae South Africa, or somewhere such. I believe he's still kickin' around – more's the bloody pity! Angus McKade's gettin' tae be an old man like mysel' now, but he's got a lad, Rory, still livin' wi' him. You know about the vicar here, an' Isobel Thursby's still alive and well. Jack Tweedie never did get married. Margaret Thursby were the on'y lass he ever cared for, but he still manages tae look after himsel'. Ma Dixon an' her lass are both dead now, an' the Rollinsons an' Atkins moved away many years since, so there's no knowing about them. There'll be none of us left at all soon. We'll all be as dead as auld Mardale."

And no one will be around to recall the halcyon days, Reid thought. At least he and Joy had managed to speak to one of the dwindling few who had spent part of their lives in the idyllic spot.

Joss excused himself, heading off slowly towards the Gents.

"Well! That was very informative!" Reid grinned across at the young student. "We couldn't have wished for any more confirmation of the legend than that. I know we were both sceptical at the beginning, but apart from the possibility of some embellishment down the ages, I'm satisfied now that the bulk of the story is true."

"Me too." She was pleased to hear that he agreed with her own judgement. "What a triumph! I never imagined we'd come up with all this."

He smiled at her excitement. "It does seem amazing to think that it's taken the destruction of Mardale to finally release the evidence of some of its past history. Of course, your discovery of the skull should merit its own place in the history of Mardale now."

"Strewth!" She was clearly shocked by the suggestion. "I hadn't quite realised what we'd started here. It's a bit daunting."

"Nonsense." He reached over, squeezing her hand. "The truth will out. If you hadn't come across the skull, someone else may well have done so. Then we might have been denied the opportunity of delving into the mystery."

She grinned back at him. "It is fascinating, isn't it? Who'd have thought it would turn out this way? I really would like to find out more about these characters now."

"So would I. They sound an interesting bunch. By the way, what do you make of Joss? He tells a hell of a good tale, don't you think?"

"He's a treasure. He brings everything to life. You can almost see these people going about their daily tasks."

Reid could tell by her earnest face that she was hooked. There was no doubt they would be pressing on with their investigations.

The old chap was making his way back now. Reid picked up his empty glass as he returned. "Same again?"

"Aye, I'll not refuse."

The drink was replenished.

"You've still plenty of fond memories of Mardale then?" Reid asked, resuming his seat.

"Aye, I'll never forget it." The old man's eyes twinkled, as something obviously amused him. "I haven't told ye yet of the 'Grey Lady', have I?"

"No."

His audience waited, intrigued to discover what new anecdote the old man would regale them with.

Joss leaned back, glancing from one to the other. "Some folk reckon tae have seen a ghost." He paused, allowing time for his remark to sink in.

Not exactly what they had been expecting. On this occasion there seemed reasonable justification for being a little more sceptical. They waited once more for him to continue.

"They tell o' a young lassie, wi' a bairn at her breast, comin' fra the direction o' Harter Fell. It all started after Margaret Thursby fell tae her death. Folk reckoned it were her comin' home – though she never did have a bairn." He took another puff of his pipe. "Even after the valley were flooded, 'tis said she were still tae be seen. The bell o' Holy Trinity church can be heard tollin' fra the depths o' the lake, an' she walks straight in wi' out makin' a ripple, an' then disappears under the watter."

Joy shuddered at the story. Reid stared at the old man with more than obvious doubt in his eyes. A ghost that answers the ringing peal of a bell issuing from a church tower that no longer exists?

Joss chuckled at their incredulous faces. "I'm on'y tellin' ye what's been said. I never saw owt, but there's many as'll swear they did. There's plenty o' like tales about the goings on around these parts. In Swindale, tis said a ghostly couple come hand in hand down the steppin' stones fra the ruins o' what came to be called 'Starvation Cottage'. Two old folk died there one winter when they were snowed in wi' out enough food or fuel. They'm still supposed to be lookin' fer some. There's plenty o' folk who'll never go near that spot at neet."

Somehow Reid could hardly take the latest revelations seriously. He imagined Joss had embroidered a few of the old wives tales. He was clearly enjoying the company and the chance to mull over old times. Maybe he was getting a little carried away. Could he be persuaded to stick to the facts? "Isn't it true that a special village was built for the dam workers, Joss?"

That appeared to have done the trick. The old chap nodded.

"Aye. Ye'll have passed the spot near the dam when ye went tae Mardale. Burnbanks were the name o' the place. Tis said up tae seven hundred men or more were livin' there when the buildin' o' the dam were in full swing. I was nobbut a lad mysel' when they fust came an' started clearin' timber where the dam were tae be built." He started to chuckle. "Me an' Isobel Thursby used tae wait till the surveyors had gaan home at neet, then creep around pullin' all their stakes out. We reckoned if we couldn't stop 'em, we'd at least make it as bloody difficult as we could fer 'em. We slowed the buggers down anyhow." His grin faded at the recollection that all their efforts had been in vain. "Still, some people made a bit o' cash out of it. The auld Dun Bull Inn did a good trade once all the workers were on site. There were never much trouble though. Some o' the lassies had their eyes set on one or two o' the young men, but nothin' ever came o' it. Folks were strict then, an' naebody got the chance tae misbehave. Any lass that got hersel' into trouble would have been disowned. Naebody seems tae bother much these days, but we were very respectable, even if we were poor."

Joss broke off again to sample a little more of his bitter.

Joy and her tutor reflected on his words. Maybe those far off days were not quite as 'golden' as they were sometimes portrayed, yet there was certainly an innocence there that seemed to have slipped away with the passing of time.

"The Dun Bull were allus a picture at the back end o' May." The pint glass had been set down and the pipe replaced in the old man's mouth. Misty eyes peered out through the smokey haze. "The rhododendrons would be in full bloom, an' the fields all round would be carpeted wi' wild flowers. It were a bonnie sight, wi' Harter Fell towerin' in the background. I've sat there many a neet, takin' in the beauty o' the place after a hard days ploughin'. Vale would be all quiet, wi' the auld church nestlin' there surrounded by yew trees that must have been almost as auld as the church itsel'. It were desecration when they pulled it down tae use as part o' the draw off tower. Many a tear were shed by the auld folk who'd worshipped there all their lives."

Joss looked to be tiring and almost close to tears himself. The professor decided it was time to call it a day.

Thanking the old man for the wealth of information, he and Joy shook the outstretched hand before making their way out into the sunshine.

Fine though the day appeared, black clouds were gathering in the west, indicating a change in the weather. Reid decided the visit to Mardale he had been contemplating could wait another day. They had not come prepared for rain.

His prediction turned out to be accurate. On the way home, a violent thunderstorm broke. Was this to finally end the long dry spell? Possibly, though it would take more than a single storm to make any impression on the level of the water in the depleted reservoir.

CHAPTER TWELVE

Inspector Grey shot a cursory glance at the windows as yet another blinding flash of lightening illuminated his office. The large, heavily built man on the opposite side of the desk jabbed a finger, indicating the torrent of rain lashing down.

"D'you see that?" Herbert Jowett had lost no time in seeking out Grey following his landing in England. After having made contact with his sister, he had hurried directly to the police station. "How long's it gaan tae be afore Mardale's under watter agin?"

Grey shrugged his shoulders. "Some time yet I imagine. It's going to take a hell of a lot more of that to fill the reservoir."

"Maybe so, but it'll be nae time at all afore the ruins start tae disappear. I want that skull back an' buried where it belongs in the auld farmhouse long afore then. You've more or less admitted it came fra there. If we've had possession all these years, it must belong tae us." The tanned face of the man grew even darker as he glowered across at the inspector.

Grey had no intention of being intimidated by the blustering attitude of the belligerent appellant. "I'll tell you once again, Mr Jowett. While there's a dispute as to the ownership of this article, I'm in no position to hand it over to either party. I have a claim here..." he held up the letter he had received that morning from Rory McKade, "...that states that the skull in question is part of the remains of Duncan McKade, or Duncan of Crieff if you prefer it. The McKades, like yourself, are also demanding the return of the skull. Their wish is to reunite it with what's left of their ancestor. As I explained to them, if either of you wish to pursue your claim it may fall to the courts to decide the outcome."

“Damn the McKades!” Jowett thumped the desk with his huge fist. “They bastards are just out tae cause trouble. You can’t believe a word they say. They’ve allus been good-fer-nothings. Just hand me that skull, an’ be done wi’ it!”

Grey’s jaw set, the fine white line of a scar starkly standing out on the lower left hand side of his face – a trophy from a confrontation with a knife-wielding thug in his past. Who the hell did this man think he was? He was way out of his depths if he imagined he could throw his weight around in this neck of woods. Clearly he was used to ordering around his minions and to getting his own way. On this occasion he was to be sorely disappointed.

“You heard what I said, Mr Jowett. Either you and the McKades come to an agreement between you as to who is the rightful owner, or you go to law about it.”

Jowett’s face distorted with rage. “You’ve not heard the last o’ this!” He spat out the words with venom as he rose to leave. “I’ll have a solicitor in touch wi’ your superiors afore the days out. You’ll rue the day you ever crossed me!”

The inspector calmly watched the man depart. A nasty piece of work. Clearly the type of person most people would not wish to have as an enemy. Nevertheless, his threats cut no ice with Grey. Did he really believe he could force a change of mind? If so, he was certainly labouring under a misconception. Even more so if he thought Grey would lose any sleep over the matter.

Walking over to the filing cabinet, the inspector picked up the skull that was at the centre of the controversy. It was rather a grisly reminder of the events that had taken place so long ago. A picture of the weapon slamming down on the unfortunate victim’s neck sprang to mind. Hardly the most pleasant way to end your days – your head lopped off to be impaled on the point of a lance.

Given the choice, Grey decided he would prefer to hand the skull over to the McKades. At least they could finally give it a decent burial. A smile crossed his face as he watched the teeming rain cascading down the windows. The adjacent car park had already taken on the appearance of a children's paddling pool. It seemed his wish could soon be granted. As Jowett himself had pointed out, if the rains continued for any length of time, he would have little chance of succeeding in his endeavour to return the macabre object to Mardale. Serve the arrogant bastard right. It was a pity he had nothing better to do than concern himself with such nonsense.

Replacing the skull on top of the cabinet, Grey smiled to himself, patting it casually on the crown. "Just bide your time, lad," he said cheerfully. "One of these days you may well end up back on what's left of your shoulders."

CHAPTER THIRTEEN

The previous day's storm had passed, leaving in its wake a more bracing atmosphere. Merlin Reid stood before the open window of his study, inhaling the cool, sweet, morning air. It was a great relief to be rid of the oppressive heat for a while. Outside, a weak sun struggled to penetrate the slightly overcast sky without, it must be said, any tangible sign of success. Nevertheless, the weather was suitable for the visit to Mardale that he and Joy had planned.

Both had agreed to rise early – in the optimistic expectation that by doing so they might avoid the worst of the traffic which could rapidly clog the narrow winding lanes leading to the vale. The publicity regarding the discovery of the skull – not to mention the legend associated with it – would obviously arouse the curiosity of a great number of people. There was little point in setting out at a time when the masses were likely to be gathering.

Intrigued by the prospect of discovering just how much of Joss Pattinson's account of life in the valley might be corroborated, Reid quickly prepared for the off. The ghosts and ghoulies element of the story may be totally implausible; however, the majority of the old man's chronicle of the history of Mardale seemed genuine enough. There was certainly plenty to investigate. Joy was profoundly moved by the report of Margaret Thursby's death and of the memorial cut into a boulder by the man who had fallen in love with her. The young student would not be satisfied until she had sought out the spot. Joy was clearly a sucker for anything romantic. On the other hand, Reid himself was keen to follow up on the factual aspect of the ancient legend, hoping to seek out the cave under Kidsty Pike where Duncan of Crieff was reportedly hidden while recovering from his wounds. That should not prove too difficult. The ordnance survey map of the area indicated a clear path leading up to Riggindale Crag – the almost vertical rock face below Kidsty Pike, where the cave was said to be situated. The professor estimated a walk of approximately two and a half miles to the spot from the car park at Haweswater. He smiled wryly to himself. Even with his creaky joints, that should not be too onerous a task. Nothing was going to prevent him from delving into the wealth of history which was undeniably associated with the remote dale.

Having eaten a hearty breakfast, the professor and his companion collected wellingtons and walking boots. Best to be adequately equipped to tackle any terrain. Shortly afterwards they were on their way.

It was as well that they had set out in good time. In spite of that fact, the journey was still somewhat prolonged by the extra traffic en route. Clearly they were not the only ones who had chosen to make an early start. The herd of cows they also encountered along the way – painstakingly making their lumbering way into the grounds of Thornthwaite Hall – only added to the delay. At least on reaching their destination it was possible to park without a great deal of trouble.

A further visit to the crumbling remains of the village was decided upon before they set out to explore the surrounding fells. Wellingtons donned, they made their way along the track, muddied now by the preceding days raid and already churned up to some extent by the first visitors to arrive that morning.

The downpour that had occurred was certainly having quite an effect. The stream, which when they were last there had wound its languid, but determined way towards the much diminished lake, now gurgled and frothed – the mud-stained swirling brown water flecked with creamy-white crests as it hurried along its boulder-strewn course. Though the level of the lake appeared to have fallen slightly since their previous visit, it was clear that that process was about to be reversed.

As they had driven into the valley they had both seen, and heard, the thundering white water descending precipitously down the gill which thrust its relentless silvery fingers through rock and vegetation on the opposite side of the reservoir. If more rain should prove to be in the offing, Mardale could eventually return to its obscure, watery grave.

The relative silence that had existed in the vale up to that point was suddenly shattered by a siren echoing along its entire length. Everyone turned to stare at the ambulance that was now threading its tortuous way though the other traffic on the narrow, twisting road that traversed the mountain side some way above the lake.

"I wonder what's up?" Joy shot a concerned glance at Reid. "I didn't see any sign of an accident as we came in."

"Nor I." He suddenly became aware that a police van was closely following the other vehicle. "I did notice a police car when we parked though. I assumed their presence here might be in case too much traffic piled up and needed marshalling. Having said that, I wondered at the time why there was no sign of any constables in attendance."

The ambulance had pulled up now, close to the track leading to the ruined village. Two stretcher bearers issued forth, followed by uniformed policemen from the van. All began making their way along the track.

Reid turned his attention to the scattered remains of Mardale. A knot of people were gathered around the ruins of Oxtors Farm, creating a gaudy splash of colour against the drab background of the silt covered base of the reservoir. The majority appeared to be tourists, clad mainly in hiking gear. Vivid red socks were clearly visible, rolled down over sturdy walking boots, a plethora of bright T-shirts and cotton tops adding their tinted highlights to the scene. Backpackers and walkers, all had turned out for a glimpse of the spot where Duncan of Crieff's severed skull had been unearthed. Yet there seemed something unnatural about the group. Formed into a semi-circle, they appeared absorbed by some other event which was evidently taking place at the site.

Reid quickly realised that his assumptions were correct. A short distance beyond the crowd it was possible to make out two police officers. He took hold of Joy's arm. "You don't mind if we carry on? I would like to check out exactly what's happening over there."

By the tone of her voice it was obvious that she was not too keen, having already sensed that the proceedings had something to do with the arrival of the medical team. "Okay, Prof. But if it's anything nasty, I'd rather not go too close."

He could understand her hesitancy, though being a former G.P. it was not in his nature to walk away from any incident which might require medical assistance. Realising it was unlikely that he would be called upon to render aid – since the police were clearly in control – his years of training nevertheless drew him to the spot.

It was slow going. The sticky conditions were hardly to his liking. Arthritic joints hampered his progress at the best of times, and as they approached the ruins, conditions under foot became even more difficult. He was pleased when they finally drew near to the group of spectators. Behind Joy and himself the small force of police and ambulance men had gained ground.

"Is that you, Prof?"

Reid turned, as the unmistakable gruff tones of Inspector Grey rang out.

"I might have known you'd be here! How the hell did you get wind of this?"

The professor smiled, waiting for Grey to catch up. "I'm not quite with you, Inspector."

"Thank God for that!" Grey chuckled at Reid's bemused expression. "I was beginning to think you were psychic. Come along with me – you could be in for a bit of a shock."

Joy anxiously drew back. "You go ahead, Prof. I'll wait here if you don't mind. I had enough of a shock the other day." She made her way over to join an elderly lady sporting a small haversack, who was conversing with an equally elderly gentleman similarly equipped. Both gave the same impression of also being hesitant about approaching the scene of the incident too closely.

Reid joined the inspector as the crowd parted to allow them and the stretcher party through.

The sight that greeted them was not a pleasant one. A large man lay crumpled in the mud, his head supported by the jacket of one of the constables who had been first on the scene. A pool of blood stained the sodden ground below the all too obvious wound on the back of the man's head. The jacketless constable came forward to greet the inspector.

"Sorry, Sir. I think we've just lost him."

The paramedics went forward to examine the body, quickly confirming the constable's words.

"He's right, Inspector. We're too late."

"Right. Come away from there."

Grey turned to the constables who had accompanied him to the scene. "In that case, you'd best get back to the van and bring out the screens. Radio back to the station and have them send the pathologist and a photographer out here. Let 'em know it's a murder case. You don't get an injury like that by tripping and falling on a rock."

The jacketless constable endorsed the inspector's opinion. "I'm sure you're right, Sir. The rock that caused the injury was close to the feet of the victim, as you can see." He pointed out the chunk of stone which must once have formed part of the ruins alongside. "We haven't touched it, but it is possible to make out traces of blood and hair on the one corner."

Grey stepped forward to see for himself. In spite of the fact that the sediment had been well churned up by countless boots over the preceding days, he placed his feet carefully, returning in his own footprints. It was a fairly pointless precaution considering the disturbed nature of the ground, nevertheless the action came instinctively.

"As you say, Constable, that's almost certainly the instrument used in the attack."

The young officer looked pleased to have Grey's confirmation of his judgement.

For a while Grey stood silently surveying the scene. The body lay close to the corner of what appeared to be part of the remains of one of the outbuildings once belonging to the farm. Anyone approaching the house would, of necessity, pass by that point. It had not escaped his attention that the piece of rock used in the attack was virtually unmuddied, unlike the rubble which lay partially submerged in the sodden ground. It took little imagination to conclude that a loose chunk of the crumbling wall could have been lifted clear by the attacker, who could have remained hidden by that same wall from the view of his approaching victim. One swift stroke and the deed would have been done. Once the pathologist had finished his work, Grey intended to test his theory by seeking to replace the stone in its original position. There looked to be a small patch of walling, which by its lack of weathering, indicated the recent removal of one of the stones.

Merlin Reid had remained silent while Grey carried out the inspection. By now his curiosity was getting the better of him.

"Do you know who this man is, Inspector?"

Grey nodded. "Sure, I know him only too well. He was in my office the first chance he got after flying in from South Africa yesterday. He goes by the name of Herbert Jowett!"

Grey could tell instantly from the sudden, sharp intake of breath that the professor realised the implications immediately.

"That's right. The damn prophecy's now been fulfilled! That man came to see me, terrified out of his wits at the prospect of this happening. I have to admit I thought he was paranoid at the time, but there's no doubting now that he wasn't quite as crazy as I thought. You can imagine what the media will make of all this. I have enough trouble with 'em at the best of times, but this is going to be a bloody circus!"

Reid could well believe it. So Grey finally did have a murder inquiry on his hands. The professor made no comment as the inspector moved back to quiz the constables who had been first on the scene.

"You found no sign of a skull?"

"No, Sir." The men exchanged puzzled glances. They were not from the Penrith station, having been dispatched from Craigend when the call came in about the incident.

Grey set about putting them in the picture. "You'll be aware that a skull was removed from this site and that there was a subsequent connection made with regard to this ancient legend?"

Both men nodded.

"Then you'll probably also be aware that the professor here…" he indicated Merlin Reid with a wave of his hand, "…brought me into the case when one of his students discovered the damn thing. Be that as it may, you certainly won't need me to remind you that Penrith station isn't manned at night since so little crime take place in the town. A patrol car's usually all that's needed to respond to most emergencies. When the station was locked up last evening, the skull was sitting on top of my filing cabinet. During the night, some bugger managed to force the door and make off with the bloody thing."

A smile crossed the faces of both young constables at the thought of a police station being burgled.

Grey also saw the funny side of the incident, chuckling as he carried on. "I know villains are usually more inclined to break out of the nick, but at least this time I've got a damn good idea who was responsible. Certainly two characters spring immediately to mind. Unfortunately, that's one of 'em lying there with his head crushed in. As soon as I heard something was amiss here, I guessed he'd be involved. The question now, of course, is, if the skull's not here, has the other bugger got hold of it?"

The constable in full uniform spoke. "The group of people who came across the body are still here, Sir," he indicated four couples standing a little forward of the rest of the crowd. "We asked them to stand by until you had a chance to have a word with them. I'm not sure if they might be able to assist. They seem a sensible lot. One of the men rang through to the Craigend station while the others remained here attempting to render assistance. There wasn't much they could do. They said the man was unconscious, and it was clear he was in a bad way. They were frightened to move him in case it caused him any more harm. They just made sure he was able to breathe by clearing away some of the mud near his nose and mouth. By the time we got here, the blood was congealing in the wound, so we carried on making him as comfortable as possible while we waited for the medics."

"You did right." Grey was pleased with the way the men had handled the situation. "By the looks of him, there was no way anyone could have done more to save him."

He crossed to where the small group were standing. They still appeared quite shaken by the incident. Thanking them for their efforts, he assured them they had done all that was humanly possible. One of the women broke down in tears on hearing of the death. Grey indicated to her husband that he should take her away. He then addressed the remainder.

"I don't suppose any of you witnessed anything to do with the actual attack? No sign of anyone hurrying away, or bending down to pick up a fallen object?"

All shook their heads. One of the men voiced his opinion that the event must have taken place quite some time before they arrived on the scene. He was sure no one was in the immediate vicinity. The others backed up his statement.

"I don't recall thinking he'd been attacked." A lady in the group looked at her companions as if for support. "I think we were all too shocked and concerned about the poor man to consider how he'd come by his injuries."

"That's true." Another of the ladies spoke up. "We just assumed that he'd met with some kind of accident. If anyone was still close by, they must have been hidden from view behind some of the old walling."

"But you saw no one leave at any stage?"

"No. There were a few other people about, but we seem to have been the first to get here after this horrible event had happened. All the other folk were some distance away, looking at the other ruins. I suppose they were trying to find out where the skull had been dug up, as we had been."

The man holding her arm agreed. "I imagine they'd come early to avoid the crush, just like us. Even then, the car park was already beginning to fill up when we arrived."

Just as Grey feared. It would be simple for the attacker to mingle unobtrusively with the other sightseers before making off – assuming that the person in question had still been around when other visitors began arriving.

"None of you came across any item which might have been discarded, or left behind inadvertently by the person responsible for this?"

Again there was no positive response. Grey could see no point in continuing with the questioning.

"In that case, would you all mind giving your names and addresses to one of the constables? If we require statements at a later date we'll be in touch."

He motioned to one of his men to take the details, directing the other to question anyone else among the rest of the crowd who may have witnessed anything suspicious.

The constables with the screens were just arriving back at the scene. Grey returned to where the body lay to supervise the arrangements.

Merlin Reid decided to take his leave. The news of Herbert Jowett's death had come as a great shock – as had the information about the theft of the skull from the station. There was no doubt now that there was more to this than any of them had ever envisaged. He was not looking forward to breaking the news to Joy. She had been apprehensive all along since discovering the skull. The realisation that someone now lay dead – almost certainly as a result of that discovery – was something she was going to have to come to terms with.

She was still standing where he had left her, in the company of the elderly lady and gentleman. It was the old woman who spoke.

"What's happened?"

He had hoped to pick his own time to acquaint Joy with the facts. Unfortunately, the subject could not be avoided.

"I'm afraid a man has lost his life here."

"Oh, dear." The old lady shook her head, then strode briskly off in the direction of the car park. Neither she, Isobel Thursby, or the elderly man, Jack Tweedie, had bothered to mention that they were both former residents of Mardale.

Reid took hold of Joy's arm. It would have been impossible to have missed the look of alarm that had instinctively spread across her pale, serious face. "Sorry, Joy. It's Herbert Jowett."

She took a deep breath, then shrugged her shoulders. "It's no surprise. As soon as I saw the crowd here, and the police, I guessed it had to have some connection with the family who'd lived at the farm. I kept trying to persuade myself it was just a silly legend after reading the report of the curse in the papers, but the fear was always there. In a way, it's almost a relief to get it over with."

He gently led her away from the crowd. The adventure was beginning to turn sour.

"Shall we make our way home?"

"Oh, no!"

He was surprised by the decisive tone of her voice.

"Are you sure? I realise what a shock it's been."

"I'm sure, Prof." She turned her pale, determined face to look him straight in the eyes. "We can't just turn our backs on this. I need to know why it's happened. Surely there has to be some logical explanation. I'll never settle now, not until we get to the bottom of it."

"I haven't told you the rest of the story yet."

"What else is there?" Her voice betrayed the pent-up emotions.

"The skull was stolen from the police station last night – and there was no sign of it at the farm."

She was quiet for a while as she considered his words "You mean that man could have stolen it and been killed because he had it in his possession – and someone else wanted it?"

"We really shouldn't jump to conclusions, but that is a possibility."

"The McKades?"

"Like I said, it's not up to us to judge. Inspector Grey may come up with some other solution."

"But you have your doubts?"

He tried to concentrate. The death of Herbert Jowett had come as a hell of a shock. "From what we've learned so far, the McKades look to be the most likely candidates. Grey's sure to be aware of that. We might be in a position to render a little assistance with the information we've already come across, but the inspector's obviously going to pursue his own investigations."

She forced a weak smile. "I realise that, but don't you see, we have to try to help. I feel responsible for that man's death. Somehow I want to make amends. I need to do something constructive. If we went back now, without following up on this, I'd just sit and fret."

He was heartened by her positive response. There was good sense behind her reasoning.

"Good girl, my own sentiments entirely. I'm not absolutely certain how much Inspector Grey knows about the case at this stage, but I imagine we're a few steps ahead of him. He had dropped the investigation before this cropped up."

"Maybe he'll wish he hadn't!"

Reid nodded. "At least he's not the kind of man to resent the offer of assistance from anyone who might provide useful information. That does leave us in a position to respond if asked."

His reply seemed to please her. She quickened her step, as though keen to depart the scene of the incident. "Let's just carry on with what we planned then. I still want to see that memorial to Margaret Thursby. You don't imagine old Joss was having us on, do you?"

He shook his head. "I can't see any reason why he should."

They were crossing the old packhorse bridge now, grateful to be on firmer ground. Soon they would be well clear of the clinging mud. It would be a relief to get back to the car and exchange their wellingtons for the relative comfort of their walking boots.

"Look!" Joy suddenly stopped in her tracks, pointing ahead. "It's those newspaper men. They must have stayed on after all."

The pleasure in her voice – plus the colour that was rapidly returning to her cheeks – indicated that the young reporter might well be playing some small part in aiding her recovery from the shock of Herbert Jowett's death.

Tony Hoskis had recognised her too. "Hi!" He raised a hand, though that action was hardly necessary; her attention was already keenly focused on him. "What's going on, Joy? We heard the police were here." He came bounding over, leaving the photographer in his wake.

She grabbed his arm. "Say hello to the professor first. This is my tutor, Merlin Reid."

"Pleased to meet you, sir." The young man grinned as he shook the outstretched hand. "I'm Tony Hoskis and this is my side-kick, Ray Jacobs. Sorry we missed you at the Hall, but we had a deadline to meet."

"That's very understandable." Reid could see that the young man was impatient to discover what was happening behind the screens in the distance. "Anyway, feel free to call on us again if you've the time. By the way, in answer to the question you first put to Joy, I'm sure you'd be interested to learn that a man has just died under suspicious circumstances at the site of Oxtors Farm. Inspector Grey's handling the case at the moment, but I doubt he'll release the man's name before the next of kin have been notified."

The reporter made no attempt to pump him for more information. It was clear that he understood discretion was being exercised.

"Thanks for the tip off. Let's go, Ray." He grabbed some of the photographer's equipment. "We'll probably take you up on the invitation to visit the Hall again," he called over his shoulder as they sped on their way.

The smile on Joy's face confirmed Reid's opinion that she would be delighted if they did. The anticipation of seeing the young man once more might cause her to forget the remorse she was obviously feeling with regard to the tragedy that had just occurred.

They continued on, soon approaching the car park. Harter Fell rose impressively in the background.

Once booted up, they stood for a while surveying the range of splintered crags which towered ominously above the valley. If Margaret Thursby had leapt from one of these prominences it was hardly surprising that she had failed to survive. Reid shielded his eyes from the sun, attempting to pinpoint the most likely position from which anyone might have made such an awful plunge. A sector to the right looked the most promising location. Various tracks traversed the base of the mountain, one leading in the desired direction.

"Shall we try this path?"

"Sure." Joy was happy to allow him to decide where they went – and at what pace. He was hardly likely to set off at any great speed.

The track led steadily upwards, undulating with the contours of the land. As they gradually ascended, the air became fresher, a breeze making the climb more tolerable. After a while they approached the area where the fissured face of the rock rose almost vertically from the ground.

"This looks a likely spot." He paused to take a breather, pointing out several large boulders that littered the slope ahead.

Joy appeared impatient to investigate.

"You carry on," he suggested, smiling at her excited expression. "I'll just rest the old legs a minute."

"Okay, if you don't mind."

She made off, as he seated himself on one of the smaller, more comfortable looking rocks. He watched her as she moved from boulder to boulder. Eventually there was a triumphant cry.

"I've found it! Do come and see what else is here!" She was beckoning furiously.

No peace for the weary. He levered himself carefully up from his very temporary resting place.

The reason for her excitement soon became obvious. On the side of a boulder facing away from the cliff, and towards Mardale, the inscription to Margaret Thursby was clearly visible. On the ground below, a posy of wild flowers had been carefully arranged so that people using the path on the slightly higher ground might not easily notice it there as they passed by.

He read out the text that had been painstakingly carved into the rock. "In loving memory of Margaret Thursby, who fell to her death close by on the 24th of May 1934. May she now find peace."

Joy pointed to the small floral tribute. "There's a note attached."

He took up the flowers, once again reading out the message that accompanied them. "God's will be done." No indication of the identity of the person who had placed the posy there. The flowers were already beginning to wilt, in spite of being placed in the shade of the overhanging boulder. He judged they must have been picked early that day – or the evening before. Was there any significance in the wording of the message? Or the fact that Herbert Jowett had died that very morning? Or was he merely reading into it much more than the few words were ever intended to convey?

Detaching the note, he considered further. What if it were of some significance? Before he had time to examine it thoroughly, the scrap of paper was torn from his grasp – almost as though by an invisible hand. A sudden gust of wind took it, whirling it first up towards the cliffs, then back over their heads and down across the fells. They watched as it fluttered like some frolicking butterfly, eventually to disappear over the rocky outcrops below.

As suddenly as it had arrived, the wind abated.

Joy shivered as she turned to gaze up at the soaring crags behind them. "That poor girl. Can we go now, Prof.? This place is beginning to give me the creeps. I feel as though we're not welcome here."

They retraced their steps.

"What do you make of the message on that note?" Joy had been silent until they had moved some distance away from the scene of Margaret Thursby's fatal fall. She made no comment about the somewhat inexplicable loss of the scrap of paper. Perhaps she had accepted, as he had, that fingers, once strong and supple, now no longer retained the grip they had before the onset of arthritis.

He considered her question before attempting to answer. "Difficult to say, Joy. It may just be coincidence. Someone who knew the girl in the past may have returned to Mardale to view the ruins. We can't rule out the simple possibility that that person then took the opportunity to lay flowers at her memorial at the same time."

"I suppose that's as likely an explanation as any other." She grabbed at the chance to believe it. "I hate to think that the man who'd been in love with her could be involved in any way with the murder."

"Jack Tweedie? Yes, so do I. He seems to have suffered enough in the past."

They carried on in silence until reaching the point where the tracks divided.

"Do you still want to go on, Joy?" He hesitated before attempting to alter course. "If so, we need to head off over Mardale Beck to seek out the cave."

“Yes, I’m game.” Her smile was back. “I still want to see how much of the story Joss told us is true.”

Reid led the way again after consulting his ordnance survey map.

The normally boggy ground at the head of the lake was still relatively dry, in spite of which they made their way along the constructed walkways and bridges that traversed the muddier areas. Once across the reed-blanketed morass, they followed the clear track which wound its way back towards the depleted lake at a point where The Rigg, a wooded finger of land, extended out into the water. Almost doubling back on itself, the track then rose sharply alongside a dry stone wall, leading ever upwards towards Rough Crag and the heights of Riggindale Crag. This was where Joss had indicated the cave lay. It was also, Reid recalled, an area which contained the nesting place of the only known breeding pair of golden eagles still existing in England. After long years of absence, the secluded mountainous region had finally coaxed the rare birds of prey to return once more to the place where, in the past, their predecessors had soared without fear of disturbance. Now, unfortunately, they had to be monitored and protected by the RSPB. He cast his eyes skyward in the forlorn hope that he might spot the majestic pair; he was not to be rewarded. No doubt if they were aloft it would be some distance away from the intrusive presence of man. The uncovering of Mardale had certainly brought a massive influx of visitors to the remote dale. Luckily the invasion should be short-lived; besides, an eagle’s territory could spread to over 3,000 acres.

The climb was a fairly exhausting one, though very rewarding. Regardless of the ache in his arthritic joints, Reid was convinced it was worth the effort. A few stops on the way had enabled them both to regain their strength and to look back, gaining a panoramic view of the scene below. It had been possible to make out most of the ruined buildings, with many of the dry stone walls still standing, as they had for centuries, outlining the boundaries of farms and fields.

Oxtors Farm still had its band of sightseers, the screens and cordoned-off section of the murder scene indicating that the police were still active on the site. Reid had his doubts that they would discover anything of much significance there. Nothing other than the rock used in the attack had been apparent in the vicinity of the body.

At last. The cave was just ahead. They had reached a fairly level area, strewn with boulders and rough chunks of rock which had clearly broken loose from the towering crags above. A dark cavity in the face of the massive formation was clearly visible. Reid forgot his weariness. Taking hold of Joy's arm, he excitedly pointed it out. "It's here! Just as Joss said it would be."

They scrambled forward to investigate.

The jagged rent in the face of the crag was of sufficient height to allow them to walk erect into the fairly capacious interior. Though gloomy inside, the place was reasonably dry. Whether that would be the case at other times of the year was difficult to assess. Maybe not precisely the kind of spot one would choose to hole up in when badly injured, though no doubt preferable to lying out on the open fell. It would clearly afford protection from the elements, and one could imagine that with some dried bracken for a bed it would seem like heaven to a wounded fugitive. Duncan of Crieff must have thought that all of his prayers had been answered when he was brought to this place by his rescuer. Little did he realise the fate that later lay in store for him at the hands of Abraham Jowett.

"Well, Joy. Confirmation indeed of this part of the legend. Everything Joss told us seems to be borne out so far."

She beamed with pleasure. "So he wasn't having us on after all. I had a few doubts when he started to come out with the ghost stories."

"So did I." He chuckled at the recollection. "Still he never claimed to have seen one himself."

"That's true." She tried to force another smile. "I could have enjoyed this experience so much more if only there hadn't been such a terrible tragedy. What an awful pity that someone had to die."

He put a comforting arm around her shoulders. "Maybe we should try not to pay too much attention to this so-called curse. Let's just treat it all as a bit of an adventure. I know that man's death is an awful thing to have happened, but at least this should prove to be the final chapter of that story."

"There's still the murderer to find. Do you really think we might be able to help?"

"Why not?" He smiled reassuringly at her serious face. "As I've already indicated, Grey will probably be delighted if we can offer him any assistance. I may contact him once he's had time to sort himself out."

They made their way back out into the daylight, little realising that the remains of Duncan of Crieff – the man who's dreadful fate had almost certainly sparked the mornings terrible events – lay within twenty yards from where they stood.

CHAPTER FIFTEEN

Ralph Braithwaite's home turned out to be a modest, semi-detached council house in a back street of nearby Craigend. Grey hoped the man would be present. A small van parked on the drive seemed to indicate that he was. A quick dash through the rain and Grey was knocking on the front door. He wondered momentarily whether Ellen Braithwaite had had chance to inform her son of his uncle's death. The answer appeared to be yes. As he opened the door, it was apparent that the man had been expecting him.

"Are you the police inspector who called on my mother?"

"That's correct." Grey formally introduced himself.

"I suppose you'd best come in then."

He was led through into the small, untidy living room.

"Take a seat."

Grey did as he was requested. Ralph Braithwaite settled himself opposite. He was a rough-looking, heavily built man, who appeared to be in his mid-thirties. Grey could hardly fail to notice the similarity in size to Herbert Jowett. There was no doubting that he came from the same stock.

"I've not long gotten in. It's nae use tryin' tae work in these conditions." Braithwaite sprawled back in his chair, apparently totally at ease.

"I suppose not." Grey realised he was lucky to have caught the man at home. "I'm sorry I had to be the bearer of such disturbing news to your mother – and to yourself, of course."

"Dunna fret yoursel' about that." Again there was no sign of distress at the demise of Herbert Jowett. "All my mother an' I want is tae get my uncle buried an' tae have the skull put back alongside the auld house. You surely can't deny us that after what's happened. Ma won't settle till she knows the skull's safe agin. If we don't get it handed over immediately the farm'll be under watter afore we can do owt about it."

Once more Grey tried to fathom whether he was being strung along. Someone must know the whereabouts of the skull. It was inconceivable that anyone other than Herbert Jowett or one of the McKades had stolen it. Now was not the appropriate time to divulge that he had no idea where the damn thing was anyway. Best to force the man on to the defensive.

"Can you account for your movements between eight o'clock last evening and nine o'clock this morning, Mr Braithwaite?"

Ralph looked suitably taken aback. "What the hell for?"

"I am conducting a murder inquiry here, sir." Grey was not prepared to mince his words. "I understand that you, your mother and your sister, may benefit from the death of your uncle."

"An' about bloody time too!" Anger was taking the place of the consternation that had originally registered. "Has my mother told you how that auld sod treated her? He's never given her any o' the money that's hers by right. She scrimped an' saved all her life tryin' tae bring us up on a pittance."

"So I understand. All the more reason then that your uncle's death should cause you little concern."

The man eyed Grey coldly. "You're bloody reet, but you're barkin' up the wrong tree if you think I had owt tae do wi' it. What about the McKades?"

"I've spoken to them, Mr Braithwaite. As you might guess, they deny any knowledge of the murder." Grey persisted with the question that had been ignored. "I still require you to acquaint me with the details of your whereabouts during the relevant occurrence."

Ralph Braithwaite shrugged his shoulders. "I did what I usually do after a day's work. Had a shower tae cool off, watched television, hit the sack about twelve. I was up about seven thirty, as normal, an' out doin' some wallin' afore nine."

"Anyone who can confirm that?"

"Probably not. I work mainly on contract. Most folk just trust me tae turn up an' do the job. I give 'em a price, an' once the work's done, I sends 'em the bill. There's not many as bothers me. I does the job reet, an' that's all they worry about."

Not exactly a sound alibi. Grey sat silently and considered the possibilities. Mrs Braithwaite could well have been aware of the time her brother left the house. What if she had alerted her son to that fact? And what if she were lying and had driven Herbert Jowett herself on his fatal last journey? Either way, it would probably mean that some kind of conspiracy would have to have taken place. The fact that her car had been left at the Haweswater car park could well be a red herring. Her son may have driven her back in his van. There was just the possibility that Herbert Jowett may have been murdered by someone accompanying him to the farmhouse. That would then more easily account for the fact that the killer was in a position to mount an attack. Rather than lying in wait, the person responsible may have seized the opportunity to grab a rock in passing, and strike the fatal blow. If time allowed, burying the skull somewhere in the vicinity of the farm would then be feasible. The mud churned up by a multitude of feet would render it almost impossible to detect any further disturbance of the soil. The Braithwaites could not be ruled out. Their protestations of innocence were not wholly convincing.

Another crack of thunder. The rain beating relentlessly against the window reminded them both that time was running out for Mardale. Even if any clues had remained at the scene of the killing, they would surely be washed away by the downpour. Pinning the crime on any of the suspects could prove to be extremely difficult.

"Have you spoken to your sister?" Grey wished to find out the exact extent of the family's possible involvement.

“Ma’s gaan tae have a word wi’ her. We’re not lettin’ on too much about this damn curse. She’s easy upset. I don’t want your lot round there. I expect the bloody Press’ll be nosing around afore we know it.”

The man looked genuinely concerned.

“I’m sure we can avoid calling on your sister at this stage, Mr Braithwaite.” Grey was prepared to spare the woman the attention of the media which could result from such a visit. “Perhaps you can just answer one question on her behalf. Does she own a car?”

“Her husband does, but she can’t drive. She’s too nervous tae ever attempt it.”

“Right.” Grey decided he was satisfied for the moment. “I’ve informed your mother that we shall be doing all in our power to bring the killer to book. If you come up with anyone other than the McKades as possible suspects, get in touch with me right away.”

“You’d be wasting your time, Inspector. It’s the bloody McKades reet enough. At least they’ve done us a favour. As long as it’s only my uncle tae suffer, I don’t give a cuss!”

Grey could well believe it. Herbert Jowett was not exactly the flavour of the month. Still, whatever qualities the man possessed or lacked, his murderer had to be apprehended. Grey said his goodbyes, then made another run for the car. It was time he discovered what forensics had managed to dig up.

* * *

Ellen Braithwaite had hurried off to her daughter’s home after ringing her son. She was never keen to meet up with Jean’s husband. They had never seen eye to eye. He had always held it against her and Ralph that they had failed to secure any of the money due to the family. Ellen suspected the man would never have married her daughter but for the fact that he believed she would soon come into a goodly share of the fortune. It was little wonder that Jean had changed from being a confident young woman to the extremely anxious one she was now. Cedric Bull treated her with callous indifference. Ellen tried not to interfere, since Jean refused to listen to any words spoken against him, but Ralph had let it be known he despised the man. If he had his way, Ellen knew that her son would move heaven and earth to prevent Jean's husband from laying his hands on any of the cash that was finally due to the family. Unfortunately, it was Ellen herself who would have to decide that issue. She would be Herbert Jowett's next of kin. She had realised many years ago that one day she might be faced with this dilemma. Now the time had arrived, she was not looking forward to the prospect. But Jean was her daughter, and as such was entitled to share in anything that came their way. Ralph was going to have to accept that.

"Hi, Ma." Jean Bull was a little surprised to find her mother on the doorstep. "Come on in. I've only just arrived back mysel'. I've got the kettle on. Want a cup o' tea?"

"Yes, please."

Ellen made her way into the sitting room. It was tidy, as always. Jean was a good housekeeper – a trait that she had inherited from her mother. And that was not all that she had inherited. She had a good figure, a strong constitution and, until she had married, a pleasant, confident, outgoing personality. Only when her husband was present did she lose that confidence. Jean really was a nice girl – too nice for the man she had married. Ellen smiled to herself. Perhaps every mother thought that of her child. Still, it was time to sort things out. She was determined that her daughter should now have a better deal out of life.

"Here we go." Jean came in with the tea things. "I've put you a scone, Ma." She knew her mother could never resist her home baking.

"Thanks, love." Ellen was sure that her daughter must be wondering if there were any special reason for the visit. It was not the time of day she usually chose to drop in. Best to get it over with before the police released any of the details of Herbert's death. At least it was nothing that was going to upset her over much. She was as aware as the rest of her family that her uncle was a bad lot.

"I've just had a bit o' disturbing news about your uncle Herbert, Jean..." She made no attempt to disguise the fact that she was hardly distressed by what she had to disclose. "...you remember I told you he was comin' ower tae have a last look at Mardale afore it went back under the watter?"

Her daughter nodded.

"Well, the police have just been tae see me. Your uncle's been killed at the auld house."

A look of disbelief spread across Jean's face. "Good grief, Ma! How did that happen?"

"It were no accident. Inspector Grey says he were hit wi' a lump o' rock. Someone must have bin expectin' him tae turn up there. Or he just bumped into one o' the auld folk who still held a grudge agin him. I told you long ago that nobody could stand Herbert, or his da. The auld bugger has finally got what he deserved."

"That's a bit hard, Ma." Jean could see the good in almost everyone.

"Maybe. But you never got tae know him. Herbert only ever cared fer himsel'. We should have been well off, Jean – and now we're gaan tae be. All the money should come my way, an' I'll see tae it that you get your share."

Jean's face lit up. "At least that'll please Cedric. You know how he's always said we should have had our share o' the fortune."

Ellen knew only too well how Jean's husband would react. Somehow she was going to have to find a way to protect her daughter's interests. Unfortunately, that could prove to be extremely difficult.

"What about these stories in the paper?"

Ellen had been expecting the question. All the speculation about the legend – not to mention the family's involvement in it – was going to be difficult to explain away. "I told you afore, lass. It's all made up by these reporters. They'll say any thin'."

"But what about uncle Herbert. Surely it's more than just a coincidence if he's been killed?"

Ellen struggled for an answer. She would rather keep her fears to herself. "It's just a silly story blown up out o' all proportion. Herbert might have been killed, but that doesn't mean it's anythin' tae do wi' a curse. A lot o' people hated your uncle. It wasn't on'y us as he upset. Nobody could stand him. The Kings ruled wi' a rod o' iron, and God help anyone who stood in their way."

"But you used tae say it were great livin' at Mardale, Ma." Jean had never been made aware of all the facts before.

"So it were. Mardale were a beautiful spot reet enough, but it were the Jowetts' little kingdom. Herbert felt he could do as he pleased and his father never discouraged him in any way. That's why, if there were anyone who wanted tae get their revenge on Herbert, they'd have had tae wait till they were safely away from the place. Nobody would have dared try anythin' while they were still in the valley. Herbert's da would have had the hide off 'em!"

"You mean it's someone from the past then, who's waited all this time tae pay him back?"

"It has tae be. One o' the auld villagers must have spotted him there an' just decided tae strike him down. They'll all be the same as me, wantin' a last look round. You know I went up there the other day wi' Ralph so we could see the auld house. It's bound tae be the last time I'm ever gaan tae get the chance."

"Cedric said there were no smoke without fire when he read about the curse. He got quite excited about it. Said if it were true we might see some o' the money at last. I hardly think he'd have reckoned on things happening this soon though."

Ellen was hardly surprised that her daughter's husband had been excited by the prospect of easy money. He'd have little regard for Jean's feelings with regard to the curse. No matter that she could be endangered if the threat were real.

"Well, Ralph thinks the same as me. He reckons it's just an auld wives' tale. Now don't you go frettin' about it. Just be grateful that we shall come in fer the money now."

That brought a smile back to her daughter's face. "I suppose you're right. I thowt we'd never get it, Ma. I hope it'll be worth the wait."

"You can be sure o' that!" It was Ellen's turn to smile now. "There were plenty tae start wi' and I know the auld bugger kept reinvestin' it. That were allus his excuse fer not sending us any. I once saved up fer a solicitor tae send him a letter, but all we ever got out o' it were a copy o' what the cash were tied up in. That an' a list o' all the reasons why he couldn't lay hands on it. We got promises but bugger all else. It's there all right. And it's our turn tae benefit now, lass. We're gaan tae be rich at last!"

CHAPTER SIXTEEN

Tony Hoskis had turned angrily to his colleague after the brush off from Inspector Grey at Mardale. "Miserable old sod! He could at least have given us some idea of who this dead bloke is."

Ray Jacobs smiled at the young reporter's indignation. "Who cares? There's still got to be a bloody great story in this."

"That's for sure! If this stiff is one of those Jowett characters, we've got a bonanza here. This curse business will sell us a million!"

Jacobs was excited by the prospect too. "Right, I'll set up the equipment here and see if I can get any good shots. In the meantime, interview some of the crowd. See if anybody's come across any useful information."

"I'm on my way."

It was a pretty fruitless search until the reporter came across the old man to whom he'd spoken on the previous visit.

"Hi there, remember me? Tony Hoskis. You were kind enough to give me an interview the other day."

"That's reet." The man didn't look particularly enthusiastic about repeating the experience.

"I don't like to bother you, but you seem to be the only past resident of Mardale that I've come across. The last time we spoke you told me you were aware of the legend and the feud between the Jowetts and McKades."

"So?"

"Well, I wondered if you had any idea of what's happened here today. You don't know who this guy is whose head's been smashed in, I suppose?"

"Who do you think?" It was obviously a rhetorical question as the man made no attempt to await a reply. "It's that auld bugger, Herbert Jowett. I told you the legend shouldn't be ignored."

"You're sure it's him?"

"I'm sure reet enough. I saw him lyin' there afore they put up the screens. He were allus a girt big bloke, e'en in his youth. You couldn't mistake him. An' now the bastard's finally paid fer all his wrong doin'."

"Can I quote you on that?" Hoskis could tell by the man's expression that it was unwise to have raised the question. "Sorry. Forget I asked. Could I just have your name?"

"Bugger off!" Jack Tweedie turned on his heels. He had no intention of becoming involved with the police if he could avoid it. Herbert Jowett was dead, and that was all that he'd been waiting to ascertain. Maybe now, Margaret Thursby, the girl who had been his own dear childhood sweetheart, could rest in her grave.

"Guess what!" Hoskis had excitedly made his way back to join his partner. "The dead guy's definitely Herbert Jowett. The old chap we spoke to last time seems convinced of it. I knew we were on to something good here. I blew it a bit at the end though. Still couldn't get him to give me his name."

Ray Jacobs stifled a smile at the young reporter's inept handling of the interview. He clearly still had a lot to learn. "Never mind, we've got what we wanted. We can ring up the police before we send in our report. By then they might be prepared to confirm the identity of the bloke."

Tony brightened up. "You're right. I bet that supercilious inspector's going to get a shock when he finds out we've already sussed out who the stiff is anyway. This is turning into a bloody good story, Ray. I'm damn glad you talked the boss into allowing us to stay on."

Ray tapped the side of his nose. "Piece of cake. I told him we might get an exclusive." Ray failed to let on that he had also dropped a hint that Tony had cast his spell over the young student at the heart of the mystery. "Here they come!"

He quickly took a succession of shots as the stretcher bearers emerged from behind the screens, struggling valiantly through the mud with their heavy burden.

"Well, the old chap was right..." Tony Hoskis scribbled away furiously, recording the dramatic scene. "...he said the dead guy was a big bloke. Those poor bastards look as though they'll be glad when they get on to drier ground."

The crowd of onlookers parted to make way for the labouring ambulance men, allowing Ray Jacobs the opportunity to acquire a few close-ups of the shrouded figure. Once he'd completed the task, he turned once again to his companion.

"I think we could do with visiting our young student friend again now, Tony. Once we get the police to officially release the name of the dead man, she and that tutor of hers could be good for some more background material."

"Just what I was thinking." The young reporter grinned at the older man. "They seem to be pretty clued up. With their local knowledge, they might be able to push us in the right direction. Could be useful for checking up on some of the people involved. Anyway, I fancy seeing her again. We usually get lumbered with a load of ignorant pillocks who can hardly string two words together, don't we? At least she's got her wits about her."

"And she's not a bad looker." Ray Jacobs could spot the gleam in the young man's eyes. "Tell you what, you can handle her on your own this time – if you'll excuse the pun. See if you can get her to go out for a meal, or down the pub. She might just provide a bit more information than you'll get from a straight interview."

The young reporter chuckled. "Suits me – I could do with a night out."

"And ply her with plenty of drink. That Professor Reid appears to be well in with the police. If he knew the name of the victim, it may mean the pair of 'em have been sniffing around. No point missing an opportunity like this."

Tony Hoskis nodded. "You could be right. You're a shrewd old sod. Any chance I might book my expenses down to the firm?"

Ray laughed at the young man's cheek. "And you reckon I'm shrewd! You get a night out with a nice bit of crumpet, and you want the paper to pay for it. You're learning fast, lad! I don't see why not though. Get a receipt. If you come up with anything good, they're hardly likely to complain."

"Brilliant!" Tony thrust his pad and pen into a capacious pocket. "I reckon we've finished here then. Let's find a pub and see about getting confirmation of that poor sod's identity. Once the word's out, you can bet the rest of the media are going to descend on this place like a plague of locusts. We've beaten the bloody lot of 'em this time though." He grinned with delight at the thought of achieving his first scoop.

Ray Jacobs had seen it all before. "Come on then." He gathered up his equipment. "Let's get back to the van."

It took some time for the reporters to negotiate the crowded, narrow lanes that were the only form of access to and from Mardale. The storm that had broken on the way back hardly seemed to have deterred the hordes of determined sightseers who were still making their way towards the site. Clearly they had realised this could be their last opportunity to gaze at the spot where Duncan of Crieff's skull had been discovered. As yet, they would almost certainly be unaware of the latest dramatic developments.

Harassed, sodden-looking policemen, stationed at strategic positions along the lanes, appeared to be struggling to control the volume of traffic that was now converging on Mardale. The newspaper men chuckled with delight at the thought of their rivals attempting to follow up on the story. By the time they arrived, with the way the rain was now teeming down, the ruins of the village should be well and truly obscured once more.

Deciding to make for Shap, the two men chose the Kings Arms as their port of call. Tony Hoskis made straight for the phone, eventually managing to make contact with a member of the Penrith police force. No statement had been issued about the murder victim he was told, but one was expected shortly. He should ring back a little later. He most certainly would. In the meantime, a preliminary report to the news desk was called for. He may still be wet behind the ears, but many of his more experienced colleagues would give their eye teeth for this story. There was no way anyone was going to beat him to the draw.

"Any luck?" Ray Jacobs pushed a pint of bitter across to the young man as he came to find him in the bar.

"Not yet, but the news editor's delighted with what we've got so far. I've told him we're pretty certain it's Herbert Jowett, but that we're just awaiting confirmation. He wants the pictures as soon as you can wire 'em through of course."

"He can wait till we've got through these first." A plate of sandwiches had just appeared. "Get stuck in and we'll sort that out later. By the time we've eaten these the police might be prepared to confirm that it really is that bloke."

The old man at the next table allowed the flicker of a satisfied smile to cross his features. He made no attempt to communicate to the newsmen his identity. Joss Pattinson had heard all that he wanted to know. It appeared that the man who was once destined to become King of Mardale was finally dead – and not before time! Hadn't everyone always said that one day the legend would be fulfilled yet again?

* * *

Merlin Reid and Joy Elliot had not been as lucky at dodging the storm after their visit to the cave. Though they had realised bad weather appeared to be on its way, by the time they spotted the ominous black clouds sweeping over the crest of the mountains it was too late. The cave was behind them and no shelter was at hand. Reid handed Joy the keys to the car. "You go on ahead. You can get along much faster on your own."

"No way!" She rammed them back into his pocket. "I reckon I shall get just as wet anyway."

She was probably right. The way the rain was coming down, neither of them could avoid a soaking.

"Ah well, at least it's refreshing." He grinned at her rain-spattered countenance. "And we're not alone. Look at that lot down there." He indicated the crowd of people now rapidly moving away from the scene of the murder. "I think I'd rather be up here. It's a bit better underfoot for one thing."

She giggled as his feet nearly went from under him. "You were saying?"

He regained his balance almost immediately. "Maybe I shouldn't tempt fate. It's more slippery than I thought." He planted his feet a little more carefully.

"The police seem to have finished though, Prof." She drew his attention back to Mardale. "It's lucky this didn't come a few hours earlier. I wouldn't have envied them their task if it had."

"Nor I." He halted for a moment to view the scene. The lashing rain almost prevented him from doing so. A flash of lightening, followed immediately by a peal of thunder, persuaded him that this was not the time, or place, to be hanging about. Joy had spun round, a look of alarm on her normally placid face.

"Let's go, Prof. I don't like it up here."

He took hold of her arm, quickening his pace. "I'm not that keen myself. It's just as well we're not up on the tops."

Another flash, forking along the summit of Harter Fell, added weight to his words and impetus to their sodden feet. Soaked to the skin, they put their heads down, forcing their way forward into the rain-laden gale that was now sweeping in their direction. Already the rocky ground beneath their feet was looking more like the bed of a stream.

It came as a great relief when they finally got down to the lower level. Thank God for the elevated walkways. The boggy section around Mardale Beck, which had appeared relatively dry when they made their way across earlier, now oozed with excess liquid. This had to be the beginning of the end for the exposed village. Once the catchment area leached its surfeit of storm water, the lower lying areas of Mardale would quickly become submerged. If Inspector Grey – or anyone else for that matter – planned a return visit to Oxtors Farm, it now looked out of the question. If the farm had concealed any secrets, they were now almost certainly destined to remain there…

At last. They had made it to the car. Reid opened the boot first, grabbing the two blankets he always kept ready for any emergency. The occasional accident victim had always been grateful for his thoughtfulness. Now he and Joy were equally thankful to make use of them. Once inside, he wrapped the dry material around the bedraggled young lady, towelling her dripping locks with one of the corners.

"Thanks, Prof." She shivered, but managed a smile. "You look after yourself now. God, I feel a mess."

"Joy, you are a mess!"

She burst out laughing. "You brute! If I wasn't all wrapped up, I'd thump you!"

"If you weren't all wrapped up I'd never have dared say it." He chuckled, pleased to see she still retained her sense of humour. "Never mind, once we get back and have a hot shower you can make yourself glamorous again. I'm sure that young reporter is going to find an excuse to pop back and have another word with you."

She flushed a little at his words. "Do you really think so? I imagined he'd be too busy now that this looks as if it's turning into a murder inquiry."

"Oh, he'll be back." Reid had spotted the tell-tale look in the young man's eyes.

With the blanket now tucked beneath him and draped loosely around his sodden shoulders, he was attempting to extricate the car from the ruck of vehicles that surrounded it. At least there was a police presence, the hapless constable making a brave effort to stem the tide of incomers while endeavouring to allow others to depart the scene. He had his hands full. It was obvious that the people arriving were intent on seeing the remains of Mardale while they still had the chance. Reid could only wish them the best of luck. By the time they were able to vacate their cars without getting a soaking, the place would be awash.

The constable was waving him out at last. Good. It was no joke sitting around in wet clothing. He was pleased to be on the move. "Soon be home, Joy." He smiled as she snuggled deeper into the confines of her blanket.

* * *

That was better. They had both showered and taken afternoon tea. Now they sat enjoying the comfort of warm, dry clothing, as the torrent of rain battered against the window panes.

Joy had made a good job of prettying herself up – no doubt in anticipation of the young reporter calling. She still looked a little wan, but Reid was convinced she had gotten over the initial shock of Herbert Jowett's death. They had both had time to consider the implications of that particular event. It was impossible to ignore the curse reputedly wrought upon the family by Duncan of Crieff's widow. There were many unanswered questions. By whose hand had the man met his death? Was it just by chance that it had coincided with the removal of the skull from the farm? If Jowett were the man responsible for stealing the object from Grey's office then where was it now? Could it have been carried off by the person who had attacked him? Reid had resisted the temptation to discuss any of the details with Joy since they arrived back. Best to give her some time to come to terms with what had happened. It was to be hoped that Grey would soon discover the killer. She would rest a lot easier once that occurred. He began to wonder how Grey was getting on with the case.

His musings were interrupted by the ringing of the telephone. Tony Hoskis was wanting to have a word with

Joy. Reid was pleased to see her response when informed of the fact. She wasted no time in heading off to speak to the young man.

She returned quite quickly and with a huge smile on her face. "Tony's asked me out to dinner tonight. You don't mind if I go, do you, Prof?"

"Of course not. Do you good to have some young company. You might get a few more compliments than you get from me."

"That's true!" She fixed him with a fairly good attempt at a stern look of disapproval. "I haven't forgotten what you said about me in the car yet."

"Get off with you!" He grinned at her as she started to chuckle. This was the Joy he was used to. Tony Hoskis would find her a pleasant companion.

"See you, Prof." She strode off to make sure she was entirely presentable.

Another phone call. This time it was the Windermere Biological Association with the information that he had requested on the approximate time the skull had been lying in the mud at the bottom of Haweswater. About forty to sixty years, he was told. There was no doubt that the contents of the skull matched the sample taken close by. And yes, that would indicate that the skull could well have been displaced from its niche as the walls slowly crumbled. Yet more confirmation that this was no hoax. Just as well, considering the far-reaching effects of the discovery. The rest of the tests for the pollen content of the sample were still being analysed. He thanked them for their efforts. Now it was time to keep his side of the bargain. He had promised to let them know of any developments.

"You asked me to keep you up to date with events at this end."

"We certainly did! Has something happened?"

He could guess the effect his words would have. "I believe we've got our victim of the curse. A man's been murdered at Oxtors Farm."

"Christ!" There was a moment's silence. "Don't tell me it's actually one of the family who originally lived there?"

"I'm afraid that's still confidential, but you can draw your own conclusions. Inspector Grey should be breaking the news soon anyway so in the meantime, if you don't mind, I'll pass on your information to him about the skull."

"Of course. My God! So we may have been indirectly taking part in a murder hunt. Wait till I tell the others. They're not going to believe this!"

Reid rang off and dialled the number of the Penrith police station. Grey may, or may not, be interested to learn that the skull was definitely genuine. That hardly concerned the professor. All that mattered was that it gave him a damn good excuse to give the inspector a call.

CHAPTER SEVENTEEN

Inspector Grey was his usual affable self once informed that Reid was on the line and the nature of the call. Having disposed of the pleasantries, he quickly got down to business. "I'm told you have news from the boffins at Windermere."

"That's right. I don't know if it's of any interest to you at this stage, but I've just had it confirmed that the skull had been lying in the silt for between forty to sixty years after spilling from its hiding place. Certainly there's no question of a hoax."

"Good. I'd hate to think someone had deliberately set this lot up!"

The skull's connection with the legend having apparently been almost totally authenticated now, at least the possibility of a more calculated plot had been eliminated. Grey sounded relieved. "By the way, I've just released the details of the murder to the media. I know they wouldn't have received the information via you, but those bloody news hounds had already managed to ferret out Jowett's identity. I've got a description of the man they said identified the body, but they swear he wouldn't reveal his name. He's definitely one of the ex-residents though. They'd spoken to him before on their first visit to Mardale. He was the one who told them about the feud."

"Yes, I remember reading about it." Reid wondered who the man might be. Clearly someone who was determined to keep his identity to himself. Still, for the moment that was not the issue. Could Grey be persuaded to divulge more? "Have there been any other developments? Or am I being too presumptuous?"

Grey chuckled. "Yes, you are! Still, when were you ever anything else? All I can say at the moment is that Jowett did die as a result of the blow to his head and there's no evidence of any motive linked to robbery. His wallet containing his return ticket to South Africa, plus credit cards, not to mention a considerable sum of money, were all still present on his body. Makes you think, eh?"

"Sure does…" Reid cast his mind back to the conversation he and Joy had had with Joss Pattinson. "I suppose you've already been to see the next of kin – and the McKades, of course?"

"I have. Needless to say, none of them matches up to the description of the man the reporter spoke to. At this stage we're assuming he was just an innocent spectator who'd been drawn back to view the remains of the village where he'd spent his childhood. As he must have known Herbert Jowett in his youth, it wouldn't take much to put two and two together if he saw the size of the body. Jowett must surely have stood out as a young man."

"So I've been told." The professor acquainted Grey with the details he had acquired from old Joss.

"You have been busy!" Grey sounded quite surprised. "You don't let the grass grow under your feet, do you?"

"Well, I had got a head start. And you were the one who told me I was welcome to dig around."

"That's true." Grey was chuckling again. "I might have guessed you'd have something up your sleeve. Anything else I should know?"

"Possibly." Reid wasn't totally convinced that the morning's discovery was relevant, though in the light of what Grey had just said about the elderly man who'd spoken to the reporter, it could have a bearing on the case. He outlined the story of Margaret Thursby, and of the man who had lost his childhood sweetheart so tragically. "There is one other thing." He described the floral tribute left at the memorial stone with the note and its cryptic message, 'God's will be done,' concluding by admitting his incompetence in losing the scrap of paper.

"Christ! Sounds like another possible suspect." Grey appeared startled by the news. "I guess we can't rule out this Jack Tweedie then. If he matches the description we got from the reporter, he'll need to explain his presence at Mardale. He could have been hanging around to make sure he'd made a proper job of killing Jowett. Doesn't seem to tie in with the missing skull though. Anyway, I'll let the Superintendent know. The big boys are on the case now that we've established it is murder. I reckon we'll be doing all the leg work, as usual, and he'll be claiming all the glory."

Reid was aware that Grey was not seriously complaining. The inspector was certainly never cut out to be a desk bound officer. Whatever was going on, he had to be in the thick of it. Once the challenge was presented, Grey was relentless in his efforts to bring any criminal to book.

The inspector sat smiling to himself after replacing the receiver. 'The Magician' had certainly done his homework. Somehow he usually managed to come up with something useful. Jack Tweedie now had to be included in the list of suspects. The question was, which of those suspects had most reason to wish Jowett dead? And where was the damn skull? It might still be worthwhile obtaining a search warrant for the McKades' place. If Jowett had the object in his possession when arriving at Mardale, then there seemed no good reason for anyone other than the McKades to murder him to acquire it. Tweedie certainly didn't appear to fall into that category. Was there a possibility that the McKades, if guilty, might not have had chance to reunite the skull with the rest of the remains? It appeared unlikely, though a lot depended on precisely where the remains were situated. Maybe time had prevented the implementation of any such plan. It would have been impossible for anyone – with the possible exception of one of Jowett's relatives – to have known for sure that the man was going to turn up with the skull or when such an event might take place. Only the certainty that Jowett would move heaven and earth to replace the skull at the farm could have caused someone to lie in wait for him.

Grey headed off to speak to the superintendent. He would put the case to him.

* * *

Cedric Bull's piggy little eyes lit up at the prospect of money finally coming to the family. He had waited a long time for this. Too bloody long. Herbert Jowett had certainly outlived his stay on this planet.

Cedric's wife, Jean, had delayed relating the day's news until they had finished their evening meal. Now he sat back in his easy chair, considering the possibilities. "You say your mother's definitely going to see that we get our share?"

Jean failed to register that her husband had used the words 'our share'. The fact that the money would come to her, he had chosen to ignore. But her delight at the thought of how the unexpected wealth was going to change their lives excluded any consideration of his choice of words. She could hardly contain her excitement.

"Yes, love. Ma said uncle had no one else who could claim the money and it would come direct tae her. Once everything's been sorted, she's gaan tae decide how she'll split it up. She said she's handing most of it over tae Ralph and me." She beamed across at her husband. "It's what you've always wanted, dear. You might be able tae give up the plumbing at last." That was the thing Jean wished for most of all. Cedric hated the job, but there was little else in the way of work. The fact that he was self-employed meant he was in no position to turn down whatever was offered. This often resulted in him being called out at all hours of the day and night. Jean had high hopes that a change in circumstances might bring about a change for the better in their relationship.

Cedric sat contemplating his wife's words. He still had serious doubts about how easy it might be to come by the money. Hadn't Ralph always hated him? And the bugger held a great deal of sway over his mother. He could still throw a spanner into the works. That would be the last straw.

"What about your brother?"

Jean understood her husband's concern. Ralph was very much a product of the Jowett dynasty, even though he was not descended directly from the male line. Since their father's death, Ralph had taken over all of the family's affairs. Jean loved her brother and believed he loved her too, but he had always been dictatorial. She had been forced to defy him to marry Cedric. Though that marriage had taken place over six years ago, her brother had still not come to terms with it. She also had doubts about her mother's ability to persuade Ralph that she and Cedric should be allotted a fair share. As always, Ralph would want his say. There could be trouble ahead. For the moment she could only endeavour to placate her husband.

"We just have tae trust mother. She seems determined about gettin' it settled proper. I know Ralph can be a bit of a pain at times, but it's mother's money. She's the one tae decide who gets it."

"Easily said, but you know what Ralph's like. You know he's never liked me – though God knows why. And what makes him think he's always got the right tae rule your life or your mothers? I'm sick of the way he carries on. It's time you stood up for yourselves. Just make sure he doesn't try anything on!"

Jean could see that her husband was getting into one of his states. God help her if she didn't manage to get hold of the money. Cedric was hard enough to live with at the moment, without any added complications.

* * *

Cedric Bull had been correct in his assumptions. At that very moment, Ralph Braithwaite was on his way to see his mother. The thought of his brother-in-law getting his greedy little hands on part of the family's fortune was anathema to him. Ralph had never let on to his mother that he suspected

Cedric of regularly being unfaithful to his wife. The man would never be without an excuse to spend an evening out, often complaining that he was always on call, but Ralph had noted that his van was often parked outside the house of a widow in Craigend. He had gritted his teeth, keeping the secret from his sister. She was a good lass, but she had a blind spot as far as her husband was concerned. Ralph had long since decided that Jean was best left in ignorance of the facts.

He had reached his mother's house now and stood waiting impatiently for her to unbolt the door. He hoped he was not too late to prevent her from committing herself to handing over any part of the fortune without first considering how to ensure Jean kept total control over it. That bastard of a husband of hers was never going to get the chance to squander his sister's legacy on another woman.

Ellen Braithwaite had been expecting her son.

"Come in, love. What a performance! Have the police been ower tae your place?"

"They have, Ma." He followed her inside. "I hope they've not caused you too much hassle. The nosey buggers are into everything. They seem tae know all about uncle's money comin' tae us."

"Aye. I told 'em, son. There didn't seem much point in tryin' tae keep it quiet."

Her son didn't look very convinced though he chose not to admit it. "I suppose you could be right. Maybe it's best not lettin' 'em find out these things fer themsel's. They'd probably only bother us all the more." He settled down on the old settee. "Anyway, sod the lot of 'em. At least we'll be getting it at last. The auld bugger deserved all he got an' we deserve what we're gaan tae get."

Ellen was aware what would be uppermost in her son's mind. He had not come to discuss his uncle's death. That was something neither of them had any regrets about. Why should they have? Like her son said, the auld bugger deserved it. No, the only thing on Ralph's mind would be the repercussions resulting from Herbert's death. She waited for him to continue.

Ralph was not intending to mince his words. "You do realise, Ma, that we've got tae decide quite quickly what's gaan tae happen about Jean?"

Ellen took a deep breath. "I have had a word wi' her."

That was exactly what Ralph had feared. Just like his mother to rush in without thinking. "I hope you've not told her you'll just hand the money ower. You know what'll happen if that husband o' hers get hold of it."

Ellen's face clouded. "She must have her share, Ralph."

"Aye, I know she's got tae have her share. Don't you think that's what I want? But what's gaan tae stop him fra fritterin' it all away?"

Ellen had been struggling with that problem all afternoon. She had still not resolved it. How could she suggest to her daughter that she should deny handing over any control of the money to her own husband. And even if the money were transferred into an account in Jean's name only, Cedric would surely make it his business to see that she parted with it. Yet Ellen was not prepared to see her daughter go without. Better that Jean gave it all to Cedric – whatever the consequences – than have it withheld. Jean would never forgive her if she reneged on her promise.

Ralph could sense his mother's hesitation. She was too weak to handle this. He had to take control. "You can't do it, Ma. You'd best put it in my hands. If Jean's share goes in the bank an' you let me dole it out, I'll make bloody sure that bastard can't rip her off. You've seen what can happen with your own brother. Look how he grabbed hold o' everything. We can't risk that happening agin. Not tae our Jeanie."

Ellen was weakening now. What her son said made sense, yet she could hardly bear to put her daughter in that position. But then, what if she didn't agree to Ralph's suggestion? He would never let her forget it if his sister were once more deprived of a better life by her horrible husband's greed.

“You’ll have tae tell her then, Ralph. I’m havin’ nowt tae do wi’ it.”

That suited him fine. At last he could put Cedric Bull in his place. Jean might bring the family fortune home, but it would be spent wisely or not at all.

* * *

Tony Hoskis had been a little late in calling for Joy Elliot, though once in the car he quickly explained the reason for the delay. He and Ray Jacobs had got their heads together in an endeavour to establish the identity of the old man who had given them the information at Mardale. Like Merlin Reid before them, they had come to the conclusion that the ex-residents of Mardale would not have moved far from their original base. A word with the landlord of the Kings Arm,s giving a good description of the man, got an immediate response. “That’ll be Jack Tweddie. There’s only one or two o’ the auld folk left now. He lives just along the road.”

Tactful questioning elicited the address. No mention was made of the fact that Jack Tweedie had declined to volunteer his name when approached earlier. The old man quickly received a visit.

Like many people in the past sought out by the media, Jack Tweedie was astounded to find the pressmen on his doorstep. He had been far from pleased, repeating his previous demand that they “Bugger off!”

Tony Hoskis had pleaded unsuccessfully for a further interview, being dispatched with a torrent of abuse. Ray Jacobs had hardly improved the old man’s temper by seizing the opportunity to snatch a hurried shot of him as he returned indoors. Jacobs had no doubt that the other newsmen, who would undoubtedly descend upon the area, would seek out the man anyway, along with anyone else associated with Mardale. This story was far too important to consider the sensibilities of every Tom, Dick and Harry.

"So Jack Tweedie was there?" Joy was surprised by the young reporter's account.

"You know him?" Tony Hoskis was also taken by surprise.

"I know of him." She recounted the tale old Joss had passed on.

"Good grief! No wonder he didn't want to get mixed up in it then. You don't think he could have anything to do with the murder?"

Joy shuddered. "How horrible. Suppose he had? It certainly seems as though he hated the man, but then, so did a lot of other people according to Joss."

"Just depends who hated him the most." Hoskis concentrated for a moment on his driving as he looked for directions. The signpost quickly put him on the right track. "I suppose if you thought someone had caused the death of a person you loved, you might be driven to take revenge."

"Or some other force might drive you to it." Joy did not like the way her mind was working. "Do you think it's possible that this curse is for real? I've been bothered all along, since I first set eyes on that awful skull."

Tony squeezed her knee. "If it were meant to be, no power on earth would have changed it." His hand was slow to move away. She hardly noticed. 'No power on earth?'

They soon arrived at a converted country house. Tony jumped out to open the car door for her. This was nicer than she had expected. A fairly shy girl, she had hardly ever had much time for boyfriends. The lads at school had teased her unmercifully about that, but none of them had ever appealed to her. This man did.

Tony took her arm, leading her up the small flight of steps and into the attractive reception area. Ushering her into the lounge bar, he helped her out of her coat. Soon he was back at her side.

"What would you like to drink while we wait for our table?"

She hesitated. She was not much of a drinker.

"Try a gin and tonic." Tony was a dab hand at cajoling young women. Especially young women whose tongues he hoped to loosen.

"Okay, just a small one."

This really was very pleasant. She had hardly imagined that they would end up in such a charming setting. Somehow she had been anticipating a pie and a pint at one of the local pubs.

"Here we go." He handed her the drink, then settled down into the comfortable armchair opposite, lifting his pint glass.

"Good health, Joy. I am glad you decided to come."

God, he was a handsome man. The slightly irregular smile that lit up his tanned, finely chiselled face was echoed in the depths of his magnetic blue eyes, sending a shiver down her spine. For the first time she had the chance to devote her thoughts entirely to him, without the distraction of his partner. She liked what she saw. Casually, though smartly dressed, in white jeans, T-shirt and suede jacket, he looked entirely at ease – unlike herself. She wondered if her nervousness showed. She suddenly remembered the touch of his hand on her leg; it was pleasant, though disturbing. Just how many other girls might have succumbed to his manly charms?

"I imagine you and Professor Reid must have spent some time trying to work out exactly what's been going on?"

His question brought her back down to earth.

"Yes. It's been an exciting time. I shudder every time I think of that man being murdered, but it is fascinating to be part of the action."

"I'll bet it is." He smiled his devastating smile once again. "You and the professor seem to have already come up with one or two facts that even the police aren't unaware of."

"I think you're probably right." She returned his smile a little demurely. "Mind you, I think the Prof. will soon let the police know about anything he feels might be important. Since the skull was stolen from the station, Inspector Grey probably needs all the help he can get with the case. It must be embarrassing to lose the main piece of evidence they had."

Tony Hoskis almost spilled his pint. "You mean to say they've let someone steal it from right under their noses?"

Joy realised she might have spoken out of turn. The gin and tonic was already causing her to drop her guard. "Oops! I think I may have been a little indiscreet."

The reporter tried to hide his delight. "Nonsense. That's bound to come out sooner or later." He didn't want her to clam up now. "You needn't be concerned. I'll not attribute it to you. That's if I use it at all."

"I hope you won't." She was concerned to think she might have broken a trust. "Do you have to mention it in the paper?"

Damn right he did, but he wasn't letting on to this young innocent.

"Leave it to me." He winked across at her. "Anyway we haven't come here to talk business, have we?" He didn't want to put her on the defensive. Time enough to broach the subject again later "Let's have another drink before we go in to dinner."

Her protests were ignored. Making his way to the bar, he was soon back with refills. "Come on, Joy. We might as well make a night of it."

What the hell! She accepted the drink. Surely she could trust him. She raised her glass. "Good health, Tony. Only don't make me drink too much. I'm not used to it." She started to giggle. "I suppose it is funny when you come to think about it. Fancy someone pinching a skull from a police station."

He joined in with her laughter. She was going to be a pushover. He kept the conversation away from the murder at Mardale for the time it took to finish their drinks. She would be more at ease once they were dining.

And so it proved. The Chardonnay he'd ordered to accompany the meal clearly went straight to her head. He chose his words carefully, not wishing to appear to be interrogating her. He was a past master at introducing the topic of interest by degrees.

"You can't help feeling sorry for those poor devils who had to lose their homes at Mardale, can you?"

"Just what I said." She was trying to look serious, but suddenly she was giggling again. Alcohol always affected her that way. "Sorry, I'm not really laughing about those unfortunate people. I was just thinking about the look that must have been on Inspector Grey's face when he found that skull missing."

Tony Hoskis chuckled too. No wonder Grey preferred not to talk to him when he attempted to get the interview at Mardale. Clearly he had good reason to keep everything quiet.

"Who do you think might have stolen it, Joy?"

She seemed to have lost any inhibitions she might have had about discussing the subject. "I suppose it was the man who got murdered. He was obviously desperate to get the skull buried back at the farm. And you can't blame him, seeing what's happened."

"You can say that again." Hoskis was still angling to find out if the girl knew more. "Of course, these McKades seemed to have good reason to want the skull back in their possession too."

"Yes. I feel sorry for them in a way." She paused for a moment to sip a little more wine. "Fancy being committed to returning that skull to the rest of the remains of their ancestor. You can hardly believe that all the descendants of that man could have hung on with such grim determination."

Tony stopped eating long enough to refill her glass. He smiled as she appeared not even to notice. "I suppose it's all a matter of pride. If they felt they were the rightful owners of the land at Mardale, the resentment would have fuelled their resolution. It must have been even more galling for those who were there when the valley was sold off. Just imagine how they felt watching the land disappear below the water and someone else walking off with a small fortune."

Joy nodded. "They must have been gutted! You can see why the ones left now are so determined to get their own back. And possibly by whatever means necessary."

"Does make you wonder what lengths they'd go to."

She thoughtfully sipped her drink once more before replying. "I suppose they could have been the ones who stole the skull from the station. There doesn't seem to be any evidence that they have it, but I imagine Inspector Grey's followed up on it."

"Well, there's no news of any arrest." It was Tony Hoskis who looked thoughtful now as he tucked into his meal. "I wonder where the McKades live?"

"Oh, they're at Shap." Joy was almost forgetting that the good-looking young man sitting opposite her was a reporter and as such had a vested interest in probing for every scrap of information he could unearth. "They've got a smallholding just on the outskirts, so we were told. Everyone who was moved out of Mardale was resettled by the water board."

Just as Hoskis had surmised. The McKades would certainly be getting a visit from him and Ray Jacobs in the morning. Forewarned was forearmed. It should be a simple matter to seek out their address. The rest of the press squad – along with the television boys – were not going to be allowed to steal a march. Joy Elliot was proving to be a most valuable asset. He smiled across at her glowing face, refilling her half empty glass once more. She appeared a little light-headed. "Here's to us, Joy." He lifted his own glass, encouraging her to follow suit.

"Definitely!" She started to giggle again, clinking glasses with him. "I'm really enjoying this, Tony. I was feeling a bit down after that man was murdered, but I'm feeling great now. I think I needed something to take my mind off it."

"You deserve a treat." He was actually sincere for a change. She had been a great help with the story and he doubted she had much chance to go out and enjoy herself on the meagre funding most students received.

"You are nice." She was almost blushing as she looked him directly in the eyes. "I am pleased you thought of doing this."

How grateful would she be, he wondered, reaching out to stroke her hand. "Nonsense. It's my pleasure." He almost felt embarrassed to think that the paper would be picking up the bill. Still, she wasn't to know that. What difference did it make anyway? As long she was enjoying herself he might as well reap the rewards.

"Do you think it'll take them long to catch the killer?" She was looking serious again.

"I don't imagine so. There can't be many people who'd have cause to murder a stranger. And if Herbert Jowett's been away in South Africa – as everyone seems to think – how many people would still be around who were carrying a grudge? It would surely have to be someone from his youth or someone who might benefit from his death. At least Grey confirmed he hadn't been robbed."

Joy shuddered again at the thought of the killing. Tony Hoskis decided it might be wise to change the subject for a while.

"Are you ready for coffee?" He didn't wait for a reply. "Let's take it in the lounge. I'll get them to bring us a liqueur as well." He moved over to draw back her chair as she arose.

"Thank you, Tony." He did seem the perfect gentleman.

One liqueur had led to another – and yet another – as they chatted away the evening. Now Joy excused herself, as Tony headed off to settle the bill and collect their coats. God, she felt inebriated. She was having to concentrate very hard not to reel as she picked her way carefully through the gaps between the tables. She tried valiantly to steady herself.

She had another fit of the giggles in the toilets. Just in time she realised that her dress was caught up in the back of her panties. What if she had gone out looking like that? The other people there would have choked on their drinks. She tried to stifle the sound of her laughter as she rearranged her clothing. How embarrassing. She had to control this. It was not like her at all.

Someone else was coming in. She quickly crossed to wash her hands and powder her nose before anyone realised the state she was in.

Still smiling to herself, she rejoined the young reporter.

It was just a short journey before they turned into the drive leading up to the Hall. Gravel crunched beneath the tyres like shattering egg-shells as Tony brought the car to a halt.

The house was in total darkness. Joy realised it was rather late. The professor's room was at the rear of the building so there was no knowing if he was still up. Joy turned and smiled at her escort. She felt uncomfortable. She had never considered exactly what she would do after a man had shown her a good time. Should she ask him up to her room for coffee? Somehow that had the ring about it of inviting him for something more.

"Thank you for a lovely evening," she blurted out. "I would ask you in, but I'm not sure my tutor would approve."

He looked disappointed. She guessed he probably had hoped for something more, yet she hardly knew the young man.

He was unfastening his safety belt now, as well as her own. He was taking her into his arms, drawing her close to him, searching for her lips. Head still spinning from the effects of the alcohol, she put up no resistance. This was heaven. Slipping her hand behind his neck she responded warmly to his kiss.

Was that a mistake? Was she leading him on? His hand was fumbling now to undo the buttons of her blouse. She wriggled uncomfortably as his hand slipped inside, his lips were still pressed against her own, preventing her from protesting. Did she want to protest? Suddenly she knew that she did. His hands were all over her now, lifting her skirt, one hand between her thighs. She wasn't ready for this. She managed to turn her face away from him. "Don't Tony." She was crying now, ashamed that she might have given him the wrong impression. “Please stop. This isn’t what I want.”

He attempted to kiss her again, ignoring her pleas. She turned her face, preventing him from locating her lips. “Please, Tony. I’ve never done anything like this before.” Her eyes were streaming with tears as she struggled to remove his hand from its intimate contact with her body.

“It’s OK. I’ve got a rubber.”

She continued to struggle. Suddenly he gave up. “Sod it then!” He seemed to realise that he’d gone too far. He handed her a handkerchief. “Don’t cry. It’s not the end of the world. I hadn’t really planned it this way, you know. Maybe I’m just used to getting my way with women. Most of them want it as much as I do.”

She attempted to dry her eyes, still sobbing quietly. “I’m sorry. I suppose it’s my fault. I should have realised.” She fumbled for the door handle. “I meant what I said about it being a lovely evening though. I just wish I hadn’t spoiled it for you.” She jumped from the car, bursting into tears once more.

He made no attempt to follow. The revving of the engine and the grinding sound of rubber on gravel gave every indication that he was furiously driving away.

She stood for a while trying to compose herself. She didn’t want her tutor to see her like this or to realise what had happened. She would keep it to herself. She dried her tears once more, adjusting her clothing before quietly letting herself into the silent house.

She needed a shower. All of a sudden she felt dirty. Surely she hadn’t really led him on? Not enough to justify him going so far anyway. She should never have drunk so much. She could maybe have prevented things getting out of hand if she hadn’t. Her tears started again in the shower, lost among the myriad of tumbling, rushing droplets that enveloped her trembling body. She wanted to scrub away the memory of his all-embracing hands and the dread of what might have occurred had he not desisted. A lesson had been learned.

CHAPTER EIGHTEEN

Joy awoke with a start. She had cried herself to sleep after the upsetting incident which had ruined what had, at first impression, promised to be a perfect evening out. Now it was time to get a grip of herself. She headed for the shower, still feeling the after-effects of the drink. Her head hurt though that was nothing compared to the hurt she felt in her heart. Still she had this intense desire to cleanse herself thoroughly.

That was better. She stepped from the shower, drying herself before the mirror, gazing at her own naked body. Somehow she had almost expected to see the imprints of the hands that had fondled her. She bridled at the recollection. Why did men have to force themselves upon women before they barely had time to become acquainted? Tony had seemed such a gentleman. Was he only interested in her for his own gratification? And for the information she might impart? She guessed so. Her lower lip trembled as she fought to control her emotions. She might willingly have given herself to him – had she had time to get used to the idea. She was no prude. But now she was angry to think that she had been used. The anger took away some of the shame. She looked at her body in a different light. He didn't deserve to be the first man to take her. When she finally parted with her virginity it would be to someone who had much more consideration. A man who wanted her in a loving way, not merely as a one night stand.

She made her way down to breakfast feeling slightly happier. No real harm had been done after all. Just a blow to her silly pride.

Her tutor was seated at the breakfast table when she appeared, having already selected his meal from the heated serving trays prepared by the cook. In front of him were the morning papers – the *Today's News* prominent at the top of the pile.

"Morning, Joy." He greeted her in his usual cheery way. "I trust you had an enjoyable evening?"

She forced a smile. "Yes. It was a lovely meal." She purposely changed the subject before he had time to inquire further. "What have the papers got to say about the murder?"

He pushed the *Today's News* issue in her direction. "Read it for yourself. As you might have guessed, this is the only one with the full story. Looks as though Tony and his pal have been hellishly busy!"

The headlines were sensational – which came as no great surprise. 'DEATH OF A KING!' Joy read on.

> 'Yesterday, the legend of the Mardale skull was dramatically brought to a terrifying conclusion. Herbert Jowett – the man once destined to become 'King' of Mardale, until that tiny hamlet was deserted to the waters of a man-made reservoir – was found brutally murdered at the shattered, crumbling remains of his former home, Oxtors Farm. A curse had been placed on the Jowett family several centuries before by the wife of Duncan of Crieff – chief of the McKade clan – who was slain by the man who founded the Jowett dynasty. The skull of Duncan of Crieff was walled up in the farmhouse following the death of a member of that ill-fated family by drowning; a death that had been predicted should the skull ever be removed from the precincts of the farm. This was the first ever recorded victim of the curse. Perhaps it would also have been the last – had the sands of time not finally run out. Spilt from the ruined building after years of submersion below the shimmering waters of Haweswater reservoir, police action following the discovery of the skull by Joy Elliot – a young student – led to the skull being removed by Inspector Grey. Transported to the Penrith police station for safe-keeping, information from a reliable source now leads us to believe that the skull was then stolen from the station a short while before the body of Herbert Jowett was discovered. HOW, and by whom, must surely be a pertinent question. And, had the skull not been removed from the

farm, would Herbert Jowett still be alive today? Inspector Grey was not available for comment.'

There was much more along the same lines though Joy was just grateful that she had not been named as the informant. At least Tony Hoskis had kept his word as far as that was concerned. She read on, realising how much she had inadvertently revealed to the young reporter. The story of Jack Tweedie's ruined childhood romance and of the memorial he had cut into the boulder took up another page. There was a blurred photograph of the old man as he had attempted to avoid the attention of Ray Jacobs. He looked vaguely familiar. Could she possibly have caught sight of him at Mardale she wondered?

She glanced up at her tutor. Did he realise just how much of the story had come from her lips? If so, he was tactfully ignoring it.

"You've got to hand it to these lads, Joy. They waste no time digging up the dirt. I imagine Grey's not going to be very pleased at having his name splashed all over the paper as the man who lost the skull."

"I suppose not." She felt awful about letting that slip. Still, now having first-hand knowledge of how reporters worked, she felt pretty sure they would have come up with the information somehow.

"Tony must be pleased with himself." The professor indicated the other newspapers. "None of these have anything like the amount of detail he's amassed about the case. Proves it pays to be quick off the mark."

Joy put the paper back, trying not to look too guilty. "Yes. I expect he's delighted. I imagine his career could receive a tremendous boost as a result of all this." She made her way over to the breakfast trays, selecting just a small plateful. She really had very little appetite.

Reid had just about finished his meal and excused himself. From Joy's general demeanour he suspected her encounter with Tony Hoskis had not gone as well as expected. Pity, he had hoped she would be bubbling over with news of the event. It would have been nice to see a smile back on her face after all the trauma she had experienced over the past few days.

* * *

There was no smile on Inspector Grey's face either as he perused the article. "Bloody reporters!" He threw the newspaper in the bin. "Sod the bastards! God help them if they expect any cooperation from me in the future!" They were about to make him a laughing stock. The article would also have alerted the Braithwaites to the fact that the skull had gone missing. He had hoped that by not informing them of the theft, one of them, if guilty, may have let something slip. They were still among the prime suspects in the case. Related or not, hatred and greed were always going to be sound reasons for despatching someone to an early death. And, that being the case, he could also not rule out the possibility of their conspiring with the dead man to steal the skull. It would not then be difficult to grab the opportunity to set someone else up, after murdering the man themselves.

The buzzer on his desk interrupted his train of thoughts. Superintendent Morrison required his presence. No doubt he would have a few choice words to say about the newspaper report. Morrison was another who preferred to play his cards close to his chest.

Grey was not wrong in his assumptions. Morrison quickly proved that he was less than pleased that news of the skull's disappearance had leaked out. Nor was he happy about the story of Jack Tweedie finding its way into the headlines.

"Damn it, Grey!" was his reaction. "We haven't even interviewed this man yet. Now the bloody papers have got hold of it. By the time we get on the scene, the place will be crawling with reporters."

Grey had hardly failed to recognise that fact. It still amazed him the speed with which the media seemed able to pick up on the smallest clue. Obviously the public were more prepared to speak to the press than they were to the police. Whatever the reason, it was not going to help the reputation of the force if they were constantly beaten to the draw.

Morrison quickly decided to pay Jack Tweedie a visit. Grey was to accompany him. At least an interview with the man might throw some light on the affair.

* * *

As expected, the media were out in force. Droves of them had descended on Shap the moment the full story broke. Deprived of a visit to the ruins of Mardale by the waters now engulfing the forsaken village, they had lost no time in wheedling out the address of Tweedie from the same source as the *Today's News* reporters. Morrison ignored their pleas for information, forcing his way through the throng. It took a while before Tweedie responded to the superintendent's repeated ringing of the doorbell.

"Come in." A burly, rather distinguished-looking man ushered them quickly inside after realising they were uniformed officers. "I don't know what the hell you want, but you can tell that lot outside to piss off for a start. They've been driving me mad from the moment I got up this morning!" He led them into a neat, well-furnished living room.

Morrison ignored Tweedie's demand that he see off the crowd of reporters, plunging immediately into his interrogation of the man.

"You must have some idea why we're here."

Tweedie grudgingly indicated that they should sit.

"I imagine it's these bloody stories in the papers about me an' Margaret Thursby. That's nobody's business but my own though. And why are all that gang o' nosy sods out there. You'd think I was a bloody murderer. All I've ever done is tell one o' they reporters about Herbert Jowett. I wish to God I'd kept my trap shut!"

"Perhaps if you tell us about Jowett we might be able to convince them that they're wasting their time." Morrison sat back awaiting a reply, clearly indicating that his words were not merely a request.

Jack Tweedie stared back at the superintendent. He could not control his anger. "Herbert Jowett were a slimy bastard!" he vehemently exploded. "He made Margaret Thursby's life a misery. He an' his father drove her to her death an' I'm not the on'y one as could tell you that. I'm bloody delighted the auld bastard's had his comeuppance, an' you can bet that goes fer most o' the folk as ever knew him." Tweedie's eyes blazed with fury, his features twisted by the bitter memories of his lost love.

Grey could sympathise with the old man, though that sympathy did not extend to absolving him if some crime had been committed. "You don't deny you were at Mardale at the time the body was discovered? Could you explain to the superintendent here just how it came about that you were present there?"

Tweedie shrugged his shoulders. He appeared to be struggling to regain his composure. Pushing back the lock of greying hair that had drifted out of place, his age-mottled hand returned to grip the arm of his chair with such force that the colour drained from his fingers.

"Why the hell shouldn't I be there?" He was on the defensive now, arms crossing over his chest as if to hold the world at bay. "I'll likely never see the place agin. I'd heard all about the skull – that were reason enough. I'd not long got to the auld farm when I saw the police gathered round the body. I knew it were Jowett as soon as I spotted him lying there."

"You were also there the previous day – when you spoke to the same reporter?" Morrison shot the question at the old man ignoring his obvious discomfort.

"That's reet. I've been up there quite a bit since Mardale started to appear. That day was the fust time you could make out the outline of the auld bowling green alongside the Dun

Bull Inn. I used to watch my father play there when I were nobbut a lad."

Morrison clearly thought Tweedie was straying from the point. "You're not denying then the fact that you were keen on Margaret Thursby when you were a young man?"

Tweedie looked to be getting enraged once more. "That's my business! I told thee, it's nothin' to do wi' anybody else."

"It is if it's connected in any way with this murder!" Morrison was not in the mood to compromise.

Neither it seemed was Tweedie. "You can get stuffed! If you think I've got anythin' to do wi' it you'd better arrest me."

Morrison's face was a sight to behold. "If you persist in obstructing the course of justice I may just do that!"

"Please yoursel'." Tweedie held out his hands as though signifying he wished to be cuffed. Grey did his best not to smile. The old gent was tempting providence.

"Don't push your luck!" Morrison appeared almost lost for words. "Right! Can anyone verify what time you left to go to Mardale on the morning Herbert Jowett was murdered?"

"I live here on my own." Tweedie was certainly not very communicative.

"So I understand, but did you not see any of your neighbours? Or speak to one of them?"

The old man scratched his head, looking thoughtful. "Can't say I did. You can ask em' yersel' if you don't believe me. I told you, when I got to Mardale, Jowett were lyin' dead in the mud. Not long after that the police put screens around the body." He looked across at Grey. "You were in charge I reckon. A constable came an' spoke to the folk gathered there and took names an' addresses. I gave him mine, same as all the others. You can check on that – I watched him write it down. I told him same as I've told you; I didn't see anything!"

Grey glanced across at the superintendent. Did he get the same impression that the man might be holding something back? Tweedie may have passed on his address at the time, but he'd definitely not indicated when questioned that he knew Jowett. Had that been the case, the constable would have informed Grey immediately. Nor had Tweedie mentioned that he was a past resident of Mardale. That too would have been reported and Tweedie would have been questioned more thoroughly. Was it merely that he wished to avoid courting publicity? Or was he deliberately being evasive? Morrison certainly didn't appear to be wholly convinced by his answers.

"Did you visit the memorial stone at the foot of Harter Fell? The boulder where you carved out a message commemorating the death of Margaret Thursby."

Tweedie's worn face took on a look of utter desolation. Almost as suddenly it was replaced by a look of total defiance. He glared at his inquisitor. "I've said all I'm saying. You can do what you bloody well like. Why the hell can't you leave me to grieve in peace? I don't want hordes o' folk trampin' all round that spot. It's not meant to be a site fer bloody picnickers an' the like. That's our special place – mine and Margaret's. If you start on about it, it'll never be the same agin."

Morrison was by now convinced that he would get nothing more out of the man. He was utterly determined to stand his ground and was clearly extremely distressed. The reason for his concern could well be as he stated – or it could be that he feared for himself. It must have come as a great shock to him to realise how much was known about his past life. Grey had done well to gather so much valuable information. Unfortunate that the press had managed to get hold of it too. That meant the man would have had time to prepare his defence before the interview. Never mind. Jack Tweedie could stew for a while. If he were involved, he should now be aware that he was far from being in the clear.

"Right. We'll be continuing with our investigation, Mr Tweedie, but consider what's been said. If you decide you want to get anything off your chest, contact me at the Penrith station." Morrison rose from his chair, handing out the proverbial olive branch. "By the way, let me know if those reporters get too much out of hand. About the best we can do is threaten to charge 'em with obstructing the highway."

Tweedie made no reply. Following them to the door, he slammed it shut behind them. Morrison winked at the inspector. "I'm sure that old bugger knows more about this than he's letting on. One thing's for certain though – that Jowett character certainly had a talent for making enemies."

A quick check around the neighbours produced no tangible results. No one had noticed Tweedie leaving on the morning in question, or, if they had, they were keeping it to themselves. Most of them seemed to genuinely like the old man, expressing concern about the distressing effect the media might be having on him. Certainly, no one thought him capable of committing such a crime.

Morrison led the way back to the car. "Well, another one without a satisfactory alibi. At least he didn't attempt to unload the blame on to anyone else. That could be a point in his favour – or he could just be a damn sight more shrewd than he'd have us believe."

Up to this point the superintendent had ignored any suggestion that he might take out a search warrant on the McKade residence. Grey wondered if Morrison were deliberately ignoring his advice in order to show who was in charge. So be it. If the McKades did happen to have the skull secreted away, the chances were that it would not be at their smallholding. And surely they would bide their time a little while longer before attempting to dispose of it. They were hardly likely to risk drawing attention to themselves at this stage. As they were next in line for a call anyway, there was little likelihood of them getting the idea they were off the hook. And guilty parties rarely managed to hide their secrets for long without coming to grief.

It was just a short journey to the McKades' tiny farm. As in the case of Tweedie, this too was the scene of media attention. Grey noted that it was the pressmen he had encountered at Mardale who were encamped there. The same bastards who had spread the story of the theft of the skull. Neither he nor Morrison responded to their urgent demands for an explanation as to how it went missing.

Striding up to the door, the superintendent thumped loudly upon it with the knocker. The older man eventually appeared – after first checking them out from the window. He stood well back from the entrance as he let them in.

"Bloody nuisances!" he yelled out at the pressmen who were attempting to snatch photographs. "Sod off!"

The door was slammed shut. He now turned his attention to the officers.

"See what you lot have done. They sods out there are gaan to drive us mad. Why don't you clear 'em off? We've nowt to do wi' Jowett's death."

Morrison ignored the expected tirade, speaking firmly and with no suggestion that he would brook any nonsense. "Is your son here? I want to speak to you both."

Angus McKade could recognise the voice of authority. "I'll fetch him. He's out the back." He made his way sluggishly through the kitchen door.

Morrison swept the room with his eyes. It was a dingy place, needing the touch of a woman. He recalled Grey informing him that Rory McKade's wife and child were away. Was that merely a coincidence? Maybe. Maybe not.

There was no sign of affluence here. What a difference it might have made if the ancestors of these people had retained possession of the land at Mardale. Their bitterness was easy to appreciate. Uprooted, without any further hope of their complaints being considered, they must have been doubly disenchanted by their treatment. No wonder they had snatched at the chance to lay claim to the skull. Apart from the desire to reunite it with the rest of the remains, the prospect of instilling the terror of the curse in the mind of Herbert Jowett must have appealed to them greatly. The question was, had they taken any part in bringing about the fulfilment of that curse?

Angus McKade was now returning with his son. Morrison introduced himself to the younger man, persuading them both to sit before attempting to cross-examine them. He had decided on an indirect approach, giving them the chance to make a clean breast of it if their involvement were merely restricted to stealing the skull. Fixing them with a coolly appraising stare, he got down to business.

"You'll be in no doubts as to why we're here. Firstly, I'd like to ask you once more if you took any part in removing the Mardale skull from the precincts of the Penrith police station?" He held up a hand to silence any immediate reply. "Think before you speak! I'm prepared to overlook that theft – even if you are guilty. My only concern at the moment is to seek out the killer of Herbert Jowett."

Rory McKade showed no hesitation. "I've already informed the inspector here; it were nowt to do wi' us."

"Very well." They had had their chance. "Then let's consider the facts. By your own admission, you were determined to get hold of that skull. It's also clear that you had good reason to hate Herbert Jowett. And as there appear to be no others, apart from the Jowett family and yourselves, who might conceivably wish to acquire the skull, that leads me to the conclusion that Herbert Jowett stole the skull and that one, or both of you, had decided to lay in wait for him – knowing full well how determined he was to replace it at the farm. I suggest you then struck the blow to his head, regardless of the consequences, and made off with your trophy. It might be best if you admit to that and plead that your intention was only to disable the man while you made your getaway."

The look on both the men's faces had turned from defiance to consternation.

"Hold on!" Rory McKade had jumped to his feet. "You can't pin this on us just because we wanted the skull!"

Morrison remained unmoved. "There was no sign of the skull alongside the body."

“Maybe.” Angus McKade’s tired, lined face was showing the strain as he attempted to offer a plausible explanation. “Jowett must have buried it afore he were killed. Like Rory said, we aint got it. What’s wrong wi’ you lot gaan an’ diggin’ around fer it?”

Morrison pointed out of the window at the darkening sky, with rain beginning to pelt down once more. “In case you haven’t realised it, it would be impossible now. The farm, and almost all the rest of the remains of Mardale, are now under about a foot of water. We’ve had to withdraw our men from there already.”

Almost a glimmer of a smile crossed the old man’s face. “Well, at least they bloody reporters out there are gaan tae get a soakin’.”

Grey smiled at the prospect too, watching as the newsmen turned their backs into the driving rain. Serve the miserable sods right. They wouldn’t last long in this weather. It looked to be settling in quite nicely. What better way to dispel them?

Morrison ignored the old man’s remark. “If we accept that Jowett buried the skull before he was murdered, that still doesn’t let you pair off the hook.”

Angus McKade shook his head. “Narry a soul seems tae be takin’ any notice o’ the curse on the Jowetts. Who’s tae say whoever did him in wasn’t driven tae it? What if it were done wi’out their intention? There’s good reason tae heed the legend’s foreboding. It were reet on the last occasion.”

“Let’s not get into the realms of fantasy!” Morrison was not falling for that line. “Are you trying to tell me that one of you did it, but you had no control over your actions?”

“Like hell we are!” Rory McKade angrily refuted the suggestion. “If you reckon you’ve any evidence against us, you’d best come out wi’ it.”

“You still deny any knowledge of the skull’s whereabouts?” Morrison disregarded McKade’s outburst.

“How many times do you need tellin’? Me an’ fadder have got nowt tae do wi’ it. We’ve not seen the soddin’ skull an' we've not killed Jowett." Rory McKade stood there, fists clenched, indignation written across his weathered face.

There seemed little point in pursuing the questioning. Evidence was clearly lacking and without it any arrest was out of the question. Morrison heaved his bulky frame from the worn armchair. "If that's all you have to say in your defence we'll leave it there for the time being. If you can find any witnesses in the meantime, who can verify that you couldn't have been at Mardale when Jowett met his death, so much the better for you. You may yet need them."

He left them to chew over his words, heading for the door with the inspector in attendance. Once outside, he stood for a moment considering the layout of the area. The smallholding nestled in a fold of the land in an area sparsely tenanted. Chickens scratched for insects in a small copse to the right-hand side of the house, the group of trees effectively shielding from view the rickety lean-to where a scruffy pick-up truck was parked. Cowsheds and outbuildings were scattered indiscriminately around the fields.

"You say you've checked that pair out, Grey? The neighbours have been questioned?"

"Anyone who has sight of the place. As you can see, there are few who might."

"So no luck there?"

"No one who could account for the McKades' movements on the morning Jowett died. Unless someone had happened to glance out just as they drove away, or arrived back, there wouldn't have been much chance of a sighting."

"Not much bloody help then!"

Ignoring the pressmen, Morrison strode briskly to the car. He was not one to court publicity at the best of times and this was certainly not an occasion that called for a change of policy.

"Damn reporters!" He brushed the raindrops from his dour face with the back of a brawny hand. "The scourge of the profession, Grey. We can't make a move without the bleeders sticking their noses in."

“True.” Grey was gratified to see the luckless pair scuttle off to their own vehicle. “At least they looked to be giving up here for the time being. Probably realised they’re not going to see anymore action today.”

His words were borne out as the men sped off.

Morrison allowed himself a rare chuckle. “Let’s hope the rest of ‘em follow suit. This weather should soon drive the miserable sods into the nearest pub. Best bloody place for ‘em too, as far as I’m concerned!”

CHAPTER NINETEEN

The rain persisted. Merlin Reid gazed from his study window at the sodden garden below and the almost totally obscured mountains which lay shrouded beneath the now somewhat unfamiliar capping of dark grey cloud. Not the kind of day to be venturing abroad. The drought had certainly ended with a vengeance. He and Joy had been fortunate to have concluded their work at Mardale before the rains came. The sample of sediment they had obtained should prove invaluable in the coming months, when normality and order would hopefully be restored to their lives. Yet there was no way he could concentrate on the task of organising the impending trials. The murder of Herbert Jowett refused to leave the forefront of his mind.

Giving up on the project, he made his way to Joy's room. She would have long since finished her breakfast and it was extremely unlikely that she was faring any better with settling down to her studying. She might welcome the chance to discuss anything that was on her mind.

"Come in, Prof." She managed a smile as she answered the door, though it was apparent that the air of despondency he had noticed earlier had not left her. Grabbing up the scattered news sheets she had been scrutinising, she made space for him to sit. "I was wondering if you'd pop in."

He made himself comfortable, attempting to assess whether her demeanour was entirely due to the blame she might be attaching to herself over the death of Herbert Jowett. He could only conclude that that was the case.

"I feel sorry for Mr Tweedie." She blurted out the words as though it were all her fault. "Why did they have to bring him into this? Hasn't he suffered enough in the past? The poor man must be hating all this publicity."

"I guess so." Reid could imagine the man's consternation. "No doubt a lot of people are going to suffer the attention of the media before this case comes to a conclusion. Of course, there's still no telling who might actually be responsible for the killing."

She shook her head, looking even more downcast. "I wish we'd never found that skull. This is turning into a nightmare!"

"Buck up, Joy." He reached over to take her hands into his own. "There's no way we could ever have expected things to turn out like this. I realise we can't ignore the facts, but we can't turn the clock back either. I still feel the only way we can deal with this problem is to provide Inspector Grey with any information we can come up with."

"You're right." She put on her brave face once more. "We've learned quite a lot in the last few days, haven't we? I'm sure we must have helped already, don't you think?"

"I certainly do." He grinned reassuringly across at her. "Grey's a nice bloke, but he's still a policeman. He's not exactly in a position to adopt the same approach that we have. I can't imagine old Joss confiding in him in the same way, even if he were to be asked. People are wary about saying the wrong thing. They're always going to be a bit on their guard when dealing with the authorities, especially if it means letting down any of their friends."

She nodded in agreement. "I suppose that's true. The police can't have an easy task getting information from anyone who's afraid to speak out, can they? And even if someone did have an idea of who might have committed a crime, it's not to say they'd let on about it. Certainly not if it didn't particularly concern them."

"Just so. And how many people are likely to be concerned by the death of Herbert Jowett? I can think of no one who seems remotely distressed – with the possible exception of yourself."

She appeared almost shocked by his words. "Yes, I suppose that's true. And would I be so bothered if it wasn't me who had been responsible for discovering that wretched skull? The problem is it was me. However much that man may have deserved his fate, I still feel he wouldn't be dead but for me. That's not a very nice thing to have on your conscience." She looked up, her melancholy face a picture of despair. "The only thing that might help is if we could actually play a part in bringing his murderer to justice."

Reid already had that in mind. "Well, it may be a possibility. I've given what I thought were the most relevant details to Grey, but there could be something we've missed."

Her interest was certainly rekindled. "Can we go over again exactly what we do know? It's a horrible day out there and, if you feel you could spare the time, I'd much rather do that than try to study."

He needed little persuading. "Right. What are we absolutely sure of? Let's try to stick to the facts. I think that, however much we might doubt the substance of the legend regarding the skull, we both agree that everything that we've seen and heard so far bears out the fact that most of the past residents of Mardale have complete faith in the tale."

"Agreed." She had no qualms about accepting that.

"And that the McKades and Jowetts were the only people who really might be expected to go to extreme lengths to get their hands on that skull, for whatever reasons each family might have."

Again she saw no reason to argue.

"In that case, some member, or members, of either family must have been responsible for stealing the skull from the Penrith police station."

"I can't see who else."

"And the most logical conclusion has to be that it was Herbert Jowett who carried out the theft. I know that isn't an established fact, but it could go a long way towards explaining his death. It's obvious that we can't rule out an attack on him by the McKades. If they had allowed the injustices of the past to fester in their minds, they may have decided this was their last chance to get even. It would certainly appear to have been the last chance they would ever have of retrieving the skull."

"What are the options?" She could sense that he was not prepared to accept anything at face value. As with his approach to every experiment they undertook, nothing was accepted until it was proven beyond doubt.

"There is the possibility that Jowett was murdered by a member of his own family. I know that sounds pretty awful, but Grey let slip that Jowett's sister and her children would come into a great deal of money now that he's gone."

"And what about Jack Tweedie?"

"Yes, he can't be discounted." Reid gazed across at her troubled face. "He certainly seemed convinced that Herbert Jowett or his father contributed in some way towards Margaret Thursby's death. That is, if we're to believe all that Joss Pattinson told us."

"Then there's that strange note with the flowers at the boulder."

He had not forgotten. 'God's will be done.' "You can interpret that in a few different ways."

She looked to be mulling over a problem.

"Something on your mind?" He knew he need hardly ask.

"Well, I know we were supposed to be sticking to the facts, but when you said, 'If we're to believe all that Joss Pattinson told us', I just wondered about his ghost story. You remember the part about the Grey Lady wandering from the direction of Harter Fell with a baby in her arms?"

He could barely hide the trace of a smile that momentarily flickered across his lips.

Joy flushed a little. "I know it sounds silly – especially as there was no mention of Margaret Thursby ever having a child – but what if she were pregnant when she died? I've never believed in ghosts, but what if someone made up that story because they knew something? Or thought they knew something? If Margaret Thursby had been pregnant, in those days it could well have seemed a good enough reason for her to take her own life. She was the parson's daughter. The shame of it could have turned her mind."

Reid felt a mite embarrassed at being amused by Joy's initial words. "Sorry if I misunderstood your reasoning. As you say, it's not a known fact, but it is a hell of a good theory."

She perked up at the compliment. "You really believe it could be a possibility?"

"Certainly. There may have been some kind of conspiracy to keep it quiet if it were true. That's assuming anyone other than the girl herself actually knew about it. Whatever the circumstances, in a tiny community such as that, rumours might soon start flying around. Anyone with an axe to grind could have decided to invent the ghost to put the fear of God into the man they thought responsible."

Joy's face had a determined look. "We owe it to that poor girl to lay the ghost… sorry – that wasn't intended to be a pun." She grimaced at her own words. "I mean to discover what really happened. I've wondered from the start how anyone could possibly be driven to take their own life. I suppose there isn't any likelihood that it wasn't suicide?"

"You mean someone may have killed the girl, then made it appear to be her own doing?" He had to admit that the thought had never crossed his mind.

"Remember what Joss said? The Jowetts were all big men. 'A yard across the shoulders' were the words he used. Could Herbert or his father have decided to get rid of her? If one of them had struck her a blow that either knocked her out, or proved to be fatal, she might have been carried to the top of the fell and thrown to her death. It would be one way to avoid the consequences of their actions."

He considered her words. A case could be made out for either of those premises. Jack Tweedie seemed convinced that the Jowetts were responsible for Margaret's death. If one of them had also been responsible for getting her pregnant, then the motive was certainly established. Proving that point, however, would be an almost impossible task. Herbert Jowett would be taking any knowledge he had of the event to the grave, as had Margaret Thursby

"There's not, of course, any evidence to prove Margaret Thursby was pregnant, or that either of the Jowetts were liable if that happened to be the case."

"I realise that." She struggled to establish why the thought had first crossed her mind. Women's intuition? Maybe. Whatever it was, she was convinced she could be on the right track.

"Anyway, back to the facts." Reid was always the realist. "There's still no explanation as to what's happened to the skull. Assuming Herbert Jowett did steal it, then what occurred when he went to replace it at the farm? We know he was murdered, but was that before he attempted to bury it there or after the task was completed? If it were before, then someone could have grabbed the skull and made off with it."

"Or, if it happened to be one of the man's own relatives, the person responsible would still bury the skull in order to fend off the curse."

"Precisely, Joy! Only if they panicked after killing the man or realised they might get caught if they hung around too long, would they take it away with them?"

"And what if Jowett did bury it before he was killed?"

"It wouldn't make much difference, would it, Joy? If someone was watching and waited until he had completed his task before attacking him, they could have unearthed the skull again afterwards, or alternatively left it in position if it were one of the family."

"And what if it were neither a relative nor one of the McKades?"

"In that case I'd assume the person concerned wouldn't be in the least interested in what happened to the skull. The only intention would have been to attack Jowett when he was off guard."

"That hardly rules anyone out then, does it?" Joy looked terribly disappointed that they had failed to come up with anything concrete. "We've no idea where the skull is, whether it may ever be seen again, or who might be responsible. The police aren't going to find this very easy, are they, Prof?"

He had arrived at the same conclusion. "I don't think so. They obviously realise they've got several potential killers out there, but with Mardale back under the water, where do you search for clues? Unless they can come up with any definite evidence, their only chance would appear to be to try to eliminate some of the suspects from their enquiries. If any of them have a watertight alibi it may narrow down the quest a little. If not, it may mean they have to wait for someone to crack."

"So all we can do is wait too?"

"For the moment." He cast his mind back once more to the conversation they had had with Joss. "There's no doubt Herbert Jowett made a lot of enemies. Who can say which one of them finally decided to take their revenge? There might be someone out there that we don't even know about."

"Is there any point in mentioning anything to Inspector Grey about what we've discussed?"

"Not at the moment, Joy. We've no idea how well they're getting on with their investigation and we've nothing definite to pass on at this stage. Grey's a shrewd operator. If he's allowed to have his head he could easily have come up with almost the same kind of ideas that we've put together."

"He's hardly likely to know much about Margaret Thursby though."

The professor acknowledged the fact. "True, but unless the superintendent is totally running the show, Grey could be pursuing some of these lines of inquiry right now."

She looked a mite disappointed. "It's a pity we don't know exactly how much they have discovered. It might have helped us to work out what's going on."

"You could be right." He toyed with the idea of ringing Grey in an attempt to pump him for any such information.

Unfortunately, he could come up with no legitimate excuse to do so.

* * *

Superintendent Morrison and Inspector Grey had made their way to Ellen Braithwaite's home. Morrison wanted to hear for himself what the woman had to say. Mrs Braithwaite had asked them inside and now sat opposite them. Introductions over, it was Ellen who spoke first.

"So, you've lost the skull." The accusation was directed at Grey. "You never told me that yesterday when you came. I thought we might still have a chance of gettin' it back."

"I regarded it as fairly irrelevant." Grey had been expecting some such comment from the woman. "I would have thought the death of your brother would have been of much more significance to you."

"Aye, I expect you would." She glanced defiantly at both of them. "Well, you must know who's got it. There's only the McKades who'd have killed Herbert tae get hold of it. That's if they didn't steal it themsel's from the station. Whichever it were, we still want it back. Herbert's dead, an' it's all because o' the curse."

Morrison had not come to listen to the woman's complaints. "What concerns me at the moment is finding your brother's murderer. You may be correct in your assumption that the McKades hated Herbert Jowett, and that they had every intention of laying their hands on the skull if that were humanly possible. That doesn't, in itself, prove them guilty of the crime. As you've admitted to the inspector here, your family may well have had a much better motive for disposing of Herbert Jowett. Since you'll be the automatic beneficiaries under his will, you consequently come under as much suspicion as the McKades. Not one of you appears to have the slightest concern for the dead man."

“Why should we have?” Ellen appeared apprehensive, yet not cowed. “My brother never treated us right. You can’t expect tears shed over him.”

Morrison changed tack. “Have you, or your son, been over to Mardale in the last few days?”

She seemed to be considering his words before replying. “We went last Sunday. We both wondered what the place might look like after all these years. The water were still up around the auld house at that time, so we couldn’t get really close. I could see most o’ the walls had collapsed though. It went through my mind about the skull, but I never knew exactly where it had been walled up in the house anyway. Tell the truth, I never even knew fer sure if it were ever there at all. It were only after it were found that I were certain the legend must be true.”

Morrison was disappointed. If Mrs Braithwaite or her son had denied visiting Mardale it might have been possible that their presence there could have been established by an inspection of their footwear. Any sediment from the bottom of the lake adhering to their shoes, or their clothing, would probably have been easily identified. Such a test now, even if positive, would hardly be sufficient to incriminate them.

“There are other questions I need to ask.”

She nodded. “Please yourself, but you’re wastin’ your bloody time. Do you really think I’d murder my ain brother?”

“It has been known.” Morrison had seen plenty of cases where considerably less provocation had resulted in a similar outcome. “Now, you told Inspector Grey here that on the morning of the crime you came down to find your brother and your car missing?”

“That’s reet.”

“And how did you then spend your morning?”

“It were my usual wash day. I collected together the sheets an’ pillow cases an’ changed the bed. Then I sorted out the other dirty things an’ got ‘em in the washer. While I waited fer it tae get done I did my cleanin’.”

Morrison mentally noted the reference to washing. The woman could well have laundered any soiled or blood-stained clothing at the same time. "You didn't go out at all?"

"No, I was in all morning."

"Anyone who can confirm that?"

"Well, I were here when the inspector came and told me o' Herbert's death."

"You saw no one else before that?"

"Not as I recall."

Another one who appeared to be without an adequate alibi. Morrison was beginning to realise the difficulties ahead. "How about your neighbours? Did you not speak to any of them?"

Ellen smiled. "What neighbours? Most o' the houses round here are holiday homes. Locals can't afford 'em. We only see one or two o' the newcomers about on odd weekends."

Grey nodded at the superintendent. "That's the case in a lot of these villages. Once anyone moves away to find work the houses are often snapped up by outsiders."

"Quite so." Morrison rose from his chair. "Right. We'll leave it at that for the moment. Thank you for your cooperation, Mrs Braithwaite. We shall no doubt be in touch again quite soon. Should the skull turn up you will be informed."

Ellen showed them out. She appeared delighted to see the back of them.

"Right. Let's get over to that son of hers." Morrison led the way to the car, heaving his bulky frame into the passenger seat. "One of these buggers must know something about this man's death and for my money there's a fair chance it could be the pair of 'em. They appear too eager to lay the blame on the McKades for my liking."

Grey could find no reason to argue with his superior's assessment. Why were the Braithwaites so keen to point the finger at the McKades to the exclusion of anyone else?

They caught Ralph Braithwaite just as he was about to leave after finishing his lunch. He looked none too pleased to see them. Like his mother, once they had got over the formal introductions, his first words concerned the missing item. "How come you never mentioned the skull had been stolen?"

Grey was not pleased to be constantly quizzed about the episode. He was more used to firing the questions. "Let's just say I was waiting to see if you had anything to say about the matter."

That seemed to take the wind out of his sails.

"What the hell d'you mean?"

"I mean that we have no idea, as yet, who stole the skull. It may have been your uncle acting on his own. On the other hand, he could have had an accomplice."

Ralph shook his head. "If you think I had owt tae do wi' it, you can think agin. I never even saw him. All I knew was that you'd found him dead. If he hadn't got the skull wi' him, you can bet your boots the McKades saw him off tae get their hands on it."

Once more the McKades were being cited as the villains. Morrison was becoming more suspicious by the minute. "How do we know you took no part in it? Can you show any proof that you couldn't have been present when the skull was stolen or when the murder was committed?"

The man swallowed hard, shaking his head. "I told Inspector Grey there were no one I knew of as could swear tae where I was. It's no fault o' mine if I work on my ain."

"Right, then explain to me how you spent the morning of your uncle's death."

"It's like I said afore…" Ralph appeared annoyed at having to repeat himself. "…I do odd jobs tae make a livin'. At the moment I'm rebuildin' some o' the dry stone walls hereabouts. Folk give me a call if they're wantin' a job done, an' once I've priced it up I just get on wi' it. You've only tae look around you in this area if you need proof o' why I can't find anybody to prove where I were. Once I'm out in the country there's few folk about. Maybe the odd walker, or one o' the farmhands. If you don't believe me there's bugger all I can do about it."

Morrison was not very impressed. Were there none of these characters who could come up with a credible defence? Was it just coincidence? Or was there some form of conspiracy? "You were at home when Inspector Grey called that day?"

"Aye, I'd not long gotten in. A storm had broken an' I'd not gaan out prepared fer that kind o' weather. I'd no watterproofs wi' me an' got soaked. I don't mind the rain if I'm dressed fer it, but it were not the day tae be out in shirtsleeves."

Morrison nodded. "Perhaps not. Still, a good day to wash away any evidence of contact with a murder victim."

Ralph Braithwaite looked scornful. "That's your hard luck. Maybe you should try puttin' that suggestion tae the McKades."

Morrison had his doubts. There were too many accusations flying around for his liking. He was in no way convinced of the Braithwaites' innocence of either the murder or knowledge of the skull's whereabouts. It was not unusual for guilty parties to attempt to lay the blame elsewhere. Clearly there was a festering hatred between the two warring families. He decided to terminate the interview. He and Grey would return to the station and commence with the proceedings to take out a search warrant on the McKades' smallholding. It may, or may not, prove whether the Braithwaites were justified in their suspicions.

* * *

It had been a bad day for Ellen Braithwaite. She now sat sobbing in the back parlour at her home. Everything was going wrong. The police had obviously not believed her protestations of innocence and looked set to become a pain in the arse. She was certain that by now they would have arrested the McKades. Surely they must suspect them of her brother's murder. Hadn't she and Ralph given them enough evidence to convince them of the McKades' hatred of the Jowetts? She had hoped that by volunteering the information that she would inherit Herbert's estate she might have been left out of the investigation. Should she have kept the news to herself? Maybe it would have been wiser, yet to hide the fact would probably have made matters even worse in the long run.

Ralph hadn't looked too pleased that she had drawn attention to the family when she told him what she had done. But then, Ralph always believed he could handle things so much better. He never had any doubts that he knew best. But did he? Jean had just been on the phone. Ralph had broken it to her that he was to control the money she was to receive. She was devastated. She could not believe that her own mother would put her in such a position.

"How could you agree to such a thing, Ma?" she had wept. "Cedric will go mad! You can't let Ralph do this to me!"

Ellen had tried to explain that her son only had Jean's interests at heart, but her daughter was distraught.

"It's none of his bloody business! You told me I was gaan to get my share. What good is it if Ralph's to decide how I can spend it? You promised me, Ma. You've said all my life that I'd come into the money one day."

Ellen had attempted to calm her daughter, assuring her that Ralph was only concerned about Cedric spending the money unwisely. It was not exactly the most diplomatic way she could have phrased it.

"The bloody cheeky sod! What's it to him how we spend it? Cedric was right about Ralph. He said he'd interfere. You've got to ignore him fer once, Ma. I told Ralph I'd never speak to him again if he did this, but he refuses to listen to me. He says I'll thank him in the end, but he's got another think coming. You've got to make him change his mind."

Ellen had sworn to do her best, though she knew that it was hopeless. Ralph would never agree to allowing Cedric Bull the chance of ever laying a finger on the money.

So this was to be the outcome of Herbert's death. They hadn't even come close to discovering what wealth there might be in store, yet here they were arguing amongst themselves about its distribution. Was this the curse still at work? Was all the disunity a direct result of the terrible plague that had been visited on the family? She made her way into the bathroom, washing the tears from her drawn face. Somehow this had to be resolved – and soon.

CHAPTER TWENTY

It was early the following morning when the duty sergeant unexpectedly burst into the office where Morrison and Grey were discussing the implementation of the search warrant.

"Excuse me, Sir!" The sergeant's flustered appearance made it clear that something of the utmost urgency had compelled him to interrupt the proceedings. "There's another body! We've just had a report in that Ralph Braithwaite's been found dead. Just like the last victim, his head's been caved in."

"Christ!" Morrison leapt to his feet. The visit to the McKades' place could wait. "Come on, Grey. Where's the body?" The question was directed at the sergeant.

"Just on the outskirts of Craigend, Sir. Your driver's being given instructions on how to get there now."

"Good work." Morrison hesitated only momentarily. "Get the pathologist informed. At least this time we shouldn't risk having the scene of the crime disappear before we've had a chance to properly examine it."

Grey followed closely behind the superintendent as he hurried to the car.

Morrison grimaced at the inspector as they moved off. "Another victim of the curse, Grey?"

"You can bet that's how the media are going to portray it."

"That's not all they're going to imply if I'm any judge." Morrison sat weighing up the prospects. "The bastards are going to crucify us over this."

"That'll come as no surprise!"

Morrison shook his head. "Perhaps we should have considered the possibility of such an event occurring. I don't give any credence to that bloody curse, but maybe we ought to have calculated the risk. Some lunatic out there might be using this legend to his, or her, advantage."

Grey nodded. "At least it now appears that the person who murdered Herbert Jowett wasn't Ralph Braithwaite. Not unless you accept that he could have had a hand in killing his uncle and someone else then saw it as a good opportunity to see him off too."

"Well, if this keeps up it'll cut down on our list of suspects considerably." Morrison looked troubled in spite of his seemingly flippant attitude. "I think we'd best put some kind of watch on Mrs Braithwaite and her daughter. The last thing we need is for one of them to be struck down too. We'll never hear the end of it if that happens." He instructed the driver to radio through the command. Who could be certain that the remaining members of the Jowett clan would not fall victim to a similar fate?

Having finally left the motorway, the car was soon nosing along a quiet, narrow, winding country lane. Dry stone walls on either side hemmed in the vehicle, making it difficult to proceed at any great speed.

Rounding a corner, Grey spotted Ralph Braithwaite's van pulled into a small passing place. "This must be it."

The constable who stepped out from behind the vehicle, waving them down, appeared to confirm the inspector's words. A patrol car had quickly been diverted to the spot as soon as the news came in.

"Just along here, Sir." The constable led the way once they were out of the car.

Ralph Braithwaite lay in an almost identical posture to that of his uncle when discovered at Mardale – face down, the back of his head stove in. Grey took in the scene as Morrison went forward for a closer inspection. It was self-evident that the man had been working on repairing the wall bordering the road. Part of it was in a collapsed state, with a small section looking to have been recently restored. Grey's mind flashed back to the scene at Mardale. It was an almost uncanny carbon copy of that event.

"The chap who found him is pulled into a gateway a little further along." The constable indicated a tractor a short distance off. "He's a bit shaken. He knew Ralph. Apparently he was the one who'd asked him to come and fix the wall. I said he'd best wait down there till you came."

"You did right." Morrison answered almost absent-mindedly as he continued studying the body. It was clad in waterproofs; the rain, which had eased slightly overnight, now beating a soft rhythm on the impervious material. It was probably one of the last sounds Ralph Braithwaite had heard. That, and perhaps the voice of his killer. It would have probably been difficult for anyone to have crept up on the man unawares. Someone could have engaged him in conversation, waiting until he was off guard before striking the blow. The assailant could have approached on foot, though the odds were that he, or she, had alighted from a vehicle. The solid, rain-washed surface of the roadway unfortunately gave no clue as to the identity of either the vehicle or the person involved.

"Looks as though he was struck as he bent to pick up some of the walling material, Grey."

"I would judge so."

"The rock here appears to be the one that caused the damage." Morrison indicated a solid piece of stone alongside the body. "Precisely the same method as used last time. One assumes that it was just lifted straight off the wall and brought crashing down on the back of the man's head. Simple. Even if the killer had brought along a weapon there'd be no need to use it. Just grab the first thing to hand. Doesn't make our job any easier."

Grey had been thinking along the same lines. No doubt any tests for fingerprints would prove just as inconclusive as on the previous occasion. "At least we know this one was premeditated. There's no way anyone just happened to come across the man. That could have been true in Jowett's case, but this is hardly a spot where people are constantly passing."

Morrison nodded. "As you say, this man was definitely targeted."

The pathologist was just arriving, along with the photographer and the rest of the crew. Morrison had a quick word then left them to get on with it.

"Let's see what the tractor driver's got to say, Grey." He led the way to where the man had pulled off the road.

Scrambling down from his cab, the man still looked shaken. His tanned face appeared drawn, almost pale beneath the bronzed exterior.

"Superintendent Morrison." A large hand was extended towards the farmhand as the introductions took place. "And this is Inspector Grey."

The man nodded. "This is a bloody awful thing to happen. Who the hell could do anything like that?"

"That's what we're here to find out." Morrison indicated they should stand in the lee of the tractor, away from the worst of the driving rain. "You were the first to come across the body?"

"I guess so. There was no sign of anyone else around. There's hardly any traffic uses this road, especially at this time of the morning. It was about twenty to nine when I got here. Ralph was always an early starter." He shivered as he recalled the sight of the dead man. "Poor bugger. He was only trying to do his job. If I'd have got hold of the bastard who did this, he'd have been lying alongside Ralph by now!"

Morrison ignored the understandable headstrong reaction of the man.

"You say this road isn't frequently in use?"

"Only by the likes of me an' a few others. It doesn't lead anywhere in particular. Just access to the fields and the few farms round about."

His words only confirmed Grey's conviction. Ralph Braithwaite had almost certainly been shadowed as he made his way to this place. It was inconceivable that the murderer just stumbled upon the man.

"If the person who committed this crime were driving, would he have to return the way he came?" Morrison broached the question more in hope than in expectation.

"Oh no, there are various turnings off further up the lane." It was clear that the reason for the query had not been missed. "No one's passed me in either direction since I arrived though."

"Did you move the body in any way?"

"Not likely!" The man looked at the superintendent in astonishment. "You've seen the state of him. I know a dead man when I see one. I just got my lad to run back to the farm and ring your lot."

"Just as well." Morrison reached out a steadying hand to grip the man's shoulder as he began to shiver. "Look, I'll send one of the constables down to get a brief statement from you, along with your name and address. We don't want to keep you hanging about here any longer than is necessary."

"Thanks." The relief showed. "What about Ralph's ma?"

"We'll deal with that."

The man looked pleased to be relieved of the onerous task of breaking the dreadful news. Grey was not quite as pleased. He realised he was the logical choice for the unpleasant job.

He and Morrison returned to the scene of the killing. Access to the road had been restricted to police vehicles. The screens were already in place around the body.

The pathologist, who appeared to have finished his inspection of the corpse, came forward as they approached. "Not much to go on here. By the state of him, I guess he died almost instantly. Killed between eight and nine this morning judging by the temperature of the body. The piece of rock there is clearly the implement used in the attack. Either this was done by the same person who murdered the last victim, or it's a copycat killing. You can take your choice."

Morrison had no wish to consider the latter suggestion. One murderer was enough to be going on with. "You found no trace of anything that might give us a clue as to what kind of maniac we're looking for?"

The pathologist gave a thin smile. "Early days yet, Superintendent. There's hardly a sign of any struggle. No visible footprints. The killer had no need to step off the road. As you can see, the verge here is very narrow. It was simply a case of reaching out for one of the rocks capping the wall and slamming it down on the victim's head. There could be traces of blood on the killer's clothing, but that's only a conjecture. First catch your killer, eh?"

"Easier said than done." Morrison moved closer for another look at the scene of the crime.

"Nasty business, Grey." The pathologist sorted through his equipment as the inspector lit up his pipe. "The younger they are, the worse it seems. He looked to be in the prime of his life, unlike the last victim. Wasn't married, was he?"

"No."

"Damn good job. One less to grieve for him."

Grey gave no answer. Puffing away at the shag tobacco, he was still considering how he was going to break the news to Ralph Braithwaite's mother.

The superintendent raised no objection to Grey's suggestion that he and the policewoman who had previously accompanied him to pass on the news of Herbert Jowett's murder should now relay the news of the latest death in the family. God! Grey realised how much he hated this job at times like these. There was no chance the woman was going to accept this as easily as on the last occasion.

"You get off then." Morrison had finished making his notes. "I'll see you back at the station. I'm sure we can leave things here in the pathologist's capable hands for the time being. I'll arrange for a fingertip search around here in case there's the slightest chance of finding anything. Not very bloody likely by the look of things!" He shook his head as he walked away.

* * *

Rory McKade stared moodily out of the window. “When are they bastards gaan tae clear off?” His father shook his head. The *Today’s News* reporters had arrived spot on nine that morning, just as the McKades were about to leave. Now there was no chance of making a move without being followed. “Be patient, lad.” The old man tried to calm his agitated son. “They’ll not last much longer in this weather. It’s nearly 12.30 now. They’ll be off tae the pub soon if I’m any judge. They know bugger all about what we’re about.”

The young man paced the floor, as he’d done most of the morning. “I want this over wi’, da. Now we’ve finally gotten hold o’ the skull, I want it reunited wi’ the auld un’s remains while we’ve got the bleedin’ chance!”

* * *

The blood drained from Ellen Braithwaite’s face as she answered the knock on her door. The sight of Grey and his companion, and the expression on their faces, was sufficient explanation of why they were there. Kate, the police constable, took her arm. “Can we come in?”

Ellen nodded, almost stumbling, as she led them inside.

“Don’t tell me it’s Ralph.”

Kate helped her to a chair.

Grey could not shirk his responsibility. “It is bad news I’m afraid.”

She broke down. “He’s dead?” She knew she didn’t really need to ask. Kate knelt beside her, cradling the sobbing woman in her arms.

“That bloody curse! I thowt it were all over when Herbert were killed.” She broke down again, her body shaking as she wrapped her arms around herself, rocking backwards and forwards. Kate attempted to comfort her but was pushed away.

“Bugger off! It’s all your fault!” She was shouting angrily now, glaring at Grey. “Why didn’t you give us the skull, like we asked? Ralph would have been alive now, but fer you." She shot another venomous glance in his direction. "What about my daughter? Is she gaan tae get slaughtered too?"

Grey shifted uncomfortably. "We've got men looking after you both. One's stationed outside here in a car a little way along the road and one's at your daughter's home. They're both in plain clothes."

"You never looked after Ralph! No one took heed o' the bloody curse! How could you let him die?" Ellen was almost screaming now.

Kate tried to calm her. "Would you like us to take you over to your daughter's home? Or to ring her – or go and speak to her?"

The woman had stopped sobbing now. She struggled to pull herself together. "Take me there." The sobbing quickly began again. Kate was allowed to help her to her feet.

"Can I get your coat?"

"It's by the door."

Kate helped her on with it. "Come on now, we've got the car outside. What about your handbag? Is this it?"

The woman made no reply, rummaging inside for the front door key.

Kate gently took it from her trebling fingers, locking the door behind them. "Here we are." She guided her into the car. "Can you just give the driver directions?"

The journey took just a few minutes. Kate took control again, taking Ellen by the arm to lead her to the door.

The young woman who answered Kate's knock looked totally bewildered. "Ma! What are you doing here?"

Ellen Braithwaite attempted to reply, choking as the words failed to materialise. She fell into her daughter's arms. "It's Ralph!" She finally managed to force out the despairing words.

"Oh, Ma!" Her daughter clung desperately to her.

"Can I come in for a minute?" Kate stood patiently waiting to see if she could offer any further assistance.

Ellen Braithwaite turned on her. "Haven't you lot done enough? I don't want you in here. You're all the bloody same!"

The door was slammed in Kate's face. She stood silently for a moment, then sadly walked away. Try as she might, she could never entirely distance herself from the suffering of the bereaved relatives she all too often came into contact with.

* * *

On his return to the station, Grey had gone immediately to the superintendent's office. It was a new ball game now. Herbert Jowett's death had thrown up a variety of suspects – Ralph Braithwaite clearly being one of them. Now he had joined his uncle as the latest victim. Did this rule out the rest of the Braithwaite family as suspects? From the reaction of his mother and sister, Grey could only assume that it did. Money was perhaps not the motive in this case after all.

Morrison listened to Grey's assessment of the family without interruption. Now he sat back, thoughtfully chewing the blunt end of a ball-point pen. Finally he spoke. "If we accept that the Braithwaite family are in the clear, we have to consider what motive the other suspects might have for murdering Ralph Braithwaite."

Grey could see the snags. "It does rather mess up our line of thinking. If the McKades had sufficient hated of Herbert Jowett to kill him to gain possession of the skull, why then attack Ralph Braithwaite? It would only make sense if they were attempting to divert suspicion from themselves of being the original killers. Surely there'd be nothing more to gain?"

"Not unless they thought Jowett had the skull with him when they attacked him, but discovered they'd made a mistake." Morrison had clearly been considering all the options. "What if they realised Ralph Braithwaite could have the skull instead? They may have come to the conclusion that they'd slipped up. Maybe they realised that they'd killed the wrong man. Braithwaite could have stolen the skull, intending to meet his uncle at the farm so the pair of them could bury it there together."

Grey could see the sense in that. "If that were the case, Braithwaite may even have witnessed what occurred at the farm. He may have welcomed seeing his uncle murdered. It would mean his mother would come into the money without any effort on their part."

"Exactly. He could have cleared off before the McKades even realised he was there. If so, he'd have had no chance to bury the skull at the farm and could still be hanging on to it. After all, he'd have had difficulty getting it back to Mardale once we'd put in an appearance there."

Grey considered the suggestion. "It certainly might account for why Braithwaite failed to come up with any alibi to cover his movements at the time of his uncle's death. And the McKades could, I suppose, have decided to keep an eye on him. They may even have seen him put the skull into his van when he left home."

Morrison appeared to agree. "If they had killed once in an attempt to lay their hands on it, a second murder might not be out of the question. Especially if they had any inkling that he could have witnessed the killing."

Grey could imagine the consequences. "Braithwaite may have kept quiet about it if it suited his purpose, but what if he broke under questioning? The McKades might realise he could then admit to us that he'd stolen the skull and that he was aware of their part in the murder?"

Morrison saw how the inspector's mind was working. "Whatever conclusion the McKades drew about that, killing him could have solved both their problems. He'd be out of the way and they might end up with their trophy."

"Precisely! I imagine forensics are working on the van in the hope that something might turn up?"

"They're dusting for prints." Morrison picked up the report that had arrived shortly before Grey returned. "The McKades certainly fit the bill. Braithwaite's wallet was still in his coat pocket – £25 and a credit card inside. Again the theft of money wasn't the motive behind the murder. And if it were the McKades, they were pretty smart. They must have taken the van keys from his body to enable them to get hold of the skull, then locked the van again afterwards and pushed the keys back into his pocket. They'd certainly want to make sure it appeared as if nothing had been disturbed."

"All surmise, of course." Grey realised there was no evidence of any kind, at that point, to substantiate the theory. But neither was there any evidence of anyone more likely to have committed the murder. "Jack Tweedie certainly doesn't look much like a candidate now."

"You're right." Morrison could think of no possible reason for the man to murder Braithwaite. "Unless you put forward the same argument that he'd do a copycat killing just to throw us off the scent, he stands to gain nothing. I'm sure we can rule him out. Funny thing is though, I could have sworn he knew something about Jowett's death. There was something about his manner that had me puzzled."

Grey's fingers itched to light up his pipe. Like Morrison still chewing on his Biro, Grey's brain functioned better once he had something clenched between his teeth. "What about this search warrant on the McKade place?"

"I've been making arrangements to get the men together while you were out." Morrison grabbed his jacket. "They should be here by now. These bloody cutbacks are a nightmare. By the time we get the reinforcements we need, half the bloody criminals have already flown the coop."

"Have the press been notified of this latest death?" Grey posed the question as he followed Morrison out.

"Not yet. I thought we might just delay it until we've had a crack at these buggers. You never know your luck; we might be able to announce that we've got the killers at the same time."

The superintendent, Grey, and the police contingent, arrived shortly after the reporters had left the smallholding. Soon enough though. The McKades were just about to climb aboard their dilapidated wagon.

"Christ!" Rory McKade made a grab for the shoe box that his father was carrying as Morrison and Grey alighted from the police vehicle. His attempt to hide the object was unsuccessful. The skull of Duncan of Crieff spun to the ground as box and top parted company.

"Well, well! What have we here?" Morrison strode across in triumph, retrieving the fallen object. "Recognise this, Grey?"

Grey certainly did. "That's it, Sir. Look at the staining it received during its submersion."

"Right. Book 'em!" Morrison grinned with delight at the sheer luck of the encounter. "Being in possession of stolen goods should do for the moment."

"Hold on!" Rory McKade backed up against the lorry as Grey indicated to a couple of the constables that the men should be taken away. "Can't we talk about this? We've done nothing wrong. The skull were left on our doorstep this morning."

Morrison looked scathingly at the man. "Really? And I suppose you were just about to bring it to the station?"

Rory McKade shook his head. "You know better than that. You know what we were gaan tae do wi' it. It rightly belongs tae us anyway."

"We'll decide that!" The superintendent was not pussyfooting around any longer. "We'll also decide how you came by it. Now get into the car or you'll also face a charge of resisting arrest."

The man still made no attempt to move. "Look. Can't you just take me in? Da's an auld man. He's never done owt wrong. I can sort all this out if only you'll let me."

Morrison was beginning to lose his cool. "You're both involved in this. I don't know if you're just trying to pull a fast one, but you're in real trouble this time!"

Rory McKade could see there was no use arguing. "What about the animals? Someone has tae see tae 'em."

"We'll sort that out at the station." Morrison took hold of the man's arm. "Now, move!"

There was no disputing the command. Both men meekly made their way to the cars.

Morrison sent them off before returning to Grey. He had deliberately avoided making any reference to the discovery of Ralph Braithwaite's body when dealing with the McKades. There was plenty of time for that. If they were guilty of that crime – and Morrison now had little doubt that they were guilty of at least one murder – a little patience might payoff. One of them should crack under interrogation.

"What a stroke of luck, Grey." The superintendent was delighting in his moment of victory, his ruddy face beaming with pleasure. "I was beginning to think we'd never see that blasted skull ever again. The buggers won't get out of this with that bloody cock an' bull story. Get some of the men to collect up their clothing or anything that looks at all suspicious; you know the procedure. I'll get back to the station. Those crafty sods aren't going to get the chance to get their heads together."

Grey set about the task. He would follow as soon as possible. Nice change to clear up a case so speedily. Morrison would be in his element. Plenty of Brownie points to be earned. No wonder he was grinning like a Cheshire cat as he departed the scene.

As Grey finally made his way back to the station, he speculated as to why the McKades had taken so long to set off with the skull – if they were to be believed about its appearance on their doorstep. Clearly it must have come into their possession early that morning, again if their story were to be believed. That they intended to bury it along with the rest of the remains was hardly in dispute. A heavy garden fork and spade were loaded in the back of their vehicle. The only logical conclusion seemed to be that if they had attacked Ralph Braithwaite, acquiring the skull in that way, then they must have returned to the smallholding to pick up the implements. At that point they must surely have been disturbed. Why else would they still have been hanging around? The newsmen who were constantly prowling around the area could well provide the answer. There had been no sign of any of them as Grey and the superintendent drew up at the smallholding, though it was conceivable that they had put in their usual appearance. At least it would make a pleasant change if the media had played a helpful role for once.

* * *

Joss Pattinson had smiled wryly as the sodden *Today's News* reporters entered the bar at the Kings Arms. As Inspector Grey had correctly surmised, they were indeed the men who had prevented the McKades from disposing of the skull. And they were not the only media men sheltering from the elements. Shap had become something of a Mecca since the murder of Herbert Jowett.

Joss winked at the landlord. He was enjoying this. So far the newsmen had not discovered his connection with Mardale and the landlord had agreed not to disclose it. Joss was not intending to court the attention of any of them. He was well aware of the distress being caused to Jack Tweedie, the McKades and the Braithwaites. Luckily, most of the other residents of Shap were also canny enough to ignore the pleas of the television and press crews for information. It was a close-knit community who took care of its own.

"Not much action today." Tony Hoskis had seated himself along with Ray Jacobs at a table near Joss, distancing themselves from the other reporters gathered at the rear of the room.

"Bit of a washout really." Jacobs lifted his pint glass. "Cheers! Have a roll." The plate was pushed in Tony's direction.

"You still think we're covering the right place?" The young reporter was desperate to keep up the momentum.

"Sure. I can't see the police letting up on that pair for long." Jacobs spoke quietly, not wishing to share their knowledge of the whereabouts of the smallholding with the rest of the media. "There's still no news of the skull and there's only the McKades who seem to fit the bill as far as wanting to get hold of it."

Tony Hoskis nodded. "You're right. I'm surprised the 'plods' haven't moved in before now. If that skull isn't buried at Mardale, the McKades must know something about it. We shouldn't hang about here for too long. I'd hate to miss out on anything at this stage."

Ray Jacobs smiled at the young man's impatience. "Bide your time. We'll dry out a bit while we eat our lunch. The weather might have improved a bit by then."

Tony looked doubtful.

Jacobs attempted to reassure him. "If we rush off too soon, this lot," he nodded in the direction of the media crews, "will guess we're on to something. I reckon they're waiting to follow our lead. We might as well take advantage of the fact that they probably haven't yet twigged where the McKades live, or that they haven't realised where the action's going to be. When we're ready to make our move, you slip off to the toilet while I get two more pints in. I'll pop them on the table here, then head for the toilets myself. By the time they realise we're not coming back, we'll be well away."

Tony Hoskis smiled at the plan, though he was barely convinced by his partner's conviction that it was reasonable not to hurry. The morning may have been entirely uneventful up to this point, yet some inner sense warned him that they were unwise to have left their post.

CHAPTER TWENTY-ONE

Once installed at the station, Rory McKade had been permitted to convey the news of his arrest to his wife. In spite of her distress, he had refused to allow her to visit him, or to return to their home, insisting that she remain at her mother's. He was not prepared to subject her and their young son to the harassment he and his father had been forced to endure at the hands of the press. She took some convincing but eventually agreed to his demands. She was requested only to make arrangements for his animals to be taken care of by one of the neighbours.

Father and son were separated – the younger man being the first to be conducted to the interview room. Both had declined the offer of legal representation. Both insisted that they saw no reason for it. They would surely change their minds once they became aware of what charges they might eventually face. Or were they carefully manoeuvring to avoid any suggestion that they did know of the charges that might follow?

Directly the formalities were over, Morrison began the questioning while Grey listened in.

"Right, Mr McKade, tell me precisely what did happen this morning."

The man looked uncomfortable, seemingly struggling to find some plausibly explanation.

Morrison sat back, impatiently waiting for him to begin.

McKade shifted uneasily in his seat. "You'll not believe me, whatever I say."

"Try me!" Morrison glared at the man.

McKade took a deep breath. "Okay. I got up about six thirty, same as always. Had a bite o' food, then fed the stock an’ milked the cows. I gave fadder a shake later, then got him a bit o’ breakfast. He usually gets up around eight o’clock. He’s a bit frail now. We sat talkin’ fer a time till he’d finished eating, then I cleared away while he went tae see if we’d any post. There weren’t any, but he looked out the front door in case the postman were about.”

“And what time would that have been?”

“Just afore nine. It were then he saw the shoebox. He just brought it in, thinking it were a few cakes or some such left by one o’ the neighbours. That sometimes happens when my wife’s away fer a few days. Anyway, Da’ put it down on the kitchen table an’ took off the lid. I think he almost had a heart attack when he saw what were in it.”

“And where were you at this time?”

“Just headin’ fer the back door. He called me an’ we both realised it had tae be the auld un’s skull. We’d waited all our lives tae get our hands on it. We didn’t stop tae bother who might have left it there. We grabbed our coats, an’ were just about tae set off an’ bury it wi’ the rest o’ the remains when we realised the bloody press had arrived outside agin. I couldn’t believe it! We had the bloody thing an’ couldn’t get tae bury it.”

“So what then?”

“We just hung around waitin’ fer the bastards tae piss off. As soon as they did, we got hold of a spade an’ fork, then you bloody lot came along. Another few minutes an’ we’d have been gone.” A look of despair shot across his face. “What now? I can see you don’t believe me, but that’s the truth!”

He was damn right. Morrison didn’t believe a word of it. Well certainly not much of it. The only thing that rang true was the bit about the press turning up. That, at least, did account for the delay in the McKades setting off as soon as they got their hands on the skull. How that particular event came about was the matter to be resolved. Morrison was not yet ready to disclose that Ralph Braithwaite’s body had been discovered. If the McKades were guilty of murdering the man – and the superintendent had no doubt that they were – then the longer he kept them in the dark the sooner they might slip up.

Sarcastically, Morrison posed the question "So you're not claiming it fell off the back of a lorry then? That's the usual answer we get whenever we question suspects..." Not bothering to wait for a reply he continued, "…and you never even considered who might have left this skull on your doorstep?"

Rory McKade shrugged his shoulders. "God knows. When we couldn't get out tae bury it we started wondering. Somebody might have planted it on us. We just decided we'd get it put back wi' the auld un's remains as soon as we could. That were all that really concerned us. It's the only thing our family's ever wanted. A pledge is a pledge and this looked like the only chance we'd ever have of redeeming it." He suddenly looked Morrison straight in the eye. "It's bloody Ralph Braithwaite, ain't it?"

Grey saw the look of satisfaction spreading across the superintendent's face. Had Rory McKade finally slipped up? Or was he actually prepared to admit to the crime?

"That bastard's tryin' tae frame us! He must have killed his uncle fer his money, then took off wi' the skull. That crafty sod's allus hated our guts. Now he's tryin' tae put the blame on us. He put the skull on our doorstep! He told you we'd got it, didn't he?"

Morrison was disappointed. For one moment he'd been certain the man had decided to confess. Now it appeared he was cunningly attempting to cover his tracks. If he were responsible for Ralph Braithwaite's death, what better way to escape detection than to feign righteous indignation by blaming the dead man for Herbert Jowett's murder and inventing a plot against himself and his father?

"No one told us you had the skull." Morrison was careful not to play into the man's hands. Rory McKade may have spent the morning planning the details of his defence should he be caught with the object. "As a matter of fact, we were calling on you this morning to search your property." The warrant was spread out for McKade to see. "And that we have now done. If we find any more evidence to back up what we already have, you haven't a leg to stand on. I put it to you that you've had the skull ever since you murdered Herbert Jowett. For some reason, you were unable to rid yourself of it immediately and you've been waiting for your chance to dispose of it ever since."

"That's bloody ridiculous!" Rory McKade was showing signs of the strain, his rough hands clenched into tight fists, his face contorted with anger. "If we'd had it all this time we'd easily have gotten rid of it!"

"Just so!" Morrison smiled grimly at the man. It was a statement that he might come to regret. "So perhaps you haven't had it all this time. You have only just acquired it."

McKade eyed Morrison warily. What was the bastard up to now? "That's what I've been trying tae tell you!" he groaned, lifting his eyes to heaven and shaking his head as though totally unable to comprehend.

"And what if that were so?" The superintendent posed the hypothetical question, the smile fading from his lips. "You only acquired it this morning? What if Ralph Braithwaite had been in possession of it all this time as you suggest? What if he had stolen the skull from the station here? What if you had murdered Herbert Jowett in the belief that he had it? What if you then realised that Braithwaite was the only other person who could have taken it? And what if Braithwaite had witnessed you murdering his uncle?" Morrison paused to let it all sink in. "Did you murder Ralph Braithwaite this very morning in order to silence him and to take possession of the skull?"

The effect was dramatic. Rory McKade shot bolt upright in his chair, eyes staring from the depths of his drained, pallid face. "What the hell are you on about? Are you telling me Ralph's dead?"

"Are you telling me you're not already aware of that?" Morrison scathingly answered McKade's question with his own. "I'm telling you he's dead, right enough. I'm also telling you that I believe you had a hand in his murder. How did you go about it? You must have followed the man. Did you suggest that Braithwaite should hand over the skull and that you would keep quiet about him stealing it? It was a bit late for him to get it back to the farm, wasn't it? And he could still claim the family fortune. Was he too frightened to trust you? So did you then let your father take over the conversation while you stole behind the man and attacked him? As you said yourself, you'd have buried the skull back with the rest of the remains before now if it had been in your possession… You took possession this morning!"

McKade almost appeared on the point of collapse. He glanced at Grey, as though appealing for help. "I don't believe this! You can't be bloody serious!"

"Oh, we're serious." Morrison kept up the pressure. "If we find your prints, or those of your father, on Ralph Braithwaite's van, then you're for the high jump. You might just as well admit it now."

McKade shook his head. He looked devastated. "You'll find no prints. We've not been near his van."

"You deny being involved in his killing?"

"Of course I bloody do! I told you how we found the skull. It were left there on our doorstep."

Morrison closed the interview. Rory McKade would be fingerprinted. His father should already have undergone the process. The old man was now to be brought in for his interrogation.

Angus McKade sat glowering as Morrison attempted to question him. No amount of cajoling, or threatening, would loosen his lips. Morrison was finally losing patience.

"You're not helping yourself, or your son, by this attitude. You were both in possession of a stolen item when apprehended this morning. Any court will take your refusal to answer my questions as to how you came by that skull as an admission of guilt."

The old man stared silently at the table. He had lived long enough to realise that the superintendent was out to trap him. Any discrepancy between his version of the events and that of his son would be seized on immediately.

Morrison decided only shock treatment was likely to work. "Very well. Your son, and in all probability yourself, are in danger of being charged with the murder of Ralph Braithwaite."

That had the desired effect.

"Damn ye!" Angus McKade shot a look of pure hatred at Morrison. "So that's what all this is about. You never told us Ralph Braithwaite were dead."

"I'm telling you now!" Morrison was convinced the old man knew about the killing. He must have been involved. Given the circumstances, Ralph Braithwaite was hardly likely to have turned his back on Rory McKade. The man must have had an accomplice. "You might as well save us all some trouble and come clean. You and your son were the only people who could possibly have considered murder as a way of getting hold of that skull. We're well aware of the hatred you felt for that family."

The gravity of the situation was beginning to sink home. Angus McKade seemed to shrink into the depths of his chair. His face became a picture of despair as he fought to come up with some explanation. "We didn't do it!" The words were issued through tight-drawn lips. "And that's all you're gettin' out of me!" It was clear that he meant what he said.

Morrison stood up. "Very well. That's all for now. You'll be held in custody on the charge of being in possession of stolen goods. You can expect further charges to follow once we've examined all the evidence. I'd advise you of the need for a solicitor if those charges do follow."

The old man was led away. He would again be separated from his son. Morrison was determined there would be no chance for them to concoct a tidy version of events.

"Well, Grey. I suppose we'd better let the media in on this." Morrison realised he could delay it no longer. "I'll call a press conference and we'll get it over with. They're bound to make a meal of it. Some of those bastards won't think twice about blaming us for this last death."

Grey shrugged his shoulders. "Goes without saying."

Morrison picked the skull up carefully, using his chewed up pen. "It's as well we've got this back. At least the public can see that we've not been sitting on our backsides. I won't release the McKades' names as yet, of course, but the media can have the usual 'suspects are being held for questioning'."

"Let's hope that satisfies them."

"Don't bank on it!" Morrison set down the skull again, looking at it thoughtfully. "With hindsight, it's always easy to suggest that we should have foreseen this second death occurring."

"Wouldn't that have implied a belief on our part in this ridiculous curse?"

"Maybe so. I don't imagine that'll stop Mrs Braithwaite laying the blame on our shoulders though." Morrison headed for the door. "Check up on the fingerprints, Grey. We need to nail the McKades as soon as possible. Forensics can have a crack at the skull and the shoebox. If the van's thrown up anything useful, we could have this sewn up by the end of the day."

* * *

Joy Elliot turned on the television more out of desperation than a desire to watch any special programme. The rain showed no sign of abating, hardly encouraging a move outdoors, and there was no way she could devote her thoughts to studying. Having discussed with her tutor all the facts they had gathered regarding the murder of Herbert Jowett, she still had a recurring dread that they were missing something. Reid had now returned to his own room, seemingly intent on making some progress with his official duties. Left to her own devices, she could not blank out the thought of Margaret Thursby and of how she might have met her death. Old Joss's conviction that Margaret had been driven to take her own life by Herbert Jowett was the only source of comfort she could cling to. Dreadful though that appeared, it did make Jowett's murder seem slightly more acceptable. Maybe she should not feel such awful guilt over the death of a man who appeared to be something of a monster.

The news that Ralph Braithwaite had been murdered suddenly shook her out of her daydreams. Her whole body began to tremble as the newscast continued.

"The nephew of the man regarded as the uncrowned King of Mardale, Herbert Jowett – whose death had been linked with the legend of Duncan of Crieff – was discovered early this morning with fatal head injuries. Superintendent Morrison, who is leading the investigation, reports that the man died in almost identical circumstances to those relating to his uncle. His skull was crushed by a heavy blow from behind. The implement used is believed to be a rock taken from the dry stone wall which was being repaired by the dead man. The police have already taken two suspects into custody but refuse to confirm that charges will automatically follow. The 'Mardale Skull', which reputedly forms part of the remains of Duncan of Crieff – and which was stolen from the Penrith police station – has now been recovered."

The newscast moved on to other subjects.

Joy Elliot neither saw, nor heard, the rest of the news. One death on her conscience was hard enough to bear. She had scarcely had time to convince herself that that man had perhaps deserved to die, when now another member of the family had lost his life. Again she was forced to accept that she must, in part, be to blame. She could not duck the issue. Burying her face in her hands, she burst into tears. Would the agony never cease?

Merlin Reid had also tuned in to the broadcast. The significance of the tragedy was not lost on him. Joy would be devastated. He made his way in the direction of her room, hoping she might not have heard. Best if he could break the news gently.

Arriving at her door, he realised that she was well aware of the new development. Her sobs were evident above the sound of the television. He knocked, entering without waiting for a reply. She rose and came towards him, eyes streaming with tears.

"Oh God, Prof!" She threw herself into his arms, desperate for reassurance.

He held her tightly, letting her tears flow. She had been under enough strain without this.

"It's all right, Joy." He stroked her hair, almost as one might pet an injured puppy. "You can't accept responsibility for this. What's done is done."

She still remained cradled in his arms. He could think of nothing more to say that might ease her pain. Gradually the sobbing began to decrease. Gently he relaxed his grip, eventually allowing her to ease herself away. He gave her his handkerchief, turning to switch off the television set.

"Do you think that's the end of it now?" She had sunk into an armchair, shaking, dabbing the tears from her cheeks as she attempted to stem the flow.

"We can only hope so. They say the skull's been recovered. If that's the case, I imagine they must have the culprits."

"Thank God!" She struggled to stifle any further show of emotion. "I want to see an end to this, Prof. I can't take much more."

"I know, Joy." He grasped her shoulders, once more attempting to comfort her. Unfortunately, he realised just how many problems still lay ahead. The suspects in custody had evidently not yet been charged with the murders.

Joy was slowly beginning to compose herself. That was apparent from the fact that she too appeared to have reached the same conclusion. "We don't know for sure that it is them."

"Let's wait and see." He was aware that was not going to be easy for her. He wondered just how much evidence Grey and the superintendent had gathered together.

* * *

Morrison had just received something of a bombshell. Once the news of the arrests had been announced, an unexpected phone call had caused another major rethink. A man who had volunteered his name, but who had insisted that it should be kept secret, had made contact. Apparently he had been informed by one of the McKades' nearest neighbours that she had witnessed the McKades being arrested. What's more, the man admitted that he and the woman had been having an affair. He quickly glossed over that fact, pointing out that he would never reveal exactly which lady he was referring to. Clearly she was one of the householders who had earlier denied seeing any signs of the McKades at the time of Herbert Jowett's murder. Now that events had moved on, her conscience was pricking her. She and her lover had seen the McKades about at the relevant time. They had seen them through the bedroom window. They had seen them as they'd frolicked naked on the bed, chuckling as they just about managed to keep out of sight. They had not drawn the curtains as they had no wish to attract attention to the house once the lady's husband had departed for work. The man would not give details of the husband's occupation. 'Did they take him for a fool? That would soon give the game away!' If they wanted his cooperation they must honour his conditions. The woman's husband must never be made aware of his wife's infidelity. The conditions were agreed. Morrison inquired about the movements of the McKades on the morning just past. The man could not help. It was not a day on which he visited and the woman had only seen the McKades being taken away while coming home from her shopping. She knew then that she had to do something. She'd had a guilty conscience all along about lying to the police when they made enquiries at the time of Herbert Jowett's death. Having assured her husband that she had spent the morning in question walking a friend's dogs, she could hardly change her mind when the police questioned her and her husband later. Hence the phone call now.

Though not exactly what Morrison had wanted to hear, it certainly appeared to entirely rule out the McKades with regard to the murder of Herbert Jowett. Did this now confirm the suspicion that Ralph Braithwaite was guilty of that crime? Things could be beginning to fall into place at last.

* * *

The results of the fingerprint tests were not promising when passed on to Inspector Grey some time later. No trace of the McKades' prints were present on Ralph Braithwaite's van, or on the rock used in the attack. Grey was not particularly surprised. Anyone with an ounce of sense would have avoided leaving their calling card. However, there was one teasing detail which did not quite add up. Ralph Braithwaite's own fingerprints were clearly defined on the door handle of his van, and on the keys taken from his pocket. There was no evidence of anyone attempting to wipe away any other prints which might possibly have existed. That action would have almost entirely obliterated Ralph Braithwaite's own prints. If someone had affected entry it had been done with a great deal of expertise, and a great deal of cunning.

The skull bore the prints of both the McKades, along with those of Herbert Jowett and others not yet identified. Here was a breakthrough. But was it an entirely welcome breakthrough? It clearly indicated that Herbert Jowett had been the person who stole the skull from the station. How else could his prints have appeared on it? Unfortunately, Ralph Braithwaite's prints were not present. If he had ever been in possession of it he had taken care not to touch the skull with his bare hands. The fact that the McKades' prints were there was hardly relevant. Their statements had obviously contained no denial of handling the skull. Grey realised that his own prints, and those of the pathologist who had originally examined it after its discovery, were likely to account for the ones not yet verified. Thankfully, that could soon be established.

The shoebox gave little away. Faint evidence of previous handling was there along with a vague suggestion of the McKades' prints, though cardboard was not exactly the best medium for conveying information on such a subject – and again, the McKades could hardly deny contact.

It was not the conclusive proof that Morrison was looking for, though neither was it proof of the McKades innocence in respect of the killing of Ralph Braithwaite. What it certainly proved was that Herbert Jowett met his death at the hands of someone who then snatched the skull and ran.

Grey considered the latest evidence. Could Ralph Braithwaite have murdered his uncle at the farm? Why not? He could either have aided and abetted Herbert Jowett in the act of stealing the skull or he could have been the one who lay in wait for him. Did he then panic and rush off with the skull if he'd somehow been disturbed? The McKades could well have been the ones who made an appearance. Had they then realised that Braithwaite must have the skull secreted somewhere? And was it possible that that very morning Braithwaite had intended hiding it in some cavity in the wall that he was working on? It was apparent that someone had followed him to the spot where he met his death. It all appeared to add up – but did it?

Grey hesitated before passing the new evidence to his superior. He would have preferred more time to consider the implications. He wondered if Merlin Reid had heard the announcement of the death. What would he make of it? Reid had certainly contributed already to the enquiries. Might he have anything else up his sleeve? The crafty old codger always managed somehow to avail himself of information that never came Grey's way. Grey allowed himself a smile. 'The Magician' was not a policeman. His was the interest of a man divorced from the strict code which Grey had to adhere to. Nothing was to be gained by denying him access to the information at hand. The man had proved in the past that he was trustworthy. Morrison could wait a little while longer. The inspector reached for his pipe, then the phone.

Merlin Reid was surprised but delighted to receive the call. Grey had greeted him in his usual gruff manner, part formal, part amiable. "You've heard the news I imagine, Prof.?"

"Ralph Braithwaite's death? Yes. Coming after Herbert Jowett's murder, it's surely going to send out a few shock waves?"

"Indeed." Grey was a man of few words.

"Still, you've recovered the skull. Does that mean you might also have apprehended the villains?"

"Superintendent Morrison is pretty well convinced."

Reid sensed that Grey had his reservations. "You're still standing on the sidelines?"

"For the time being. I hate to jump the gun."

"You don't feel in the mood to bounce any ideas off me?"

Grey was silent for a moment. Reid guessed that the inspector was considering the suggestion as he puffed away on his trusted briar.

"Morrison doesn't exactly encourage debate. He has his own ways of conducting an investigation."

So Grey was prepared to talk. He had never been the sort of person to ignore the possibility that others might be able to shed some light on a difficult case.

"Any particular reason why you should question the superintendent's judgement?"

"It's not a case of questioning his judgement." Grey was silent again for a while. Reid was accustomed to the inspector's ponderous thought processes. He waited until the man continued.

"This business of the curse is a bloody nightmare! With the media constantly harping on about it, it's putting pressure on everyone to bring this case to a rapid conclusion. Ralph

Braithwaite's murder is just another reason to force us to take urgent action. We can't risk anymore lives being lost."

"I can see that." The professor had already considered the possibility. "Who would have thought that Ralph Braithwaite would have followed his uncle to such an untimely death?"

"Precisely! May I speak to you in the strictest of confidence?"

Reid happily accepted the provision "That's understood. What's on your mind?"

Yet another long pause before Grey finally committed himself. "We've either got a very clever pair of rogues in custody, or we've possibly got two innocent men. We caught the McKades this morning with the skull in their possession. They swear they discovered it inside an old shoebox that had been deposited on their doorstep sometime before nine. The pathologist reckons Ralph Braithwaite was murdered between eight and nine. The McKades claim the press turned up at their smallholding moments after they found the skull."

"Interesting." Reid waited impatiently to discover why Grey seemed not entirely convinced of the men's guilt. Their story appeared to be pretty weak.

"Superintendent Morrison and I formed the opinion that Ralph Braithwaite may possibly have been murdered because he was in possession of the skull. How that came about is another matter…" Grey did not wish to go into all the details. "Suffice it to say that his death, and the discovery of the McKades with the skull, appeared to justify the arrests."

"Seems pretty reasonable to me." The professor wondered exactly what Grey was leading up to. Clearly if Braithwaite had been in possession of the skull, it was doubtful that he would have risked attempting to get it back to Mardale until after the hue and cry had died down. That being the case, he would have been stuck with it once Mardale disappeared back below the waters. "So you're thinking, if the McKades had any inkling that he might have it, you can be sure that they'd have kept watch on the man?"

"That's about it. Clearly he'd need to conceal his possession of the skull. He might even have been aware of the McKades keeping watch. If he had it at home, or somewhere close by, his only recourse might then have been to carry it with him whenever he left – just in case they were prepared to break in to retrieve it. Or we conducted a thorough enough search to unearth it."

"I suppose that would make sense." Reid turned the facts over in his mind. If the McKades had originally gained possession of the skull at the time of Herbert Jowett's death, then they probably would have had no great problem in reuniting it with Duncan of Crieff's remains before now. "So why the doubts?"

"Not exactly doubts." Grey fell silent again, as though considering precisely what he did mean. "I've come across a fair number of villains in my time. Most of 'em can lie fairly convincingly, but usually it's not long before you can trip 'em up. We may still do that, but so far this pair haven't put a foot wrong."

"And you've no other evidence against them?"

"Not enough to conclusively link them with Ralph Braithwaite's death. We can only prove that they have handled the skull – as had Herbert Jowett."

"Ah, so Jowett did steal it?" Reid was beginning to see where Grey was going.

"Must have. There's no question now about his involvement."

Though it was fascinating, the news was not particularly surprising, only confirming what the professor had already surmised. He had a sudden thought. "What about the shoebox?"

"Nothing much there. Obviously, since it had recently been in their hands, the McKades' prints were just about discernible, though mainly there were just vague smudges. No definite sign of Ralph Braithwaite having handled it."

"I wasn't meaning that. What kind of footwear?"

For a moment the question threw Grey. He had scarcely had time to consider whether the make of shoe could have any possible bearing on the case. When the arrests took place it had at first appeared that the case was cut and dried, without the need to scratch around for any further clues. The inspector smiled to himself. It was typical of Reid to toss in a simple query of that nature. He had a layman's logic that ignored the more scientific approach taken by the police. There was no harm in following up on the idea though.

"You could have a point there, Prof. Forensics are still working on it, of course, and on the McKades' clothing. If they come across any trace of Ralph Braithwaite's blood on any of the items that could settle the matter anyway."

"You will keep me up to date?" Reid knew he was pushing his luck. "But I do have a young lady here who's terribly upset. She's blaming herself for these deaths. It'll come as some relief to her once she knows for sure that the killers have been apprehended. I think she could hardly live with any more guilt."

"Yes, it must be a worrying time for you both." Grey had sympathy for Joy's predicament. "Tell her not to let it get her down. Once we have anything positive you'll be the first to know."

"Thanks." Reid had his foot in the door once more. "If you think we can possibly be of any further assistance, don't hesitate to get in touch."

"Will do." Grey replaced the phone.

* * *

Jean Bull was in shock. Somehow she had gradually forced herself to cope with her mother's revelation of Ralph's death. They had clung together, weeping, for what seemed an eternity before Jean had finally managed to regain some control. She had rung the surgery, her doctor quickly agreeing to come to the house. He had administered a sedative to her mother and wished to do the same for her. She had declined. Her only means of containing her grief was by concentrating on bringing about some improvement in her mother's condition. She had little thought for herself.

Once her mother had calmed down, Jean had done her best to persuade her to spend the night there. Ellen would not hear of it. She refused even to stay for the meal Jean was preparing in readiness for her husband's arrival home. Ellen Braithwaite's dislike of her daughter's husband had only been compounded by the unpleasant atmosphere that had been created by the possibility of Ralph controlling Jean's money. Once more she had broken down at the thought that Ralph would never be there to help her ever again.

Once Cedric had arrived home, and the story of Ralph's death was retold amid a further flood of tears, Ellen had requested that she be taken home. She had turned down the offer from Jean to accompany her and to remain with her overnight. Cedric had made no attempt to press her to stay. The feeling of dislike was mutual. He was now driving her back. And he was feeling quite pleased. That fact that her son now lay dead in a mortuary elicited no sympathy from him. His mother could never now refuse her daughters demands.

Jean now reached for the tablets that the doctor had insisted on leaving for her. It was only at this moment that the enormity of the tragedy really struck home. Her last comments to her brother came back to her like a dagger to the heart. "I'll never speak to you again!" She shook with despair to think how prophetic those six angry words had proved to be. A lifetime of loving affection had disappeared with that utterance in a moment of total frustration. She would willingly give up all claim to the money if only she could take back those words and have her dear brother returned. She broke down once more, sobbing uncontrollably.

CHAPTER TWENTY-TWO

It was late the following day before Inspector Grey made contact with Professor Reid again. He was still a puzzled man. In spite of all their efforts, the police had found no definite proof that the McKades were ever in the vicinity of the scene of the crime. Neither had they been able to establish their presence in the locality of Ralph Braithwaite's home. None of the dead man's neighbours recalled sighting the McKades' van parked anywhere close by. That, though unfortunate as far as the police were concerned, hardly came as any great surprise. Since Braithwaite's home was situated in a cul-de-sac, the McKades might easily have kept watch from a safe distance. Braithwaite would be obliged to emerge onto the main road when leaving for work. Plenty of small side roads would have afforded cover to his stalkers as they lay in wait. By the same token, anyone else with the intention of following Braithwaite would have had a similar advantage.

The McKades' own neighbours were unable to verify the men's movements at the time of Ralph Braithwaite's death. The smallholding being fairly isolated, only four families were situated close enough to observe any comings or goings. None of them had been able to either confirm the men's presence at the smallholding, or their absence, although three had observed their removal by the police later in the day.

No blood stains had been discovered on either of the men's clothing. Rory McKade's wet waterproofs were examined after being found at his home, though his explanation that he had worn them only while in the process of attending to the animals was impossible to disprove. Any blood which might possibly have been transferred to the garments through contact with Ralph Braithwaite could either have been washed away by the morning's rain or easily sponged from the non-absorbent material.

Superintendent Morrison was still refusing to be swayed by the men's insistence that they had done no wrong. He had quickly concluded that their crime was solely in connection with the death of Ralph Braithwaite and that Braithwaite himself was guilty of murdering Herbert Jowett, almost certainly with the help or connivance of his mother. With the skull in the hands of the McKades at the time of their arrest, it was not a surprising inference to draw. The case against them of handling the stolen article had now been extended to encompass a charge of murder.

"Just thought you'd like to know before it's formally announced, Prof." Grey was keeping to his word, as was his habit.

"So it was them?"

"The Superintendent certainly believes that to be the case."

Once more it was apparent that Grey was not entirely convinced. Reid was puzzled as to why that should be. "Any luck with the shoebox?"

"Possibly. It turned out to have previously contained a pair of ladies brogue shoes, size 5½."

"Ladies shoes you say?" There was a note of surprise in the professor's voice.

"I thought that might interest you."

"Braithwaite wasn't married, was he?"

Grey had expected the professor to seize on that fact. "He was not. Nor was there any sign of a woman ever having stayed there. Not so much as a hair grip or a spare toothbrush."

"Curious..."

"Indeed."

"No doubt you've followed up on that?"

"Naturally. We think we may have traced the shop that sold them – it's situated in Craigend. We can't be anything like certain that they were purchased there, of course. It's a model that's sold all over the country, but they are a stock item in Craigend. Seems they're popular with the visitors as well as the locals. Great walking shoes apparently – flat heels and a good grip."

"So if they're a good-selling line, the assistants aren't likely to put a face or a name to the person who bought them?"

"Unfortunately not. Our only chance was to discover a pair of them at Ralph Braithwaite's, which we failed to do, or at the McKades' place."

"And no luck with the McKades either?"

"No. We've given the spot a good going over, but Rory McKade's wife appears to wear a slightly larger size. No sign of any brogues there either. She's away at her mother's at the moment, but we've checked her out. She denies ever having purchased that type of shoe."

"Do you doubt her word?"

"Hard to say." Grey remained non-committal. "She knows her husband's in a great deal of trouble. Even if she had once possessed any, she might well deny it. She wouldn't need a great deal of intelligence to work out that we must have some good reason to ask."

"Can't argue with that."

"You can imagine her immediately jumping to the conclusion that such an admission could have serious consequences for him, as indeed it would have. His story of finding the box on the doorstep would be blown out of the water."

"Any other leads?"

The inspector carefully considered the question. The policeman in him took the judicious view that he should keep such information to himself, yet Merlin Reid had never let him down.

“We have run a check on Ralph Braithwaite’s mother. She also denies having purchased that style of shoe, although it turns out that she does match up with the size. Obviously, that’s hardly a major breakthrough, especially when you consider that the vast majority of women fall into approximately the same category. Of course, in this case, there would be even more reason for her to deny it. She and her son would be right in the frame if it were true.”

“So she can’t be ruled out either?” Reid realised the police would be keeping their options open. Suppose Mrs Braithwaite had played some part in the murder of her brother. She could have been left in possession of the skull had a quick exit from Mardale been necessary. Was it possible the shoebox belonged to her? If so, she and her son must have conspired together. Since Ralph Braithwaite was unmarried, it was difficult to comprehend how he happened to come to place the skull in a box that had contained ladies shoes. If the McKades had murdered him to seize the skull, as the police clearly suspected, it now indicated that they were not the only killers. Ralph Braithwaite and his mother were also bound to be suspect. And, since Ralph was now dead, would his mother end up being charged? This was getting extremely complicated. Reid didn’t envy Grey the job of sorting out the mess. Best leave him to get on with it.

“Well, thanks for keeping me informed, Inspector. I’m sure Joy will be a lot happier once it’s all resolved.”

He replaced the receiver. Joy may be pleased to eventually see an end to the case, but would that remove her feelings of guilt? He was still concerned about the girl. For the second day running she had not shown up for breakfast. As Reid had himself been out for lunch, he suddenly realised he had not seen her all day. He was aware though that she had become even more withdrawn since the latest death. Nothing like her usual cheery self. Try as he might, he could not bring a smile to her pallid face. Most of her time seemed to be spent sitting in the garden or wandering down to the lakeside. She had now become obsessed with discovering the truth behind Margaret Thursby's death – convinced that it might have some relevance to Herbert Jowett's murder. That possibility seemed to be the only thing which might lift some of the burden from her shoulders. She needed the reassurance that Jowett deserved to die.

Reid shook his head. There was nothing for it but to hope that the news of the McKades being charged with Ralph Braithwaite's murder might give her a lift. He thought he had heard her moving about a short while ago. That seemed to indicate that she might be in her room for a change. It was worth a try.

"Oh! Come in, Prof." She appeared to welcome his intrusion. "Are there any developments?" She had obviously heard the telephone ring. Her question was posed with some trepidation.

"There is. The McKades have been charged with Ralph Braithwaite's murder. Superintendent Morrison is just about to announce it."

"Ah well, they must be pretty sure then." She looked somewhat relieved at hearing the news. "And what about Herbert Jowett's murder? Aren't they being charged with that too?"

"It seems not. The police still appear to be keeping an open mind on that subject." Reid was a little reluctant to relate all of the conversation he had had with the inspector.

"Did anything come from your inquiry about the shoebox?"

He had mentioned the episode to her earlier, so saw no reason to hide the truth.

"Grey seems to think so. It appears that it once held a pair of ladies brogue shoes."

She looked at him quizzically. "How exactly does that help?"

"Ralph Braithwaite wasn't married and lived alone."

Her eyes lit up. "Oh! I see what you mean. If he was the one who put the skull in the shoebox, then you'd have naturally expected it to have previously contained a pair of his shoes."

"That's the way the police are likely to view it."

"So it does rather throw open the question of who did own the shoes that originally came from the box."

"It does."

"And whoever that person was, it seems likely that they'd be mixed up in some way with these killings?"

"It would appear so." He could almost see her mind turning over.

"They're going to suspect Mrs Braithwaite of being involved in some way in the murder of her brother, aren't they? If her son was killed because he had the skull, who else is there who might have handed over such a box?" Her face fell as she considered the thought. 'What a terrible situation. She may have helped to murder her own brother and now she's lost her son. I'm really beginning to believe in this damn curse, Prof. I thought we hadn't heard the last of it." Her face crumpled, tears streaming down her pale cheeks once again.

He jumped up, gathering her in his arms. Damn! He was almost beginning to believe in the bloody curse himself. What was happening to the last survivors of the Jowett clan? Even though the Braithwaites no longer carried the Jowett name, it was clear they were caught up in some evil maelstrom that threatened each and every member of the unfortunate family. Was it possible that they were in the process of destroying themselves? What else might be on Joy's conscience before these terrible events finally came to an end?

* * *

It was not a long wait before that question was answered. Within 48 hours, Ellen Braithwaite had been arrested and charged with complicity in the murder of Herbert Jowett. Superintendent Morrison was convinced that she had either killed her brother herself or participated in the attack. There seemed no other logical explanation. Years of suppressed anger at the treatment she had received at her brother's hands must have finally driven her to breaking point. She alone would have been fully aware of the effect it would have on the man to be informed of the skull's removal from the farm. It had taken her no time at all to transmit that message to him. Who else could have brought the man scurrying back to his fate? And who else would have been so well informed as to his every move? She could come up with no reasonable explanation as to why the skull should have been found in a ladies shoebox. Morrison had his own theory. The shoebox had originally been in her possession. She had placed the skull in it and had later passed it over to her son. Her screams of denial fell on deaf ears. Both she and the McKades were now in the position of having to prove their innocence. Morrison was convinced that they would find that impossible. The news of Ellen Braithwaite's arrest was relayed to the media.

* * *

On this occasion it was Joy who made her way to her tutor's room. The arrest of Ellen Braithwaite had come as no great surprise. Joy had followed each news bulletin with growing concern over the last two days, convinced that the curse would embrace yet another member of the ill-fated family. Unfortunately, her dread of such an event occurring had proved to be well founded.

She met Reid as he was about to leave his room, apparently similarly bent on paying her a visit.

"Come in, Joy." He took hold of her arm, leading her to a comfortable chair. He took a seat opposite. "You've heard the news then?" He had quickly realised that that must be the reason for her visit, although he was surprised to see her looking relatively unruffled.

She nodded. "I think we both expected it, didn't we?"

"It looked inevitable." He was pleased she had managed to accept the situation so readily.

"Can you really believe she had a part in murdering her own brother?"

He hesitated before answering. The question was one that he had been asking himself continually over the past two days. Did he actually believe it? The evidence certainly indicated that both Ellen Braithwaite and her son might be involved. Why else would Ralph Braithwaite have been struck down? In the event that the McKades had murdered Herbert Jowett, thereby acquiring the skull in that way, then Ralph Braithwaite should have posed no threat to them. Was he a threat to anyone else? It was hard to imagine. Who might possibly benefit? Could there be any other explanation for the attack upon him? Joy was evidently looking for one, though he found it difficult to come up with an alternative. Incidents of double homicide by two different killers was a rare occurrence.

"We don't have any sound reason to question the judgement of the police, Joy. Superintendent Morrison must think there's a case to answer."

"What if he's wrong?" She was clearly desperately hoping that he might be. Her concern for Mrs Braithwaite was transparent.

Reid struggled once more to reassure her. "I suppose there is hope. Who can say what evidence may yet turn up? It's early days yet."

His words gave little comfort. Joy needed something more tangible. "That poor woman seems to have suffered all her life at the hands of her horrible brother. I realise this sounds callous, but I'm beginning to believe he may have deserved his fate, especially if all that we've heard about him is true."

"Well, there appears to be little doubt that he was a very unpleasant character, Joy," Reid was happy to confirm her opinion of Jowett. "And I must admit it's not difficult to understand that Mrs Braithwaite could finally have snapped. She must have become extremely bitter over the years."

"That's my point. It just seems so unfair that she might go to prison for a moment's madness. She's already lost her son because of this terrible affair; now she might lose her freedom too."

"If they convict her, she'll almost certainly do that." Reid could see no way that the sentence was likely to be mitigated to any great extent. Murder was murder, no matter how you chose to look at it.

* * *

Jean Bull was totally distraught. The news of her brother's death had been almost too much to bear. Now she had just been informed of her mother's arrest on suspicion of murder. The receiver slipped from her fingers, clattering across the sideboard. Automatically she reached out, replacing it on the stand. Numbly, she stumbled to the bathroom, fumbling in the cabinet for the tranquillisers the doctor had forced upon her. Thank God for his intuitive reaction to the needs of the bereaved. She filled a tumbler, slipping two of the tablets into her mouth. For one moment she considered taking the whole contents of the bottle…

What good would that do? She fought the impulse. She was not going to fulfil the terrible prophecy of doom that hung over her family. Certainly not by her own hand. She flung the bottle into the corner of the room, trembling with emotion at the thought of what she had just contemplated. Her mother needed her now more than at any other time in her life. She had always been there for Jean – and for the son who now lay dead on a mortician's slab. There was no way her mother could be left to face life on her own.

God, she wished her husband was there with her. There was no way of contacting him. Once he was out on his rounds he could be anywhere, fixing a tap or plumbing in a washing machine. What should she do? Would her mother need a solicitor? Surely there must be some mistake. She sank down on to the side of the bath, her head reeling.

Slowly she fought to pull herself together. She must put out of her mind the fears that were beginning to overwhelm her. Hadn't her mother and Ralph assured her that there was no truth in the legend of the Mardale Skull? Yet somehow their words didn't ring true. How else had the family come to find itself in this awful state? And what other disasters might yet lie in store for them? Had her uncle really travelled all the way from South Africa merely to take a last look at Mardale? She shuddered at the thought of what might possibly happen to her mother and to herself. The skull could surely never be returned to Mardale now. Some evil force had to be bent on destroying them all. They were helpless to prevent it!

And what of the other fear that had almost been driving her crazy? The dreadful prospect that her own husband could have been involved in some way with Ralph's death. She had struggled to suppress even considering that possibility, yet Cedric had gone berserk on being informed of Ralph's scheme to control her share of the family fortune. Was it possible he could have been driven to kill her brother? Perhaps by some compulsion other than the tawdry desire to acquire the money? Jean refused to believe he could ever consider such a terrible method of achieving his ends. Not without some power beyond his control taking over both his mind and body.

She rose to her feet. This was not helping. She must go to her mother. She went back to the phone, ringing for a taxi. Just time to scribble a note to her husband, informing him of where she would be. She took off her apron, letting it slip to the floor. In a daze she made her way out into the hall, collecting coat and handbag. This was unbearable. Was she to be forced to choose between supporting her hapless mother or to contemplate divulging the dreadful suspicions she had concerning the husband she loved?

* * *

Once Cedric Bull became aware of his mother-in-law's arrest, his reaction was in marked contrast to that of his wife.

Finally, everything had dropped into place. Ralph was out of the way for good and Ellen was charged with complicity in murdering her own brother. Cedric smiled to himself. If Ellen Braithwaite were found guilty of her brother's murder, who would inherit the family fortune? As Herbert Jowett had no wife, or brothers, and his sister would be ineligible, nephews and nieces were next in line. And there now remained only one – Jean, his wife. No bugger could prevent the money coming their way now. Even if Ellen somehow managed to establish her innocence, Ralph's share would surely pass to Jean. Her mother would never stand out on her own. Without Ralph there sticking his bloody oar in, Jean would get her inheritance one way or the other. He rubbed his podgy little hands together, chuckling with delight. The curse on the Jowetts had definitely come to the rescue.

* * *

The bunch of fragrant red roses came as a complete surprise – the attached note even more so: 'Sorry, Joy. You must think me an awful swine. I can only say how much I regret my actions. If you want to give it one more try, ring the Kings Arms at Shap.' It was signed: 'Tony.'

Joy Elliot stood in the doorway, vacantly watching the delivery van departing. She hardly knew whether to laugh or cry. What had brought this on? Surely there was nothing more that she could impart in the way of information? The McKades and Mrs Braithwaite were already under arrest. Only the formalities of the trial now appeared to be left to be resolved. Was Tony truly repentant? Did he actually wish to see her purely for herself? She wanted to believe that. The colour that had been missing from her cheeks for days on end suddenly reappeared. He *must* want her purely for herself. What else had he to gain?

Slowly she made her way back to her room. For once her thoughts were diverted away from the horrible recent events and she concentrated solely on herself. She had to admit that the hurt she had experienced at the hands of Tony Hoskis was mainly as a result of her feeling that she had been used. True, she had also felt violated, though he had stopped before intercourse took place. Maybe she was too strait-laced for this day and age. Perhaps she had overreacted to the situation. Perhaps it had been her own desire to give in that had shocked her so much. She stopped dead in her tracks. She had wanted him! She had wanted him so much that it hurt. It was just the wrong place and the wrong time. She had always dreamt that one day she would lose her virginity on a bed of white satin with the scent of jasmine in the air.

Suddenly she began to chuckle. Were those dreams at all realistic? Most of her friends had admitted that they had been deflowered in much less romantic surroundings. One had even confessed that it took place in the boys' toilets at school when she was just fourteen! Joy had blushed at the very thought of it. And now that she had finally made this admission that she had secretly enjoyed the excitement of the touch of Tony's hands on her body, was that not the real reason she had felt so unclean after the event?

So what was she to do? The pain was still there, though the feelings she had experienced when he had kissed her before attempting to have his way, she had not actually been able to drive from her mind. The temptation was too much. She would ring him right away. He would get one last chance. This time she would be more prepared. If he made any advances, she would decide if the circumstances were right. And she would make sure that she drank with moderation. She needed a clear head whatever decision she might come to. Her whole body trembled with anticipation as she considered what that decision might be.

"Kings Arms." The voice of the receptionist rang clear on the line.

"Is Tony Hoskis available, please? I believe he's staying there."

"Just a moment. Who's calling?"

Joy gave her name, her heart fluttering as she waited to be connected. Would he be out, still searching for more titbits to enhance his reports?

"Joy!" There was a marvellous warmth in his greeting as he came on line. "I never expected you to call. Not after the way I treated you. I've been kicking myself ever since making that terrible mistake."

She almost hugged herself with delight. He sounded quite sincere. "I never imagined I'd hear from you again either. I thought you must have decided I was just some silly little schoolgirl." She carefully avoided mentioning that her thoughts had also embraced the distinct impression of being a mere pawn in his programme to advance his career.

"I was a stupid idiot! I could see you weren't the kind of girl who was going to give herself away on a first date. I. think I drank too much, even though I was trying to stay under the limit."

Now that he mentioned it, she had been vaguely aware that her glass had hardly ever become more than half empty, while his had contained a mere drop in the base for much of the time. "You were trying to get me drunk, weren't you?"

Her accusation struck home. Give the man his due though, he gave an honest reply.

"I can't deny it. It's standard practice in our trade I'm afraid. Hospitality usually gets results and hospitality involves plying the person concerned with drinks.

Her heart sank. "So you *were* only after information?"

He hesitated before answering. "That really was only part of it. I was attracted to you – who wouldn't be? I just assumed that you were probably in another relationship already. I never thought you might take any serious interest in some guy who probably wouldn't be around for long."

"That didn't prevent you attempting to make love to me!"

Again a silence. Finally he spoke. "I've blown it haven't I? I shouldn't have contacted you again. I don't blame you for feeling bitter."

The despondency in his voice prompted her to view his apology a little more favourably. He had clearly given some thought to her feelings since his indiscretion. "I didn't say I wasn't interested. You know I wouldn't have called if I didn't want to see you again. And by the way, I don't have a boyfriend!"

"Great!" This time his expression had been one of obvious delight. "You mean you would be prepared to meet me again? I promise there wouldn't be any pressure."

She guessed what he was hinting at. "Could we treat it as though it were our first real date? After all, that would be what it would be, wouldn't it?"

She heard him chuckle.

"You know, you are a nice girl. It makes a pleasant change for me. I always seem to end up with someone who's seen it all and done it all. It'll be great to be with a girl who still has a sense of morality. I was beginning to think that was a thing of the past."

Suddenly she felt proud of her earlier reactions. Maybe men did respect a girl who didn't just give in immediately a man touched her. "That's a nice compliment. When can we meet?"

"Ah! There is a problem there." He hesitated. "I have to tell you that I've just been called away on another story now that this one appears to be wrapped up. The flowers were meant as my apology before I left. I really thought you'd never forgive me."

She was terribly disappointed. "You mean I might not see you again?"

"Hell, no! I'll be back as soon as I can make it. I'm due some leave in a few weeks' time. I thought I'd like to come back for a holiday anyway."

Her smile returned. "You'll ring me as soon as you can?"

"You bet!"

"That's fine by me then."

"Fantastic! I can't wait!"

"I'll be ready."

* * *

Jean Bull had arrived at the police station and was taken to visit her mother. It was an emotionally charged meeting. Ellen swore she had taken no part in the killing of Jean's uncle. Jean had never doubted it.

"What can I do, Ma?" She sat twisting her handkerchief in trembling, agitated fingers.

Ellen had had time to gather her wits together. "You'd best get me a solicitor."

Jean broke down in tears once more. "They can't seriously believe you had any connection wi' this."

Ellen struggled to control her own emotions. "Don't take on, lass, they'll never prove it. Wi' money comin' our way, it shouldn't be difficult gettin' a good lawyer."

Jean tried her best to concentrate. "Cedric had better handle things. I'm nae use wi' lawyers ."

"I'll not have that!" Ellen was determined. "It's family business. Ralph wouldn't have wanted Cedric gettin' involved."

"But Ma, Cedric's family!"

"Maybe. But I don't trust him. You know there's allus been a barrier atween us about the money. I don't think he ever believed me that I never got any cash out o' Herbert."

Jean could hardly deny that. Cedric had always been suspicious of her mother and Ralph's dealings with her uncle. Now was really not the time to argue. "OK, Ma. Tell me what I must do."

Ellen was relieved to avoid any dissent. "Right. Have a word wi' Inspector Grey afore ye go. I know I blamed him fer what happened, but I've had time tae think since I've been in here. I reckon he was probably only doin' his job."

"What? Dragging you in here?

Ellen took her daughter's hand to quieten her. "He seems pretty reasonable when he's on his ain. More than I can say about that snotty superintendent. Ask the inspector who he thinks would be best tae represent me. He must have a good idea o' what these solicitors are like. As soon as you can, get one of 'em tae come an' see me."

Jean forced a smile. "You always know best. I'm sure we'll soon have you out of here."

Ellen was not so confident. She would never let her daughter realise it, but the thought of how the curse was affecting all of their lives would not leave her mind. Jean was the only member of the family to have escaped entirely from some kind of direct misfortune. Ellen had already spoken to Inspector Grey about her concern, pleading with him to maintain the surveillance that had been put in place after the death of her son. Jean was now going to be out there on her own. Ellen was still convinced some evil force was out to destroy them all. How could she warn her daughter without alarming her? She tried her best to speak reassuringly.

"Well, lass, I'm sure you're right. They'll soon find out it's just a mistake, but until I do get out, I'm relying on you now that Ralph's gone." She struggled to control the tears that welled up at the thought of her dead son. "You just take extra care. I need tae know you're lookin' out fer yoursel'. There's jest the two o' us left now."

Jean threw her arms around her mother, clasping her tightly. "Don't worry. Everything'll be alright." She couldn't control her own tears anymore. "All I want is fer us tae be together agin. I don't care about the money or anything else. I just want it settled."

Ellen tried to calm her. "Be sensible, lass. I've thowt it all out. They can't have any real evidence. This Superintendent Morrison's tryin' tae make out as me an' Ralph never went tae Mardale the Sunday afore your uncle got killed. He's just tryin' tae prove we got the mud on our boots when Herbert were murdered. He keeps on about me havin' some brogues as well, but they searched the house a while back an' they found nowt. Now he's making out I got rid of 'em, so he can prove this shoebox that had the skull in it were mine. I reckon he just wants everything tae fit together so he can prove the McKades killed Ralph."

"Isn't that what you think, Ma?"

Ellen held her head in despair. "I don't know what I think. I was sure it were them as killed your uncle, but if they did, how come they never got the skull? I keep asking mysel' if Ralph could have killed Herbert. I know that's gaan tae shock ye, Jean, but don't forget how much he hated your uncle. I don't see why the McKades would kill Ralph unless they thowt he'd got the skull. It doesn't make any sense tae me."

Now that her mother had spelt it out, it didn't make much sense to Jean either. She had to accept that Ralph could be a murderer, or that he'd been killed for some reason other than the retrieval of the skull. If that were so, then the McKades were innocent. She shuddered at the thought. Who else would want to see her brother dead? She didn't even want to contemplate the question. She suddenly felt quite faint.

"Are ye ill, lass?" Ellen could hardly fail to notice the change that had come over her daughter. She assumed the pallor that had drained her face of its normal healthy glow could only be the result of the suggestion that Ralph could have committed murder.

Jean struggled to regain her composure. She could not bring herself to speak of the fear in her heart. She had to have time to think.

Ellen took hold of her daughter by the shoulders. "Pull yersel' together, Jean. I'm sure Ralph could never have done such a thing. Not even fer me. He were a good lad. He allus said he wanted me tae have justice, but he'd surely never o' killed his uncle tae bring it about."

"I know, Ma." Jean tried to force another smile. "There must be some other explanation. We'll sort it out."

Ellen gave her a hug. "Get off hame then, Jean – just as soon as you've had a word wi' the inspector. You've taken enough fer today by the looks o' things."

Jean was happy to comply with her mother's wishes. Having said her goodbyes, she made her way to see Inspector Grey. Her mother must have the best counsel available.

"It's Mrs Bull, Inspector; Mrs Braithwaite's daughter."

Grey glanced up from the pile of documents that littered his desk as the sergeant passed on the message.

"Send her in."

Jean Bull hesitantly entered.

"Sit yourself down." Grey smiled, indicating a chair opposite his own. The woman appeared frightened and apprehensive. He strove to put her at her ease. "Would you like a coffee or tea perhaps?"

She seemed surprised by his kindness. "Thanks, but I'm too upset at the moment."

"That's understandable." He could see she was close to tears. "Just take your time now and tell me what I can do for you."

She struggled to respond. He seemed a nice man, yet he had her mother under lock and key.

"How can you put Ma through this? She's the nicest person in the world! She'd never hurt a fly!"

He suddenly felt terribly guilty. His doubts about the case had still not been overcome. "Your mother is only charged with aiding and abetting your brother in the matter of Herbert Jowett's death. It will be up to the court to decide whether it was a premeditated murder."

She looked angry now. "Ralph and Ma could never have done such a thing! I know uncle were a scoundrel and a thief, but murder…?" She was shaking too much to go on.

Grey reached across the desk, gently placing his hands on her trembling, tightly clenched fists. "Your mother's a long way from being convicted. The best way you can prevent such a thing happening is to acquire a damn good lawyer and let him handle things."

She struggled to pull herself together. Getting a lawyer was, after all, why she was here. "Sorry." She withdrew her hands from his. "Can you help me with that? Ma said you'd know best who might be suitable. I don't know where else I can turn." She was near to tears once more.

He allowed her to calm down as he reached for pen and paper. "Get in touch with this gentleman. His office is in Craigend. Send him in to see your mother and then he'll doubtless want to speak to Superintendent Morrison. There's little more you can do at this stage." He handed over the address. "Try not to stress yourself too much. There's a long way to go before anyone is found guilty of either of these crimes."

That was the issue that most concerned Jean. Could she trust to luck that her mother would be found innocent? She felt compelled to pose a delicate question. "What would happen if someone were innocent and evidence was only uncovered after that person was found guilty?"

Grey was intrigued by the query at this stage of the enquiries. "In that event, there might be a retrial, though there would have to be convincing fresh evidence to justify such a course of action. Once the courts have decided, it's a hell of a job to get them to change their minds." He looked across at her troubled face. "What makes you ask?"

She appeared startled. "I… I don't know… I just wondered…"

He doubted that she'd come up with such a question without good reason. "If you have any evidence with regard to either of these offences you are bound to disclose it."

She was on the defensive now. "I don't know anything!" That, at least, was the truth. What she might suspect was another matter.

Grey was unconvinced. "If there is something you feel should be brought out into the open, you would be well advised to get it off your chest."

Her arms crossed in a gesture that indicated that was the last thing she wished to do. Her eyes would not meet his own. He was sure now that something was on her mind.

"Mrs Bull?"

She glanced fearfully at him now. He felt sorry for the woman and the situation she found herself in.

"You'd best go away and consult with the man whose details I gave you. Whether you are unsure of what knowledge you have, or whether you feel any such knowledge should be passed to him only, I must advise you to tell the truth. If it transpires that you have withheld evidence, you could face charges yourself."

She nodded. The inspector was a clever man. She would say no more. He had already realised that she had something she wanted to remain hidden.

"Thank you. I'll go and see the solicitor right away."

Jean's mind dwelt on what might happen should even the cleverest counsel fail to obtain justice. Whatever the consequences, even though that might mean her husband came under suspicion of murder, she had to see that her mother was taken care of. Grey could certainly expect another visit should her mother look to be in danger of being convicted…

CHAPTER TWENTY-THREE

Ellen Braithwaite's solicitor had consulted with his client. He had assured her he would attempt to secure her release on bail. Now he was ensconced in Superintendent Morrison's office.

Morrison had listened patiently to all he had to say. Now he sat back, leafing through his pile of notes on the case. "You do realise the seriousness of the charges against your client?"

"Of course." Frederick Bannister did not relish being treated as a fool. "I also realise you have nothing but circumstantial evidence at this stage."

"Circumstantial but nevertheless damning." Morrison pushed a sheet of paper across the desk. "Footwear and clothing belonging to both Ellen Braithwaite, and her son, have been tested and found to have traces of the sediment present at the scene of Herbert Jowett's murder. At the very least, that confirms they both visited the site. Your client takes the same size of shoe formerly in the box which was later to contain the skull of Duncan of Crieff. She has no explanation as to how her son might have come to have possession of a ladies shoebox, yet everything points to Ralph Braithwaite himself being murdered because he was in possession of that box and its contents. There's also no escaping the fact that Ellen Braithwaite hated her brother, or that she was the person who stood to gain substantially as a result of his death."

Frederick Bannister had already considered most of those facts; Ellen had made no attempt to hide them. In spite of the evidence, he had been impressed with his client's disclosure of her relationship with her brother. “Mrs Braithwaite assures me that her visit to Mardale took place on the Sunday prior to the murder of Herbert Jowett. Though they attempted to get close to the old farm the water level was still quite high.”

Morrison shrugged his shoulders. “She also assures me of that, though even if it were true, you cannot deny that that doesn’t preclude the possibility that she or her son returned at a later date. It could merely be a subterfuge meant to confuse the issue. She’s produced no real evidence to substantiate her claim of an earlier visit and has no witness to prove that such a visit ever took place. Nor has she any alibi for the hours during which her brother was murdered. She alone would have been in the position of actually knowing her brother’s plans and movements at the time of his death. While a case might conceivably have been made with regard to the McKades’ possible involvement in Jowett’s killing – since we are clearly aware of their interest in obtaining the skull – we do now have a reliable witness to verify that they were at home during the time the murder took place. In contrast to that, prior to his own death, Ralph Braithwaite was unable to account satisfactorily for his movements at the time of his uncle’s murder. We can only assume that there was some form of conspiracy between Ralph Braithwaite and his mother to dispose of Herbert Jowett and to then lay claim to his fortune.”

“As I understand it, you found no evidence of the brogue shoes, by which you set so much store, at Ellen Braithwaite’s home.” The solicitor attempted to find some chink in the superintendent’s argument.

“No, though you would hardly expect otherwise. Once your client became aware of her son’s death, wouldn’t her immediate priority be to dispose of anything that might connect her with Herbert Jowett’s murder? If she suddenly realised her action in placing the skull in a shoebox belonging to herself could result in it being traced back, she’d have been a fool not to rid herself of the previous contents directly. That’s assuming that she still had them in her possession. The shoebox is certainly not new. By now the shoes could have been discarded at some time in the past anyway."

It seemed pointless to argue. Morrison had obviously made up his mind about Ellen Braithwaite's guilt. In spite of that, the solicitor stood his ground. "I still wish to apply for bail."

"Very well. Please make a formal application." Morrison rose from his chair, indicating that the discussion was at an end. "You may be successful, though I doubt your success will be long lived. Unless you make some progress in procuring witnesses in her defence, she'll undoubtedly go to trial and in my opinion, will be sent down."

* * *

Inspector Grey still had his doubts about the case. Neither Ellen Braithwaite nor the McKades had cracked, despite intensive interview techniques. As with Ellen Braithwaite, the McKades' clothing and footwear had been subjected to examination. No bloodstains, nor – in the case of the McKades – any sign of the silt present at the ruined farmhouse had been discovered. Since the McKades now had a witness to corroborate their statement that they were at home at the time of the first murder, this appeared to bear out their story of being innocent of causing Herbert Jowett's death. No charge of that murder was being considered in their case. That, at least, had simplified the matter of the first death. Either Ellen Braithwaite, in collusion with her son, or one of them acting on their own, seemed the only plausible explanation to account for Jowett's killing. Could Ralph Braithwaite have carried out the murder without his mother's connivance? The stumbling block always appeared to be the shoebox. Was it reasonable to consider the likelihood that he just happened to have such a box in his possession? The barrister who would eventually be acting for Mrs Braithwaite would no doubt argue forcefully that it was impossible to rule out such a simple inference. And without evidence to the contrary, it could lead to the conclusion that Ellen Braithwaite was innocent, as she kept insisting. Enquiries had taken place to establish exactly which local shoe shops may have stocked the particular brand in the past. It was a long shot, since it could prove extremely difficult to establish that the shoes in question had actually been purchased locally. It would also be asking a great deal of any shop assistant to cast their minds back over what could be a period of several years to describe the person who actually made the purchase. Grey held out little hope on that score.

And what of the second murder? It was difficult to envisage anyone other than the McKades killing Ralph Braithwaite in order to acquire the skull. To eliminate them from the case, it would be necessary to accept their word that the skull had been left on their doorstep. Yet how could they possibly justify such a claim? Who could have placed it there? If Ralph Braithwaite were mixed up in the murder of his uncle, he might conceivably have dumped the skull there that morning, intending to finger the McKades, yet no call had come in to direct the police to the smallholding. It had only been by chance that the McKades had been caught out with the skull in their possession. But for the appearance of the *Today's News* reporters outside their home, the skull could have been buried long before the police had a chance to lay hands on it. It didn't add up. Who else would then have had cause to murder Ralph Braithwaite? There appeared to be no justification in doubting the superintendent's total confidence of gaining a conviction in at least one of the cases. Grey ultimately came to the conclusion that, as always, the courts would have to be the final arbiters.

* * *

Joy Elliot was unable to settle. In spite of the fact that she was elated at the thought of seeing Tony Hoskis again, she could not dispel the thought of Ellen Braithwaite languishing in her cell. Her tutor might insist that Joy herself was innocent of any blame for the woman's predicament, yet how could she convince herself of that fact? She already had two deaths on her conscience. To see a woman who had suffered so much anguish go down for a term of imprisonment was more than she could bear. She had to do something. There was a gnawing feeling that some cruel injustice was about to take place. She had to speak to the professor.

He was not too surprised to find her at his door once more. They had both been struggling to come to terms with the disastrous consequences of her discovery at Mardale. For once, he felt powerless to buttress her against the guilt she was experiencing. Directing her to a chair, he asked how he might be of help.

"I still feel there ought to be something we could do, Prof." She gazed appealingly at him. "I've been thinking, couldn't we go and talk to old Joss again?"

He considered the suggestion. There was no doubt that Joss would be the most likely person to know of any information that had not come to light. Mardale had been his life – and Mardale and its residents still appeared to be almost his only source of interest. The events of the last week or so must have had a profound effect upon him. And how few of his contemporaries were now left to witness the macabre happenings that had come to pass.

It was debatable whether the police had taken the trouble to seek out the old man. And even assuming that they had, how forthcoming would Joss have been? Inspector Grey had certainly not indicated any such contact, but then Grey was not in overall charge. Had that been the case, Reid felt certain that the course of the investigation might have taken a different turn. Maybe Joy was right. It would do no harm to speak to Joss once more, besides she needed something to take her mind off the awful consequences of her part in this sad saga.

"We could give it a try if you think it might help."

She cheered up immediately on hearing his words.

"I do! There might be something everyone's missed! If I can do anything at all to make up for the trouble I've caused I have to make the attempt."

He looked at his watch; 11.45. They could get to the Kings Arms in good time. "OK. Get yourself ready. I'll just let cook know that we're eating out, then we'll be off."

They were pleased to see Joss installed as they entered the bar. For a moment he stared at them blankly before recognition finally dawned.

"Come fer another crack, 'ave ye?" His wrinkled face broke into a broad grin. "You've missed all the fun here. They reporters have all gaan now. They'll be camped outside the Penrith police station if I'm any judge."

Reid grinned back at the old chap. "You may be right, unless Inspector Grey's seen them off. Still, we didn't come here to see them. We'll join you again if we may. Can I get you your usual?"

"That's good on yer, lad."

Joy had to stifle her smile yet again at the way Joss addressed the professor. 'Lad' did seem a little inappropriate. She pulled up a stool, settling down alongside the old man.

"Well, lass, I told ye there'd be some mischief." The grin had faded now. "Nobody's gaan tae miss Herbert Jowett, but it's a shame about Ralph Braithwaite."

"And Mrs Braithwaite." Joy could not rid her mind of the woman's plight.

"Aye, Ellen's in some trouble there." Joss reached out to take the glass Reid proffered. "Good health." The glass went straight to his lips.

Reid joined them, bringing over drinks and a salad lunch for Joy and himself.

"So what do you make of all this, Joss?"

"It's a rum do." Joss eyed the professor up as though unsure whether he should give an opinion. The reporters who had invaded the small community had left behind a sour taste. Almost every resident had been approached in an attempt to dig up whatever dirt might still be undiscovered. The media men had been met with an almost total wall of silence. No one appeared to have succumbed to their blandishments. The sight of the siege at the homes of the McKades and Jack Tweddie had troubled almost everyone in the village.

Reid could sense the old man's reluctance to speak. He respected him for it, but silence could help no one. It was time for a last effort.

"Joy here, wondered if there might be anything we could do to clear the air. She feels responsible for what's happened."

Joss glanced sympathetically in her direction. "It's nae fault o' yours, lass. The seeds o' this were sown many years since."

"Maybe, but I was the one who stirred it all up."

He could see she was having problems with her conscience. "How do ye reckon I might help?"

That was better. Joy's serious face took on a determined expression.

"Talk to us. You probably know more about Mardale and the people who lived there than anyone else."

"That I do!" He looked somewhat relieved to be free at last to converse on his favourite topic. The events of the past few days had shocked everyone who knew the families involved, provoking sympathy for most of those who had suffered, plus a good deal of speculation about the cause of the killings. Joss had his own opinions.

"I don't reckon Ellen murdered her brother fer a start. She might have hated him fer takin' off wi' all the money, but blood's thicker than watter. I know a lot o' folk have no sympathy fer any o' the Braithwaites – on account of 'em bein' part decended fra the Jowetts – but Ellen were allus one o' the best o' the bunch. Ralph inherited some o' the Jowett arrogance though. You could never win an argument wi' him. I suppose he thowt he were a descendant o' the auld 'Kings', an' as such, a bit more special than the rest o' us.

Come tae think o' it, I guess he'd have taken on the title once Herbert died, if we'd have all still been at Mardale."

Joss broke off to slake his thirst, glancing contemplatively across at their engrossed faces. After downing a prodigious amount of the amber liquid, he replaced his glass on the table, wiping the back of a bony hand across his thin lips. "It were Ellen's daughter I allus felt sorriest fer. I reckon she only got married in order tae spite her brother – an' tae get a life o' her ain. Ralph were dead set agin the marriage an' did all he could tae prevent it. He never did get on wi' Cedric Bull. Can't say I blame him. Cedric were never much o' a catch. Still, Jean seems reasonably happy. At least, as happy as most folk these days." Joss appeared none too ecstatic about the modern way of life.

"I suppose you're wonderin' about the McKades?" He could see that his question was unnecessary. "Well, they're the most likely tae have killed Herbert. I told ye they despised all the Jowetts. Angus brought his son Rory up tae hate 'em as much as he did. Can't see why they'd kill Ralph though. He'd done 'em no harm, unless he were standing in the way o' 'em gettin' their hands on the skull. I've never known anyone so set on settlin' old scores."

"You still think this is all tied in with the curse then, Mr Pattinson?" Joy felt she had to check once more.

"What do you think, lass? It brought Herbert Jowett back here tae die. See what's happenin' wi' the Braithwaites as well. There's not a male descendant o' the auld kings left now, an' Ellens charged wi' murder."

Joy was attempting to put that thought out of her mind. She still had other questions she would like answered.

"You told us about Jack Tweedie the last time we were here. We managed to find the boulder where he'd carved out the memorial to Margaret Thursby – and we found flowers and a message there."

"Did it say who'd left it?" It was Joss's turn to take a keen interest now.

"No. It just said 'God's will be done'."

Joss scratched his head. "Not many people would have known about that place. There's few enough of us left now."

"That's what we thought." She waited to see if he might come up with any explanation.

He sat quietly contemplating for a time. "Could have been Jack Tweedie as left 'em I suppose, though I don't reckon he'd have left a message like that. He were never much fer religion, especially after Margaret's death. He told me there were no God as could have let her kill hersel'. He gave up gaan tae church after she were buried. Put flowers on her grave regular though, at first."

It was Joy's turn to look thoughtful now. "Do you think Margaret could possibly have been pregnant when she died?"

Joss appeared totally shaken by the suggestion. "Who told ye that?"

"No one." A shiver of excitement ran up her spine. The old man gave every indication of being aware that it might, in fact, be true. "I just wondered if she might have been. She had to be in some desperate state of mind to jump to her death."

Joss remained silent for a while. How had this slip of a girl managed to unearth the rumour that had rocked Mardale at the time of Margaret Thursby's unfortunate death? The rumour that had miraculously been kept from the ears of her despairing father. He had presided at her burial never suspecting he might also have been burying his future grandchild. Joss stared across at Joy's earnest face. Finally he spoke.

"It were never proved. Not like today – in them days, there were none of these forensic thingumajigs as far as I knew."

So there was a suspicion that Margaret had been carrying a child. Was that the reason for the tale of the Grey Lady bearing a baby at her breast? Joy shuddered. Was it, as she suspected, just a figment of someone's fervid imagination? Perhaps a tale made up to terrify the father of the unborn child?

Joss gave no clue. "Margaret were a lovely lass. The sun went out fer a lot o' folk when she died. No one wanted tae believe she were wi' child. If it were so, she must have been forced into it. She were a nice, clean livin' lass. Not the kind who'd bring shame on her family. Whatever the truth might be, the secret went wi' her tae the grave!"

"You told us Jack Tweedie believed the Jowetts had driven her to her death." Joy was desperate to unearth whatever secrets remained hidden. "Do you think it's possible one of the Jowetts could have made her pregnant?"

The old man looked uncomfortable. Even after all this time he found it a distasteful subject. He stared back at her earnest face, realising it would serve no purpose to conceal the truth.

"Jack Tweedie certainly came tae believe it in the end. It were a long time after we'd all left Mardale, an' Herbert Jowett had left the country as well by then. I think it were Margaret's sister, Isobel, as let on she were sure Herbert were responsible. Jack swore he'd kill him if ever he set foot back in this country."

Joy and her tutor exchanged startled glances.

Joss tugged nervously at his bottom lip. "As like as not he never meant it. Jack were a nice bloke, but a bit of a hot-head as far as anything tae do wi' Margaret were concerned. I'm sure it were just said in anger."

"But what if he had some form of evidence?" Joy was beginning to realise how damning it now sounded.

Joss shook his head. "I doubt he'd any real proof. Like as not Isobel just put two an' two together an' decided it were Herbert. We all knew he were allus after the lasses, but they knew it too. Most o' 'em kept well clear o' him if they could."

Joy glanced at the professor's serious face. She could imagine what was now going through his mind. Should these details be passed on to Inspector Grey? She had no doubt that the answer could only be yes. Her tutor could hardly be expected to ignore the implications. Jack Tweedie could well believe he had every justification for carrying out the assault on Herbert Jowett. It would not be difficult to make a case against him. To have been made aware of Margaret Thursby's possible fate at the hands of Jowett may well have been more than he could stand. The opportunity to avenge himself would surely have been overwhelming. If he had taken off with the skull after the killing – conceivably in order to thwart the final act of Jowett – might he not then have left it on the McKades' doorstep at a later date? It could have been his way of compounding his revenge by handing it over to Jowett's sworn enemies or of diverting suspicion from himself. After all, it had been established that he was present at Mardale on the morning of Jowett's murder.

Reid had taken over the conversation, though Joy's mind hardly took in anything that was being said. For some strange reason her thoughts were now directed away from Jack Tweedie's possible participation in the crime. She was missing something here! Something that Joss had said! One tiny fragment of the old man's utterances had struck a chord somewhere deep within her subconscious. Suddenly, and without any shadow of doubt, she had become convinced that there was yet another possible explanation for the murder of Herbert Jowett.

On each occasion the professor and she had spoken to Joss, the word 'clean' had come into every mention he made of the Thursby sisters. Casting her mind back, Joy struggled to recall the phrase he had used on their first visit. 'Good clean lasses they were, even though their mother wasn't there to look after them.' She remembered the gist of the conversation well, though she had had to translate his words a little from the strong old Westmorland dialect. And what had he said about Isobel Thursby? 'She looked after her father once he'd had a stroke, and kept the house, and herself, as clean as a new pin.' Why had the memory of the Thursby girls remained in his memory forever associated with cleanliness? Joy was sure she knew. She was also sure she now understood why she had first considered the possibility that Margaret Thursby might have been pregnant. What had been her own reaction after the unpleasant sexual encounter with Tony Hoskis? Almost one of disgust with herself for allowing things to go so far – and an urgent desire to scrub herself clean. How much worse would she have felt had she not managed to prevent him from forcing himself upon her? She recalled reading of cases where women had been raped and had been obsessed ever after with a desire to wash away all traces of the encounter. She was finally convinced that Margaret Thursby had been abused by Herbert Jowett. As a maid in the household, she might easily have been subjected to unwelcome attention. Too terrified, or embarrassed, to speak of such matters to her father, she may have put up with it until she realised her condition. As Joss had pointed out, she would have been mortified to bring shame on the family. More so, since her father was the parson. A young girl in her position might prefer to die rather than live with the disgrace.

And that left Isobel Thursby. She had been forced to take Margaret's place as maid in the Jowett household. How long would it have been before she too was subjected to the same treatment? And, like her sister, Isobel may have accepted her fate with the same fortitude. No wonder she had later been able to deduce the condition of her sister at the time of her death – and to be almost certain of the man responsible. The only question that now remained was how had she managed to live with that knowledge for so long before confiding in Jack Tweedie?

* * *

Isobel Thursby had spent most of the morning paying a further visit to her sister's memorial at Harter Fell. As was her normal practice, she had gathered wild flowers to lay at the foot of the boulder. Yet again she had attached a note. It read: 'Revenge is sweet. An eye for an eye, a tooth for a tooth!' Now she was down on her knees in the nearby church of St Michael's. Much of her time had been spent there since the day of Herbert Jowett's death. Hadn't God's words originally come to her there, urging her to kill the evil man who had constantly abused both her sister and herself? The man who had brought about Margaret's destruction, and that of his own unborn child; either by his own hand, or by the unendurable guilt that had forced Margaret to take her own life. The man who had also made Isobel herself pregnant, just weeks before the mass exodus from Mardale, forcing on her the choice of joining her sister in the grave – or leaving her father's home to seek an abortion. Tears stained her hollow cheeks as the memories flooded back. Horrified at the prospect of giving birth to Herbert Jowett's child, yet longing to hold the baby that had become an integral part of her own body, she had struggled with her conscience before finally coming to the dreadful conclusion that her unborn infant had to die. Making the excuse to her father that she was joining a convent, she had sought out a backstreet abortionist before throwing herself on the mercy of the sisters.

Now she had murdered once more. God had told her to go forth and kill the last of the Jowett descendants. She smiled, recalling how simple it had been to dispose of Ralph Braithwaite. Once you had mastered the art, it came easy. And now Ellen Braithwaite was charged with murder. Isobel reflected on that. God worked in mysterious ways. She had given no consideration as to what might be the result of returning the skull to the McKades. The skull she had taken from the hands of Herbert Jowett as he lay dying; intending to rob him of his last wish by granting the McKades theirs. She had simply left it on their doorstep on her way to deal with Ralph Braithwaite. Perhaps the McKades were also evil men. Why else would God wish to punish them?

She rose to her feet. Surely Jack Tweedie would never speak of witnessing her attack on Herbert Jowett. When he came across her at Mardale, had he not told her that he was there to do precisely the same thing? And now there only remained Ellen Braithwaite's daughter to deal with. So far she was childless. She must die before it was too late. No other descendant of the Jowetts, however far removed, must ever walk the streets again.

* * *

Joy suddenly became aware that the conversation between her tutor and the old man had come to a halt. She pulled herself together. She could not leave before discovering where Margaret Thursby's sister lived.

"Didn't you say Isobel Thursby's home was close by, Mr Pattinson?"

"Aye, that's right, lass." He took a long puff at his pipe before continuing. "She lives in the little cottage up by the post office. It's not that long since she passed the window here. Just a few minutes afore you got here as a matter o' fact. Headin' fer the church as like as not. She's allus up there – except when she's out walkin' on the fells. Never settled since we all left Mardale. She's still a tough old lass though – an' never lost her faith in God."

Reid could sense the change that had come over Joy. She was fidgeting in her seat, clearly desperate to be on the move. He sank the last of his pint. "Well, it's been a great pleasure talking to you again, Joss." He stood up, shaking the old man's hand. "Must be on our way now, though I hope we'll see you again sometime."

"I'm allus here." He smiled across at Joy. "Take care o' yersel', lass."

She could hardly wait to get outside. "Can we go up to the church now, Prof?" The words spilled from her lips in a ferment.

"Of course." It was plain for Reid to see that she could barely contain her excitement. "What on earth is it?"

"Don't you see?" She didn't wait for a reply. "It could be Isobel! If Margaret were interfered with by Herbert Jowett, you can bet Isobel suffered the same fate."

He struggled to keep pace with her. She was almost running up the road. "Steady on, Joy!"

"Sorry." She had almost forgotten the stiffness in his legs.

He forced himself to speed up. He could see now exactly what she was getting at. Maybe Jack Tweedie was not the obvious suspect that he had at first appeared to be, following Joss's disclosures. Everyone could have been barking up the wrong tree. The matter of the legend; the skull; its discovery; its subsequent loss. All these may have combined to confuse the issue. Certainly the initial discovery had triggered off the killings, but what of the events since then? Everyone had been so concerned by who might have stolen the skull – and for what reason – that little consideration had been given to any other issue. So many people appeared to have had their lives blighted by Jowett in one way or another. The McKades and the Braithwaite family were perhaps not alone in their suffering.

Joy grabbed his arm. "I'm sure I'm right." She didn't care to explain how the incident with Tony Hoskis had brought about her flash of inspiration. "Don't you think that the skull being discovered could have sparked off Isobel's deep-rooted hatred of Herbert Jowett all over again? The thought that he might return to blight her life once more must have shaken her to the core."

"I can well believe it!" The professor was becoming more convinced by the minute.

"If I am correct, just imagine the horror of her coming face to face again with the man who had raped her and her sister and knowing that she should have spoken out long ago about his conduct. What if she's carried the guilt for all these years then suddenly saw the chance to take her revenge."

"There's no denying she'd have cause enough to consider it."

"And who could blame her? She must have realised that Jowett would be drawn back by the news of the skull. Everyone in the village seemed to be aware of his fear that it would be moved from the farm one day."

They had rounded the corner now and were heading up the hill leading to the church. Garrulous rooks circled above it, disturbed perhaps, by the woman on her way out of the church grounds.

"It's her!" Joy crushed Reid's arm as she hissed out the message. "That's the woman who was at Mardale the day the body was discovered. Don't you remember? I stood talking to her while you went forward with the inspector."

"My God, you're right!" He recognised the tall, upright figure of the woman who had been standing alongside Joy when he returned to her after witnessing the corpse of Herbert Jowett. She had walked briskly away after he had answered her inquiry about Jowett's state of health. She could well have been waiting to check if the man had actually died from the result of her frenzied attack. He recalled the knapsack she had been carrying on her back. A simple way of mingling unobtrusively with the rest of the tourists, while at the same time, affording her the possibility of transporting a weapon should she need one.

Also the ideal way to carry off her gory trophy after she had disposed of Jowett. Who was going to suspect an elderly lady of being the perpetrator of such an awful act?

"Take hold of yourself, Joy. Just carry on up the hill. We don't want to put her on her guard."

They strolled past the preoccupied lady.

"Did you see?" Joy was almost out of breath with excitement; her heart was pounding as she struggled to gasp out the words. "She was wearing brogues!"

Reid had seen. It was not conclusive proof, though it was sufficient to warrant a check on the woman. "Okay, let's give her a minute, then we'll follow her. If she does return to the cottage that Joss indicated, at least we'll be in no doubt as to her identity."

Isobel Thursby did indeed return to the cottage.

Reid hesitated. Was the woman still a potential danger? Even the very brief glimpse he had had of her intense, strained face, indicated that she may be. He had seen that expression before on the faces of disturbed patients he had encountered at the hospital; a haunted expression; an expression which caused him great anxiety. More so, since he now recalled that she had had the same expression at Mardale, a fact that he had put down at the time to her concern for the man who had just died.

There was a phone box outside the post office. No sense in taking a risk. A quick call to the Penrith police station and he was connected through to Inspector Grey.

"What is it, Prof.?"

Grey listened to the story in astounded silence. The brogue shoes seemed to clinch it. He knew the professor well enough to understand that his advice was sound. There was no denying that there was justification in taking his words seriously.

"Good God!"

Reid smiled at the response. "You've got Joy Elliot to thank if there is anything in this. Call it female intuition if you will, but that girl's got a good head on her shoulders."

Maybe. But Grey knew Merlin Reid had had a hand in it somewhere along the way. 'The Magician' had probably pulled something out of the hat yet again.

Before the inspector had time to express his gratitude for the tip off, Reid's concerned voice echoed down the line. "Christ! She's on her way out to her garage. You don't think she's likely to make an attempt on the life of Ellen Braithwaite's daughter do you?" That was the possibility he had been worrying about since acknowledging the fact that Isobel Thursby may have murdered Ralph Braithwaite as well as Herbert Jowett. If her mind had snapped – as now appeared increasingly likely – there was no telling what she was capable of.

"Damn!" Grey was galvanised into action. The prospect, however slight, of another innocent victim being slaughtered was one that could not be ignored. "Can you give me her description and the make of her car? We did have a man posted outside the daughter's house, but in spite of her mother's concern, I couldn't manage to persuade the superintendent to keep him there once her mother and the

McKades were arrested. He was convinced there was no longer any danger."

Reid quickly gave a description of Isobel and of the car that was now pulling out onto the main road.

"I'll get someone over there immediately." Grey called out the message to the duty sergeant. "Now I'd better have a word with Morrison. He's going to get a bit of a shock. He's already made his mind up that we've collared the villains. He can hardly ignore your evidence though. If the woman was at the scene of Herbert Jowett's killing, then there's ample reason to bring her in for questioning, even if she doesn't show up at Jean Bull's home."

The professor was relieved to know that Grey had the matter under his control. There was no time for Reid himself to make it back to his car in time to follow the woman; she was already out of sight. He considered ringing back to ask for the daughter's address. Would that actually help? Was he jumping to too many conclusions? Isobel Thursby was probably only off on some shopping trip. In any case, by the time he had sorted out directions, the police would be responding to the threat – if one actually existed. He prayed that this proved not to be the case. Joy would be devastated if there were yet another death.

She was waiting impatiently outside.

"What's happening?" Her question came before he hardly had time to open the door.

"Inspector Grey thinks we may be onto something." Reid was reluctant to mention his own fears.

"Great! They believed us then?"

"I think Grey's convinced that Isobel has a few questions to answer. The brogues, and her being at Mardale at the time of Jowett's death, do seem to indicate her possible guilt. If your assumption of her and her sister being abused by Herbert Jowett has any foundation, then it's hardly surprising that she may have finally cracked. You could well have hit on the solution, Joy."

“Thank God for that!” She realised she had just about come to the end of her tether.

* * *

So too had Isobel Thursby…

Jean Bull’s home was only minutes away, a fact that, had it been known to Merlin Reid, would certainly have made him think twice about leaving the matter to the police – and would have caused him to ignore the painful joints that normally prevented him from embarking on any swift form of action.

Isobel’s car came to a screeching halt. No one in sight. She carefully checked to make doubly sure. She picked up the heavy shopping bag. This time she would be using the hefty coal hammer hidden inside its depths – the hammer that had accompanied her on the last two occasions, when its use had been rendered unnecessary by the availability of more suitable weapons with which to mount an attack on her victims. She pulled on the flimsy, daintily embroidered cotton gloves. The same gloves she had worn on the last two occasions. She left the engine running. It had to be accomplished quickly, just like before. She made her way to the door.

Jean Bull responded quite quickly to the ringing of her doorbell. “Hello, Mrs Thurs—” Her words of welcome were cut short by the look in Isobel’s eyes. A look of demoniacal fury. The blur of the hammer only just warned her in time; she raised a hand, ducking to one side to protect her head. The hammer crashed down on her shoulder, paralysing her left arm. She had no time to scream with the pain; the hammer was raised once more. She tried to force the door shut – impossible with one arm out of action – Isobel was much too strong for her. She was thrown across the hall by the sheer power of the woman. Once more the hammer rose in the air; once more Jean attempted to fend off the attack. This time she took the full force of the blow on her remaining sound arm; this time she did scream! She was now powerless to protect herself. She waited in agony for the next blows that she was certain were about to end her life…

Neither woman had heard the squeal of protesting tyres that announced the arrival of a patrol car. Desperate fear in Jean Bull – and a ruthless determination to kill in Isobel Thursby – had removed all sense of reality. The hand that stayed the blow, which would almost certainly have despatched the unfortunate victim, seemed to come from nowhere. Alerted by the scream that had issued from the open door, a burly constable had sprung to Jean's defence.

It was Isobel Thursby's turn to scream now. She fought like some demented animal in an attempt to shake off the restraining hand, only one thought driving her on; the face of Herbert Jowett grinning up at her from the shoulders of the cowering figure down on its knees before her. The same face that had grinned down on her as she had been subjected to repeated acts of rape. The face of the man who had killed her sister; killed her sister's baby; killed Isobel's own baby…

It took both of the constables who had answered the call to finally bring Isobel Thursby under control. An ambulance was quickly summoned to take away the sobbing victim of her attack. Had Inspector Grey not managed to make contact with a patrol car dealing with a minor incident close by, Jean Bull would surely have followed her brother and uncle to a slab in the mortuary.

CHAPTER TWENTY-FOUR

Isobel Thursby's arrest and the charge of murder on two counts quickly followed. So too did the release of Ellen Braithwaite and the McKades. A check on Isobel's shoes had confirmed that they coincided exactly with the make and description present on the box which had contained the skull. Traces of blood, that matched both Herbert Jowett and Ralph Braithwaite, were discovered on her clothing. She appeared totally unconcerned when confronted by the evidence. "God told me what to do," she had insisted. "God will take care of me."

The courts quickly decided otherwise. Faced with the overwhelming evidence, Isobel was found guilty of both murders, but judged of unsound mind. The state would take care of her. She was committed to a mental institution. Joy was destined never to become aware that she had been correct in her assumption that the story of the Grey Lady had been manufactured to unnerve Herbert Jowett. Isobel had been unable to come up with any other method of seeking revenge for her sister's death at that time, nor for the degradations that Jowett had subsequently subjected her to.

Jack Tweedie attended Isobel's trial, though saw no reason to give evidence of what he had witnessed at Mardale. His one regret was that he had not foreseen the possibility of Isobel going on to kill once more after disposing of Herbert Jowett.

Joy was unhappy to see Isobel Thursby locked away, but took comfort from the fact that the poor woman might now find peace. Joy had discovered her own peace with the realisation that she had almost certainly saved the life of the last potential victim. She had also prevented three innocent people from suffering the fate of being wrongly convicted of murder. Now she could look forward to resuming her life. And to resuming her acquaintance with Tony Hoskis!

Angus McKade and his son Rory were, in the end, given permission to bury the skull of Duncan of Crieff with the rest of the remains. Ellen Braithwaite, and her daughter Jean, had finally decided that the curse had run its course.

Jean recovered well from her injuries. Her life finally took a turn for the better. Possibly it was the realisation that he had almost lost her that prompted her husband to change his ways. Maybe… That or the fortune that finally came her way! They remained childless. Isobel Thursby's last wish had been granted – the Jowett dynasty would fail to continue after the eventual demise of Jean Bull.

Joss Pattinson never did lose his unshakeable conviction that the curse imposed on the Jowett family had solely been responsible for Isobel's murderous attacks. And never was he dissuaded that she was merely the instrument of some malevolent force manipulating her every move from beyond the grave.

Nor was he alone in that assumption…

THE END

www.ingramcontent.com/pod-product-compliance
Ingram Content Group UK Ltd.
Pitfield, Milton Keynes, MK11 3LW, UK
UKHW020415250726
13967UKWH00007B/2651

9 781780 033402